THE RAIDER WITHIN

SHELLY JARVIS

PAPER MAGE PUBLISHING

If you can love someone with your whole heart, even one person, then there's salvation in life. Even if you can't get together with that person.

HARUKI MURAKAMI

CONTENTS

CHAPTER
ONE

HIRO

"Chief?"

My head jerks up. The words jar me, as they always do. Even after four months...

Has she really been gone that long?

No. Longer.

It's been at least six months; the solstice choosing rite was last week, reminding me of the bond we made at a makeshift ceremony on Nigel's ship, and the way she abandoned me almost immediately afterward. It was also a stark reminder of what could happen if someone decided they didn't want to keep putting their faith in an absent chief and her shit-for-brains spouse. Not a single person challenged her, challenged me, to be Chief. And I can't figure out why. I'd vote myself out in a heartbeat.

Maybe, like me, they believe she'll come back. Maybe, like me, they're damned fools.

I push the thought from my mind, ignore the ache in my chest that ignites every time I think of Nova. I refuse to give myself time to dissect that particular pain. All that matters, really, is that I miss her. Doesn't matter why. At least, that's what I tell myself at night when I stare at the ceiling over our bunk in the *Curiosity*. I shake my head, wishing I could dislodge the stabby Raider girl who seems to occupy my thoughts rent-free.

She left me, left us all, and even though I know why, I still hate her for it almost as much as I love what she's willing to do for her people. We returned to Coco's farm a week after leaving the Hole in the World only to find chaos. There were people missing, and *pieces* of people removed from the bodies of those Nova cared about. I didn't know them, but that didn't stop the ache the sight produced. No one should have to die like those people did. Then to learn that the Règle had caused that in an effort to bring Nova back to the station? I have no doubt she felt responsible—it's what sent her hurtling to the station in the blink of an eye to save those that were taken—but it left me ill-prepared and in charge of a bunch of Raiders.

The man who spoke my name before my brain dove down the Nova rabbit hole stands stock-still in front of me even while my thoughts ramble on. He gives me the respect and patience I don't deserve. I wonder what these people would think if they knew who I was before. What would Nova think, if she knew the real me?

Dark eyes, a tentative half-smile greet me when I finally acknowledge the man waiting for my attention. He's handsome; tall and lithe, built for running, among other more enjoyable things. I could easily think of a few activities that would put his body to good use. My mind runs with that thought for just a second before I shut it down. Though I'm sure Nova wouldn't mind if I spent some quality time with this man, or anyone else, for that matter, I'm committed to my Chief. Besides, she ran off to the space station before I got her permission to fool around.

"How can I help you?"

The man's smile broadens at my question, as if I matter. But really, I'm just trying to hold it together and do things like Nova would, so she doesn't come back to a world where all her hard work has fallen apart.

"It's the bracelet," he says, adjusting his dark-rimmed spectacles. "We've had a breakthrough."

It took hearing those words for me to realize who he is: Javian Balunovic, the tech guru we picked up from the Hole in the World, thanks to some negotiating by that brawny beauty, Thoa.

"When you say breakthrough—"

"We can use it," he says, cutting me off. He winces when he realizes he interrupted me, but presses on. "It will get us onto the station."

His proclamation has a dual effect—it is both a cascade of bricks crashing against me and a pair of wings sprouting from my back, allowing me to fly. We can get to the station, we can save Nova. But it also means taking these people she loves, people I have grown to love, into the belly of the beast.

I nod. "Good work, Javian."

"Thanks, Chief," he says, cheeks bright as fire. "There's still some bugs to work out—"

"Keep at it."

I rise and walk past him. Though I hear him stammering some techno-jargon at my back, I ignore whatever else he planned to say. I'm not trying to be rude, but I am not a details person, and his words mean little to nothing to me. As long as the device works, that's all I need to know at this point. Until it's time to use it, my attention needs to turn to the big picture and make sure our people are ready.

As I walk, I flag down Apolline, one of my inner circle, and they slide into step alongside me. I hook a thumb over my shoulder and ask, "What do you know about Javian?"

They shrug. "Keeps to himself. Spends most of his time down in the pit."

"The pit?"

Apolline smirks. "It's what some of the others have taken to calling the research area in the base of the city."

I frown at this, but don't say anything. I understand *why* they would think of it like that. I would've too at one point. But now I know better. Those people working tirelessly in research and development are some of the brightest minds this world has to offer. They're the ones who will change this place for the better when the rest of us realize fighting can only take us so far.

"Any family?"

"Not that I know of."

"Do some digging," I say. Just before I dismiss them, I add, "Find him a gift, a reward of some kind."

They raise their brows. "Intimate?"

I think of Javian's dark eyes for only a second before shaking my head. "Just a thank you. He's the one who will bring Nova back to us.

There's not really a gift grand enough to say thanks for that, so do what you can."

———————

THE AFTERNOON SUN IS BLINDING AS I STEP OUT ONTO THE AEROPORT STREET. Serves me right for sitting indoors for the last few days. Since we turned north, I've spent more and more time inside. As someone who lived in a temperature controlled environment for twenty-four years, the cold doesn't agree with me. And the fluffy white rain that spits from the sky as we travel toward Old York is wholly unpleasant. I'd heard of snow before, seen how beautiful it was in old movies from before the cataclysm, but experiencing it is far worse than anything I was prepared for.

The market is bustling as I pass through. Vibrant hues of cerulean, amaranth, and vermillion beam from stalls containing garments, carpets, and paintings. I pass a table covered with celadon ceramics dipped in silvers and golds which sits next to a cart boasting a wide array of root vegetables, some of which are very much out of season.

Vendors shout over one another, looking for their next customer. Since Herol Hamrick, current ruler of Aeroport, convinced the floating city's denizens to take up the fight against the space station, we've been traveling all over the country, spreading the word as best we can. Because we're on the move, Aeroport doesn't have as many visitors now to keep their inventory moving, so Herol thinks our trip to the old city will give a boost to the trading market.

I'm eager to find my way around Old York. It was a popular destination in the old entertainment programs I watched when I was a kid, and something about the city has always held a bit of mystery and intrigue for me. It always seemed big and dirty and full of more people than it should be able to hold. In those ways, it reminded me of the space station. I always related to those people living in small apartments, working a crap job they hated just to survive.

But then there were the movies that showed art and beauty and the majesty of the city. Though parts of the station had that as well, those things seem to be more prevalent with the people I see now. The Raiders and the recruits we've accumulated over the last few months surprise me everyday with something new and grand, and those things are very much a symbol of what this world can be.

I pass the metal arches on my way to city hall and tap them for good luck. I have no idea what it means exactly, but I noticed several of the sailors do it religiously and I've taken up the habit. I pass the oil fountain where a group of Raider children are practicing their bladework, and step into the darkened hall. Herol is there, propped on one of the five council seats, a stack of papers spread before him.

He looks up when I enter, a smile spreading across his face. "Chief Hiro, to what do I owe this pleasure?"

"They've done it."

"Who has done what and how does it affect *me*?"

I smile. Herol is a man after my own heart. No matter what's going on around him, he has his priorities, and those priorities are always dependent on his interests. But this news is bigger than either of us, and I know he'll want to hear it. "The techies have figured out how to make the device work. We can get to Nova."

Herol stares at me for a second, lips parted slightly in an expression that registers a little awe and a lot of confusion. "If you're joking with me…"

I shake my head. "Serious. Javian came to see me just a few minutes ago and I came straight here."

"How does it work?" he asks.

"No idea," I say, giving him my brightest smile. "I didn't listen when Javian was explaining it. But it does work, and that's all I care about."

Herol climbs down from his seat and walks over to me. He puts his arm around my shoulders in the fatherly way he has recently adopted when he wants to tell me I'm a dunce.

"I understand the excitement, Hiro. Really, I do. Getting Nova back is of the utmost importance to all of us, and having the tool working is a huge breakthrough that needs to be celebrated. But don't get too far ahead of things or set yourself up for disappointment. We need to figure out how to get a large number of us up there if we're going to be successful in storming the space station, and using the device one at a time isn't the way to do it."

This is not the response I expected, certainly not the one I wanted. I don't care if his words make sense; I don't even care about storming the station. I just want to get Nova. "But *I* could get to her. I know my way around the ship. A one man operation—"

"Would fail," he said, though not unkindly. "They know you, they could be watching you right now."

"I still have this," I say, pulling the small disc from my pocket. "Nova's sister made them to keep the star-people from listening."

"I know, and hopefully it still works. But we don't know what happened once they were taken. Maybe they shut off the devices and things are back to normal, with them listening to us plot and having a good laugh."

"So, what are you saying? You think I should give up on... on Nova?"

"No," he said, fast and firm. "Never give up on that girl."

"But you make it sound hopeless."

"Even if it is, even if there's no reason to believe it will ever work, you can't give up on her."

"Why?"

"Because she would never give up on you. I didn't get a chance to know her well, but that much is obvious to anyone who meets her."

He's right, of course, in more ways than one. We have no idea what happened when the Règle took our people and no way of knowing what Nova walked into when she followed. They could be tracking our every movement, listening to our every word, waiting for the right moment to destroy us all.

But Nova would never stop fighting.

Neither will I.

CHAPTER
TWO

CAMERON

The alarm blares long and loud. It's a grating sound that I feel in my teeth. I swat at the thing, miss, and it continues taunting me. Bets' arm slides across my chest and she turns it off with one firm tap.

"Call off," she mumbles.

I smile as she presses herself against my side and wraps her leg around mine. "I can't, love."

I open my eyes in the dark room, despite their tired protests. I didn't get enough sleep last night. I rarely do. As she traces a finger across my chest, I shiver; sometimes lack of sleep is a good thing, the time used for more titillating exercises.

Other times, dark times, it's because of the nightmares. Gnashing teeth and impossible, beastly mouths that come from a place inside my brain that's lost to me.

"You can," Bets says, her voice clearing away the dark thoughts. "I give you permission."

As my eyes adjust to the blackness around us, I can make out the shape of her. She's tall and broad, with thick shoulders that hold me close and hips that do things I can't think about this early in the morning. Not if I'm going to go to work, at least.

"I guess you can do that, technically," I whisper, my lips tickling against her ear.

"Damn right I can," she says, a smile in her voice.

She reaches over and grabs hold of me, pulling my body against hers. I rise above her, pinning her arms above her head. I lean down and press my lips to her brow, her cheek, her neck, her lips. She writhes beneath me and I know what she wants, but I like to make her work for it, at least a little.

"Call off," she breathes, her voice husky with desire. I can hear the edge of hunger in her tone. "Tell them the Règle has a special task for you."

I press my tongue to Bets' collarbone and trace it along her skin until a moan escapes her. I pull up, putting too much space between us, and say, "But you're not the Règle. Not yet, anyway."

"Almost."

"That's not good enough to get me out of work."

"Fine," she says. She hooks an ankle around mine and shifts me over, rolling on top to pin me down. She grinds her hips against mine and I feel my body pulse in time with her movements. She pauses, though I'm nearly at the point of begging her not to, and says, "You don't have to call off, but you're definitely going to be late."

I scan my bracelet under the timeclock, wincing when it shows me nearly twenty minutes late for work. Second time this week. If I'm not careful, Bets and her magical vagina are going to get me fired.

Probably won't matter when she becomes the Règle, but we don't know exactly when that will be. The role passes to the next of kin when the current Règle dies; Bets was sixteenth on the list and never thought she'd be called to serve, but now she's here, one away from controlling the entire station, and the current Règle is barely clinging to life.

She tells me there has been a lot of turnover in the position as of late. Seven Règles have died in the last eighteen months. I ask her how they died, if I should worry about her; what she tells me, I don't remember, but I'm too embarrassed to ask again. There's not a lot that sticks since my accident, and I can't clearly recall anything from before, but I don't want to add more to her plate by letting her know how hard it is for me to remember things that are happening *now*.

Sometimes when Bets tells me the story of how we got together, I get pictures in my head, like traces of memories. They're fragments, really. I see her in neon lights—she was running a bar, running from her destiny; I see a flicker of my reflection in a window while she stands behind me; I remember, or think I do, the way our bodies intertwined, hot and sticky and hungry.

Or maybe I'm only remembering last night. Or last week. That's about as far as my memory goes these days.

"You're late, Cam."

I spin and salute my commanding officer. "Apologies, Sarge."

He shakes his head, smirks. "We both know there's nothing I can do about it. If I were to guess, I'd say she's probably the reason you *are* late."

Heat creeps up my neck and I know my skin is turning blotchy, but I don't confirm his suspicions. Sergeant Hicks and I are friendly, but we're not friends. He goes easy on me because he wants my favor once Bets becomes Règle—I'm not fool enough to think otherwise.

"Assignment, Sarge?"

He sighs and runs a finger down the tablet in his hand. "You're escorting that little blonde terror today."

I scrub a hand over my red curls. They're nearly to the bottom of my ears now, and constantly in my way. I should probably shave my head again, but I like the feel of Bets' hands pulling my hair at the precise moment she—

"You there, Cameron?"

"Yeah, yes, sorry. Can't seem to focus today."

Sarge gives a light punch against my shoulder and says, "Get your head in the game, Forsberg. You know that bitch is gonna put you through the ringer."

"Yessir," I say, smiling and nodding as Sergeant Hicks heads off down the hall.

As soon as he's out of earshot, I spit out a curse at his back. I hate the way he talks about the prisoners. Sure, some of them are hard to deal with. They're rude and belligerent and, occasionally, violent. But they're people, and it doesn't cost us anything to treat them that way.

Even the little blonde terror.

I turn and walk down the opposite hall, hoping I don't run into any other guards before I get to my destination. Despite Bets' assurances that I loved my job before the accident, I can't seem to find common ground with my coworkers now. Maybe the accident changed me; maybe for the better. I'm not sure I would've liked the old Cameron Forsberg.

Stevens leans against the door I'm headed toward, looking as if he doesn't have a single care in that empty head of his. He smiles when he sees me and I can't help but smile in return. He's the most amiable person I've ever met—or at least of those I remember. He's about as deep as a cup of water, but he's as likable as they come.

"Oy, Cam, how goes it?"

"Not bad, mate," I say.

"Late again?" he asks, a smile tipping up the edges of his lips. He takes a deep breath and adds, "You smell like sex."

I feel the heat tickling my ears as I try to change the subject. "How's the menace?"

He snorts. "She's wild today. Glad I'm not going in."

"Me, too. She'd tear you up."

"No doubt."

He pats me down—standard procedure before letting anyone enter the room of a patient or convict—though Stevens is a little looser on the guidelines than some of the others. Still, he confirms I have my taser and nothing else, then buzzes me into the room.

The girl is on all fours, crawling around the floor and howling. Though it's entirely unprofessional, I immediately burst into laughter at the sight of her.

She stops her circuitous route and slowly turns her head toward me. A growl emanates from her, low and deep. Now I understand why Stevens said she was wild.

The little witch tilts her head and asks, "Which one are you today?"

"Same as last time I was here," I say. "And the time before that."

"But not the time three weeks ago," she says, a smile creeping across her face.

Sighing, I shake my head. The poor girl asks me the same question every time I come in here, though my answer never changes. She's convinced I'm her long-dead sister…

"Noooovaaaaa," she calls, climbing up onto the bed.

"That's not my name, Ivy."

"Not today, but maybe tomorrow. You'll be Nova again soon."

"Okay," I say, not in the mood to argue. "But today I'm Cam, and I'm here to change your bedsheets. Can you get off the bed, please?"

The girl flashes a grin from her dirty face. I don't know how she gets dirty. The walls are white, the floor is black—

A sharp pain shoots behind my eye and I stagger back, my hand going to my taser in case Ivy uses the moment to strike. But she doesn't move from where she's crouched on the bed. She watches me, her grin growing wider, as she lifts her shift-dress and defecates on the sheets.

"Seriously?" I ask, exasperation thick in my tone as my headache finally dulls.

"I wouldn't do this if you were Nova today."

I sigh. "But I'm not Nova. I'm never Nova. My name is Cam."

"If I make you angry enough, you'll be Nova. She always comes back when the anger gets too strong."

"There's nothing to be angry about," I say. "Annoyed, maybe. At least you shit the bed *before* I changed the sheets."

"I could go again after."

I shrug. "Go for it. I'll let you sleep in it."

"*Tinora,*" she hisses.

Jerk, I think, the thought striking me from nowhere. Even without knowing her Raider-tongue, I understand the meaning behind the word.

"What does that mean?"

"You know what it means," she says. "Jerk."

Ivy climbs off the bed and goes to the corner. She folds her arms against her chest and rocks her narrow body back and forth, her eyes never leaving me as I fold her sheets enough to avoid the pile of feces she's gifted me.

"Where's the new one?" she asks.

"You know the drill. It will be on your bed when you get back."

"Back from where?"

She already knows this, so I'm not sure what she gets out of asking.

"Your escorts will be in shortly to take you to the showers to get cleaned up. Maybe if you're nice to them, they won't have to sedate you."

"I want them to sedate me," she whispers.

Though the anger in her eyes never dissipates, there's something else there, too. Fear?

"Why?"

"It's better that way. Easier, for when the doctor comes."

I flinch. There's something unsettling in the meaning behind her words. "Ivy, does the doctor do something to you that he shouldn't?"

"Everything the doctor does is something he shouldn't."

"I know you think that," I press, "but he's supposed to be helping you. Does he… does he touch you? Hurt you?"

Ivy steps across the floor so quickly, I barely have time to reach for my taser. The dirty sheets are the only thing between us as I swing the device up to rest against her side, but she doesn't reach for me, doesn't try to harm me; Ivy stares at me, her eyes boring into mine, begging me to see the world in the strange way she does.

"Send Nova," she whispers.

She steps back, returning to her corner, and I back out of the room. My heart is hammering against my ribs and even after I'm in the hall-way, I can't seem to catch my breath. Stevens puts a hand on my shoulder but I shrug him off and head toward the laundry. Something about the girl clings to me. As much as I don't want to think about it, I can't shake the haunted look in her eyes.

Eyes the exact shade of green as mine.

CHAPTER
THREE
CAMERON

Bets and I sit at the best table in the finest restaurant, wearing our fanciest clothes. Neither of us like it. I'm a guard, for star's sake, and before being called into the succession line for the Règleship, she spent her time bartending at the Dirty Onion. We're not made for fancy nights of schmoozing with high society.

But here we are.

It's a nice place, I must admit, even if I don't know which fork to use, and the dress I'm wearing is way too glam and makes me uncomfortable. And Bets looks like a billion credits, decked out in a low-cut burgundy dress that draws my eyes directly to her breasts, no matter how much effort I exert to not look at them. Her brown bob has been coiffed in a way that's stylish without making it so elaborate that it doesn't look like her. The Règle's personal stylist dressed her, dressed both of us, actually; but while I look like a kid playing dress-up in the flashiest gown their parents own, Bets looks like she belongs here, even if she says she doesn't feel like it.

We spent the first forty-five minutes of our evening out doing a meet-and-greet around the room. I couldn't guess the number of people we met tonight—rich people who paid quite a bit to be here tonight in the hopes of getting in Bets' good graces before her rise to power. I don't remember a single name because 1.) I don't care and, 2.) my traumatic brain injury tends to mess with my short term memory. At least, that's the excuse I'll use when she asks me questions later.

Now though, we've finally got some privacy and a moment to ourselves. The rest of the patrons are at their tables, and only occasionally glancing at us as they pretend to talk about other things. I glance around too, but not at them. I'm enthralled by the opulence of this place.

The ship itself is plain no matter where you look. There are rooms with decoration and color added, especially those where the affluent do their dealings, but this restaurant looks like it's from another world. There's polished wood—*actual wood*—on the floors. The ceiling is dark paneling, but delicate gold filigree fixtures hang over the individual tables, creating pockets of light through the dim room. I didn't know lights could even do that until we came here. Everywhere else on the ship there are running lights or panels; individual lights seem so luxurious. I'd hate to imagine how much dinner here costs. Probably more than my monthly salary. Luckily, we're not paying. Perks of being the future Règle.

Even the seats we're on are softer than anything my ass has ever touched. We're perched in front of a window, a rarity in itself, that stretches from one side of the restaurant to the other. I've never seen the planet below through more than a porthole, but tonight we've got a prime view to stare down at the dead world.

"What do you think it was like down there?" I ask absently as I watch the blue and white swirl below us.

Bets grimaces. "Why would you ask that?"

My brows furrow. "Haven't you ever wondered what it was like?"

"No," she says. Her voice is firm and final.

I can tell she doesn't want to talk about it anymore, but I don't understand what's wrong. She gets this way sometimes. I think I'm supposed to know why, but I don't remember.

I slide my hand across the table and place it on top of hers. "You look gorgeous tonight."

She purses her lips as her eyes slide up to mine. "You're just saying that."

"Not at all, babe. That dress really highlights your ass-" she glares at me and I add, "-ets. Assets."

A smile crawls across her face and I know the trouble has passed for now. She asks, "How was work?"

"Weird," I say, sipping on my fizzy orange drink. "I had to change the sheets for one of the patients today and she thought it would be a good idea to hop up and shit on the bed."

"Gross."

"Very."

"You need a new job."

I shrug. "It's not usually that bad. Just one girl who gives me a hard time."

"Why is that?"

"No clue. But I'm starting to think I should talk to Sarge about taking me off her rotation."

"Probably a good idea. Speaking of Sarge, did you get in trouble for being late?"

I smirk at her, and heat creeps up my neck as I remember the things she did to me this morning that made me late for work. If I play my cards right, maybe there will be a repeat performance tonight, in fancy dress this time.

"I did *not* get in trouble, but that's only because he wants to stay in good with my girlfriend."

"Right," she says, clearing her throat. "I've been wanting to talk to you about that."

"About Sarge?"

"No, about being your girlfriend." Despite the tightness of her dress, Bets shifts out of her seat and slips to one knee, still managing to look regal. She pulls a small box from her purse, pops it open, and asks, "Cameron Elaine Forsberg, will you do me the honor of being my wife?"

WE ASK FOR DINNER TO GO, BECAUSE I'M TOO EAGER TO RIP OFF MY *FIANCÉE'S* clothes. I'm desperate to see that fancy dress on the floor of our bedroom, so when the boxed food arrives, we practically race from the restaurant. The excitement of the evening burns bright in my veins, reminding me with each beat of my heart how much I love this woman. It doesn't matter that I can't remember before the accident; I love her now, in this moment, and I can't imagine anything else being as perfect as our future.

I hear clapping as we leave and I try to smile back at them, but my eyes are too focused on Bets to see much else.

She pulls me down the hall and we're running as fast as we can, stopping to steal kisses in empty alcoves as we go, but we're too far from home and I can't wait to be with her. I drag her through a door marked *Employees Only* and we fall against the wall of the service corridor. Her skin glows luminescent as I press myself against every part of her, hungry to taste and touch and tease my angel, my love. I bury my face against those perfect breasts who've been taunting me all evening, freeing them from the dress-prison that will keep my mouth from them no longer. She moans into my hair and it echoes down the hall behind us. The sound is so enchanting, I almost wish there was someone there to hear her.

I let her catch her breath. She pants against me as I hold her, a glorious smile on her face as she stares off into the darkness. When she lets out a deep sigh, I know she's back from her rapture. I smile and ask, "Ready to go home, future wife o' mine?"

"Oh, no you don't," she says, spinning me around so my back is against the wall. "It's your turn."

I run my hands through her soft brown hair, ruining the delicate designs the stylist created, while she lets her tongue trail along my body. I stare at the glittering gem on my finger as I let her consume me.

When she finally breaks away, I haul her up and press myself against her. Leaning up, I whisper, "I love you."

"I love you, too. Now let's get home so I can finish what you started."

The alarm blares into my dreams, jerking me awake. I sit up and swat it off, both annoyed and grateful to be awake. At least this time it rescued me from that strange nightmare that seems to be recurring as of late. I don't know what it means; it's always a handful of disjointed pictures that blur into one another, followed by gnashing teeth coming for my throat.

Bets is beside me in the dark and I trace a finger down her bare back. She stirs a little, and I know from experience that it wouldn't take much to have her awake and hungry in seconds, but instead I get out of bed and let her sleep.

I get ready for work in record time without the distraction of my insatiable future wife, and decide I'll make a coffee run before my shift. There's a dingy little shop I've been wanting to try on the wrong side of purple-thirty-triangle, but Bets never wants to go there. Rare mornings like this are my only chance to explore on my own, trying to reclaim some semblance of who I might have been, and I take these stolen moments every time.

There's not a lot of traffic out at this time of morning. I pass a handful of bleary-eyed people headed to jobs of their own. A couple nod at me, respecting, or at least acknowledging my position as a guard. I wonder if they'd still nod if they knew I mostly clean up after bratty teen rebel-wannabes.

I order and wait for my drink. When the man behind the counter hands it to me, his sleeve shifts up just enough for me to see a bird tattooed on his wrist. He tucks a strand of silvery-purple hair behind his ear and gives me a strange half smile.

As I step away, I wonder if I knew him before the accident or if I'm imagining it. Maybe I got coffee here every day and he wonders why I never make smalltalk anymore. Something about him felt so familiar, but when you're always searching for familiarity in a world that's constantly disappearing at the edges, it's easy to confuse a friendly face for more than it is.

I decide that I'm reading too much into it and turn my coffee up to take a drink when I see something written on the side of my cup. Scrawled in sloppy writing across the side, it says, *Nova, say hi to Ivy for me.*

I spin back to the coffee shop, to the green-eyed man with the raven tattoo, but he's gone and someone else is at the register. My eyes dart around the empty corridor, desperate for a chance to talk to this stranger. There's no trace of him.

A ding from my wrist lets me know work just started and I'm late again. With a sigh and one last look, I give up on raven-dude and jog off toward the cells where ~~they're~~ we're holding Ivy. I've been able to dismiss her so far, but a second person calling me by that name seems like more than just a teenager out of her head. The thought ignites something in me, a spark that I haven't felt since I woke from my accident, and a tiny part of me starts to fan the flame that maybe I am something more than who Bets tells me I am.

"Cam?"

I startle at the voice, turning to see one of the doctors that ~~hurts~~ helps the patients. He's a bit taller than me, lithe, handsome. His thick black hair is parted to the side, and his dark eyes crinkle when he smiles from under his well-trimmed beard and mustache.

"Doctor," I say, nodding toward him.

"Yosh," he says, offering his name and a kind smile. "Off to work?"

"Yeah."

"I'll walk with you, if that's okay."

I press my lips together, hoping it doesn't look like a grimace, and say, "Sure."

We walk through the corridors in silence. At first I worry about the quiet, that awkwardness will bloom between us as we travel, but that never quite happens. The doctor and I are not familiar with one another aside from occasionally passing as we move between patient rooms. Still, there's something easy, nearly comfortable, in the space between us. I consider asking him if we were friends before my accident but something holds me back. If we were and I've lost the friendship we once had, I think I would miss it all the more. So, I don't ask, and he doesn't mention it. We let companionable stillness stay with us instead.

He stops at an unmarked door in the corridor right before the entrance to the patient wing where I work, saying, "This is me."

I stop with him, and the awkwardness finally hits. I suddenly realize I don't know what to do with my hands. We stare at each other for a moment, before I swallow down the anxiety that has decided to lodge itself in my throat.

With a nod to his door I say, "Okay then."

The doctor's eyes crinkle again when he smiles, but there's a sadness there that I can't place. He nods in return and says, "Okay."

"I'm going," I say, hooking my thumb over my shoulder in the direction of my job. Heat creeps up my neck, into my cheeks, until I can feel warmth at the top of my ears.

"Be safe, Cam."

"Yeah," I say, though my brows crease at his words. "You too."

I turn on my heels and walk away. My encounter with the doctor has left me anxious, though I don't know why. Because it was unexpected, because he is so easy to be around, because he is too pretty, because I finally felt like I could take a full breath?

There's no time to digest whatever just happened, so I try to brush it out of my mind and hope I won't see him again for a while. As easy as it is to be in his presence, it also feels like dangerous ground.

I step into the corridor and clock in, my thoughts turning to what my workday holds. Hopefully the girl will be calm today so I can get some answers from her. Or, if she's wild again, maybe I'll head back to the coffee shop and try to stake out the purple-haired person who clearly knows something I don't. Either way, I'm getting answers. Even if they're answers I don't like.

CHAPTER
FOUR
IVY

The door slides open and one of the guards peeks around. I meet her eyes, taking pleasure in her flinch when she finds me looking at her. I'm not strong and brave like my sister; I can't kill these people with a stare, as they seem to think she can. But I can match her in wildness. I can be her twin in ferocity, mirror her anger and contempt for those who keep me here, even if I'm all bark and no bite.

The guards don't seem to know the difference.

The doctors, though, they know. And I know the guard checking in is just a precaution before they send in one of the doctors. Usually they tie my hands, just in case, but not today. Today, they drugged me.

I wasn't sure at first, but it didn't take long before I felt the calmness coursing through me. It isn't the first time, but it's definitely the strongest dose. My anxiety has faded from a constant river flowing through me to nothing more than a trickle, a drop of nerves barely registering in my psyche. Like this, I can't even muster enough indignation to hiss at the guard checking on me, nor can I be bothered that I'm failing at this minor task.

"She's settled," the guard says over her shoulder.

In the background, someone admonishes her for taking her eyes off me. They're giving too much credit to a station-born girl who grew up around these corridors. Even if I could get out of here, there's nowhere for me to go. It's not like I could gain control of the station and fly us off somewhere away from the planet, turning this stationary prison into the vessel of exploration it should have been. At least, I don't think I could...

I blink back the thought, unsure where it came from. It's too heavy for my drug-addled brain. Besides, there's something far more pressing happening right here, right now.

"I told them I didn't want to see you again," I say, my voice slurring out the words. Whatever they've given me today is strong.

He shrugs. "They don't really care what you want. You're a prisoner, after all."

I narrow my eyes at him, trying and failing to muster the rage that is tempered just out of reach. Instead, I focus on the hand twitching inside his jacket pocket. He's nervous.

There are two doctors who come to see me. One is cruel, fond of violent treatments and putting his hands where they don't belong; the second is kind, always trying to soothe me and talk away my anger and fear. I hate them both equally.

"I may be a prisoner, but I'm still a citizen. I know my rights."

"You don't have any rights. You forfeited them during the rebellion."

"Is that what they're calling it? The rebellion?" I ask, a laugh catching in my throat. It fizzles out before it can fully form. "That's a strong word for a bunch of escaped convicts trying to get away from this place and find a free home elsewhere, only to be corralled back and locked away again."

He shrugs. "You were going to come back and cause harm to the station. You had to be stopped."

"*We*," I growl. "*We* were going to come back. Or have you completely disassociated yourself from us?"

"I didn't have a choice. I was taken to the ground against my will. The Règle knew I was innocent in the attempted coup."

"What about Krew? And Baz? Were they innocent? Or have you forgotten them so completely that it doesn't matter anymore?"

Dr. Okada swallows hard before he speaks, and I can't help wondering if it's the name of his lover or his brother that he's forcing from his mouth, swallowing them down into the darkness so the thought of them can't hurt him. "I can't speak for them. I only know what happened to me."

My anger bubbles up over the dam the medicine has built inside me and I growl, "You're a traitor." Though I want to rage at him further, I can't sustain those feelings for more than a moment.

He shakes his head but doesn't argue. "I'm here to help you, Ivy. Will you let me?"

"I don't want your help, Yosh. I can't trust you. I'd rather have Dr. Shaw."

Yosh runs a hand over his face, then brushes away the dark hair that has fallen into his eyes. He mutters, "Shaw is dangerous."

"At least I know what I'm getting with him," I say. I rub at my temples, trying to fight the headache that's forming behind my eyes. It's hard to hold onto my hatred while I'm drugged, hard to focus on all the reasons I want Yosh to go away. If I make him leave, Shaw will take his place. I might *say* I'd rather deal with him, but my resolve gives out when the shock therapy sessions start.

"I know what you think of me. I understand why. But I can't sit by and let him mistreat you."

"Isn't that how you got yourself into trouble last time?" I ask. "You helped another girl who Shaw was hurting, and it got you kidnapped to the ground. That's the story, right?"

"Maybe you're right. If I'd left your sister alone and let Shaw 'accidentally' over-stimulate her brain, she'd be dead and none of this would have happened. But I didn't. I tried to save her. Because I..." he trails off. Okada clenches his jaw, the only sign he's given that my words are having any effect on him.

"Because?" I prompt, my curiosity overpowering my rage.

He shakes his head, refusing to answer. Instead, he says, "Maybe I should learn that lesson; letting him shock you to death is probably the right decision."

I stir, forcing my body to stand. He's not afraid of me like the guards. He pretends to be, for their benefit, but we both know he doesn't look at me with the same reverence as with her. They seem to think I can access Nova's abilities, but Okada knows better. He holds his ground.

"What other options do I have?" I ask. "Watch them destroy my sister over and over, stealing her brain when her memories become inconvenient for them? I'd rather be dead."

He steps closer and I raise my hands toward him. I want to throw my fists until he cries out, but I am not strong and brave. I am not the girl they fear. Yosh catches my hands with his and I feel something pressing between our palms. I try to pull my hand away to look at it, but he shakes his head, a movement so small I'm not sure I saw it.

"I'm not your enemy," he says, his voice quiet and his words rushed. "I want to help you. I want to help Nova. I've been working on something to stabilize her memories so the Règle won't have to keep erasing them. If I can figure that out," he glances at our joined hands for a fraction of a second, "then one shot should do the trick. It might take a few days to settle, but it could definitely work."

"Why are you telling me this?"

"I want you to know that I'm going to help Nova."

"Because the Règle wants you to."

"Yes, but also because *I* want to."

I realize with suddenness exactly why he wants to save her. "You love her."

Yosh meets my eyes but doesn't acknowledge what I said. "You have to do this. Not for me—I don't care what you think about me—but for her."

"Who will she be, if you can get her memories to stabilize? The real Nova, or the persona they've created for her?"

He hesitates then, his eyes trailing to the corner of the room and back. I've always thought a camera was in the room, but I've never been able to pinpoint its location. It seems like Okada just did.

He says, "I have to give the people their best chance of survival, the best life they can have without everything going to pieces. Who do you think would be best for that?"

His answer is phrased in such a way that both Nova and Cameron could be the answer, depending on who is asking the question. If we're both listening to his words right now, which of us is he lying to? There's no way for me to know.

He releases my hands and I drop them to my side. I throw myself back on the bed and hide the thing he's given me under the hem of my shift. "How do I know you want to help us?"

"You don't," he says, shrugging. "But who else can you trust?"

"I can't trust anyone."

He nods. "I hope you'll feel differently the next time I see you."

I swallow, all the fight drained out of me. "Me, too."

He walks to the door, turns to look at me one last time before he leaves. "Next time you see Cam, tell her hi for me."

"She won't remember you."

He shrugs. "You never know."

Then he's gone and I'm left wondering what the hell I'm supposed to do with the syringe full of liquid that's resting against my leg.

CHAPTER
FIVE
CAMERON

I step into Ivy's cell, close the door, and fold my arms across my chest. She's sitting on her bed, leaning against the wall with her arms behind her head like she couldn't be more relaxed.

"Which one are you today?"

"What happens if I say I'm Nova?"

Ivy smirks. "You're not, though."

"How can you tell?"

She looks me up and down before saying, "There's no blood on your uniform."

My brows lift in surprise. "Nova is violent?"

"Nova is a person. She's complicated and messy and she does a lot of messed up stuff."

"That doesn't sound like someone I want to be."

"You don't always get to choose," she says. Her words hint at a secret she isn't willing to share, of dreams traded in for a much harsher reality.

"What if you could? What would you choose?"

"Doesn't matter. I'm here, and whatever else could've been is gone."

"That's sad."

"We're all sad. We're all just containers for dreams and desires that are never going to come true."

"Is that what Nova told you? Because she's wrong, you know. You don't have to give up on yourself. We could work together to get you rehabilitated and help you have a real life after this place."

"Why? So I can have a pretend life, like you? No thanks."

The comment digs deeper than it should. Maybe because part of me wonders what I'm missing from before my accident, or maybe her words just resonate with whoever I was before. She's wrong, though. I have a beautiful life with an amazing woman who I'm going to love forever. The rest is just background noise.

"I'm happy with who I am and the life I have. People can take bad situations and make the best of them, if given the right opportunities. Even you."

"Not you, though, no matter how much you protest," she says. "Because you're not really a person, are you, Cam? You're a figment of the Règle's imagination, made into her pretty little plaything."

I press my lips into a grim line. Whatever I'd hoped to get out of this session with the patient, it's clearly not going to happen. Which makes sense, really, since she's delusional. Coming here was a mistake.

As I step back toward the door, she says, "You're getting closer to the truth, you know."

I pause, my hand on the door handle. "The truth as you see it may not be the same as the one I see."

Ivy laughs. "What triggered you this time? Did you lose your temper again and almost go full-Raider? Or catch a rerun of that deathmatch TV show you starred in? Maybe Benjy sent another one of his cryptic messages? Or was it—"

"Benjy?" I ask. The name tickles something in my brain that I can't scratch. "Is that the guy with the bird tattoo?"

She shrugs. "Never met the guy, so I couldn't say. I just know that a while back, two, maybe three times ago when you were Nova, you told me someone named Benjy had triggered your memory."

"Two or three times ago?"

"Yeah. Not sure which. The Nova transitions start to run together each time you restart."

"Wait," I say, "what are you saying? What happens to me—or what do you *think* happens to me?"

"You remember."

"Remember what? I don't remember anything—"

"—since the accident," she says at the same time I do.

"I've never told you about that."

"*You* haven't, no, but my sister has. Only bits. We never get long to talk before—"

The creak of the door behind me interrupts her words and she smiles, as if she'd been expecting a visitor and they arrived precisely on time.

"Everything okay here?" Stevens asks, hand at his taser like he expects he'll need to use it.

"Fine," I say. I try to catch Ivy's gaze, though I'm not sure what I expect to find there, but her eyes are locked on him.

"No need to call in the squad yet," she says. "She's still Cameron."

A strange expression crosses his face for the briefest of seconds. Relief? Then his eyes shift to me and he winces.

"What's that look about?" I ask.

"Nothing. Just worried she got to you. She's wily, that one."

My eyes shift to Ivy who smiles as if Stevens' very appearance proves her words are true. "She has a lot to say about who I am. A lot more to say than the people who I've worked with for the past few years."

Stevens gulps visibly, and it's almost comical the way he's so clearly trying to hide something. "It was traumatic. We don't want you to have to relive it. That's all."

That is most definitely not all. Everything about him has changed over the course of seconds. "You know, no one will tell me directly about the accident. They tell me it's too painful, it's too awful, it's too traumatic to relive. So, how am I supposed to recover from something that no one will talk about? How can I avoid having this terrible thing happen again if not one of you will tell me what happened?"

He pauses for too long before saying, "It's complicated. I don't think I could explain it if I tried."

"Try."

His eyes widen and he stutters, "I... can't."

I nod as I purse my lips and say, "Why don't you tell me the truth about what's going on? Right now."

Ivy says, "He's not allowed. And he's probably scared, though I'm not sure if it's of you or the Règle. Maybe both. You've never made a move toward him, but he's seen what you can do. It's enough to scare anyone."

I watch the way Stevens' face contorts at her words. He's not made for keeping secrets, but this seems like way too much to be real. Swallowing the lump that has formed in my throat, I choke out the words: "It's true?"

"Of course not," he says, forcing a too-loud laugh. "This little witch has gotten into your head."

"You know what happens when people get in Nova's way," Ivy says in a strange sing-song voice. She throws herself back onto the bed with a cackle and rolls around like she's having the time of her life.

"And you know what happens to those who defy the Règle," he grinds out through clenched teeth.

Ivy sits up, shrugs. "She's going to switch soon, Stevens. You're one of the decent ones, so I'd hate to see you get your face smashed in."

Stevens swallows, a visible lump bobbing down his throat. This man really is afraid of me.

No, not me; he's afraid of Nova.

"Stevens," I say, "no one has to know what you tell me."

The look on his face turns sad. He might be afraid of Nova, but he pities Cam.

"The room is bugged," Ivy says. Stevens says nothing, but she goes on as if he confirmed it. "I thought so. They've caught her so fast each time I've been the trigger."

"Each time? How many times has this happened?"

"A few," Ivy shrugs.

Stevens murmurs, "Too many."

"You might as well tell her. You know they'll be here soon and she'll forget again."

Stevens scrubs a hand over his head. When he speaks, the words rush out as if they've been dammed up and waiting for a breach. "We keep eyes on you, we do everything we can to keep you contained, but you keep killing the Règle. They catch you when Ivy is the trigger, but whenever you figure things out without your sister, someone dies."

"How many times?" I ask.

"You've tried to rescue me six times," Ivy chimes in. "Three other times you had just figured it out and hadn't formed a plan yet."

"And you've killed the Règle five times."

"Well that's just poor security," Ivy says. "Never happened when my father was in charge of the division. At least, not until the end when he finally stood up to you bastards."

"So, wait: six times I've tried to rescue you, three times without a plan, and five murders. That's fourteen times. Fourteen times I've been another *person*?"

"Probably closer to twenty, if I were to guess. There's probably a few we're unaware of."

"How long has this been happening?"

Ivy raises her hands. "No clue. They won't let me keep a calendar in here. I've asked."

"Nearly a year," Stevens says.

Ivy sighs. "Longer than I thought."

Stevens' words send me reeling and for a moment I think I might pass out. I suck in a strangled breath, then another, until the darkness recedes from the edges of my vision and I can focus again. "I've been flipping between two personalities for a YEAR?!"

Stevens and Ivy both raise their hands to try to calm me down. Ivy says, "Keep it together, Cam. We're in uncharted territory today."

Ivy steps toward me, arms outstretched as if she wishes to embrace me. Stevens says, "Take a step back, kid. I don't want to tase you."

"One hug before they get here," she says. "I just want a moment with my sister."

He sighs, like he can't believe he's going to let his heart lead for a minute, then nods. She approaches, but I don't know how to react. She steps in anyway. Her arms wrap around me and I look for something familiar in that gesture, but it's as foreign to me as everything else in my life. Just before I pull away, I feel a tiny pinch on the underside of my arm. I jerk back from her; her smile is tight, strained, as I watch her slip something back in her pocket.

Was that a syringe? Did she just drug me?

I open my mouth to ask what she's done, but she shakes her head the tiniest bit, and my insides screech to an obedient halt. I don't know which instincts to trust—those rational, surface feelings that are screaming inside my brain that I need to go to a doctor immediately because this kid just poisoned me, or the ones that lie underneath, so deep they're nearly ingrained in my bones, that tell me Ivy wouldn't hurt me.

"Sorry," she mouths. She steps back and says, "You're looking pale, Cam."

All else seems to fade to the background and I nearly forget everything happening, including that I'm half sure she just stuck a needle in my arm. I laugh, a high, thin sound that doesn't sound right to my ears. "Cam? Nova? Which one is it?"

"If you don't remember anything, then it's Cam," she says. "And that's an interesting turn, because Cam has never asked these questions before. It's always been Nova coming in here asking questions."

Stevens says, "If you were Nova, I'd stun you until security gets here. But if you're Cam, it's all good. But not completely Cam? I have no idea what to do."

"And that begs another question…"

I spin toward the words, my heart sinking when I see Bets in the doorway. I take a half-step toward her and stop.

"What am I supposed to do with you now that you're someone in-between?"

Before I can stop them, the words stagger out of me: "Tell me it's not true."

"What good would that do?"

"I don't understand," I say, verging on tears. "We have a life together, we just got engaged!"

Bets nods, but the expression on her face is far more calculated than any I've seen on her before. "Things have been good. I really thought we were moving forward. The relationship has been solid, you haven't seemed too curious about your past, and the sex"—she expels a breath and shakes her head—"mind-blowing. But alas, all good things must come to an end."

Her gaze flicks behind me and I turn, too late, as something sharp pricks my neck. Stevens. What has he done?

Ivy wails, "You sonuvabitch!"

"Control her," Bets says, as guards flood the room and head straight to Ivy. Bets traces a finger down my cheek and says, "My predecessor passed today—very tragic, no *idea* what happened—so I'm the Règle now. Can't have you running amok, knowing how you've behaved toward those in my position previously."

As she speaks, the edges of my vision curl, fade to a fuzzy black, and I feel myself falling, falling, falling…

CHAPTER
SIX

CAMERON

"Cameron, can you hear me?"

I blink. My eyelids are heavy, protesting. Bright light surrounds me. I try to lift my head, my hands, anything, but I'm just so tired.

"Don't move, babe. You're okay. I promise."

Her voice is so sweet, so soothing; it makes me wish I knew who she was. I mumble, "What happened?"

It's quiet for a long time, or what feels long, and I wonder if maybe I didn't actually say anything. Then that sweet, soothing voice says, "My love, you've been in an accident. But don't worry; the doctors are taking care of everything and you're going to be just fine."

CHAPTER
SEVEN

HIRO

I hammer the staff against the metal makeshift stage, sending echoes booming across the square. All eyes stare up as I say, "Tonight, we honor the sun who gives us the day, who withdraws so we may have night. Like the sun, we give ourselves to whom we choose as we share the right to wed. Like the sun, we turn away as we desire, offering instead a period of rest."

The words are repeated out through the square by the translators, making sure every group of Raiders knows what we do tonight, and why. Once the translators have finished their work, I shake the staff, listening to the rattle of the beads, and thinking back to when Nova held this staff a year ago.

I open my mouth to continue, but the lump forming in my throat stops me. Caita steps up beside me and dips her head in respect. I nod my permission for her to speak and she says, "Chief Hiro, it is your right to choose first. Who will you have as your mate?"

I swallow back the emotion lodged inside me. Looking out over the assembly, I can't help but consider the question. Our numbers have grown dramatically since we came to Old York. All told, I lead nearly a thousand Raiders committed to the cause against the star-people. And I could choose anyone from among them as my mate.

My eyes catch those of Nadja, the beast handler. Her gray and white cat is curled at her feet, but I've seen her training the creature and know how ferocious it can be. She is a beautiful woman, and though she is double my age, I'm certain she'd make a fine mate. No doubt she could teach me a few things, and I would be an eager student.

I scan farther into the crowd, where Rego stands alongside his protege, Fatboy. The young Raider's nickname betrays the man he's grown into—a man who is as pleasing to the eyes as any I've ever seen. He's kind, jovial, and loyal to Nova. With Rego's guidance, he'll be a chief of his own group of Raiders some day, once this band has achieved its goal and Nova is home. Today, though, he could be mine, if I wished for it.

Perched at the edge of the crowd is our techie, Javian. He never chooses a mate, to my knowledge. I'm not sure he's even a Raider at this point, though he's committed to the cause. Our eyes lock for a long moment, and I envision what the next few months would be like if I went home to him everyday. Making him breakfast, listening to his stories as he talks about his work in the lab, drinking in the scent of him every morning as he unfurls his long limbs from mine.

I shake my head, dislodging the thoughts, and look away from him. It dawns on me then that I didn't even consider the merits of sleeping with him, though I'm quite certain it would be delightful. When did I become someone who let his mind run rampant with thoughts of *cuddling*?

I take a deep breath and let my eyes wander again, surveying the many bodies gathered before me, trying to shake off the weird feeling that lingers in my chest when I spy the hot scientist. I ignore the way my heart squeezes tighter at the sight of him; the true pain of my philandering heart is knowing that I could have any of them, and they'd eagerly come to my bed, but doing so would diminish the legend I've built around their missing Chief.

With a deep breath, I say, "I choose Nova-du, true Chief and wife of my heart."

There's a pause as the translators deliver the message across our mighty band, then in near unison, the Raiders bring a fist against their chests and stomp their feet, cheering, "Nova-du, Nova-du."

Oh, Squirrel, I miss you.

A smile spreads across my face. She would absolutely hate all this attention, and here I've gone and turned her into some great myth among the Raiders. To the newer people, the ones who haven't met her, the stories of all she's done are passed to them like the texts of an old god, and she is regarded with as much reverence.

When quiet falls again, I impart the right of guiding the choosing ceremony to the translators. Each has been trained as a chief would be, and the groups break up into smaller sections to choose from those who speak their language.

Mostly. There are some who speak multiple languages, or at least enough to get by in the other groups. Some of the translators move among the groups more freely. And there's always a star-crossed coupling here and there between people who can only understand one another with the language of their bodies.

Zeb is a hot commodity no matter where he's located in the crowd, and though he turns down everyone who chooses him, he never has less than four trying to win his heart.

I get it. He's a mountain of a man, handsome, strong, loyal, kind. There's nothing bad to say about him. Sometimes I see the way he looks at Caita and I think maybe he'll choose her at the next ceremony, but his devotion to little Sarah keeps him from choosing a mate. He's committed to being the father she lost and won't let his affections be divided.

Maybe we're alike in that way. Him with Sarah, me with Nova. Not sure if we're devoted, or just fools. Probably a little bit of both.

The ceremony lasts late into the night, with mates trickling out of the circles until early morning. Folly and Gareem pass by with their new mate in tow. He's a good-looking fellow with thick black curls around his ears. I smile at them, but they're too preoccupied to pay me any attention. I wonder if they ever miss me like I miss them. It's not the same as the way I miss Nova; with her, it's like an ache in my bones. With them, I miss their warmth, the comfort of their figures on soft rugs, the way their bodies rose to greet me.

I need to get laid.

The last of the couples and throuples and quads are making their way to their homes and I can finally head back to my bunk. Most of the Raiders have taken up residences in the old buildings on the underside of the city, in tenements that peek above the water. Newer parts of the city have been built to connect the tops of the skyscrapers, though some of the bridges are too precarious for me to even think about crossing them. Those are the places that belong to the outcasts of the city, the ones who come to the Raiders and find the first home they've ever known.

I can't imagine what it would have been like to walk through this place before the water came and erased everything Old York once was. Sometimes when I close my eyes, I think I can still hear the sounds of the long-dead city.

I still sleep in my old room on the *Curiosity*. Caita has tried to talk me into moving to a permanent place on more than one occasion, but I brush her off, though I don't know why.

I sigh. I'm lying to myself again. I know *exactly* why. Joking with Nova in that bed is the last happy memory I have with her. The worst thing is, I know I'm starting to give up hope. If I leave that room, my last tie to her, I don't know if I can keep doing this.

We're docked in the middle of a building with the side blown out of it. A lot of the buildings have held up surprisingly well, despite the years without anyone caring for them. I can even recognize some from old movies. This one even has most of the old windows on the west side of it.

I cross onto the ship and head below deck, eager to crawl into that damned bed and fall into dreams, hopefully those involving me getting some action. When I step into the room, there's a shape curled up on the bed.

My hand grabs the blade at my side and I brandish it toward the intruder. He unfurls himself and stretches, standing up to show his massive form. Broad shoulders, arms thick with muscle and covered in swirling black tattoos, dark curls pushed back from his furrowed brow. The last thing I need is to see a specimen like that in my bed. I'm barely keeping it together as is.

"You scared the shit out of me."

"Me?" Thoa asks. "You're the one holding a knife."

"We both know you could take it if you wanted to." *He could take just about anything he wants*, I think. I slip it back in its sheath and ask, "What are you doing here?"

"Waiting for you. We need to talk."

Though this isn't how this dream normally begins, I'm okay to go with it. Usually, he wouldn't be wearing pants. I cross the room and begin to undress, willing my brain to carry out the full fantasy before I wake. "About what?"

"It's done."

"What's done?"

"The device. I met with Javian earlier this evening. We're ready to go whenever you are. They can get everyone onboard in a matter of seconds."

I turn to face him, my eyes going wide as I realize this is very much not one of my dirty dreams. "Seriously?"

He nods and I swallow hard, my mouth suddenly dry. I try to step toward the bed, but find my body shaking so bad I can't move my legs. Thoa is at my side a moment later, wrapping his massive arm around my waist and helping me sit down.

After a few minutes, I finally manage to say, "We can get her. We can really do this."

"Yeah," he says, a smile brightening his beautiful face. His azure eyes are alight as he says, "It's been a long time coming, but we're ready. We're going to save Nova."

I VISIT JAVIAN THE NEXT DAY. MY ADVISOR, APOLLINE, DISCOVERED THAT HE has a fondness for oranges, so I barter for a couple to take to him. I stand outside the door to his lab, rotating the oranges in my hand as the citrus smell permeates the air. For the briefest moment I try to figure out why my palms are sweaty.

When I finally get up the nerve, I step forward and rap my knuckles on the door in time with the beat of my heart. It's hammering against my ribs, far faster than it should. I'm having trouble swallowing, too, now that I think of it. Maybe I'm coming down with something…

Javian opens the door, his cheeks flushed, his hair an ungodly mess. It looks like he's been raking his fingers through it to try to tame it, and all he's managed to do is make it stand straight up. He stares at me for a moment as if trying to figure out who I am and why I'm bothering him, and not for the first time, I wonder how he can contain so much light in eyes so dark.

"Is this a bad time?" I ask.

"Oh, gods no," he sputters. "Please come in, Chief."

He wipes his hands down the sides of his blue pants, and I wish I could do the same. To my pants, of course, not his. I swallow hard—there's that pesky sickness coming around again—and will myself *not* to think about my hands on his pants.

"I brought these for you," I say, extending the oranges. Javian's face lights up and I bask in that moment, short as it is.

"I can't accept these. They're too rare."

They are, and they cost more than I'm willing to admit, but I don't want him to know that. "You *can* take them, and you will. If you don't, they'll go to waste."

"You don't like them?" he asks, brows rising in surprise.

"They're fine, but not my favorite. I like pears."

"They're *my* favorite," he says, staring down as I pass the orbs to him. "How did you know?"

"I have my ways."

His eyes flash up to mine and I see him trying to work out my secrets. What he hasn't yet figured out is that I'd tell him anything he wanted if he'd ask. I'm certain I couldn't keep anything from him if he pressed. But he doesn't. He never does. Maybe that's what I like about him. Javian never seems eager to take things from me, even the things I give willingly, and I appreciate his desire to be his own man.

Javian leads me through his workshop. There are strange things throughout—beakers, burners, piles of ingredients that I couldn't name if I tried—and I suddenly realize I have no idea what this man does.

I stop just before we move to the next room and ask, "What is all this?"

Javian's ears tinge pink. "Just some... experiments."

"Thought you were our tech guru."

"I am, I guess. But I've been reading some of the old books the Raiders have found since we've been in Old York, and I wanted to try some stuff."

"Those texts are hundreds of years old," I say, brows furrowing. "What could you possibly learn from them?"

"I wouldn't expect you to understand. You come from above, where life continues to progress. But a lot of what people once knew has been lost down here. I thought maybe I could bring some of it back."

I nod, but my distrust of doctors and scientists is starting to seep into my thoughts. Javian has always struck me as someone to be trusted, until now. Should I really let a few "experiments" change that?

I shake my head, trying to dispel my bias. "I'm surprised you could find anything usable in those books. They weren't in great shape."

"There's definitely been some guesswork with it. Some of the texts were completely faded or damaged, and I've had to piece together quite a bit of it. Most of it still doesn't make sense, but if I could figure out even a little of it, what might that do for our society?"

His desire to help is clear on his face, and any blooming doubts because of my distrust of doctors is overridden by my faith in him. "I have some things from above that may help. I'll have Apolline bring them over later."

The look of amazement on his face sends a weird fluttering through my stomach. I definitely need to rest later. As much as I hate doctors, maybe visiting one wouldn't be a bad idea. Copperhill is due to arrive tomorrow, and if I'm going to see *anyone*, Davie would be my best bet. She saved Rego from death's door; I'm sure she could handle a cold or whatever is causing this weird, warm feeling in my chest.

"Are you feeling okay? Do you need to sit down?"

My eyes track back to Javian. "Yeah, yeah I'm good. Just a little distracted."

"Do you want to see the new tech, or…"

"Please," I say, flashing him a smile. "That's why I'm here, after all."

"Right," he says, lips stretching in a tight smile.

We go into the next room and Javian explains the tech he's working on. Most of what he says is lost on me, but his confidence in what he's talking about is what's important. I don't know how to do the things he does, but I trust in his expertise. Without him, there'd be no chance of rescuing Nova. And that's my priority.

"So, yeah," he says, drawing my attention back to him. "That's how it works."

"And you're sure it *will* work?"

"Definitely. You could go right now, if you wanted."

It's tempting. I could go, save Nova, and be back by dinner. Or, I could get caught. Besides, knowing her as I do, I'm sure Nova wouldn't be happy with being the only one back on the ground.

"That's great news," I say, trying to keep my tone level, though I'm not sure why I don't want Javian to hear my excitement. "What about the rest of the plan?"

He sighs. "I can get them there, but it's still a little sloppy. With a little more time—"

"We're out of time," I say, cutting him off.

He bites his lip, his eyes going soft. "I know you miss your, uh, wife, and I know you're eager to get her back, but if you want to do it efficiently and keep our people safe, I think I could do a better job of it with a little patience."

I chew on his words as I try to dismiss my haste. Of course I'm in a hurry to get to Nova, but it's already been so long that a little more time might not matter. Finally, I ask, "You think, or you know?"

"I know. I can make this work and protect our people, if you can wait a little longer."

"How much longer?"

Javian looks over to the jumble of wires and bracelets piled on his work table. "A few weeks, maybe a month."

"A month?" I ask, rubbing a hand over my face. He nods, but his expression is full of pity. I meet his eyes again, taking in all that they show me, and return his nod. "Do it."

"You're sure?"

"Don't give me the chance to change my mind. Just get to work. In a month's time, we're going, whether you're ready or not."

I turn and leave, unwilling to give him another chance to show me the pity he holds for me. I may be a broken man, but I'll not have the whole world seeing it. Besides, I need to find a place to rest before my heart beats right out of my chest.

A few minutes later—once I'm away from Javian, strangely enough—my heart settles back to normal.

CHAPTER
EIGHT
CAMERON

Bets tugs my hand as she drags me to the next stall. We're in a market—Pœwani, I think she said. She wants to show me where we fell in love in the hopes that it will trigger some memories. Does she know how desperately I want this to work? Can she see it in my eyes when she looks at me, her face so clearly full of love, and I stare back feeling nothing?

I *need* those memories. In my addled brain, they feel important. Bets says we'll make new ones, but those fragile things are who I am. They brought me to this point, made me fall in love with this woman...

Without them, this ring on my finger feels like a chain binding me to a stranger. Maybe the other me was madly in love with her, but I'm not. I don't know her. Sometimes when she talks, my mind wanders to who I must have been before. I can't seem to reconcile my current feelings with the life I must have had. Sometimes when she talks, I want to smack the hell out of whoever I was before, because I can't imagine how they could've fallen in love with *this* woman. There is something deep in my gut that doesn't feel right when I'm with Bets; it's constantly whispering *run, run, run.*

She knows something is wrong. Last night, she tried to kiss me and I recoiled. It was involuntary, an unintended response I couldn't control.

There was something in her eyes then—betrayal? Anger? Suspicion? I don't know for sure, but whatever she felt, it was more than hurt.

Today she planned this impromptu trip around the market, where she greets adoring people eager to shake her hand. Some have even bowed to her, the new Règle. Meanwhile, she drags me behind her, never letting me out of her sight. When I suggested she greet the throng without me and let me hover along the edge of the crowd, genuine panic spread across her face before she could rein it in. She doesn't like for me to be out of her sight.

Maybe it's because of my accident. She refuses to tell me what happened. Though she promises we'll talk about it after I've had "time to heal," I can't help but wonder if she had something to do with what happened to me. Not on purpose, I don't think. Bets is adored by many who seem to regard her as a kind person, and she seems to truly love me. It's just… I don't know. Something is off. I can't put my finger on it, but I *feel* it. Every sweet thing she does for me sends my guts writhing.

She squeezes my hand and smiles back at me as she pulls me out of the crowd and toward a filthy-looking bar. *Vuile Ui* is written above the door and I scrunch up my face, mouthing, "Dirty Onion?"

"You remember?" Bets asks, excitement coloring her tone. I wince, shake my head, and point at the sign. She asks, "Since when do you speak Dutch?"

I tap the side of my head with one finger and say, "No clue. You didn't know?"

"One of your many secrets," she says. Her brows crease for a fraction of a second before she's smiling at me again. "Don't worry, I'm sure this will jog your memories. It's always worked in the past."

I stop dead but she keeps walking until our arms are stretched wide between us. "What does that mean? Have you had to bring me here before?"

"That came out wrong," she says amidst a nervous laugh.

"You make it sound like I have a habit of losing my memory."

She closes the gap between us and places her finger under my chin, tilting it so I meet her eyes. "Don't be ridiculous, babe."

My doubt crests into full-blown suspicion, sending prickles of heat to the tips of my fingers. They *ache* to do something… violent? Though I'm not sure why my mind went to that, something about it feels right.

"You've got exactly ten seconds to explain yourself or I'm leaving."

She swallows. "It's just, well, I always bring you here when we're having trouble."

"Trouble?"

"No relationship is perfect," she says. "I do my best, but I'm not perfect. Especially with this new position. I mean, the Règle? It's so far away from who I was when we first met, and sometimes I have to come here—*we* have to come here—to remember who we were and try to realign our feelings for each other."

"Oh," is all I can get out. I don't believe her.

She nods, encouraged by my syllable. "I didn't want to bring it up. I've been trying to make things good between us, but I know the accident has made things hard for you. And, well, I was worried you were pulling away from me. I don't know what I'd do without you."

The expression on her face breaks me. Even if I'm not feeling particularly keen on her right now, she's doing her damnedest to keep us moving forward. It can't have been easy for her to deal with my accident, taking care of me, and now to be fighting against the very person who once proclaimed their love for her. At least, I assume I proclaimed it. Whatever. Maybe I only whispered it. Maybe I only vaguely agreed because I was lonely or bored or horny. Either way, this whole situation has been rough on her; the least I could do is make a little effort.

I pull her close and wrap my arms around her. When I pull back and look at her, I say, "Welp, I'm an asshole. I'm sorry."

She brushes a red strand of hair back from my face and says, "It's okay."

"It's not. I've been pushing against you as if you're my enemy instead of the woman who has worked to make me better. Bringing me here was a kindness, not an act of attrition."

"You didn't know."

"But I should've," I say. "You've been amazing through this whole ordeal. And obviously if you want me to come to some place called the Dirty Onion, there's a reason for it. So, lead on, Bets. I trust you."

I don't, but she hasn't given me a reason not to, so I'll just keep saying it until it is true. Or until I break.

Her face lights up and she takes my hand again, dragging me into the hole-in-the-wall bar that means nothing to me, but seems to make her happy. The place is lit almost entirely by a neon sign above the bar. It's probably safer that way; you can't see all the dirt that gives this place its name. She makes small talk with the hot bartender, his crazy-deep dimples appearing cavernous thanks to the shadows of the room. Though I check out his ass while he makes our drinks, even that can't help me out of the funk I'm in.

I smile when Bets needs me to, I pretend to enjoy my time as I listen to her stories. She seems to believe we're on the same page, at least for now. My acting is at least good enough to hide the truth of my feelings, though I don't know that I'll be able to do it for long. No matter what my words say, no matter how much I pretend to go along with her, I can't shake the sense that something is wrong.

My only consolation is the knowledge that it will all come out in the end. I hold that in my heart with a certainty that I have about nothing else. Whatever Bets is hiding won't stay hidden forever.

I SLEEP FOR WHAT SEEMS LIKE DAYS. THERE'S NOTHING ELSE FOR ME TO DO. No job, no friends—none that I remember, anyway—and even if I suggest something simple like taking a stroll, Bets acts like it's a huge undertaking. Stars forbid I plan to go out on my own. Her head nearly exploded when I suggested walking to the coffee shop and back.

I like to imagine she wasn't always like this. In the stories she tells and the memories I try to create from the nothingness in my brain, she was carefree and wild, a free spirit. I have to think of her that way, rather than the woman I'm sharing an apartment with, despite the evidence before me. I can barely stand living with Bets as things are; I don't think I could fall in love with this version of her.

Despite the circumstances bordering confinement, there's something terribly freeing about losing your memories. I find myself not giving a single shit about what anyone thinks, and that alone is glorious. I don't know if the old Cameron felt that freedom, but I highly doubt it. Being engaged to Bets makes me think the old Cam was bogged down by worry and wanting to please those around her.

I'm glad old Cam is gone.

When I decide to sneak out while Bets is asleep, I'm certain it is against the old Cam's better judgment. I can't even imagine how angry it will make my fiancée if she finds out. I want to feel bad, especially after how hard she's been trying to make me happy, but I just... don't? I feel bad in *theory*. That will have to be enough.

Once Bets is snoozing soundly beside me, I slip out of bed and into the bathroom. I hid some pants and my binder here earlier. Once I'm dressed, I sneak out of the bathroom and close the door, leaving a sliver of light creeping underneath so maybe she'll assume I'm having stomach trouble. I slide my feet into some pink fluffy slippers, hoping no one will notice them, but ready to tell them to piss off if they do.

The apartment door hisses open on its hydraulic hinges. I consider not closing the door all the way, since the clanging of the metal slab closing shut is likely to get me caught, but in the end I don't want to risk her safety just so I can go on a walkabout. So, I close the door and take off at a brisk pace down the hallway, turning at the first junction I reach. If she follows, maybe I can at least get far enough ahead to have five minutes to myself. That doesn't seem like too much to ask.

When it's been fifteen minutes and she still hasn't screeched out my name, I start to relax a little. I don't know where I'm going, but the steady beat of the grates below my footfalls is calming. I wonder how many times I've walked this way before, passed by these same people. There aren't many out right now, and that's both good and bad; no witnesses if the Règle asks around, but less opportunities to hide.

The fact that I want to hide from my future wife is certainly a bad sign for our marriage. Even if I get my memories back, I don't know if I'll still feel the same about her. Could the old Cam still love her after all the new Cam has felt? But that's part of why I'm out here, wandering around. I need something, anything, to trigger a memory and give me a reason to stay with her.

I've just turned down a new corridor when my picture flashes at one of the hologram stations: *Missing*.

"Damn it," I mutter.

"Well, that's not good," a man says.

I look up to where he stands perched at a coffee counter. His green eyes are sharp, staring between me and the hologram. I consider running, trying to hide, but the man hasn't made a move to call security. Instead, he just stares at me with a half-smirk on his face, the other side of his mouth pulled down by a scar.

"Please don't call them," I say, letting out a shaky breath. For the first time since I woke up in the hospital, a surge of fear pulses through me. I have no idea why, but it's strong and urgent and undeniable.

"'Course not," he says, never losing the smirk. My racing heart stills at the ease of his words, until he continues: "But normal security rounds are in about... oh, two minutes or so. If you're going to avoid them, you need to move."

I run my fingers through the curls tangling around my ears as I look down the corridor at my options. There aren't many. Plus, I have no clue what the normal rounds are like, so I could walk into guards at any moment.

"Back here," the man says, motioning me behind the counter.

I dive behind and tuck myself into the space between a stack of cups and the man's legs. Seconds later, the pounding of boots fills the space around us as a group of guards run by. When their footsteps retreat, I start to get up, but the man nudges his foot against my knee and presses down, holding me in place.

"Morning," he says.

"You see a girl wandering through here this morning?" a new voice asks. "Tall, red hair, looks lost."

I hold myself completely still, hoping the coffee man doesn't change his mind and decide to rat me out. A beat later, he says, "Not much traffic this morning. The usuals, but no one out of place."

"You sure? It's urgent that we find her. There will be a reward in it for you, if you've seen her," they ask, the suspicion in their voice almost palpable.

"Can't say I have. But I saw the hologram when it popped up, if that's who I'm supposed to watch for. If I see her, I'll let you know."

The guard grunts and I think they're moving away, but the man's foot doesn't budge. I count down in my head, ticking off numbers as I try to steady my body. The act is familiar and eases me into a strange calm. Maybe it was something I did in another life.

"You look familiar," the same guard says.

"I get that a lot," coffee-guy says.

Tick, tick, tick.

"Step out from behind the counter, please."

"No problem," he says.

His foot lifts off me as he heads around the corner.

Tick, tick, tick.

The barrel of a gun edges around the counter. Then a face. Followed by a whole body. Gun and guard lock onto me as I smile up with a sheepish grin. "Hello. Lovely morning, isn't it?"

They start to turn toward coffee-man. "I thought you said—"

Crack!

Something big and heavy and metal cracks down on the guard's face. Blood sprays out of their nose as they crumple to the ground. The man kicks the guard's gun toward me as he rifles through their pockets. He pulls out a taser and smiles.

Eyes flickering toward me, the man says, "Grab the gun, kid. We've gotta get out of here."

"What. The. Hell?"

"Not a lot of time. If you're running, now's the time."

"I'm not going anywhere with you."

His smirk never fades. "You've said that before, Nova."

"I don't know who you think I am—"

He waves his hand dismissively. "Yeah, we've done this before, too. Look, this is the first time I've drawn this much attention, so we might not have an easy time meeting after this. If you want to know the truth, we need to go. Now."

He steps away from the counter and I jump up, watching him head down the side corridor. As his silvery-purple hair moves out of sight, I grab the gun and chase after him. This is absolutely the stupidest thing this version of me has done, but something about it feels right. Righter than anything else in my life. So screw it. I follow a stranger who just knocked out a guard to save me from going back to the apartment I share with my fiancée/captor.

As I race down the corridor, fear and adrenaline pulsing through my veins, I smile, knowing I'm exactly where I'm supposed to be.

CHAPTER
NINE
CAMERON

The stranger leads me through a door marked *Employees Only*. I can't help but smile, knowing the very act of going somewhere I shouldn't would enrage Bets. As soon as I step through, I get a wave of deja vu.

"Whoa, wait," I say. "This seems familiar."

The man's smirk grows a little broader as he says, "It should. You were just here a couple weeks ago."

"I was unconscious a couple weeks ago, in a coma, recovering from an accident."

"Nope, you were very much here," he says, then pivots and steps toward the wall, saying, "actually it was more here, and there were a lot of sounds. A lot."

He steps away then, walking down the corridor, leaving me staring after him, my cheeks on fire. It takes me a few seconds to follow after him, my insides squirming in embarrassment. As we walk through the dark, I say, "I'm sure you're mistaken."

He chuckles. "Absolutely not."

"Even if it were true, why were you just standing there watching?"

"I heard a woman screaming and came to make sure no one was being murdered. Because I'm nice. Turns out the Règle's just a screamer."

"Voyeur."

"Perv."

I open my mouth to protest, but what can I say? I have no memory of the event he witnessed. It's still embarrassing knowing this guy watched an intimate moment, but as far as I'm concerned, the girl that was here two weeks ago was essentially someone else entirely.

I catch an amused light in his eyes and realize there's nothing to be embarrassed about anyway. This man isn't judging my actions—if anything, he seems a little impressed. Now I *really* wish I could remember. Maybe it would be one positive memory of Bets to measure against all the bad vibes I feel around her.

"Where are we going?" I ask, changing the subject.

"That's a good question," he says. "I wish I had an answer for you."

"You don't know?"

He laughs, a nervous sound that makes him sound like a wild thing. "Our normal encounters have been mild. Subtle. I've been able to trigger your memories with a few words, or once, with my tattoo. We're off the books with this one."

"Normal encounters? Are we friends?"

"I wouldn't say that," he says, ducking under a low-hanging tube the size of my waist.

"Okay, but we know each other."

"Yeah, yes, we do. Technically, you hate me. But when you finally get your memories back, I think that will change."

"That doesn't make sense. Why would remembering that I hate you make me like you more?"

"Because I've been helping you for months. Every time they take your memories from you, I try to help you regain them. Well, every time I've had a chance."

I stop in the near-darkness, his words echoing through my mind: *every time they* take *your memories from you...*

"Take?" I ask, my voice barely more than a whisper. "*Take* my memories?"

"You're brand new, aren't you? Haven't had time to work any of this out on your own? I usually don't see you until you're starting to get suspicious, so I figured you knew at least a little."

I swallow, fight down the terror trying to build inside me, and tick off numbers in my head again until I'm calmed down. Once I can take a breath without feeling like there's a weight on top, I ask, "What's happening to me?"

"I'll fill you in as best I can," he says, "but we need to get to a safe spot first. We're not far."

I follow the coffee-dude through the tunnels below the space station's floors. I can hear people talking above us as we pass under larger inter-sections, and the pounding of boots seems to be growing more prom-inent. Neither of us comment as the flood of guards grows stronger, but there's a tension building around us that is so tangible it prickles against my skin.

After we've been walking for a quarter of an hour, the man turns back to me and presses one finger against his lips in the universal sign of *Keep your mouth shut.* I roll my eyes at his back as he turns. I already wasn't talking, so what else does he want from me?

He steps to the side of the corridor unexpectedly, sliding into a narrow space in the wall that I wouldn't have noticed without him. He sidesteps again and I slip in beside him. It's tight. The walls press against me front and back, and my nerves kick in so hard I start shaking. I don't know how the old Cameron felt about enclosed spaces, but I am not a fan.

As we move farther into the crack in the wall, coffee-dude must feel me vibrating next to him, because he presses his arm against me, brushing his fingers to mine in what feels like a comforting gesture. It's nice on his part, but it doesn't help. I'm about to tell him that I need to get out of this place—NOW—when a voice rings out above me, cutting through all my thoughts.

Bets.

She's fuming, cursing at someone I can't see. I can't see *her* either, but her voice leaves no doubt. I can't make out exactly what she's saying, but she's yelling about an escape and someone needing to fix things, being unable to fix things. She screams about someone who can't be managed and must be dealt with.

I want to hear the whole thing—part of me thinks it would cure my memory loss to see this part of her, a part I've surely seen before, though she's hidden it these last few weeks. But the coffee guy's hand grabs my wrist and pulls me onward. Bets' voice fades, but I swear I can still hear it ringing in my head.

Finally, I step out of the narrow space and the room opens before me. I take a deep breath, relishing the feeling of my chest expanding fully without the wall forcing me to take shallow breaths. The man moves around the room, lighting tiny candles that smell like one of the perfumes that Bets likes.

"We can talk here," he says. "Not too loud, though."

"Who are you?"

In the dim light, I see his smirk has returned. "The name's Benjy. And you are?"

"Cameron," I say, a slight chuckle with it. "Thought you said we knew each other."

"I don't know you as Cameron, but I know your real self."

"What does that mean?"

"Cameron is an alias, a name you once used to hide from the Règle; now, it seems the Règle is using it to hide the real you."

"If I'm not Cameron, who am I?"

"Did you hear the Règle screaming about needing to get someone under control?" he asks, changing the subject.

"Yeah, um, Nora or something."

"Nova," he smirks. "That's you."

"That's definitely not me."

"Because the Règle told you so after stealing your mind again?" When I have no answer for him, he continues. "Your name is Nova Kennedy, and you are a royal pain in the Règle's ass."

"But we're engaged."

"That's the kicker. It's pure kismet. She's drawn to the one thing that can ruin her."

"I would never…"

He laughs. "Never say never. You're a ruiner; it's what you do, what you're *meant* to do."

I shake my head, unsure about the things this stranger is telling me. What the hell am I even doing down here with him? He could be making everything up, working against Bets to try to break her from the inside.

Except part of me surges forward to meet his words, like a moth to a flame. I know he's telling the truth, even without remembering.

"What happens now?"

"We rest," he says.

"There's no chance I'll be able to sleep after everything that's happened."

"You'd better figure out a way past it. If our last few encounters have taught me anything, it's that sending you out into the station too soon after finding out the truth usually ends up with you caught and another dead Règle."

"Excuse me?"

"Oh, yeah," he says, "you're fierce when you're you. The real you. I have no idea how you took them out, or why they keep giving you the chance to do it again. Well, I saw why the new one lets you back into her life, but damn. They're just asking to be murdered by letting you live. Eventually they're going to figure that out and take care of their mistake."

He tosses me a blanket as he stretches out on his own. His eyes close immediately and within seconds, a little whistle blows between his parted lips. With him already asleep, I won't be getting any further answers about who I am.

I try to follow his lead, but my head and my heart are racing. As I've been doing all week, I count in my head to try to relax, letting the simple monotony soothe me. Just as I'm about to drift off to sleep, a sudden thought jerks my eyes open: *We're sequestered in a hole in the wall; so where do I pee?*

I WAKE TO THE HUMMING OF A SONG THAT STICKS TO MY BRAIN LIKE TREE SAP. Part of me wonders how I know the cling of sap between my fingers as clearly as I know my own name; then I realize, I *don't* know my name. Not if the coffee-man's wild words are true. Not if the squirm in my gut when Bets calls to Cameron means anything.

But somehow I know tree sap.

The song drifting down to me is like that. Languorous, sweet, but gummed up in my head so firmly I can't dislodge it. There is a deep part of me that wants to sing the refrain when the time comes, but the words never quite surface.

I roll over and let the melody soothe me back into dreams that are full of green grass under dirty toes, the scratch of bark under fingertips, and a dozen other things that Cameron has never felt, but *knows* all the same.

CHAPTER
TEN
CAMERON

The next time I wake, there is no sweet song. There's no snoring Benjy, either. There's nothing but the hum of the station under my body as we rotate around the dead planet that haunts my dreams with things that cannot be.

I stand and stretch my aching limbs. The pain feels refreshing, earned. The mattress at Bets' place is the softest thing I've ever touched; somehow, sleeping on the cold floor last night felt more natural than climbing in her bed these last few weeks.

It doesn't take long for the boredom of this empty room to kick my curiosity into gear. I circle the room, inspecting the walls, the floors, the ceiling. Once I've done that a few times, I find myself edging closer to the handful of belongings Benjy has stashed here. In addition to the blankets we used last night—this morning?—he's got a bent spoon, half a sleeve of crackers, a dog-eared book, and a ceramic cup with a broken handle.

I pick up the book and open it to a random page. The light is brighter than it was earlier, but still too dim to see anything besides a jumble of dark lines across a dirty page.

"Can you read?"

"Of course," I say, eyes darting up to Benjy as he leans against the hole's entrance.

He smirks. "You're holding the book upside-down."

He pushes past me and dumps armfuls of something on his bed, but my mind is puzzling something together and I pay him little attention. His words have knocked something loose in my head—a memory, I think, of a woman asking me the same thing. We were in a white-walled room with onyx floors, bare aside from my bed and maybe a desk. The thought gets fuzzy if I press into it too hard, but if I'm careful, I can see the edge of it.

Benjy passes his hand in front of my face and the memory slips away. His brows are raised like he's waiting for a response and I realize he must have been talking to me while I was lost in my broken mind.

"I'm sorry, what did you say?"

"I asked if you're hungry," he says, handing me something warm wrapped in a napkin before I can even answer. "Where were you just now?"

I tap my temple and say, "I was stuck in a memory."

"A good one?"

I shrug as we sit side by side and unwrap warm nutrition bars. They're not my favorite thing to eat, but they're edible while they're warm. I shove the food in my mouth, sucking in air to cool it as I chew. This one is pasta and red sauce flavored, I think. Sometimes it's hard to tell. I had real spaghetti for the first time a few days ago during one of Bets' events, and since then, I've had a hard time swallowing the bricks that are supposed to taste like that.

After two more bites, I say, "I don't know if it was good or bad."

"If it's not sex or fighting, it's probably not worth remembering anyway."

I smile, but his words don't sit right with me. They're the kind of thing someone says when they've never had to worry about who they are, or wonder what came before, or felt lost and detached from past, present, and future. He doesn't mean any harm, he just doesn't understand.

"Where did you go?" I ask, putting some distance between our conversation and my screwed up brain.

"Scouring the station for this worthy meal, milady," he says, waving his hand with a flourish. "You're welcome, by the way."

"Thank you," I say around another bite of flavored brick.

"I also wanted to see how screwed we are, so I wandered around the market a bit listening to hot gossip."

"Learn anything?"

Brow furrowed, he says, "Yes. The reports say you were kidnapped by an old man. Old! Such bullshit."

Choking down the food in my mouth, I say, "The nerve. You can't be more than, what, sixty?"

"Sixty?" he screeches.

"Obviously I was joking. You don't look a day over forty-five."

"Dammit. I've only just turned thirty-three." He brushes back a strand of silvery-purple hair, his hand stopping above his ear. "It's the hair, isn't it? I need to go darker."

I jab my elbow lightly against his rib. "Did you learn anything *useful*?"

I feel him squirm beside me and realize all this casual talk was a way to avoid whatever horrible thing he needs to tell me. Looking at the food cooling in his hands, Benjy takes a deep breath and says, "They're going to kill her."

"Who?"

"Your sister."

THE FIRST WEIRD THING ABOUT LEARNING MY SISTER IS ABOUT TO BE executed, is learning that I have a sister. Benjy can't tell me much about her: she's blonde, a teenager, and locked up in the rehabilitation ward. He's never met her, but says Nova—er, me—has talked about her when she's—I'm—in my right mind.

It's exciting to realize there's someone out there who might be like me, someone I'm connected to and might be able to help me make sense of my jumbled brain. Maybe she could trigger some memories, remind me of what it was like growing up, tell me a story of how we picked on each other or played together or something else that sisters do.

The second weird thing, which pops in my head almost immediately after the first weird thing, is the intense desire to do everything within my power to protect her. There is a woman on this station who I don't remember knowing, and she's about to die because of me and my menacing overlord fiancée.

"Did you get any details?"

He shakes his head. "Overheard a couple guards talking, but I was afraid to get too close."

"How do we rescue her?"

"We don't."

My head jerks toward him, but he won't meet my gaze. "She's going to die because of me."

"No," he says, shaking his head. "She's going to die because of the Règle."

"Same thing. Bets is only going after her to draw me out."

"And the fact that you're ready to rush to her side proves that she knows what she's doing. The Règle knows you far better than *you* know you. She's trying to play you."

I push myself up and pace the length of the small space. "Ruining my life is one thing. Hell, even if she wants to kill me, that's... well, it's not great, but maybe more understandable. But wanting to kill Ivy is..."

Benjy laughs.

"What? Why are you laughing?"

"You said her name."

"Yeah?"

"I didn't tell you her name. You pulled that out of your memories."

My eyes go wide as I stop pacing, realizing he's right. And if I can remember that, what else has Bets' threats shook loose?

"I need to see her," I whisper.

"Ivy?"

"No, Bets."

"Screw that," he says, rising to meet me. "That's a terrible idea."

"It's the only thing I can think of that might give us a chance to rescue my sister. You've already said that Bets will expect me to rush to Ivy's side. Maybe this will surprise her, throw her off her game."

"Or," Benjy says, holding up his index fingers like he has a brilliant idea, "maybe we keep hiding and try to get your memories back."

"What good are my memories if Ivy dies in the meantime?"

"I definitely hear what you're saying, but have you considered that the only person who can solve this issue is the one locked inside your mind?"

"There's no time."

"Seriously Nova?"

"I'm not Nova," I huff. "And that sucks, because she sounds like a badass. But she also sounds like she's kinda the worst, because she keeps getting caught and other people are getting hurt on her behalf. So, I'm just Cameron, but maybe Cameron is the solution this time."

Benjy sighs. "Honestly, she does cause a load of trouble wherever she goes. Might be nice to try another option."

A sudden thought strikes me and I can't resist asking it. "Who is Nova to you, anyway? A friend? A lover?"

Benjy snorts a laugh for a little too long before saying, "Oh, that was a good one. Hilarious."

"Okay, so we weren't lovers. You're too old for me anyway." Benjy casts a hurt look my way, and I ask, "Friends, at least?"

"Yes? I mean, there was a point where we definitely could have been friends, if things hadn't gone sideways."

"What happened?"

His green eyes swivel to the empty corner of the room as if he's hoping something there will save him from this conversation. "You may hate me again after I tell you."

I shrug. "If I'm going to see Bets, I might not remember you for much longer anyway."

"Good point." He swallows, then in a rush of words, he blurts, "I betrayed her, I betrayed my people, I destroyed everything we'd been working for. I traded in the lives of people I cared about, exchanging them for a lie. Nova probably should've killed me."

"But she didn't."

His eyes return to mine. "No, she didn't. And I owe her for that."

"Good. I'm sure I'll need to cash in on that in the near future."

"What, this isn't enough?" he asks, arms outstretched to take in the room.

I laugh and say, "Though the accommodations are quite stunning, it sounds like there's an opportunity to gain a much larger favor from this."

"Oh, sure, use my own guilt against me."

I shake my head. "I don't want your guilt, Benjy; I want your friendship."

A smile tugs at the corner of his lips and he nods. "You've got it."

"Good. Now I'm going to visit my terrible fiancée, and I expect you to do a small thing for me while I'm gone. Just so we're clear, it's so minor, I would expect it from any of my friends."

"And what's that?"

"Save my sister from dying."

"Right, tiny favor," he says, rolling his eyes. His gaze returns to me, sharp and serious, when he adds, "Don't worry. I won't let you down. That's what friends are for."

CHAPTER
ELEVEN
CAMERON

There are guards at every intersection of the station, so it's easy to find someone to take me to the Règle as soon as I show my face. Of course, I don't actually *tell* them I want to see Bets; I simply walk toward a couple of tough-looking women with my hands raised in surrender and they do the rest.

I considered sneaking around, trying to get to Bets on my own, but I don't have that kind of time. Besides, that's what she expects of me, and I'm here to subvert those misconceptions.

The brawny babes almost seem disappointed when I don't put up a fight. Maybe they were hoping for a rowdy tumble around the station rather than a peaceful walk. They take me to a large room and toss me inside without bothering to stick around. I stumble, falling against the wood floors. Real wood. I can feel the grain under my hands, rough and strange compared to the metal everywhere else on the ship. I marvel at the strangeness of it, made even more peculiar by the fact that I instantly know what it is. I've never seen actual wood before—or at least this version of me hasn't. Maybe the part of me who has is closer to the surface than I realized, making things more familiar.

I push myself up and survey the room. There are other fanciful things here besides the floors: books with gilded lettering, a painting nearly as wide as I am tall, a clear container filled with water and small orange creatures, a desk covered in a dozen things I can't name, but all of which look peculiar and important.

Across the room, there's a small cubby hole filled with grooming devices. I step close to it and stare at the woman in the mirror set into the wall above. I should recognize my own face, I think, but it feels more foreign than the wood did. Though I watch my hand lift toward my cheek, it surprises me to feel my fingers pressed into the pale flesh. I push hard against my cheek—as if I need to prove I'm awake and not trapped in some twisted dream—until the coppery taste of blood fills my mouth and I realize I must have cut myself with my tooth.

I smile at the stranger in the mirror, whose teeth are covered in blood as red as her hair. In those wild green eyes, I see someone—or something —awakened and ready to be loosed, a beast that's been lying in wait. She is fierce and dangerous, a force begging to be set free. *She* is Nova. It feels good to see her, even if I'm still trying to figure out exactly who she is.

The door squeals open behind me and I spin on my heels to find Bets entering the room. There are two guards behind her with guns already trained on me, while two others drag in the bony frame of a girl who could use a good meal or two. Her head is covered so I can't see her face, but her body is sharp in ways no person should be—a scalene when she should be a circle.

Bets' voice cuts through my thoughts. "Hello, Nova."

"Cameron," I say, shaking my head. "I'm still Cameron."

A look of bewilderment flashes across her face, replaced a second later by something much darker. In the weeks after my accident, I rarely saw her face without it smiling. The darkness suits her much better. At least it's honest.

"Well, that's a bummer," she says. "I brought Nova a gift. You won't get nearly as much out of it as she would have."

My eyes flicker to the girl on the floor. "Is that my sister?"

Bets' brows raise. "Cameron doesn't have a sister."

"Someone told me about her, told me about myself, but I don't remember any of it."

Bets nods and steps farther into the room, tapping her index finger against her chin. "And that should be enough. It was, in the beginning.

You didn't react to anyone you knew before, didn't realize there *was* a before, and for the life of me, I can't figure out why that changed."

"Because the real me was still in here," I say, pressing my hand against my chest.

She waves my words away. "We've tried the same procedure, different procedures, experiments that could've left you completely incapacitated... nothing has worked like that first one. And boy, was it a doozy! That first procedure wiped you clean and we had the most remarkable time falling in love with one another, without the burden of being enemies."

"Did it never occur to you that I was still your enemy? Or that what you did to me, what you kept doing, made me your captive, not your lover?"

"That's not how—"

I cut her off. "Every time you kissed me, every time you *touched* me... The real me didn't consent."

"We were in love."

"To call what you did to me 'love' just proves you're incapable of it. You made me a prisoner in my own head, taking what you wanted without regard for me, my body, or my choices."

"I didn't force myself on you. I didn't make you stay with me. You made those decisions."

"Every choice I made was built on a lie. You compelled me to be with you by removing every other option. And now you're what, trying to buy goodwill by bringing my sister to me?"

Her jaw clenches and she swallows visibly before spitting, "I wouldn't piss on you if you were on fire."

"Strange way to behave toward someone you claim to love."

"Hard to love someone who gets closer to killing you every time her personality shifts."

"Well maybe that wouldn't happen so much if you'd keep your goons out of my head."

"I'm trying to keep us together. Clearly that isn't something you're interested in."

My mouth opens as if I'm going to respond, but what am I supposed to say to her? She's living in a fantasy with someone who doesn't even know her, and expecting things to work out because she *wants* them to?

I take a deep breath and try to think of something to say to draw her back to reality. When nothing comes to mind, I give up, point to Ivy, and ask, "What's she doing here?"

It flashes through my head that I'm playing this all wrong, that I should be the nice Cameron she wants and try to find a way to save my sister, but I'm so spectacularly angry that the mere thought of it makes my hands shake. Besides, it's too late for all that. We both know it.

"I wanted to give *Nova* the chance to say goodbye to her sister. A parting gift, so to speak."

She gives a nod and one of the guards pulls the covering from Ivy's face. Purple blooms across her nose and left eye. Blood stains the split in her swollen lip. But underneath it I see a young woman's freckled face, and my heart does a somersault in my chest.

"You don't have to kill her," I whisper, taking an unconscious step toward the girl.

"I'm not going to," Bets says. I feel the needle press into my skin as she steps behind me, and as the blackness closes in around me, I hear her say, "You are. This will be Cameron's final gift to me, before becoming Nova for the last time. Cam will kill her, Nova will despair, then I will kill Nova and be done with you both."

"You love me," I slur, falling to my knees.

She bends low in front of me and tips my face up to meet hers. "All is fair in love and war."

CHAPTER
TWELVE
NOVA

I am tied to a bed.

My thoughts are sluggish and heavy, moving toward me from a distant horizon where things make sense.

Blink.

It's bright in this place. Too bright. So bright I want to keep my eyes closed against the light. But something in my gut tells me I can't.

Breathe.

My body responds to my requests, slowly. But I don't think I had to tell myself to do these things before. I shouldn't have to remind myself to complete these functions.

Blink.

It's so bright I want to claw my eyes out.

Breathe.

The air is cold in my lungs, sending an ache through my chest. No, that's not my lungs, it's my heart that's hurting.

Open your eyes.

I obey the voice in my head with haste. She isn't giving me tips to keep myself functioning. No, that bitch is making sure I survive.

As soon as I connect that voice with survival, I realize what I must do. Sliding into the background, I let the survivor take over brain control while I run the body's unconscious functions. The survivor lifts our head and looks around, a smile peeling across our face as she does.

The walls are white, the floor is black…

We remember everything.

CHAPTER
THIRTEEN
HIRO

J avian Balunovic is handsome when he's excited. Honestly, he's handsome all the time, but right now, explaining tech things to me that I barely understand, he's practically glowing. He paces around, hands blurring as they move to exaggerate his words. My mind unwillingly wanders to what else he could do with those hands.

I really am trying to listen to what he's saying, but the words are jargon and all I can actually hear is, *"We're going to save her. We're going to save her. We're going to—"*

"You're not listening," Javian says.

I squint at him, trying to pretend I don't know what he's talking about. "Of course I am. I was just so engrossed in what you were saying that I must've missed that last part."

He winces, then tries to cover it with a smile. "I know I'm boring."

"You're not boring."

He waves a dismissive hand. "At the very least, other people are bored *by* me. But I don't mind being boring, as long as you understand what I'm saying. This stuff is important and we need to get it right."

"Are you kidding?" I ask. "Your work is fascinating, truly."

"Lies are unbecoming, Chief."

"Most people are quite taken with my lies."

He smiles, genuine this time, and I can't stop my own megawatt grin from spreading across my face in response. There's something refreshing about his no-nonsense approach. This is a man who knows who he is and isn't bothered by what other people think. It's sexy.

Javian's smile fades too soon and he says, "Charm might have gotten you this far, but if you're going to use this device to save your wife, you'll need more than that."

Wife. The word strikes something inside me and I straighten. "Good thing you've got the brains."

His cheeks color at the compliment, but he says, "But I won't be with you. I'll be running things from down here, so you'll need to know this stuff once you get aboard the station."

Right, the station. I swallow against the thought. I've been ready to go after Nova since the moment she left, but now that the time is here, I'm terrified to go back up there. I've got a thousand Raiders at my back, a working knowledge of the station, and the element of surprise on my side; still, I know what awaits us, and I'm scared.

I haven't told anyone that I'm afraid. Raiders aren't supposed to show fear. Nova certainly wouldn't. But it sits in the pit of my stomach, heavy and writhing every time I think about stepping from this solid place that has become my home, back into a world that feels like a bad dream. On the station, I was a nobody; few friends, unimportant job, nothing any longer than a one-night stand. I was trapped. Now, I have nearly everything I want, and most importantly, I'm free.

"I don't want to go back," I whisper, the words tumbling out before I can stop them.

Javian reaches forward, his slender fingers resting on my shoulder so lightly, I might as well be marked *fragile*. My eyes linger on his hand for a moment before tracing up his arm, across his collarbone, past his stubbled jaw, to dark eyes full of something I can't quite read. I stare into them for too long, lost in the hunger they stir in me.

"You don't have to go," he says. "I can tell Thoa that I miscalculated. Or you can send the others and help coordinate from here."

"That's not very brave of me."

"Admitting you don't want to go seems pretty brave to me."

I shake my head. "Raiders do the things that scare them. Nova would do this for me."

"You're not her," he says. "Besides, you're the leader of the largest group of Raiders these lands have ever seen. You get to decide what Raiders do, not the other way around."

"Is this some kind of weird reverse psychology?"

He tilts his head, further sharpening the line of his jaw, and for a second I'm ready to melt into him. There's a lightness to his voice as he says, "Depends on whether or not it's working."

I smile at him. "I have to go."

"I know," he nods, dropping his hand from my shoulder. "You ready to learn about the device?"

"Teach me your ways, oh Great One."

The corner of his mouth quirks up as he says, "That would take too long. I'll settle for teaching you how to use the device. At least then I'll know you can come back to me... us... the Raiders, I mean."

My brows raise in question, but he doesn't seem to notice. He's flustered, his cheeks red, his eyes averted, as he gestures toward a row of too-familiar tracking bracelets. I let his nervous behavior continue without comment, though a large part of me really wants to call attention to it. There's something awkward and adorable about this guy, and the old me would shamelessly flirt to make him even more skittish. I would've done my best to run him off before I grew too attached, like I did on the station with Captain Alik Rolfrun every time she tried to nail me down.

But I guess I'm not the same old Hiro. Maybe this version, the one actually paying attention because I *want* to come back to this nerdy genius, is the product of time and forced change. Or maybe this is just who I am when I haven't boned anyone for a year. Either way, I'm starting to think it's a good look for me.

CHAPTER
FOURTEEN
NOVA

"You're looking well."

I press my mouth into a polite smile while I dig my nails into the palms of my hands. "Thank you. I'm feeling quite well today."

The doctor checks something off on his clipboard while I resist the urge to grab his pen and stab him in the neck. My Nova side relishes thinking of the things I could do to him, to all of them, but the Cameron in me knows I need to bide my time. There are secrets between us and the doctor, and maybe some between Nova and Cam, if I'm being honest; perhaps it's best if it stays that way, at least for now.

"My boss will be pleased. She's been watching your progress carefully."

"Please thank her for me. I get the impression I wouldn't be here if it wasn't for her."

His head tilts minutely, and I worry I've said more than I should. A beat later, he seems to shake off whatever he was thinking. "Yes, she was instrumental in your rescue."

"I'd love to thank her personally."

Don't push it, Cameron-brain says.

"Perhaps one day," he says. "But the Règle is far too busy right now when we don't have much progress to show her. We still have miles to go."

Miles. Ivy doesn't have time for that.

"How long should I expect to be here?" I ask, trying to keep my voice chipper.

He eyes me over the top of his clipboard as he jots something down. "Hard to say. This particular form of brain trauma isn't well-documented, so there's no telling how long it will take to cure you."

"I understand," I say. "Is there something I can do to help speed things along?"

"Not really," he says, placing his pen in his front pocket and walking toward the door. He gives the guard the signal to let him out and the door cracks open as he turns back to me. "Stay upbeat; don't let this place get you down. We'll figure this thing out."

I smile and step toward him, arms outstretched. For a moment, I think he'll pull away; instead, the doctor returns my smile and steps into my embrace. His hands roam over my body, covered in the thin fabric of the shirt and pants they've got me in. Asking for a hug seems to be the only permission the good doc needed to grab a handful of whatever he wanted. I try not to clench my muscles as his hands fondle my breasts, and just as he goes to step back from me, I slip my hand into his pocket and grab his pen. He's in the door's crack now, blocking it from closing, while a look of hunger passes over his features. I smile coyly at him, biting my lip, as I stare at the side of his neck, practically licking my lips as the need for vengeance builds inside me.

"Maybe I can swing by and check on you later," he says. "After lights out."

"Or maybe you don't need to go yet," I say.

I can practically see the thoughts in his head as he considers this. He *wants* me, and his desire will be his undoing. He reaches forward, tracing a finger down my side and hooking it in the elastic band at my waist. He pulls me toward him until our bodies are pressed together and I can feel his erection pressed against my thigh. I can barely keep the revulsion from my features as I imagine how many other patients he's done this to, and how many were unable to stop him from doing more.

He moves his mouth to my ear, so close I can feel his lips as he whispers, "Tonight."

He steps back, but before he can get out of arm's reach, I strike.

Though Nova aims to kill, Cam doesn't; the pen changes direction mid-swing and jabs into his eye instead of his neck, whipping out again a second later. There's a strange suction against the instrument as I withdraw it, accompanied by a thick, wet slurping sound.

The pen didn't go too deep. It's enough to injure, but not kill.

The doctor screams. There's hardly any blood, but I imagine the wound is still agonizing. Cameron-brain feels a prick of pity, despite what he was planning to do to me later, but Nova-brain remembers that this is the same doctor who used shock therapy on me the first time they kept me locked up. Nova remembers where his fingers traveled when he had me so messed up I couldn't move of my own volition. So, Nova is the one who takes charge, grabbing the doctor and pivoting him in front of my body as I step into the hall. I press the pen against his neck, making sure he knows I can make things far worse if I wish.

I let my lips tickle against his ear as I whisper, "Did it hurt your feelings when you thought I didn't remember you, Doctor Shaw? Did you think I couldn't recall all the places your hands have been? We shared so many special moments, how could I possibly forget?"

Shaw moans an answer and I can't fight the smile that streaks across my face.

There are four guards in the hall, all with guns pointed at me. *Four? They were practically begging me to escape.*

I glance at their faces, finally landing on the one farthest to my left, and closest to the door: Stevens.

"Open the doors," I order. When none of them move, I say, "I will kill this guy if you don't do what I say."

Stevens says, "Our orders are to let everyone die if it means keeping you contained."

My eyes narrow. "And you're okay with that?"

"Better him than us," the guard in front of me says. Nova-brain immediately dubs him *Supreme Asshole Number One.*

"And you're the dumbass who thinks it can't be all of you over the next two minutes? I assure you, I'm willing to give it a go."

"You'll end up dead, too," he says.

I shrug. "I've been through worse."

I push the doctor forward, using his body to shield mine. Honestly,

I'm surprised he's still standing, but as long as he is, I'm going to use him. In two steps, I lessen the gap between us and *Supreme Asshole Number One*. Though there's still a solid three feet between us, there's now a slight tremble in his hands. I stare into his dark brown eyes and ask, "How about now? Still feel okay with your orders?"

"Can someone please shoot her already?" he calls.

No one moves. I spare a glance at Stevens and he looks away, almost sheepishly. I force out a laugh and say, "They're not allowed. But I guess no one bothered to tell you that before putting you in my path."

I push Doctor Shaw at the guard and spin around behind the man, my hand slipping to his belt in a flash. I grab his taser and press it against his side in one quick motion. His arms full as he catches the good doc, *Supreme Asshole Number One* seems to barely register what's happened, even as he's falling to the floor.

Someone swears under their breath at the end of the hallway as I pick up the guard's gun. I point it toward the next closest guard and say, "I didn't kill your boy, in case you couldn't tell from your vantage point. Just shocked him with his own taser." They grumble in understanding, but I don't give them time to think. "But now I have his gun, and unlike you, I have no orders but my own. What are the chances I'll let you live?"

"Seems that you're Nova today, not Cam, so I'd say pretty slim," Stevens says.

"Honestly, I'm a little bit of both."

"Cam's good people, so I guess our chances went up a little." He puts one hand up as he slowly lowers his gun to the floor with his other. "Gonna remove my taser now."

I nod. "That blade in your boot, too."

Stevens smiles. "Cam never saw the blade. How do you know about that?"

I tap the side of my head and say, "Nova gets it."

He pulls the blade out and slides it across the floor. "Still, that's a handy trick from that distance."

I ignore the compliment. "Your friends aren't as smart as you, Stevens. They should've already put their guns down."

A whine of pain echoes behind us as Doctor Shaw contorts his body as he rolls around on the floor. It isn't as if the fetal position will help being stabbed in the eye, but he keeps reverting to that anyway. The sounds he's making... practically inhuman. He grunts and squeals like a pig about to be bacon.

"They're outright fools," Stevens says. "Then again, they've only heard the stories about you, whereas I've seen you kill three guards in this same hallway when you were Nova a couple months ago."

"But you made it out."

He nods. "I'd like to make it out today, too."

There's something incredibly likable about Stevens and self preservation. It is honest and reliable; he can always be trusted to save himself rather than a government that doesn't care about him. I give him my best smile and say, "Help me release my people. All we want is to go back to the ground and live our days in peace."

"Peace?" one of the other guards asks. "You don't know the meaning of the word."

I turn my borrowed gun on him and press the button. A thin red light blasts out of it, burning a hole straight through his neck. Specks of red flick onto the other guards, but other than that, there's hardly anything to show for the destruction I just caused. I'd nearly forgotten how precise their weapons are since the last time I'd seen one in the prisoner hold, more than a year ago.

"Holy crap," the third guard says.

"I might not know the meaning of it, but these people being held here are not broken like I am. They may be petty criminals in your eyes, but I'm the Cataclysm. I will end everything you love if I don't get what I want. No matter how many times you lock me up and erase my brain, I will *always* come back to this."

Stevens raises his hands. "You don't have to convince me to help. You had me when you stabbed Shaw in the eye. Guy's a dick."

I smile, finally figuring out what I like about Stevens: he reminds me of Hiro.

"I don't want to die," the other guard says. She does as Stevens did, sliding her weapons across the floor to me, and I breathe a little easier. Just because I *can* kill her doesn't mean I want to.

"There's a master release mechanism for all the rooms, but it's in the director's office," Stevens says.

"Where's that?"

He points at the other end of the corridor. "Two halls farther in, one up. Guards in each one."

"Lead the way."

Stevens and the other guard walk past me, though I'm certain the woman is terrified as she does. She looks jumpy, like she expects me to shoot her with the laser gun at any second.

Just as we reach the end of the hall and Stevens swings the door open, a blaring alarm issues overhead. I feel fury rushing through me and I growl, "What did you do?"

"Not me," he says, eyes going wide.

"What then?"

"That's the station alarm."

"My people?"

Stevens shakes his head. "Not a prison break. The alarm is different."

"So, what is it then?"

"It's an outside force. We're under attack."

CHAPTER
FIFTEEN
NOVA

"Attack?"

The word falls from my lips, meaningless. Though Stevens and the other guard look around as if expecting someone to jump at them at any moment, I still can't wrap my head around what's going on. If the attack isn't from my people on the station, who could it be? Are there other humans out here amongst the stars that I don't know about?

"What do we do?" the woman guard asks.

"Nothing has changed," I say.

Stevens shoots me a glare. "Not for you, maybe."

"What does that mean?"

"Maybe it's true that you just want to go on-world and be left alone," he says. "But there are people attacking *our* home who clearly don't want to just be left alone. We've gotta prepare for battle."

I chew my lip, unsure what to do. Part of me hurts for him, and I don't know if it's Nova or Cameron. This place has taken a lot from me, but not everyone here is guilty. I know what it's like to want to protect those you love.

"Help me get my people," I say. "I'll see what we can do for you after."

"Do for *us*?" the woman asks.

"We're warriors. Point us toward the enemy and let us do what we do best."

She scoffs. "You would fight on behalf of the station and the people who've kept you imprisoned?"

I pause, letting the question roll through me like an electric current, shocking me with an answer I never expected: "Yes."

If it means saving my people, the answer will always be yes.

Stevens grins, a familiar thing to Cam's eyes, a reminder that they have been friends throughout some of her iterations. A pang ricochets through my chest, remembering what it's like to have friends and family and people who matter to you. People who are *real* and not part of some manufactured drama.

I temper it. There's no time for sentiments like this; I need to keep my wits, gather those who were stolen from me, and get the hell out of here. Well, after we save these assholes from whoever is attacking them, that is.

Stevens and the woman are leading me down another hall now. It takes a moment for me to realize we've met no interference thus far. "Where are the guards you mentioned?"

He answers without turning. "They've been pulled away. That alarm is calling all hands to their battlestations."

We clear another hall, then a flight of stairs, exactly as he had instructed me. I've got my laser gun at the ready, but we don't see anyone on the way up.

Stevens stops in front of the director's office and points at the card reader. "You'll have to blast it. My access pass won't let us through."

I step to the side of the scanner, keeping him and the woman in my periphery. I square myself and aim at the card reader. The laser blast cuts through the plastic mechanism and into the wall beyond. There's a popping sound as the red light slices through wires, leaving their energy crackling in the casing that holds them. A quick buzzing sound emits, then I hear the door latch unhook.

Stevens steps up beside me as I turn off the weapon. He wedges his fingers into the crack between the door and the jamb, levering an entry. His arms and neck muscles bulge with the strain as he wrenches the gap wider.

As it finally crashes open, he pulls back panting, "Easy peasy," and flashes a grin so magnificent it could almost rival one of Hiro's.

I smile back and open my mouth to praise him just as a flash of red shoots out from beyond the door. It catches Stevens between the eyes, splashing flecks of red throughout the hallway. A tiny gray chunk sails through the air and lands on my cheek, slimy and warm against my skin.

The other guard has backed up several feet by the time I realize what's happened. I blink and she's already at the stairwell door, gone an instant later.

I can't run. Nova doesn't want to, but even if Cam could convince her feet to fly, there's nowhere to go. I need to be in the director's office, where the shot came from. I glance inside just in time to see the gun that killed Stevens now pointed at me.

Before the man—the director, I presume—can take his shot, I dive to the side of the door and out of his line of sight. I know that won't hold, as these ridiculous weapons of theirs can shoot through the thinner metal of the internal station, but at least I'm not completely exposed.

My heartbeat thumps inside my throat, racing far faster than I like. I crouch low and steady myself, taking a deep breath and counting in my head. Rego taught me how to calm myself a long time ago, when I was still a child and the nightmares full of teeth would come for me. He taught me to chase away my fears, to slow my body until it reacted the way I wished it to. Now, I return to those moments in Rego's arms, my ear pressed against his chest as I convinced my heart to beat in time with his.

Seconds pass. I keep my eyes focused on the door, never allowing my gaze to drift to Stevens no matter how much I want to. Despite everything, he was my friend and I want to mourn his loss. I can't.

When I can no longer hear my pulse thrumming through my ears, feel it pulsing in my neck, I spin out from my place against the wall and dive past the open doorway with my arm extended, firing the laser into the room. I don't expect to hit anything, but scaring him would be nice. When a scream erupts from inside the office, I'm elated by my sheer luck.

That elation slinks away as the scream continues, accompanied by a barrage of curses and several pleas to various deities. It's apparent that

I've hit him, but not in a place that would kill him immediately, and just thinking about the amount of pain he must be in makes me queasy. Not a lot bothers me, and I'm well-acquainted with the sight of blood, but the idea of a non-lethal laser blast through soft flesh is too much, even for me. A quick kill is merciful; there is no mercy in this sort of pain.

After what seems like an eternity of agonized screams, he's finally quiet. He might be dead, or the shock could have led him into unconsciousness. Or, he could be waiting for me to assume it's clear while he lies in ambush.

Rather than waiting to see which way it goes, I try a different tactic: "You dead yet?"

"Screw you," he growls through gritted teeth.

"I suppose that's not out of the question. Guess it depends on what part of you I blew off."

"I'm going to kill you, Raider bitch."

It sounds like he's across the room from where I'm standing, but I need to keep him talking to know for sure.

"Again, it depends. There's plenty of ways this could play out. But since you're injured and I'm whole, I'm the safe bet."

His words are muffled when he says, "I'm tougher than any of the bastards you've met so far. I didn't get this position by kissing bureaucratic ass, like some of those other assholes."

"I find that hard to believe," I say with a chuckle. "You're hiding in your office while the real soldiers run *into* danger. Seems like the sort of thing a weak figurehead would do."

"I'm not hiding, I'm guarding," he says, his voice sounding much closer than it was a moment before. I'm certain he's just on the other side of the wall now, waiting to make his move. I need whatever move he makes to be a mistake.

"Whatever you have to tell yourself. We both know it's a lie. Why don't you do us both a favor and just die already?"

I step feather-soft along the floor, inching closer to the open door. As quiet as my movements are, I still almost miss the pained growl emanating from his throat and the scratching thump as he drags his leg across the floor. He's nearly as stealthy as me, even injured.

Nearly, but not quite.

There's a sudden intake of breath, a hissed curse, and a thump as something hits the floor. I hope this is the distraction I've been waiting for, because I bolt out from my spot. My eyes scan the area, gun pointed where I think he is. I find him then, but rather than the fiery opponent I'm ready to meet, I'm staring down at an old man slumped on the floor. The oldest man I think I've ever seen, honestly, as Raiders tend to kill themselves off before they can get old.

He may be a tough bastard, but it's been a long time since he was in his prime. Lines crease this man's face. His white hair is thin and wispy, his skin paper-thin.

I glance around to make sure there's no one else here. There's a picture of him on the wall above his desk. Smiling. Surrounded by people—his kids, maybe—and his arms are around a handful of children. He looks genuinely happy.

The jab of pity that pangs my gut surprises me. Parts of Cameron come out at the strangest moments, and I'm not sure if I should embrace them or push them away. Cam was the nicer version of myself, the law-abiding citizen trying her best, and I can't help but wonder if she was always there and just needed to be unlocked or if this place created her.

The director meets my gaze. For a moment, I think he might reach for the gun that clattered to the floor when he fell, but he doesn't. There's a steel resolve in his gaze; we both know he has lost.

My eyes roam over him, searching for the injury. It's not as easy to spot as I expected. The laser doesn't cause the spectacular bloodbath you might expect, despite its power. There is blood at the top of his leg though, and a hole in his pants where the gun blasted away the fabric. He's lucky it's on the outside rather than the inside of his thigh; there's a much better chance he'll survive since I didn't hit his femoral artery.

"Do it already," he says.

I turn my eyes back to his. They're a lovely gray-green color, set into a face full of laugh lines and signs that there is happiness in and around him. "Are you so desperate to die that you would ask it of me?"

He clenches his teeth and I'm not sure if it's from the pain or his unwillingness to say whatever he's about to. "Desperate for it to end *quickly*. I won't have you playing your savage games or sacrificing me to one of your gods."

I laugh. It's probably bad form to chortle at a dying man's words, but I can't help it. His version of me is a stereotype I can't live up to. "First off, you're not well enough to make it into the games. Even if you were, they're not the games of savages. Your people made them and use us as entertainment. Pretty sure that makes you the monsters."

"You'll not convince me—"

"Second," I say, cutting him off, "I don't have a god. But if I did, I could find a better sacrifice than a half-dead old man."

Anger flashes in those lovely eyes just before they dart to the nearby gun. He's pale and sweaty, probably feeling weak at this point, so I don't bother trying to fight him for the weapon. I extend my leg and kick it a few feet away from him, enough to deter him if he starts feeling extra brave again.

"Whatever you're going to do, just do it," he says.

I nod and tuck my gun into my pants. When I reach for the man's belt and begin to unfasten it, he doesn't protest—doesn't even move—and for a moment I think he might've lost more blood than I thought. But his eyes are still open and he seems to comprehend that there's nothing else for him to do.

I remove his belt and strap it tight at the top of his leg. His left hand is coated red and I'm sure he had been applying pressure until his collapse. That bit of pressure, and now this mock tourniquet, should keep him alive until help arrives.

"Why?" he slurs.

"Why what?" I ask, then realize he's asking why I'm not killing him. I shrug a response. "Despite what you think about the Raiders, we don't kill for no reason. We aren't afraid to kill, no, and some of us enjoy it more than we should. But killing is just part of living, and I don't need you to die for me to survive."

He doesn't answer, and honestly, I'm not sure how much he heard. His eyes have closed, and though I can still see the rise and fall of his shoulders, he may not have much life left in him. Maybe there was more damage to his leg than I realized.

I step back from the passed out director and survey the room for the release mechanism Stevens said would be here. While I look around, I think about the words I just spoke. While the sentiment is true, I'm not sure where that answer came from. It wasn't a Nova answer, not fully, but it wasn't from Cameron either. Maybe it was from somewhere in between. Maybe this in-between person is someone I should try to find more often.

Crossing the room to the desk, I find myself entranced by how intricate the design is. Hidden away in an office like this, I expected to find something simple; this is anything but. It isn't made of metal, or even wood, but some sort of stone. Marble, maybe. The center section where the director seems to keep most of his work is all one slab of onyx, golden veins criss-crossing to and fro. To either side are several inches of tiles in various hues of red. The tiles are rough and vary in texture and composition, dissimilar to the smooth middle section. It is far too wonderful a sight to be hidden away in a secluded office.

I shuffle papers and open drawers on his desk, but it gives me nothing, so I move to the shelves along the wall to search for the thing that will save my people. It's a frustrating few minutes while I look, pulling things off the shelves and scanning the area, not knowing exactly what I'm looking for. Though I'd like a big sign that says, "Push this button," I know that it couldn't be that easy. Nothing ever is.

A memory jumps into my head and I feel a grin spread across my face. I can see Coco as clear as the day we stood side by side in the library, looking for a way to rescue the captured children in Gearhaven. Her hair was long and purple, her golden-dark skin glowing against a skintight dress. But it was her eyes that entranced me; bright green and searching for an ally in me, hoping I wouldn't betray her like she expected me to.

I shake away the vision of her, difficult as it is to let go. I didn't realize it at the time, but now I can see how strong my feelings for her were—or could have been, with time to grow those feelings. I could live in the memory of her, relishing those small moments we had before the whole world went sideways. Maybe it is too late, and all I have are the memories of her and the feelings that refused to show themselves until now. Or maybe I can look for her when this is all over and see if she is pulled to me like I am to her. For me, Coco is a flame, and I am a moth—drawn to the very thing that can confuse my navigation and throw me off-course or burn me up. But I need to keep my head on, and I can't do that while thinking of her. She's all-consuming.

Still, the memory did spark something in me besides desire. I'd found the way to the Gearhaven children by discovering a groove in the wood of the bookshelves. Maybe there's something like that here, too.

I run my hands along the shelves, feeling for anything out of the ordinary. The shelves are smooth, flawless, and infuriating in their uselessness. Whipping the chair out from behind the desk again, I fling myself down with an exasperated sigh. The thought of putting my head on the desk and crying flits through my mind, and it's so enticing, my head is on the desk before I even realize I've put it down.

That's when I see it.

On the right side of the desk, two of the tiles don't fit... right. The others around them are grooved together with such perfection, there's no doubt they were made to sit together. From above, these seemed just as perfectly aligned; with my eyes level with the desk, I can now see the imperfection of something otherwise unparalleled.

I slide a finger along the groove and let my fingernail catch between the tiles. They are loose, and though I can wiggle them, they don't move enough for me to lift them. I go back to the desk drawers, scrambling for something I can use to pry them up. There's a thin slip of metal akin to a dull knife in one of the drawers, and though I'm not sure what it's for, it seems like it will do the trick.

The metal is thin enough to fit into the groove between the tiles, and with little effort I pry them up and apart. They lift on hidden hinges, revealing a small panel built into the desk. Inside there are three silver switches flipped up, each one about half the size of my pinky finger. None of them are labeled, but the excited thump in my chest is certain that one of them will do the trick. I flip them all for good measure.

The click of every door in this hallway unlatching fills my ears and I smile. A bud of hope appears in me and I do my best not to squash it. Instead, I water that tiny sprout, remembering the faces of those captured by the Règle, by Bets. Today, *today*, they will go home. And so will I.

CHAPTER
SIXTEEN
NOVA

I half-expect a newly released prisoner to be standing at the ready to bash the director in the head when I peer out; instead, the hallway is empty. They've either been conditioned not to react to the door opening, or they're expecting a trap. Maybe both.

After a minute in the empty hallway, I yell, "Where the hell is everyone?"

A pair of dark eyes pop out around the edge of a door to my right. One dark eyebrow lifts as the rest of his face comes into view. Lips tugging up at the corners in a smirk, Baz says, "Took you long enough."

"I was trying to give someone else a chance to be the hero this time, but you bastards are hopeless without me."

"She's not wrong," a voice says.

My lips form his name as I spin toward him, but my throat closes as if trapped in a vice, and all that comes out is a puff of breath. Krew stands there, black hair grown out into tiny curls, a new scar across his forehead, but still wearing a smile that puts the stars to shame. I'd forgotten how handsome he is—sharp angles that seem like they would cut if you touched them wrong, skin as dark as a starless night, and black eyes, black holes that suck in everything around them. Even now as our eyes meet, I feel my heart tugged toward him and that consuming gaze.

"You're okay," I say.

It's not a question, but more to convince myself of it. Krew seems to understand that. He steps toward me as if in slow motion, and it takes me a moment to realize he's trying not to spook me. He seems to find the parts of me that others overlook, the ones I want to keep hidden. Now, while I'm determined to be the strong savior, he sees the fragile girl who needs saving.

Krew reaches a hand toward me and I fall against him without further prompting. He brushes his hands over my hair and coos into my ear: "It's okay. You're safe now. Everything is fine."

I so desperately want his words to be true.

After too short a moment of allowing myself to be comforted, I pull away. Straightening my spine, I fight the urge to wipe at my eyes as I attempt to return my demeanor to that of a conquering hero. I give him a nod, then turn to face the other doors.

Several people have emerged from the rooms. Some I know, but many I don't. For a moment I wonder what they'll make of me, but I shove the thought away before it can take root. This isn't the first time I've liberated captives on this station, and though this is more a medical wing than a prison, the people here are trapped all the same. And though I've done this twice now, if I have my way, it'll be the last time; in fact, my aim is to make sure they aren't able to take prisoners again. I don't exactly have a plan to stop them yet, but that's never held me back before.

"My name is Nova Kennedy—"

"Aye lass, and I'm Wynda MacNally, better known as Red. We ken who y'are," a red-haired woman says. "Most of us, anyway. The Règle doesn't keep their guests too long, so most of us were on the outside for your previous mischief, in one form or fashion."

A man next to her nods and adds, "Which begs the question, what are you doing here now?"

"And what do ya want from us?" Red asks.

"I'm here to rescue my friends. You were just in the right place at the right time."

"Friends?" a voice asks.

I turn to see Qen standing in the doorway to the next corridor. Their hair is shaved down to stubble and they look thinner than the last time I saw them, almost gaunt. Though their expression is sour, the sight of them lifts my spirits.

"It's good to see you, Qen."

"Is it?" they ask, one brow rising. "From what I've heard, you've made new friends in high places while we've been trapped here. Still palling around with the new Règle, warming her bed?"

"I've been just as much a prisoner as you," I snap. My words sound forced in my rush to defend myself, and I immediately regret it.

Qen narrows their eyes at me and says, "Yeah, I can tell. Doesn't look like those hips have missed many meals. And I don't see a whole lot of new scars. But go on and tell us how bad it's been."

They have no clue what I've been through, but this isn't the time to tell them about it. Instead I say, "Different circumstances, same prison. Maybe we can wait to compare notes until we get the hell out of here."

"How do we know you aren't here to trap us? You could be working for *her*."

Red cuts in, saying, "Oi, will ya get off it? She wouldn't release all of us only to capture us again. The Règle line is known for a merciless adherence to the laws they've created; releasing us breaks half a dozen of them, at least. And it's just plain foolish."

"I don't trust her," Qen says, ignoring the logic put before them. "I never have."

"You don't need to trust me." Looking at the assembled group, I add, "None of you do. I'm not asking for loyalty or friendship or help. You can piss off right now if that's what you want. But I'm going to make sure every cell on this station is empty, I'm going to send my people back to the ground, along with anyone else who wants to go, then I'm going to show the Règle what happens when she messes with the wrong person."

"That's a big goal," Red says.

I nod. "A friend once told me he was only able to rebel in small doses. That was good enough then, doing as much as he could, but I'm tired of doing things in half-measures. I've spent too much time worrying about everyone around me. This is for me, and I'll do it alone, with my bare hands, if I need to."

Red smiles. "You can sign me up, lass. 'Cause what I'm hearing is that there's room by your side for anyone who wants to make a mess."

I give her an answering smile and single nod. "A big damn mess."

THE PRISONERS GATHER BEHIND US AS WE LEAVE, A PROCESSION OF ANGER unleashed. I see the trial winners, Osric and Grieva, join in beside Qen; Edi, the prisoner from my first time on the station, gives me a solemn nod as they slip in behind me; Aunt Rachel's wife, Permilla, peeks out of a doorway, her face melting into relief when she sees me. She reaches forward and gives my hand a squeeze before slipping in with the others.

There are so many more unfamiliar faces falling in line. I hear whispers running through the ranks as the new people are filled in on what's happening, and hushed voices returning news of others who have already left, taking the opportunity to run while they could. I expected as much; I wouldn't have stuck around, but a surprising number of them did.

As we reach the exit, my heart sinks. The face I've searched for at every doorway is not among them. Fear reaches gnarled fingers into my chest, reminding me of what Bets had threatened to do, and I wonder, *Where is Ivy?*

Krew grabs my hand, startling me from my thoughts. "You ready?"

"Yes," I say. Then, "Wait. Where's Doctor Okada?"

A muscle under Krew's left eye twitches. "Not here. He's not a prisoner."

"I know. I saw him." The memory flickers through my mind, colored by Cameron's eyes. She didn't know him or who he had been to me, but there was still something about him that pulled us. Cameron *wanted* him, even in the briefest moments she was near him, though that was something I had never considered before. How strange…

Krew is eyeing me, brows furrowed. I push Cam's memories aside and focus on my friend. Whatever has him upset revolves around his former lover, but I don't press. There's no time to get into it now, and I have a feeling Krew has a story to tell where Yosh Okada is concerned.

Instead, I step up to the door, expecting it to be locked and need to be forced open, but it slides back instantly at my presence…

…and opens into chaos.

People are yelling, screaming, wailing. Bodies are everywhere; corpses litter the floor, piled against the walls, while those still alive throw themselves in and out of danger. Blood splatters in arcs, puddles around bodies, drips from fingertips into congealing pools. The scent of iron and feces is thick in the air, speaking the language of death.

And there, in the middle of it all, drenched in sweat and blood and smiling like a buffoon while surveying his troops, is Hiro. His dark hair is no longer stubble, but grown out and tucked behind his ears. His swirling tattoos dance up his arms on skin that is suntanned and glowing, like he's spent his life outdoors—like he was Raider-born.

My people are behind me, waiting for me to do something, but everyone else seems to melt away as I focus on Hiro. He's dressed head to heel in blood-spattered killing leathers with a curved blade held high above his head. He looks ridiculously hot. It's that sight that makes me realize that the corridor is full of Raiders. For the most part, they're not the bodies on the ground though; no, they're the ones driving back the guards.

My collection of misfits pile into the corridor, gazes casting about for some semblance of order while they cover their noses from the scent and their eyes from the sight. I hear Krew giving instructions to the group, sending them through the hall to fight or hide, depending on who they are. I'm thankful for him, as my attention is now fully consumed by the bloody brawler in my path.

Hiro hasn't noticed us. I don't know how long I could stare at him before he sees me, but I dare not wait too long for fear his people turn on mine. I call out, "Moose!"

His eyes swivel around, searching the corridor until his gaze locks on me. For one brilliant moment, there is nothing else. We stand motionless, staring at one another, lost in the moment that binds us together.

His smile isn't beaming any longer, but reserved, almost shy. I've never seen Hiro wearing such an expression. When he steps toward me, it seems tentative. I'm not certain why my heart hammers against my ribs as he closes the gap between us, or why my lungs have chosen this moment to stop breathing. But here I am, losing my ability to function as he draws ever closer.

Hiro stops in front of me, so close I can smell the salt on his skin, yet somehow it doesn't feel close enough. He reaches a hand forward and runs his fingers over a stray curl, tucking it behind my ear as he whispers, "Squirrel."

The corner of his lip quirks up as he speaks, revealing the playful face I've missed so much. I fight back a smile, lose, and say, "Hey, stranger. Been awhile."

"Too long," he says, his hand still lingering at my jawline

"Yeah, had some loose ends to—"

"You left me," he interrupts, voice cracking. His brown eyes flash gold in the flickering lights of the corridor.

The words hit me hard. "I... I'm sorry."

"Never again," he says, his eyes demanding a promise.

"Never," I breathe.

Hiro's hand slips behind my neck and tilts my head toward his. My eyes close of their own volition, my lips parting to meet his. I gasp at the moment our mouths meet. His lips are soft and he tastes like ginger and cloves. His stubbled beard scratches my cheek and I run my hands through his dark hair, clenching fistfuls as I pull his body against me. We stand there for a time-ceasing moment, war raging all around us, as we throw ourselves into our own battle.

When we run out of ammunition, we break apart, breathing heavily. Hiro says, "That was, uh..."

"Terrible," I offer, a laugh bubbling up.

Everything about it *should* have been good. In the moment, the very thought of it was powerfully sexy. And physically, it was fine. I can definitely see the appeal and wouldn't complain about kissing him again, just for the practice of it. But whatever connection lives between us is not meant for that sort of relationship. Hiro is my friend, and I love him, but not like that.

"Oh, thank the gods. My brain was racing trying to figure out how to let you down easy."

I laugh then, pull him into a hug. "I missed you."

"I missed you, too. And I meant it when I said you're not allowed to leave me again. Even if you are a horrific kisser, I still want you around."

"Me? It was definitely you that was the problem."

"Literally no one else has ever said that. I can provide references."

"No need. I'll happily hand you off to your current flavor of the week."

"I resent that," he says, hand going to his chest to feign hurt. "I'll have you know I've been entirely loyal to my wife the *entire time* she was gone, despite her abandoning me."

"You haven't had a lover while I've been gone? I'm surprised the Raiders let you get away with that during the solstice ceremonies."

He shrugs. "They didn't question their Chief."

My hand goes to my mouth as I realize what he means. When I left, the role would've fallen to my nearest family member. In this case, it was him, my new mate.

"I didn't think—"

"It's fine," he says, waving a hand. "We got by. But now that you're back, there is one incredibly important thing I need from you."

"Of course. Name it."

"Let me bang the scientist."

"What?" I laugh.

"Before you left, you said I needed your permission to be involved with anyone outside our marriage, but you left before you gave it. So, I did my part and kept it in my pants. That was clearly a disaster waiting to happen, because it had me thinking."

"And a thinking Hiro is like an unwatched fire."

"Exactly. Burning out of control, going places I shouldn't. I mean, I was so messed up I thought I might be in love with you. I am definitely not in love with you, in case there's any lingering confusion."

"Okay," I say, taking in everything as it rushes from him. "I'm not in love with you either, for the record. But where does banging a scientist come into play?"

"Right, yeah. There's this hot nerd I might actually be in love with, so, you know…"

"Oh, wow, Hiro. That's a big deal."

"Yeah, I guess. We should totally talk about it and have a whole gab session when we're not facing imminent death."

"Right," I say, looking around at the room I'd all but forgotten. My people have spread out and are clearing out the remaining guards, but this portion of the corridor itself seems clear of danger at this point. "Guess we should take care of this mess once and for all."

Hiro pulls a blade from his boot and hands it to me. "Wreck them, Chief."

"You too, Chief."

He takes a step forward, then throws one last glance over his shoulder and says, "And Squirrel?"

"Yeah, Moose?"

He flashes his megawatt grin and says, "Try not to die."

CHAPTER
SEVENTEEN
HIRO

S eeing Nova makes me feel like I'm rooted to the ground again. All this time without her, I've been swimming through air, a moment away from being blown away by the mildest of winds. Now, I feel solid. Whole.

It's weird to think that way about another person, I think as I slice through a guard trying to kill me.

I wasn't entirely convinced people actually felt that way about others; mostly I thought it was just some bull they told single people to make them feel bad for being alone. I'm sure at least half, maybe more, of the couples I knew on the station were together just to stop the loneliness; but now, part of me hopes that some of them were real. Sometimes you meet someone who is destined to be part of your life, someone who makes you feel like a real person instead of an imitation human, and I've found that with Nova.

Shame she's such a terrible kisser.

But I can live with a best friend who completes me, instead of a paramour. And now that we got that will-they/won't-they drama out of the way, I can focus on finding a romantic partner who gives me the same solidity that Nova does. Hopefully one who knows what to do with their tongue and whose teeth don't keep ramming into mine.

Another guard runs my way and I spin on instinct, slicing her hamstring. Fighting lessons with the Raiders have transformed me in a way I wasn't expecting. I mean, I used to do okay in a bar fight, of which I'd willingly participated in more than my fair share, and I *was* a guard for a while, excelling at their training program when submission of unruly citizens was the goal. Raiders though, they're a whole different breed. They use their entire bodies as weapons, focusing more on the way their flesh moves with their blades than on the blades themselves. I'm still learning their ways, but after a year of daily lessons, I'm far more deadly than I was when I left this place.

I don't realize how far I've gone away from the others until I see the door to my old apartment. The sight sends a strange pang through me; it isn't necessarily that I miss it, but I had some wild times there. The sheer volume of ass I took home…

I shake my head to clear away the sweet, sweet memories. Far too much distraction for where I am and what I'm doing. Besides, the Hiro who lived there is not the same one as the man who stands in this hallway. As much fun as I had back then, I wasn't whole. I wouldn't go back to that version of myself for anything.

Turning back toward the other Raiders, my eyes catch sight of a figure in the doorway to the next corridor. She's lovely, as she always has been: golden hair, loose instead of that braid she always wore, eyes as blue as the sky on a summer afternoon (something I couldn't have compared them to when I'd stared into them before I went on-world), a certain something in her face—the shape? the softness?—that speaks of innocence.

She has her laser gun trained on my chest.

"Captain Alik Rolfrun," I say, flashing her a grin.

"I thought you were dead."

I spread my arms out and do a slow spin for her. "Not dead."

"Let me rephrase," she says. "I *hoped* you were dead."

"Ouch. That's not very nice. I thought we were…"

"*Friends?*" she asks, a bitter laugh accompanying the word.

I slowly shake my head. No, that's not the word. I don't know exactly what I thought we were, but "friends" wasn't it. Maybe thinking we were anything is a big part of the problem. I was a complete dick to her.

"I was a complete dick to you."

Her whole body seems to pause at my words. After a moment, she says, "Yeah, you were."

"Why did you let me treat you like that?"

Her jaw clenches and unclenches. "So it's *my* fault that you treated me bad?"

"No, of course not. That's not what I meant."

"I doubt you have any idea what you meant," she says. "Now, or then. You certainly didn't know what you meant *to me,* or if you did, you just didn't care."

I let my mind wander back to the handful of times I can recall being around Alik. We worked together casually, so I saw her often in passing, but there were only a few times we were together on purpose. Still, those moments are seared into my brain.

"The first time I saw you outside of your guard uniform, you wore a blue dress nearly the same shade as your eyes. It was cut high, and with the heels you were wearing, your legs looked like they were a mile long."

"Should I be impressed that you remember that?"

I ignore her, continuing. "You bought me a drink and you were nervous about it. I wasn't sure why, because I was too self-absorbed to realize you were out of your comfort zone. We stood at the back wall listening to music while I traced a finger at the hem of your dress."

Her cheeks go red. "Again, I don't know what you want me to say. Good job remembering a moment that meant nothing?"

"Come on, Alik," I say, taking a step toward her. "It didn't mean *nothing.*"

"Completely meaningless," she says, swallowing hard as soon as the words leave her lips.

"We kissed. Your lips tasted like the strawberry lip gloss that was all the rage for a hot minute."

"Everyone's lips tasted like strawberry lip gloss until they ran out of it at the commissary."

"They tried switching it to lemon, right? But no one liked it."

"What does it have to do with me killing you right now, anyway?" she asks.

"Killing me?" I ask, genuinely surprised.

She rolls her eyes. "Why else would I have my gun aimed at you?"

"Because you want the truth, and I'm the only one who can give it to you."

Alik stares at me for a long moment while the distant sounds of fighting rumble in the background. Our soundtrack has always been a war; she and I were never meant for love songs.

"Even if I *did* want the truth, and I'm not saying I do, but if I did, I couldn't trust you to relay it. You're a liar and a cheat, willing to do and say anything to save your own skin."

I nod. She's not wrong. "I'm not the same man who broke your heart, Cap. Sure, I'm still willing to say just about anything to not die, but that now includes telling the truth. I was always afraid to do that before."

"What changed?"

"I did," I say. "I found my home; gods know this was never it. And I found people to care about, people who believe in me."

"I believed in you."

"You wanted to. And maybe things could've been good with us if I'd let you. But I wasn't ready then. Hells, I'm barely ready now. Still, every day gets me a little closer to being someone worthy of the faith you had in a worthless man."

"Why?" she asks, and I think she's going to say more, but instead she presses her lips together and glares at me over the top of her laser.

There's a lot of things I could say to answer that question, a lot of answers that would be true. But I whittle my thoughts down to the thing that seems the closest to the core of why Alik and I never worked. "I didn't think love was real. And I certainly didn't think I was worthy of even the imitation version of it."

"Didn't? As in, past tense?"

I nod, but don't add anything else to it. My actions have warranted an answer for a long time, and now that she has it, she deserves a moment to process it.

"I'm glad you found someone," she says, though her face doesn't look glad at all. "It's hard to believe someone actually tamed you. Would I," she clears her throat, "would I like them?"

I think back to when Alik and Nova met. To when Nova and *I* met. It wasn't exactly…pleasant. Ninety percent of my brain jumps into flight mode and is telling me not to tell the truth, not to remind Alik of that moment when the prisoners escaped under her watch, when I switched sides and went with the people we'd been raised to view as enemies. I could lie and tell her about literally anyone else, but in truth, it's Nova— or her absence, at least—who taught me it's possible to love another person. Even if it isn't romantic love, it's still the truest feeling I've ever known. And I've been doing so well with this honesty thing...

"Funny story, you've actually met. Remember the Raider who broke out the prisoners?"

"You're kidding me," she says.

"I mean, it's not the way you think—"

"You fell in love with that bitch who held me at laser point?"

"Technically, you're holding me at laser point now—"

"Is it inspiring feelings of love?" she growls. "No, because that's screwy. You're not in love, you've got Stockholm Syndrome."

"No, I'm not saying I'm in love with her, just that she taught me *how* to love."

Alik shakes her head. "You know, I was going to kill you with a nice quick blast through your heart, but now that seems wasteful."

"You're not going to kill me?"

"No, I'm not going to kill you."

Honesty really is the best policy, I think, elated that my truthfulness has somehow redeemed me.

"Turn around and face the wall," she says. "Hands on top of your head."

"Wait. I thought you weren't going to kill me."

She smiles, but her eyes seem to darken, storm clouds passing through that bright blue sky. "I'm not. What I'm going to do is far worse."

"What's worse than death?"

"Well, since my mortal enemy was the one who taught you to love, I'm going to take you to the woman who I assume should be your mortal enemy. Then I'll let the Règle—who's been screwing your girl for the last year, by the way—I'll let her decide what to do with the traitorous bastard who abandoned his post and aided in the murder of his people."

Alik cuffs my wrists tighter than she needs to. In one last ditch effort,

I give old Hiro the reins and let him say, "Have I told you how gorgeous you're looking these days? Why don't we grab a drink and talk about this? My apartment is—"

She spins me around and slams me against the wall. Her mouth covers mine, hungry and hard and hateful. There is no love left between us, if there ever was any to begin with. Alik takes my bottom lip between her teeth as she pulls away, biting until I taste blood in my mouth.

"That was—"

She knees me between the legs and I curl in on myself, groaning in pain.

Alik leans down beside my ear and whispers, "Thank you, Hiro. I really enjoyed that. I hope it was good for you, too."

Firm hands grip my arms and pull me down the hall. I watch Alik getting smaller as the guards drag me away, the smile on her face remaining big and cruel until she fades completely from view.

CHAPTER
EIGHTEEN

NOVA

Seeing Hiro cemented my resolve. I am going back to my home, my people, and those I love. And I'm taking a helluva lot of new friends with me.

I have no idea how many people are following me through the corridors at this point, but it's enough to send guards scattering at the sight of us. One brawny beast-of-a-man actually pissed himself when he turned the corner and saw us coming toward him.

But we are not without mercy. If they're unarmed, we don't harm them. If they're armed and surrender, we don't harm them. We actually try not to kill even the ones attacking us, if we can help it. We've gathered some restraints from the guards we've captured and are trying to subdue those we can. When you grow up believing someone is the enemy, that they're uneducated and foolish simply because they're *other*... well, it can mess with you. So, we're doing our best to show them we aren't what they think we are.

Still, there's more blood in these corridors than I want to see, more loss at every turn. There was a point when the sight wouldn't have bothered me, when I might not have noticed a world smeared crimson. No longer. I see a slash of red spray across the hall and know that's another person who might've been saved, given the chance. They have to *want* to be saved though, and a lot of them don't see us as the redeemers I want us to be. Then again, can anyone really redeem another person or do they need to do that for themselves? And if I can redeem others, is that the role I want to take on?

Some see us that way, even if I'm unsure about the philosophies of it. Some who have never raised a hand in anger, who have never spoken an ill word, but are still guilty of the sin of doing nothing—they join us. They've spent their lives being silent and obedient, but now they see their chance for something more. They lead their children behind us, putting themselves in the heart of our entourage, and it gives me hope for who we can be together.

"Nova!"

The voice cracks like a whip, sending a sharp ache through my chest. I turn to see Thoa the Bonecutter standing down the corridor to my right. The last time I saw him was in his bedroom at the Hole in the World. His hands and lips and body had crashed against mine, reducing my heart to rubble. I still remember the way his breath brushed my forehead as he whispered goodbye to me. He pushed me away...let me go...both?

Yet here he stands.

Though it's been over a year since I've seen him, everything about him seems just the same. Dark hair curls around his ears, muscles upon muscles peek out from his killing leathers—the leathers I thought he gave up—and his azure eyes stare out from tanned cheeks, an unchecked fire burning in them.

It's that spark of passion that seems out of place. I've seen it before— at the solstice when he asked me to be his mate, standing next to him amidst all the finery of Gearhaven's mayoral banquet, the look he gave me before he snuck away to join the Trials—but it's been a long time since he looked at me that way.

"Little Star, it's really you," he says.

He's closed the distance between us while my brain has fumbled for the words to speak and are still coming up empty.

"I've missed you," he says, pulling me against his chest in a tight embrace.

I consider returning the sentiment, but don't. Our relationship was always complicated, full of half-truths and missteps that pushed us away from each other. I won't restart on that same premise. The truth is, I haven't missed him. I haven't thought of him, really. Sure, my mind may have flitted to him a moment or two over the last year, in those few moments when I was myself and not Cam, but it wasn't that aching desire I once held for him.

At least, I don't think it was. There are still some jumbled moments that I can't quite remember, that remain fuzzy at the edges. But I feel like I would know if my heart had reached for him through the darkness of my time on this station. My feelings for him have cooled, tempered by time, and as much as I once loved him, I've said my goodbye to him as well.

I pull back, smile as best I can, and ask, "What are you doing here?"

His brow furrows momentarily, then clears. "We came to rescue you." He glances at the army forming behind me and adds, "Guess that wasn't really necessary. You're in the habit of rescuing yourself."

I shrug. "I'm good at gathering strays."

"That's the truth."

"How many of you are there?"

"Eleven hundred."

Thoa smiles at my surprise, giving me a moment to sort my thoughts.

It takes effort to get my face under control. "Why? How? Where did you find so many?"

"The Chief is quite persuasive, when he wants to be. Everywhere he went, he told people about you, about this place, and he built a collection of Raiders to come after you."

I smile at the thought of Hiro going around flashing his megawatt grin and people falling in line behind him because of it. He's basically a charm-monster. "I saw him and a group of Raiders earlier. He was clearing the corridors. He failed to mention he brought an entire army with him."

"I'm not surprised. His group was in charge of clearing a path, and he can be a bit singularly minded."

"What's your job?"

"Finding you."

"Well, here I am. Now what's the plan?"

"We need to get some of these civilians out of the way and into a safe place."

"Can we get them to the ground?"

He nods. "We can start that immediately. You want to go first?"

"It's like you don't know me at all," I smirk.

"Getting you home is our main goal. We can rally and build once you're there. So, whether you want to or not, you're going to have to leave."

I grind my teeth against his words. After all this time and the way things ended with us, I don't like him thinking he can force his will on me. "When I'm ready."

Thoa rubs his hand over his face, exasperated. "I'd hoped your time up here would've made you easier to deal with, maybe a little less stubborn."

Rage runs through me, removing any chance that reason or logic could be in control. I'm surprised at my own reaction; my mind tells me my time with Thoa has long been over, that I've given up the love I once held, so why am I so angry at him? Because he's here now, when it's too late? Because after all this time, all I thought we had between us, it seems as if he doesn't really know me? Because he's asking me to leave when so many are still here needing help?

My vision tunnels until there's no one but me and Thoa; my friends, my followers, the army I've amassed are gone, and all I can think of is getting away from this man I once loved.

I grit my teeth, trying to hold back my frustration. I nearly bite my tongue off in the attempt to keep quiet, before finally saying, "You're welcome to leave, but I've got stuff to do."

I'm only half a dozen steps when I hear the pounding of boots running up the corridor behind me. A blood-drenched Raider with a wicked scythe in one hand and a whip in the other reaches Thoa and pants out a message. Darkness passes over Thoa's features in a look I've seen before.

"What's wrong?" I say, returning to his side.

"You're her," scythe-woman breathes. "You're Chief Nova."

I nod, though I'm unsure why she seems to regard me like the mythical gods of old. Her eyes seem to take in every inch of my face, but she still hasn't answered me.

"What's your news?" I ask again.

"It's Hiro," Thoa says, accompanied by a wince and a bone-weary sigh. "He's been captured."

It takes a moment for the news of Hiro's capture to sink in, followed by several minutes of intermittent cursing, before I'm able to form a coherent sentence that doesn't involve murderous threats. After the initial thought-rampage is finished, my mind is still too rattled, too racing, to figure much out beyond the most basic: find and save Hiro.

"I really didn't need this today," I growl. "I have enough people to rescue—Ivy, Coco, my father, everybody else—without adding Hiro to the mix."

"I'm sure he didn't do it on purpose just to make your life harder," Thoa says.

He pulls a face as if reconsidering, based on who Hiro is as a person, and I realize he's gotten to know Hiro over the last year. He probably knows him better than I do, really. I spent weeks with him, not months. Though our friendship blossomed quickly and still feels fully-formed despite the lack of communication while I've been trapped up here, there's something to be said for having the time to develop something long-standing.

"How did this happen?" I ask, once my mind has cleared from the Hiro-induced fog. "He seemed pretty in control of what was going on earlier. Ambush?"

"He separated from his team," scythe-woman, whose name is Regina, tells us.

"Why would he do that? Teams were his idea, and he preached the importance of staying with them," Thoa says.

It strikes me then how long they must have planned for this attack. It would've taken months to gather forces, to figure out logistics, and all the while, Hiro was committed to bringing me home.

Then the bastard went and got himself captured.

Regina continues, "There was no sign of struggle. We wouldn't have known what happened if another team hadn't caught the tail-end of him being taken away."

"Could he have wanted to get captured?" I ask.

Thoa's azure gaze meets mine, full of more questions than answers. "I don't think so. There was an early plan that we scrapped that involved him getting captured, but once we were able to get the whole force zapped up here rather than one at a time, we were able to rely on numbers and surprise."

I run my tongue across my teeth and say, "So, if he did it on purpose, it's for himself."

"He wanted to kill the Règle," Regina says.

Thoa says, "We all want to kill the Règle. I don't think it would be enough for Hiro to put his life on the line, especially since he knew Nova was alive and free."

A thought wriggles in the back of my mind, half-formed. I brush past it at first, but it gets stronger each second I ignore it. Finally, I ask, "Did anyone see who captured him?"

"He was taken off by a squad of guards," Regina says. She pauses, scrunches her nose for a second, and adds, "But there was a blonde woman who seemed to be in charge."

My suspicions must be clear on my face, because Thoa asks, "You know her?"

"Maybe," I say, eyes narrowing. "There was a woman who was in love with Hiro. I met her when we freed the prisoners last time. Hiro used her affections to get us out of trouble."

"If she loved him, would she really turn him in, knowing what the Règle would do to him?" Regina asks.

Thoa purses his lips, looks from me to Regina. "You haven't had many interactions with a scorned lover, have you?"

I smile at his words, but add, "It's not *just* that. Though after the way he treated her, I'm sure that is part of it. But this woman was loyal to the Règle, to her detriment. She couldn't see anything beyond her duty."

"Even if it was her," Thoa says, "that doesn't help us now."

"It might. We don't know what her relationship is with the Règle, where her career might have taken her over the last year. She could be the key to finding him without rampaging through the whole place."

"You *don't* want to rampage? Seems like your time up here really has changed you," he says with a smirk. When my glare says more than my words ever could, Thoa's face goes serious and he asks, "Okay then, how do we do that?"

I shake my head. "No clue. We need Ivy."

"Oh, right, I forgot," Thoa says.

"You have her?"

He winces, shakes his head, and my sudden burst of hope deflates again. Thoa reaches into a small pouch tied around his neck. He pulls out a metal device no bigger than the end of my thumb and hands it to me. "Put it in your ear."

"In my ear?"

He combs his hair away and shows me an identical piece in his own. I put it in place, and suddenly there is a voice I don't recognize speaking into my ear. "*I need a name.*"

"Nova," I say.

"*Sorry, no, not your name,*" the voice says. "*I know who you are. You're basically a legend around here.*"

"And who are you?" I ask.

"*Javian. I've been working with your, uh, husband for a while, trying to figure out how to get on the station.*"

"You're the scientist?"

He chuckles. "*Not a scientist exactly. Just a tech guy.*"

"So, not the same guy Hiro told me about?"

I can nearly hear Javian blushing through the speaker as he asks, "*He told you about me? No, nevermind. Don't answer that.*"

"We need to find him," I say, slipping past Javian's question. I'm not sure how involved he is with Hiro, and I don't feel like it's my place to advertise my best friend's feelings. "When was the last time you talked to him?"

"*His earpiece went to static earlier, so I haven't heard from him for about half an hour.*"

"They must've found it when they took him into custody."

"*I think something happened to it before then. He was still fighting last time he checked in, but there was a strange pop and then nothing but static.*"

"You didn't hear anything that happened with the arrest."

"*No. I only know as much as you do,*" Javian says. "*I heard most of what was going on through Thoa's earpiece, but I didn't catch the name of the guard you were talking about. I might be able to figure something out if you know it."*

I tip my head back and close my eyes, searching for the woman's name. I know it's in here somewhere, lodged in my brain. But the constant rearranging of my personality and erasure of my memories sometimes makes it hard for specific things to pop up at the right time. I can remember the guard, remember that she had something with Hiro, but when I try to pinpoint the details, my brain tips sideways.

"Sorry, no," I say after a moment. "I know she was serving at the same time as Hiro, stationed in the same place, and she was higher ranked… Captain, maybe?"

The tap of keys sounds through my earpiece as Javian says, *"Okay, I'll start with that and see what I come up with. I've only barely hacked into their system so it might take me a minute to figure out their personnel records."*

"My sister can help you. She's a whiz at that stuff."

"Cool, give her an earpiece."

"I will, as soon as I find her. Maybe while you're looking for the Captain, you can figure out where they were keeping Ivy Kennedy in the last forty-eight hours."

"Just the last two days?"

"I know where she was before that, but she's not there now. And there's a chance she's, well, she might be dead."

Thoa's hand grips my shoulder, warm and strong. There was a time I would've melted at that touch, but now I see it for what it truly is: a shelter from the storm. It isn't some foolish romantic thing, it's simply the comfort of a friend when the whole damned world is falling apart around me. It's exactly what I need, even if every inch of my being is telling me to run from kindness, as it's too often too good to be true.

"I'll find her," Javian says.

The earpiece goes silent, but some small part of me sparks to life, reigniting hope that this stranger can somehow do what I cannot. For one strange moment, a wave of confidence in this man washes over me and I have no doubts that what he claims is true: Hiro's scientist is going to save my world.

CHAPTER
NINETEEN

IVY

It's cold in the cell they've put me in. I'm sitting on a threadbare blanket that doesn't do anything to warm me, but is at least a little cushion against the bed's metal bars that are trying to dig into my ass. Highly uncomfortable, and I am not in the mood for it.

Could be worse though. The guards in the "mental repair" unit used shock therapy, food and light deprivation, sound experimentation, and occasionally, they would beat the hell out of me.

I can handle cold.

This cell is a lot different from the one where they've been keeping me. This one has actual bars like in old-timey movies, and I can see who comes and goes. The other had a solid door and kept me from seeing anything other than whoever was directly in front of my room. This one is built for short term stays, and there's little comfort here. The other was made to keep us as prisoners for however long it took to break us, but at least we were *comfortable* prisoners.

They put me in here after a lengthy discussion about what was the best thing to do with Nova's sister. That's all I am to them—not a person with their own thoughts and feelings and desires—but an extension of the one who will be their destruction. Even now when all seems lost, I know she's on her way. I just have to live, and give her time to get to me.

I've already been doing that for a year; what's a few more minutes/hours/days?

I swallow against the thought as despair threatens to overtake me, not for the first time. But she will come, she will come. Nova always comes for me.

The Règle seemed strangely reluctant to lock me away, especially considering her recent threats on my life. I think she's afraid of Nova. Which, of course, gives me hope that my sister is actually my sister again, rather than the robot-person she's been for the last year. But I'm not totally convinced that's the case; in fact, tidbits the Règle said haphazardly have led me to believe she's still in love with my sis and trying to keep me safe—from herself, no less—to make Nova, or Cameron, happy.

Nothing more than a hypothesis at this point, but I'm curious to see how the data presents itself.

For my part, I've been quiet. Not that I had a choice. After I wailed, cried, called them a handful of creative curses, and gave them a spirited chorus of a song Stevens taught me about beer hanging on the wall, they gagged me so I couldn't make more than an exaggerated harumph.

Which is fine. Really, it is. I didn't need to talk. I was doing it to annoy them, to spur them into taking action to get the obnoxious teenager to shut up. To get them close to me. I needed them close enough to get the key for my handcuffs. These geezers are still using old-fashioned lock and key handcuffs, which I guess has its perks. Especially when used against those of us who understand how to use tech and could crush their souls with the right computer systems. So, the only way for me to get out of these restraints was to get my captor close enough to swipe the key from his pocket. He was so concerned with quieting me down while the Règle was trying to sleep, he didn't notice my hand slip into his pocket.

I haven't freed myself yet. There's still the matter of the cell door, and I don't want to give away my advantages until I can move on to the next step. Luckily, they thought the old-timey restraints would be enough, and they stuck me in a cell that is essentially a hacker's wet-dream. There are panels and wires running all over this place, some of them far more exposed than can be deemed "safe." Really, when was the last time someone inspected this place? It's a mess.

But it's perfect for me. I let my eyes trace the wires where they're visible, imagining their paths when they slip behind the wall. Their electronic actions travel like my own impulses through neurotransmitters, forging paths through junction-box synapses, until they reach their intended goals. For the wires, it's creating a prison to contain me; for me, it's outsmarting and escaping those who thought they could put me within five feet of electronics and not be thwarted by my genius. I might not be Nova, but that doesn't make me useless.

I've already figured out how to open the cell door, I've got the key to my cuffs, and for the last hour I've been counting the minutes between the guards rounds. I'm nearly ready now. I think if I wait two minutes after the next guard, I should be able to get out of here and at least down the hall. Not sure what I'll do after that, but the panel to open the next door looks pretty straightforward, so I'm going to give it a go. Even if I don't make it out, doing *anything* is better than waiting around to die. Plus, if I can make it any easier for Nova to find me, now is the time to do it.

She will come for me. She always comes for me.

The guard approaches. He's looking into the cells he passes, which he normally doesn't do. Maybe there was a shift change and the new guy is someone who actually cares about doing his job. That is less than ideal.

He reaches my cell and looks inside. When I glare at him, half his mouth tips up in a smile while the other is pulled down in a perpetual frown by a scar at the side of his mouth.

"Can I *help* you?" I growl as he continues staring at me.

His green eyes flash with something that's almost like delight. "Yeah, probably. Trying to figure out the best way to get you outta here. I wasn't sure I'd find you, so my plan didn't get too deep."

"Excuse me?"

"You're Ivy, right? Nova's sister? I'm Benjy."

I'm on my feet before I've considered he may be trying to trick me. "You know my sister?"

He tips his hat back a little and a strand of silvery-purple hair slips loose. "Yeah, I know her. We're friends even. And she's told me quite a bit about you."

"Good or bad?" I ask, unable to control the smile that spreads across my face.

"Bit of both," he smiles back. "I promised her I'd rescue you, so, here I am."

"Well, shit. I'd already planned my escape."

"Good. I'm rubbish at heroics. More into doing shady stuff to get what I want. I'm completely out of my element here."

"That doesn't really sound like the type my sister would be friends with."

"Right?" he says. "I weaseled my way into her heart."

"Can you weasel yourself away from the door? I'm gonna need you to step back so I can short out the locking mechanism."

"See, I knew you could help me. Much better plan than my idea of shaking the door until it miraculously opened."

Benjy steps back, the half-smile on his face never fading. I take out the stolen key and undo my restraints, then immediately move to the wires poking out of the wall. I can feel the hum of power coursing through them, though really, that's probably in my head. There's always been a strange connection between me and electronics of any sort, and I feel their pulse as if it's my own.

My hands dance of their own accord. There is no thought or consideration—my fingers know what to do. A minute and a half later, the cell door slides open. I step out into the corridor with Nova's friend, ready to move to the next panel.

"One thing before we go," he says.

I ball my fists instinctively, waiting for the next shoe to drop. "What's that?"

He hooks a thumb over his shoulder and says, "There's another prisoner down there. Wanna try to get her out?"

I look longingly at the door panel, the path to freedom, and press my lips into a thin line. I'm not sure why I feel the need to prove that I'm as good as Nova, but I do, and rescuing this other person is exactly what she would do. I look up at Benjy and, with a sigh, say, "Let's give it a whirl."

He leads me back to the other cell. She was far enough away that I couldn't see her, which is probably a good thing. I might not have been able to focus as well if I'd known she was so near, and in such bad shape.

"Hey, Coco," I say, staring down at her.

She looks up through swollen eyes. Her face is blotchy with various shades of purple and yellow, bruises in different degrees of healing. She's on the floor in dirty rags hanging from her body, and I'm not sure she could stand if she wanted to. Her once curvy figure is thin now, frail. I realize I'm on the gaunt side myself, if I'm being honest, but Coco looks half-starved. Knowing the Règle, I wouldn't be surprised if she was, though I can't imagine what Coco could have done to warrant such a thing, other than being lovely and existing in the same world as Nova. Jealousy can make people do some messed up stuff.

When she doesn't say anything, I ask, "Do you know who I am?" Still no response, so I ask, "Do you remember Nova?"

"No," she says, her voice croaking into existence like a door that hasn't been used for a long time. But then it resolves into, "Nova?"

"Yeah, do you remember her?" I ask. "She's my sister. I'm Ivy. I was on the farm with you before the attack."

"I remember," she says. She tries to push herself up from the floor, but the effort is clearly too immense for her.

I say, "Don't move. We're going to help you. Just stay where you are and let us take care of it."

I step to the electronic panel closest to her cell and try to wriggle the tips of my fingernails into the small gap at the edge of the panel.

Benjy sighs audibly, giving me straight up dad vibes, and pulls a screwdriver out of his pocket.

"Where did you get this?"

He waves a dismissive hand and says, "Don't worry about it."

I use the tool to pry open the panel. While I'm tinkering with it, Benjy asks, "What can I do?"

"Watch for guards."

He nods, the movement catching in my peripheral, then asks, "What do you want me to say if I see some?"

I sigh, but my eyes remain fixed on my work. "How about, 'hey, there are guards coming,' or something nice and simple?"

He nods again. "Hey, there are guards coming."

"Yeah, just like that."

"Right," Benjy agrees. "And now I'm telling you that it's happening."

I glance down the hall and see two guards coming our way, with a bloody man dragged between them. At least, I think it's a man; the face is so beat up, I can't tell much from it, and the body has been dressed in the plain shift they give the mental patients.

They've been walking toward us for around five seconds and still haven't noticed us. Their preoccupation with the lump of flesh between them has definitely been advantageous, but I don't expect it to last much longer. Any minute now—

"Hey!" one of the guards yells. "What the hell are you doing?"

Benjy smirks and says, "Keep working. I got this."

He steps down the corridor toward them and I hear him say, "Esteemed guests, welcome..." before I tune him out and proceed on the work at hand. I'm what you might call "hopeless" when it comes to fighting. Getting electronics to bow before me like the goddess I am, though...

Coco's cell door slides open. She gives the tiniest whimper of a sound, whether from the relief of being rescued or from the massive amount of pain she's in. I join her on the floor and ease her arm over my shoulders. "Come on, we gotta go."

"I can't," she breathes, pain evident in the set of her jaw.

"You have to," I say. "Before more guards show up; or worse, the Règle."

Her eyes go wide at the mere mention of my sister's crazy girl-friend, confirming that whatever has happened to her down here has been at the Règle's discretion. It's enough of a threat to get her moving, which is all I really needed. That gives us a chance of getting out of here.

We step out of the cell and I look down the hall to where Benjy stands. The two guards are now splayed out on the floor next to the man they were carrying. He turns toward me and says, "Nice work."

"You, too. Maybe you *are* someone my sister would befriend. How did you do that, by the way?"

He shrugs. "Luck."

"All right then. Get your lucky ass down here and help me with Coco."

"Should we help this guy?"

"I'd love to, but I don't think we can," I say, a tug in my gut even as the words leave my mouth. "We've gotta get Coco out of here, and I don't think we can carry both of them."

Benjy nods, but I can tell he's not happy with the decision. I'm not either, but sometimes you're left choosing between two piles of shit, and you just want to pick the one that seems smallest.

As we carry Coco past the unconscious, broken man, I glance down at him. The shock of recognition courses through me, but as bad as I feel about leaving him behind, I don't have a choice. Coco can barely move and we're out of options. Still, I know this man. Not well, as we only spent a few days together before he flew off with Nova to recruit Raiders. But he taught me a couple dirty jokes, he showed Coco's brother how to properly aim a weapon, and he shared a smile with everyone at the farm. He must have ended up here just like I did, just like Nova did, and maybe he's another trigger that will bring Nova back to us.

I try to blink away the image of his crushed nose and bloody lips, but it's burned into my vision. Whatever Hiro has done to piss off the Règle, I hope it was worth it. It looks like he may be stuck here for a while.

"Wipe him out of your mind, kid. The decision is already made," Benjy says.

I swallow back the lump in my throat. I am not built for this sort of thing, and it becomes more apparent with each passing second. "How do I stop the guilt when I know we're abandoning him to such a cruel fate?"

Benjy takes Coco's full weight as I swipe the key card from one of the guards and pass it over the door panel. He says, "It isn't easy, especially not at first. But it's not like you've got much choice. Besides, you don't know his fate. Any number of things could happen that you can't foresee. Sometimes you just have to keep reminding yourself that you did what you could, and that has to be enough."

I spare another glance back to Hiro, then nod to Benjy as we head into the next corridor. I don't trust myself to speak. Benjy's right, I think, but that doesn't make it any easier. The door *swooshes* closed, removing Hiro from view. I hope that isn't the last time I see him.

CHAPTER
TWENTY

NOVA

I t's been an hour since Hiro's scientist babe said he would find Ivy, but no word yet. It's gotta be hard poking around in a database you aren't familiar with, that you've never even seen until today, and trying to make sense of things. Despite knowing he's doing his damnedest to sort through it, my frustration with Javian is growing stronger with every silent second. If he's not careful, I will revoke Hiro's bangability.

I've been passing the time by killing guards. Not *all* the guards; in fact, some have defected from the Règle and are fighting with us, though as we go deeper into the station, they are few and far between. Those who surrendered but didn't join us are locked in the most recent block of cells we passed. Thanks to one of the guards who joined us, Nels, we learned that each section of the station has a prison block and an area of rooms for their mental patients. They're not as vast as the one I was in earlier, but they hold fifty to a hundred individual cells. Plus there's a processing center every third section, which holds groups of people until they've been sorted to their own cells. I've been through one before, but didn't realize there were multiple versions of it through the station until now. Sounds like a terrible system they've got if they need that many cells.

Nels makes it sound like there's a lot more "undesirables" throughout the station than I ever could've imagined. I don't know if we can save them all. This place is vast and it would take days to cross the entire thing. There are rumors of ways to travel around with ease, using something like the door they use to transport off-worlders here after they win the Trials, but no one seems to know if there's any truth to that. Best guess is that they're only used by the upper echelon.

As much as I'd like to set everyone free, I don't know how we'll get to them. It's hard to make plans when anything could happen when the Règle's forces come out in full force. With the ease we're having subduing the guards so far, I can't imagine this is all they've got. If there's more, what will it take to draw them out?

"Processing center in the next corridor," Nels says.

I've got him walking at my side, though I've taken his weapons. As helpful as he's been, there's still something squirrely about him. He's a slight fellow with thinning blond hair and long strawberry-blond side-burns that curl a bit too long on his cheeks. He has pale eyes, bloodshot, that dart around too fast, unable to land on anything for long. It's impossible for him to hold eye contact for more than a second. Maybe he's just nervous—he is helping invaders take over his home, after all—but there's also a very real chance that he's trying to figure out how to murder me.

"How many people?"

His fingers twitch at his side. "Hard to say. This one was closed down for a bit about a year ago due to..." he pauses, eyes shifting to me and then away. "Well, due to you, I guess."

"My old stomping grounds."

An expression I can't read crosses his face, gone a second later. "They stopped using it for a while, until they could get it, um, sanitized... and I'm not sure they're back at full capacity."

His words are far too delicate to describe the mess that happened here last year. I still have dreams about finding Alexis the Huntress and the bodies of the prisoners; they looked more like pulp than people. It sickens me to think their bodies were removed and this place "sanitized" to again be used as if nothing happened. I will not allow them to be unremembered.

We approach the processing center, a shiver running down my spine at the sight of it. Each time I blink, I see blood dripping down these now-pristine walls.

"Hold it right there!"

A squad has emerged into the hallway, laser weapons pointed at my crew. I tuck my knife into the back of my pants and take a step forward, raising my hands. "We don't want to hurt you."

The lead guard scoffs. "We've got the firepower to destroy all of you without you making it a step closer. We're not afraid of you and your sticks."

"Good," I say, easing myself a little closer. "I don't want you to be afraid."

"It will be easier on everyone if you come quietly."

"We both know that isn't true. It'll be easier on you, maybe, but not us."

The lead guard notices when I take my next step. He trains his laser directly on me. "Give me a reason to shoot you. Please. Any excuse after what you did to my brother."

"I don't know who your brother was, but I'm sorry he got hurt."

"Not hurt, dead," he spits. "Thanks to you. He wouldn't give in to you and your scummy on-world friends, so you murdered him."

"A lot of people have gotten hurt on both sides. I truly am sorry that he was one of them."

The man's finger shakes as it hovers over the trigger. "Sorry isn't good enough."

I can't reach this man through his hurt. Knowing he will become another pointless casualty, I ready myself to strike. Before I can take my next step, one of the other guards steps forward and puts a hand on the lead guard's shoulder. He whispers something I can't hear while tapping his earpiece.

"You're kidding me," the lead guard grumbles. His face seems to age ten years and his shoulders slump when the other guard shakes his head. Turning to me, the lead guard grits his teeth and says, "The Règle would like a word."

I swallow back my surprise, take a steadying breath, and say, "I have several words for the Règle."

The guard with the earpiece says, "She said to tell you she has Hiro."

I take a step toward him without another question, another thought, and suddenly Thoa is at my side. The guard holds up a hand and says, "Just her."

"If you think she's leaving my sight, you're out of your mind."

The man's jaw clenches, but he gives a terse nod. "No one else."

Thoa yells back, "Regina, hold position. If we're not back in ten minutes, kill them all."

I glance over at Thoa, surprised by his words. Ten minutes is not a lot of time before declaring an act of war. But then maybe that's why he said it. We don't have much time to see what they want, but they will be eager to return us and avoid a confrontation that doesn't need to happen.

"Ten minutes," Regina says.

I glance over my shoulder and see her flick her whip in front of her. She is a Raider, through and through, ready for anything, and she will kill them all if we are not back in ten minutes. I have no doubt.

Thoa and I follow the guards into the processing area. My eyes travel to the spot where I watched a guard slumped against the wall dying the last time I was here, unable to be saved. So many have been lost, when it never should have come to this.

"In here."

One of the guards waves us forward into a small room with a metal table and a couple chairs on each side. He motions for us to sit, but when neither of us do, he shrugs and takes one of the chairs for himself. He picks up a small black object from the table and points it at the screen on the wall ahead of us. The screen comes to life, an image of the Règle smiling down at us.

"Hello, darling," Bets says, a strained smile tugging at the corners of her lips.

She's dressed in a sparkly gown, her hair pulled up in some intricate design with gems decorating it. This bitch is literally at a party while my people, and hers, are fighting to the death.

"What the hell, Bets?"

She laughs and the screen tilts a bit, showing a group of similarly dressed people behind her watching screens displaying the carnage in their halls. "I could ask you the same thing, love."

"You're having a viewing party? Watching your own people die?" I glance down at the guard who brought us here and ask, "Is this really the kind of person you want to serve?"

He swallows hard, but says nothing. I immediately regret putting him in that situation, knowing that no matter what he says, she will likely kill him as soon as he leaves this room.

"How long do you plan to let this go on?" she asks, in a decidedly disinterested tone. Her eyes though, they give away her concern. She may be feigning disinterest for the rich bastards behind her, but she doesn't like what's happening any more than I do.

"Release my people, call off your guards, and we'll be on our way. We can stop this all right now."

Her eyes burrow into me, searching. "We both know that's not true."

I swallow, nod. "There's been too much bad blood between the on-worlders and the off."

She gives one terse nod. "There must be a reckoning."

"What do you propose?"

"Call off your people, I'll call off mine."

My brows crease, knowing it can't be that simple. "And?"

"The Trials," she says. "You'll return for one last show."

"And my people?"

"I'll make sure they get home safely. No more bloodshed."

"What about those who were born here, but want to go with them?"

Her nostrils flare, but she says, "We can make arrangements for them as well."

I know she's lying, at least about the last bit. I can see it on her face. But maybe it would give us time to figure things out until we can get everyone out safely. I need a minute to think, but Thoa has put a time on this encounter. Still, pushing for time, and also my need to know where Ivy is, I ask, "Where's my sister?"

Surprise flashes across her face, but she tames in almost instantly. "She's safe."

"And Hiro."

She pans her camera around so I can see a man balled up on the floor. There are guards nearby, but they aren't being used to contain him. Instead, there's a line of fancy dresses and suits waiting their turn to jab Hiro with an electric prod, or give him a violent kick to his midsection.

I ball my fists at my sides. "You're despicable."

The camera turns back to her and she shrugs. "Entertainment can be brutal, but it keeps the masses satiated. And your return to the Trials will do exactly that, calming the tensions running through the station. So, what say you?"

"No. She's already earned her life in those stupid games. She won't go back," Thoa says.

A flare of annoyance sparks in me, but before I can say anything, Bets says, "Oh darling, this offer isn't just for her. I want both of you there. And this time, if either of you make it to the final level, only one of you will come out alive. I won't make the same mistake my predecessors did."

I slip my hand into Thoa's without even realizing it until I feel his fingers squeeze mine. In that instant, I know that whatever decision I make, Thoa will follow me. He trusts me to make the right decision for both of us.

"I'll go," I say. "On one condition."

"And what's that?" Bets asks.

"I want you to be in the room with me when I step off into that oblivion. I want you to face me, to know that you are sending me to my death."

"Is that all?" she asks with a chuckle.

I can see the terror in her eyes though, even if no one else can. She knows what I'm capable of, that putting herself in my path could be her end, but also, almost overpowering that, she loves me, and the thought of sending me back to the Trials hurts her.

I nod. "That's all."

"Then I guess I'll see you soon, Nova."

The screen goes dark, and all that's left is the sinking feeling in my gut, knowing this will all end where it began. I'm going back to the City of Trials.

CHAPTER
TWENTY-ONE
NOVA

The guards lead us back into the corridor, just in time by the looks of things. Regina is standing at the front of our group, scythe drawn and teeth bared. There's another ten or so Raiders behind her in full killing leathers, ready to pounce.

I glance among them, meeting their eyes to let them know they can back down. My gaze catches on one familiar face in the crowd and a hiccuping laugh bubbles up from deep inside. "Fatboy?"

He steps forward, his eyes crinkling around the edges as he smiles at me. "No one calls me that anymore."

I can see why. He's grown into himself in a way I never would've imagined. He's eye level with me, but his shoulders are broad and his arms thick with muscle. Tattoos scroll out from under his leathers, tracing patterns down dark skin. For a moment, he reminds me of Thoa, but then I see the light in his dark eyes, the smile hiding within them, and the similarities fade. Maybe once Thoa was like that, but our time has been long and our road hard; the light left his eyes long ago.

"What should I call you, friend?"

"Night Stalker."

A chuckle comes from behind him and I look over to see another face I know barely holding himself together. "What's so funny, Leer?"

"Oh, nothing Chief. Just Fatboy trying to get that stupid nickname to catch on. No one is going to call him Night Stalker, no matter how many times he asks."

"Damn it, Leer," Fatboy says. "Can't you keep quiet?"

"You're lying to our Chief," Leer says.

"If Nova-du calls me Night Stalker, everyone else will too. Then it wouldn't be a lie."

I put my hand on Fatboy's shoulder, unable to stop the smile spreading across my face. "I may be willing to do a lot of things for my people, but calling you Night Stalker isn't one of them."

"Oh, sure, now you won't. But I almost had you."

Thoa's hand finds my elbow, pulling me from this carefree moment and grounding me in the seriousness of what comes next. I give him a nod of acknowledgement, not trusting my words at that moment.

I swallow hard as I turn to Fatboy and say, "I need your help. Can you spread a message to the Raiders? Quietly?"

"Anything for you, Chief."

"Thank you, Night Stalker."

Fatboy's face lights up at my use of the nickname, but fades as I whisper my message into his ear. His brows knit together and he asks, "You're sure?"

I nod. "Trust my words now, straight from my lips; I don't know what treachery the Règle may relay to you once I'm gone."

"Gone?" Leer asks, stepping closer. "But we just found you again."

"And I'm so grateful. But now I must leave again, if we are going to save everyone. I want nothing more than to stay with you all, to be with my people, but they will never let that happen. I have to finish this once and for all."

"I'll spread your words, Chief. And we'll see you on the other side."

WE WALK THROUGH THE CORRIDORS, RAIDERS AND GUARDS ALIKE PARTING TO let us through. I know my words have already traveled farther than I could've imagined, for as the Raiders eyes meet mine, they turn their backs to me and face the wall. It is the symbol of banishment among my people, and for a moment I am hurt, but then I realize they aren't sending me away—they're saying goodbye the only way they can.

The guards lead us to Bets' study, a room I've seen many times before. One of them goes to the desk and runs his fingers along the edge of tiles I've never noticed, revealing a hidden panel. Bets' desk is a replica of the one I found in the warden's office, only these tiles are in muted browns rather than the bright reds of the other one.

The guard flips a switch in the desk and a portion of the back wall slides away. I'd been inches away from that button a dozen times. Hell, we'd had sex on that desk twice, but I'd never noticed anything amiss. Guess I'd been too focused on making her legs shake.

As Thoa and I step into the secret room, my eyes immediately find a strange door set into the middle of the floor. I've seen its likeness before, at the top of the tower in the City of Trials.

"I expected you to find this a long time ago," Bets says, stepping in from yet another secret door set into the side of the room. She's wearing dark green pants and a black shirt, having changed out of the fancy dress she wore only minutes ago on the video call. Her hair is still elaborately coiffed, creating a duality in her appearance. It's nice to see both sides of her so easily, when she's hidden them for so long.

"Probably would've been easier if I would have. Could have left some of the previous Règles alive if you would have let me go home."

"Let you?" Bets asks. "I wish it would have been that simple."

"Why did it need to be complicated? Release me, release my people, stop making us into some game and treat us like humans. Seems simple enough to me."

"Of course it does. You don't understand anything beyond the tip of your blade."

"What more is there? Life on one end, death on the other. Everything in the middle passes too quickly to hang onto."

Bets shakes her head. "That was always the problem between us. You were too eager to get to the end, while I was always trying to stretch out and enjoy the middle."

"That's what you think the problem was?" I ask. A laugh comes out, but there is no joy in me. I laugh to stop myself from screaming. "After everything that's happened, I can't believe that's what you think the issue was."

"And I can't believe you don't see that everything else is built around that."

I sigh. "This is going nowhere. Just get us to the trials and honor your word and we'll never have to speak to each other again."

She swallows. "That's what you want? To never speak to me again?"

I meet her gaze, my eyes going hard despite the softness that I see coming from her. Despite all the things that have happened between us, she still doesn't want to let me go. In her own sick way, I think she really does love me. Or as close to love as she can get.

"It is what I want."

Bets lips press into a thin line and her eyes narrow. "Fine. I'll give you everything you want."

She motions her hand toward the secret door she came through and two guards enter. A broken man is slumped between them, and even after seeing how bad he was on the video call, it takes far too long for me to realize it is Hiro. They drag him over to stand between Bets and the door in the middle of the room.

"What did you do?" I ask.

Bets shrugs. "Only what I had to."

"You didn't need to do this to get back at me."

One of the guards mumbles, "Not everything is about you, bitch."

I glance at the woman and am instantly transported to the memory of standing over her and a group of guards, doing my damndest to get into the cells without killing everyone in the place. She didn't make it easy then, and in this moment I wish I would have just killed her.

Before I can say anything, the Règle says, "I did you a favor, Alik. Tit for tat. Don't make me regret it."

Alik dips her head and says, "Apologies."

Bets turns her eyes back to me and says, "You have your beloved Hiro back. Arrangements are being made even now to transport the rest of your people to the ground."

"And those who wish to defect."

She forces a thin smile. "Naturally."

"Good. Only one thing remains and our business is settled."

"And what's that?"

"Where the hell is my sister?"

"The question of the hour," Bets says.

"What does that mean?"

"It means I don't know. She was in a holding cell—the same one where your Hiro was placed—but when we retrieved him, she was gone."

I smile, unable to stop myself. Sounds like Benjy came through for me after all.

"I don't know why you're smiling," Bets says. "If she isn't safely tucked away in my cell, she's out there somewhere. Your Raiders are going to see her as a station-born who needs to die, and my people will see her as a threat. Hell, she could be dead already."

"*She's not*," Javian says, his voice crackling to life in my earpiece.

I jolt at the sound of his voice. I had forgotten about the earpiece Thoa had given me and the soft voice on the other end.

"She's resourceful," I say. "I have no doubt she'll be fine. My people will figure out who she is and protect her."

I hear keys clacking through the earpiece and a terse response: "*On it*." The earpiece falls back to silence.

Bets seems to truly mean it when she says, "I hope so. Despite everything, I never wanted to hurt her."

"Your actions say otherwise."

"The things we feel and the things we are forced to do don't always line up. Take Captain Alik, for example," she says, motioning a hand toward the young woman at Hiro's side. "She is in love with the same man you are, but her loyalty to the Règleship outweighs her heart. Her actions are that of a true patriot."

"Whoa now, let's pause right there. I am *not* in love with Hiro."

"He said you taught him how to love," Alik says, her voice dripping with hatred.

"If that's something he learned from me, it was during my absence," I say. "I mean, we're friends. We bonded, and we care about one another, but there's nothing more to it."

"I saw you kissing on the camera feeds," Bets says.

"Accidentally," I scoff. "We were happy to see each other, but knew immediately that it wasn't right for our relationship."

"You don't love him?" Bets asks.

"Of course I do, but not like you two think."

"You kissed Hiro?" Thoa asks.

He'd been silent this whole time, and I'd nearly forgotten he was there. I glance over at him, surprised by the hurt registered on his face. It's as if the situation with me, him, and Krew is happening all over again.

"Just in a friendly, happy-to-see-him way."

"You didn't kiss me; you glared at me. You weren't happy to see me?"

My eyes go wide as I search for the right words. I fumble for a second before mustering a poor explanation: "That's not it at all. Things are just *different* with Hiro."

"Hiro isn't the only one risking himself to save you," he says.

Bets lets out a slow whistle and says, "Well, this is awkward."

"Shut up," I say. "This whole situation is because of you."

Bets holds a hand to her heart as if she's wounded by my words. She says, "Wow, rude. And to think, I've helpfully prepared a solution to end all this drama, despite your attitude."

"Yeah?" I ask. "Does it involve releasing me and my people?"

She frowns as if in thought and says, "Sort of."

Bets takes two long strides toward Hiro before I have time to react. With a great push, she shoves him through the doorframe in the middle of the room. Alik dives as if to catch him, but ends up sliding in right after him. The center where the door should be flashes teal, and ripples spread out from where they entered, like rocks thrown into a lake.

Before the smile can fully form on her face, I've charged. I tackle Bets to the floor and get in a couple good punches before she uses her size advantage and rolls me over. We swing, connect, roll; neither of us truly has the advantage. Once, I could have taken her down with little effort, but my muscles have lost some of their strength in their time here, and I'm out of practice. My mind knows what to do, and my body reacts as best as it can, but it is weaker than I like and slower than I remember.

It probably doesn't help that Bets has been rolling around with me for the last year and knows too many of my moves.

On the other side of the room, Thoa has the remaining guard in a chokehold. The man's desperate struggles are futile against the brutish Raider. When the man falls to the ground, Thoa steps toward us. I am on top of Bets then, finally getting my bearings. I shake my head at him before he can interrupt.

"No. You have to go. Hiro needs you," I say, my voice urgent.

Even without looking fully at Thoa, I can sense his hesitation, feel his eyes on me. He doesn't want to abandon me again. It's been a long road getting back to this point, and he doesn't know what will happen if he goes. I don't either, but there's no other choice. Hiro needs help, and I still need to beat the hell out of Bets.

I lock eyes with Thoa for the briefest moment and he nods, reluctantly. "See you soon, Little Star," he says, and steps through the door.

I waste no time mourning losing him yet again. That particular heartache is scabbed over and doesn't reopen. With a rush of adrenaline and resolve, I slam my fist against Bets' mouth, delighted when I hear a tooth crack. She tries to cover her face, but her movements are sluggish, her reflexes dulled. She might be able to fend me off for a few minutes, but she lacks the stamina for the long haul. Even after all this time without training, without the exercise I so desperately crave, I can outlast her. I've done it enough over the last year to feel confident in this.

Our bodies clash, the room reverberating with the sound of blows and grunts. She manages to flip me over once more, but her victory doesn't last. It is a brutal dance, a duel between two people who know each other's strengths and weaknesses all too well. Bets fights with determination, but her energy wanes, while mine surges. Each swing of my fist brings me back to the woman I once was, returning the Raider within.

The room seems to close in on us, the stakes growing higher with each passing second. I need to end this now, while I can. But as much as I'm enjoying hurting her, too much of me doesn't want to kill her. More weakness I'll need to root out.

I hear boots running toward us and realize it is now or never. Bets has the same realization, and the hope of salvation gives her a sudden strength. She twists her body and pushes against me simultaneously, throwing me a few feet away. We both gain our feet and face off again, but the guards are here now. Bets smiles as they train their weapons on me. Her victory is assured, it seems.

"It was a good run," she says, panting. "You came so close to the ending you wanted."

I shrug. "In the end, everyone gets what they deserve. I guess this is what was meant for me."

Her eyes narrow at my response and she asks, "That's really it? You're giving up?"

"No," I say, a smile tilting up the corners of my mouth. "That's not really something I do."

I dive forward and tackle Bets through the doorway. We fall through together into whatever fresh hell is waiting for me this time.

CHAPTER
TWENTY-TWO
IVY

Benjy and I carry Coco through corridors full of people who pay us no mind. It was strange at first, to be walking—carrying a body, even—as escaped fugitives, but still wholly left alone. We almost took to the maintenance level that runs in side corridors and under the living area of the station. But Benjy is smart as well as lucky, or incredibly observant at the least, and he quickly realized that there was something going on that was far bigger than us and our escape. More importantly, we could use that to our advantage.

I don't know what to make of the people we pass. They seem to be ordinary folks, just standing outside their apartments waiting for a show. Electricity buzzes in the air around them. To say it has me worried would be an understatement. I can't recall a time when excitement has meant anything good for the people on this station.

"This is weird," Benjy says as we cross into yet another corridor with no resistance.

"Agree," I say. "Let's find out why."

I don't give him time to ask what I'm talking about before stopping in front of an older woman with her hands on the shoulders of a young boy around nine or ten. The boy is practically shaking out of his shoes, his head bobbing up and down as he tries to see farther down the hall.

"You look excited," I say, giving the little boy my brightest smile.

"They're coming to set us free," he says, his gray eyes sparkling up at me.

"Who is coming?"

The woman blinks her eyes at me, as if she can't believe there's anyone left who doesn't know what's going on. It is then that I watch her take me in, along with Coco and Benjy, and make a decision. She steps back toward her apartment door, pulling the boy with her. Opening the hatch, she motions us inside.

"Ivy," Benjy whispers, shaking his head.

"I've got a good feeling about this one," I say.

We follow her in and she takes us straight to the sofa, motioning for us to put Coco down. She goes to a cabinet and pulls a small black kit from inside. I've seen similar ones before, with the Chasseur when my dad was still leading them. This woman must have done something with the military or the medical field, because there's no other reason she should have a leftover medkit.

The little boy wears a pouty face as he says, "Gamma, I wanna be there when they come."

"I know, Montana, so do I. But what do we do when people need our help?"

"We help them."

"That's right, little love. Now, why don't you get something for our friends to drink while I check on their companion."

Montana runs off while his grandmother kneels in front of Coco. The woman says, "I don't know where to begin."

Benjy says, "Her ribs are bruised, if not cracked. Her left knee is definitely messed up, but I haven't had time to assess. Most of her injuries are superficial though, and she'll be able to heal with food, rest, and time."

"Are you a doctor?" the woman asks.

"My mother was," he says. "And I got hurt a lot."

The woman nods and takes something from her bag. She runs a wrinkled hand over Coco's brow and whispers, "I can give you something for the pain, and something to eat, but your friend is right about time and rest being what you need most."

Coco's head moves the tiniest bit, and the woman passes something small and white between her chapped lips.

Gamma says, "Should kick in fast. She's small, so that helps, but we need to get something on her stomach or she'll get sick."

Montana comes back in the room with a small tray holding three glasses of pale orange liquid and a plate stacked with nutrition bars. He smiles brightly as he brings them to his grandmother and says, "I picked out my favorite ones for them."

"Taco bars?" Gamma asks.

"Yuck, not those."

"They were your favorite last week."

"I like these now," he says, waving a red brick in the air. "Pascetti and meatballs."

"These are my favorite too, kid," Benjy says.

We eat nutrition bars while Gamma does her best to convince Coco to take a bite. She makes it through about a quarter of her brick before Gamma is satisfied enough to let her push away the rest of it.

"Why are you helping us?" Benjy asks, his suspicion unmasked.

He doesn't try to dance around it or pretend it isn't there, and somehow the frankness of his question seems to be a relief for Gamma.

"I owe a debt," she answers, but her eyes turn to me. "I wouldn't expect you to remember me or know anything about it really, but your father did me a favor when you were very young. He never asked for anything in return, and endangered himself in the course of what I asked of him. It has hung over my head all this time, but there was never an opportunity for me to repay him."

"What did he do for you?" Benjy asks.

I elbow him and say, "That's none of our business."

Gamma smiles. "More than I could tell you even if it was your business."

"We don't need to know," I say. "We're just thankful you're helping us now, whatever your reasons."

Montana is stepping back and forth on little feet, clearly nervous for something. Gamma asks, "What's going on, M?"

"I want their friend to get better so we can go back."

"I know, dear," she says.

"What is everyone doing outside anyway?" I ask.

Gamma blinks at me. "I don't know where you've been all morning that you haven't heard. It's been all over the station news."

"We've been indisposed," Benjy says.

"Bad timing. You missed a lot. The station is swarming with Raiders who are going corridor to corridor recruiting anyone who wants to go with them to the planet."

"Raiders?" I ask, my heart ricocheting through my chest.

Montana says, "I want to go with them!"

"Me, too," I say. And I know with certainty that I will, because Nova is here for me, for her people, and for anyone else who wants to escape this place. Nova is here to set us free.

CHAPTER
TWENTY-THREE

HIRO

Alik is standing over me with a gun. Not pointed at me this time, to my great relief. And surprise. She seems to like pointing guns at me.

"What's going on?" I ask. I try to ask. I fail at asking.

My mouth doesn't feel right. It's thick and swollen and too much. There's pain radiating through the center of my face and it takes me a second to realize that my nose is broken. I run my tongue along my teeth and they feel okay, thank goodness. I'd be right pissed if they messed up my smile.

"Stay down," Alik says.

"Huh?" I grumble as I sit up.

"Get down and keep quiet. They'll leave you alone if they think you're dead."

"Who?" but it sounds more like "Hrlllla?"

"The Raiders," Alik whispers.

Raiders? I think. *They wouldn't hurt me.*

I blink into the shadows, looking for whoever she is talking about. If I can spot a friendly face, or even an angry face who recognizes me through the mess that is my current visage, maybe I can salvage this encounter.

There is movement, wild slashing in the darkness. Even now that my eyes have adjusted, I can't make out anything or anyone I recognize. But these are not the movements of Raiders trained in the art of fighting. There are some who seem to handle themselves fine, but most of them move in a way that makes me certain they have never held a blade for anything other than cutting their food. These are not warriors; these are not people ready to bleed.

A wide-eyed man runs toward us out of the darkness. He carries a large curved blade hoisted above his head and screams as if he's being chased by a demon from the stories of old. Alik shoots her laser gun through his leg and he falls over with a heavy thud. His warcry is now just a wail of agony as he waits to die.

"Don't worry," Alik says, half-turning to me. "I won't let them hurt you."

I want to say thank you, or possibly screw you, and I want to ask why she's protecting me after all I've done to her, and I want to stop her from hurting people who have no idea what they're doing. And I can't do any of these things, because I'm on the floor, barely surviving, because she turned me over to the Règle. Where was her protection then?

I try to sit up, but my head throbs with the effort and everything starts to spin. There's a popping sound and I turn my head in time to see Thoa crouch into a defensive position. I don't know where he came from or why he's suddenly beside me, but I'm thankful for him.

Before I have a chance to say anything to either him or Alik, he pounces toward her. His killing leathers *woosh* as they rub together, and somehow that sound is the only thing I can hear in the room full of so much noise.

Alik spins toward him, her gun trained directly between his eyes.

CHAPTER
TWENTY-FOUR
NOVA

We tumble through the darkness, body over body, until we finally land in a congealed pool of blood. I can't see it, but the feel of it is unmistakable. I make sure to roll Bets over one more time and push her head down so her hair goes in it. The pettiness runs deep.

Pushing away from Bets, I force myself up into a crouch and peer out into the room. There's not much to see at first, but I can sense an overwhelming desperation on the air. I've known this feeling before, felt it myself; we are in the City of Trials, and the tower game has begun. Today these people fight for their lives, for a reward and a future they don't understand and don't truly want, but are too hungry to question.

Across the room I spot a figure I recognize: Thoa crouched much like I am, ready to strike. I am struck suddenly by how handsome he is, as if I'm seeing him for the first time. Though I can't make out the details of him, I can clearly see his bright eyes, the tattoos on his chest and arms, his marred skin from his many hunts. He is as familiar to me as the morning sun, though it has been long since I have truly looked at either of them.

There is a moment where time stills and I see what is happening in slow motion. Though I bolt from my position and throw myself across the room, it is impossible to get to him. Impossible to save him. The laser gun is too fast, the shot too close to him. No matter how fast I move, I already know I will watch Thoa die.

I cannot watch Thoa die. I cannot bear the thought of his death, and the helplessness of this moment I can't control. But the moment sits thick in front of me, paused and palpable and still, as if waiting for me to move, to fail.

My body is moving through the air even as I watch this, throwing itself toward inevitability. I feel like I'm floating in the lake where the Raiders would rest on our yearly circuitous route from mountain to desert and back again. When I was small, I was afraid of the water and the weightlessness and losing control. As I grew, I understood that when I entered the water I was giving myself permission to be free. I could let go of my responsibilities to the Raiders and the constraints I placed on myself in my attempts to satisfy them. There was freedom in letting go.

As I float through the air here, now, trying to conjure a miracle from nothingness, I give myself permission to let go.

I cannot watch him die, but I cannot save him. I cannot stop what is happening because I am not in control. There is freedom in that, and fear, and anger and helplessness and and and... I murmur goodbye to him. That is all I can do. And it breaks me.

As Captain Alik's gun fires, something on the ground shifts and knocks her legs out from under her. The laser fires into the ceiling as she drops to the ground, and Thoa's dive sends him to the side of her. As I fall on the ground where Alik was just standing and I realize that Thoa is alive, that *Hiro* was that shape on the ground who has wrestled Alik's gun away, that miracles do happen, time resumes.

I land with a thud, knocking the air out of me. With a cough and a gasp for breath, I inhale the knowledge that Thoa is alive. Thoa is alive. Thoa is alive. It beats within my chest like a tiny drum, like an echoing joy that fills my ears and heart and blood. I love him. I have always loved him. Even when I hated him, when I didn't know him, when I didn't want him... I have always loved him.

I roll toward him and put a hand on his bare arm. The feel of his warmth beneath my fingers is a comfort I didn't know I was missing.

"You're okay," I breathe.

His rough touch grazes me as he moves to stand, and though he does not respond, it is enough.

Thoa moves toward Alik. Though Hiro has her on the ground, she is struggling hard against him and he is in no shape to hold her for long. Thoa grabs her by the hair and pulls her head back, his blade coming to his hand faster than my eye can track.

"No," Hiro yells.

Thoa pauses, a mere second away from slitting her throat. "After all she has done?"

"We are better than them," Hiro says, his words garbled from his swollen face. "We do not kill for the sake of killing, we do not harm simply because we can. She does not know, and she will not unless we teach her."

Even in the dark I'm certain I can hear Thoa grinding his teeth in agitation, but he merely says, "Yes, Chief."

With a grunt, Alik is pulled to her feet. Thoa doesn't kill her, but he also doesn't treat her especially well. She is spared because Hiro is a good Chief, and no other reason. I would have let him kill her.

I move to Hiro's side and help him up. The room is dark, and I use that darkness to hide the things my face wants to show him.

"Glad you're okay," he says, his words jumbled and slurred.

"You, too. I'm sorry for what they did to you."

"Wasn't your fault, Squirrel."

"It was definitely my fault, Moose."

"It was pure jealousy," he says, and I'm delighted to see that his smile hasn't dulled. "They couldn't handle my hotness when I was one of them; in fact, that's how I ended up on-world with you."

"Pretty sure that's not what happened," I say with a laugh.

"Trust me, it is. And then when I came back and they realized they couldn't keep me, they lost it. I'm basically a god on that station."

I smile as I drape his arm over my shoulders. "If you're a god, why don't they revere you?"

"I am revered by anyone with sexual desires. Clearly the Règle is immune to my charms, which makes me feel sorry for whoever they're banging."

I don't know if he's making a jab at me on purpose or if that's just the result of his humor. I've lost track at this point of who knows what my life has been and who doesn't.

"*Is he okay?*"

Javian's voice crackles in my ear. I'd forgotten about the earpiece, about the scientist that Hiro loves, about his promise to find Ivy. *Stars, how had I forgotten Ivy?*

"He's okay," I say.

"*So is Ivy. I was able to tap into some of the station's cameras, and she's safe. She's with a man with purple hair, carrying a thin woman between them.*"

I don't know who the woman is, but now I have no doubt that she's with Benjy. "Thank you, Javian."

"Javian?" Hiro asks. "In your ear?"

"Yes," I say.

"Tell him…" Hiro says, trailing off.

"*Tell him I know,*" Javian says. "*Tell him 'me too'.*"

"We don't have time for this," Bets says, her voice cutting through everything else.

She's closer than I like, and worse than that, she's right.

"Where are we?"

"The tower," she says.

"Obviously," I say. "But you planned all this. What floor are we on? What's supposed to happen?"

"I didn't plan any of this. My whole goal was just to get you back in the tower to appease the people in charge."

"You're the Règle. *You* are in charge."

Bets laughs. "I'm a figurehead. Nothing more. And I've never been more certain of that than when they told me I had to get rid of you. That's also why they won't come after me. Whatever happens to me now, happens to all of us."

I don't know what to say, so I don't say anything.

"I didn't want things to go this way. You must know that. You know *me*, Cam."

"Nova."

She presses her lips together in a thin line. "Right. Nova."

I don't know if I know her or not. There were moments when I thought I did, moments I remember from when I was Cam, from when I was Nova, from when I was both. But I am unsure which of those moments were real, or if any of them were.

She had told me there were other people with power at the station, but nothing more. To hear that she is beholden to them, that there are people worse than the Règle, is terrifying. What happens to the station and the decent people who live there when she is removed and they are left to fight in the power vacuum left behind?

Before the thought can go any further, bright lights come alive above us. What was once dark and mysterious is now blinding in its brilliance. I blink away the spots that have come alive in my vision, but once my eyes clear and I can see everything around me, I long for the darkness to return.

Blood is everywhere. It is sprayed across the walls, pooled on the floor, dripping and gathering and covering everything in sight. And the bodies... Stars above, there are so many. They are piled in twos and threes, they are solitary and curled up on themselves, they are together, but alone in death. We are all alone in death.

At my side are Bets and Alik, Thoa and Hiro, forming an unlikely alliance—an alliance we didn't know we needed until this very moment. But we do. Desperately. Because looking back at us, no longer obscured by darkness and fear, are more than a dozen hungry faces, with eyes like daggers and teeth like knives.

CHAPTER
TWENTY-FIVE
NOVA

As we stare at one another, a voice comes radiating through the room around us. It is not Baz, like it was last time I was here. I don't know if I could handle hearing him now, knowing him as he truly is and not as the sadistic jerk who reveled in watching the torture going on below him. I wonder if this new voice is there because they want to be, or because they must be. It doesn't really matter.

"Congratulations, contestants," they say brightly. "We started with thirty-four people, and you've whittled down to nineteen. What a showing! Give yourselves a round of applause."

The voice waits until the contestants do a slow, staggered clap before they continue. "That's right. Be proud of what you're already accomplished. There was one small surprise that cropped up in this first zone already, and our viewers are going wild. Five new players have entered the tower battle, and these are familiar faces to those watching the games. But of course the other contestants have noticed the new arrivals already!"

The voice laughs in a casual way, as if they've just told a brilliant joke. And maybe they have if you're watching instead of participating in a deathmatch.

"With our total contestants back up to twenty-four thanks to our late arrivals, we'll open up floor two. And trust me, this one is going to be special. Good luck players."

The nineteen players don't move. They stare at us like we'll attack if they dare take their eyes from us. Maybe we would. Once upon a time I knew Thoa so well I could predict his movements, his thoughts, but no longer. And the others are wilder still.

"That's enough, kids. Time to get going. Leave your weapons behind and move to level two." When no one moves, the voice says, *"Now. Or we'll kill you and be done with it. No winner."*

Throughout the room I hear the clatter of weapons falling to the floor. I glance over to Captain Alik who is still holding her laser gun and say, "You, too."

"Kiss my ass," she says.

Bets gives her a nod and says, "Do it."

Alik's eyes narrow, but she does as her Règle says.

Slowly the nineteen start to disperse through the open door leading to the next level. The five of us follow just as tentatively. They fear our attack because we are dressed differently, because we showed up after everything started, because we're still breathing. They fear us because we are five strong, and though we aren't a willing team, it is obviously an advantage over them as individuals. If they do not kill us now while they have the numbers, they will not get another chance. We cannot give them another chance. We know this as much as they do; their slowness to go and our slowness to follow shows both groups what none of us are willing to say aloud.

Eventually we all make it upstairs. There are small red ovals arranged on the ground in a circle, and the contestants stand upon them. As the last to arrive, we are forced to take our places on the empty spots spread through the room. Whether the others intentionally split us up or it was just how they spaced themselves out, I do not know.

I help Hiro onto his place and move to an oval of my own. Thoa prowls behind Alik until she finds an empty position, and he moves to one a few spaces away. Bets is on the far side of the circle from me. As I stare at her, I can't help but think of the choosing ceremony of the Raiders. In a circle much the same as this, I turned away from Thoa. Stealing a glance at him, I wonder what our lives would have looked like if I'd taken him for my mate. There is no doubt it would have been different. I do not know if it would have been better, or if things happened the way they needed to and we were always destined to lose one another over and over. Maybe losing him all these times in all these ways was the only way for me to understand what it means to love him.

He does not spare me any attention. Whether he thinks of that night so long ago, I do not know. His gaze remains on Captain Alik—a hunter stalking his prey.

"*Welcome to the second level,*" the voice says. "*After that dizzying free-for-all on level one, we wanted to slow things down a bit. For this level, you'll be paired against another player. One of you will live. The other will not. To choose your combatant, we'll have you move in front of them to challenge them. Once a challenge is issued, it cannot be withdrawn or refused. The winner of the challenge will move upstairs to level three to wait for the next part of the trials. If anyone leaves their spot for anything other than their own challenge, they will be shot dead. So, let's get started.*"

"Who goes first?" a big man across the room asks.

"*Let's have our youngest get us started. I believe that's...*" the voice pauses, as if searching for something they can't remember. "*Ah yes, looks like that is Georgia Keeney at fourteen years old.*"

"Holy shit," I mutter.

Fourteen is way too young for this. Hells, I was twenty last time I was here and I was too young. I survived, but at what cost?

The girl steps forward into the middle of the room and spins in a tight circle, surveying each person. She looks so small, especially next to some of the men gathered on the far side of the group. I wouldn't describe her as frail—little thing has some arms on her—but she definitely looks like the underdog in any challenge she makes.

Her bluntly chopped brown hair hangs in a curtain over her eyes, giving cover to the calculations she makes. Finally she stops spinning, making her decision. Georgia Keeney steps forward until she is eye to eye with her combatant. In a thin voice, she says, "Fight me."

And there is nothing I can do.

I give her a nod and walk side by side with her into the ring of players, knowing I will have to kill this child to survive. Another death that shouldn't happen, another death caused by my hands, another death to weigh me down. But I will kill her because it is the only way to save everyone else.

As soon as we reach the middle, she attacks. Before I know what's happening, the kid is on my back, clinging onto my neck with one arm and using her free hand to scratch and scrape at my eyes. Her hold is tight, thanks to those muscled arms of hers, and I realize this isn't the easy fight I was expecting.

I gasp for breath, and the edge of my vision is starting to go black. From some far off place I hear a voice I know, a voice I love, yelling, "Nova-du! Show them who you are."

Thoa.

I turn my body, with Georgia Keeney on my back, so that I can see him. He is still on his oval, but it looks as if he is barely able to hold himself there. He wants to run to me, wants to save me. It is what we do for each other. To do so now would be the death of him. And if I let this child kill me, he will surely run to my body, and he will be shot. I cannot allow that.

Our gazes lock; his azure eyes are so full of fear and concern, but there's also hope there. I will not let him down.

Slowly I become aware of a loud grunting sound and I am unsure if it is Georgia or me. She has nearly stolen my final breath, and I feel a heaviness weigh down my limbs. Her grip around my neck is firm, and though I claw at her with my fingers, I cannot loosen it. Instead, I pitch my body forward with as much force as I can muster. Georgia may be clinging to me but she is still small, and the movement bucks her off me, allowing me to take a breath.

The influx of air refreshes my senses and reminds me what is at stake. While the girl is scrambling to retake her hold of me, I shift my body and send her stumbling across the circle. Georgia spins to face me again, lowering herself as if she's ready to pounce. Maybe she is—it's how she managed to get the upper hand the first time—but I won't underestimate her again.

Georgia prowls around me looking for an opportunity to attack. I wait and watch, letting her decide when she is ready. She is wily and agile, too much so for me to be confident that an offensive move from me would be successful.

The moment she strikes, I throw myself out of her path and let her hit the ground. I jump on top of her before she has a chance to rise. Georgia squirms under the weight of my body, but I am taller and stronger and better fed after being on the station for the last year. I hold her still with my legs and use my arms to pin her into submission. No matter how she struggles, she cannot overpower me. Her only advantage had been surprise; now that it is lost, her destiny is clear.

She stares up at me, her expression full of panic.

"I'm sorry," I whisper.

"I don't want to die," she whimpers.

"I don't want to kill you."

Georgia swallows, gives one terse nod. She doesn't want to die, but she is ready for what comes next.

"Close your eyes," I say. "I'll make it quick."

She closes her eyes. I expect to see tears sliding from her eyes, but they do not come. Instead, it is my tears falling onto her face that I see. My eyes crying for another person's death that I won't have time to mourn, because there are others that must be killed and others that must be protected and others, and others, and others...

Georgia Keeney is dead at fourteen years old. She was a child who was surely loved by someone, who lived a life that was hard and brutal, and who died far earlier than she should have. She deserved so much more than this.

I rise, leaving her body in the center of the circle of combatants. A door at the side of the room *wooshes* open and I walk through it, unable to look back at the child I left behind, at the friends who may die in the moments to come, at the room where death lingers cold and dark and interrupted only by the briefest signs of fleeting life.

Taking a deep breath and relishing the pain in my neck—for it means I am still alive—I climb the stairs to level three where I will sit and wait for those who do not die.

CHAPTER
TWENTY-SIX
NOVA

There are flowers on the third level. Grass. Flat, heavy stones placed sporadically through the room. It is all fake, a mirage after the desolation of the last level. But it is calm and tranquil, a balm after what just happened below. I move to the far side of the room, sit on one of the large rocks, and watch the door to see who will join me next.

I want to cry for Georgia. I try. My mind holds her face behind my eyelids every time I close my eyes. Her bird-like features peck at me, dig into my brain, but the tears won't come. I think of the other children who I've cried for, who have been saved and lost through this journey—Sarah from the station, Coco's brother Wolfie, Tess and Edith Ann Roody and all the other children who were being kidnapped and sold, my own sister—and I mourn for the loss of their childhoods, for the loss of my own. Though I do not cry for any of us, I still mourn; I long for something better for the children who will come after.

I don't know how long my thoughts are in this dark place before the next victor comes. He is tall and broad, wide shoulders and arms as thick as my thighs. His dark skin glistens with sweat, and it is clear he didn't win easily. My thoughts immediately turn to Thoa, who would be a good match for this brute.

He approaches, eyes narrowed at me. "Who are you?"

"Nova."

"Argus," he says. Brows furrowed, he pauses for a moment before adding, "I am sorry you had to kill the child."

"So am I."

He grunts an affirmation.

"I am sorry that you had to kill as well. Were they—"

"I will not talk about it." Another pause, then, "You are not from this place."

"I am," I say. "I lived with the Raiders for most of my life. Until I won the tower battle and was sent away from my home."

"You lost your prize? Was it so little?"

"The prize was not what we are led to believe. It took everything from me."

He sits on the ground a few feet from me, close enough to talk but far enough away that I don't feel threatened. It is a kindness, and we both know it. He could easily pick me up and throw me like a ragdoll if he wanted to. Once, I might have withstood a battle with him, or even come out ahead. But I am not the fighter I was the last time I was here. Faced with someone of his size and strength now, I don't know how well I would do.

"I have nothing for them to take."

His tone is flat, resolved. Though the words speak of pain, there is no bitterness there that I can detect. Argus is a man who has suffered, who has lost, and who understands that this world does not care. He does not yet know how much less the world above cares in comparison.

We sit in silence for a long time before the next combatant joins us. She is close to my height, but thinner, hungrier. Her curly hair is pulled back into a ponytail to keep her angular face clear, but the left side of her face is scratched to hell and there's a bruise blossoming under her eye.

"Argus," he says when she approaches.

"Nova."

The girl stops in front of us, still panting. Finally, she says, "Leah."

Argus motions for her to sit. She finds a place farther away, putting me between her and Argus. I understand the inclination, but even after only a few minutes with him I feel at ease. He doesn't kill because he wants to, but because there is no other way out.

"You can rest here," I say, trying to give her some peace. "We will be enemies as we climb the tower, but for now we are the victors, and we rise together."

The girl chuckles and shakes her head. "You are a fool to think we are not already enemies. I would kill you right now if I did not need to fear Argus coming for me after, if I were alone with him."

Her words place a heavy mantle over us, and we do not speak again as foe or friend. After many long, quiet minutes, a new face appears in the doorway. My heart skips through my chest and I stand up, buoyed to my feet by the sight of him.

Thoa staggers toward me. His ankle is hurt, and his chest and arms are red from the beating he took, but he is here, and he is whole, and he is all I need. I run to him, grab his face and pull his lips to mine. We collide in hunger, mouths answering one another with ferocity. Every other sound in the world goes quiet and all that remains is the rush of blood in our ears, the thunder of our hearts bursting from our chests, the breathless gasps as we dig deeper into each other, refusing to let go.

He groans softly, low in his throat, and pulls me closer. Our bodies press together with such sublimity that I know nothing will ever fit between us again—not breath, nor thought, nor sound. I dissolve into Thoa, in this moment that is wonderful and terrible all at once. We kiss as if our lives depend on it; I sink into his skin, soaking him like rain, coating him like honey.

We have never had the right opportunity, time has never been on our side, and it likely never will be. But we don't need things to be perfect, we just need one another. We will take these broken pieces and make each other whole.

I don't know how long we are there; time has lost all meaning and all that matters now is being with Thoa. But soon, or maybe not soon, another figure comes through the door. I see her in my periphery, and it takes far too long for my mind to work out who she is, who she *was* to me.

Bets doesn't say anything to us. She doesn't try to push past us or make her way to the other victors. Bets just stands there, waiting. I pull at Thoa's leathers and move him out of her path. The sight of her face sends a pang through me; I do not love her, I do not care for her at all, but I did at some point and I do not want to see her hurting. She is. It is clear in the set of her jaw, in the crease of her brow, in the slump of her shoulders.

She moves past us and goes to stand near Argus. Bets does not fear the man who could tear her limb from limb if he wished to. Perhaps she even wants him to.

I stand with Thoa at the edge of the room while the next four winners emerge. The first after Bets has skin as dark as Krew's, though it is not the flawless night sky that he is. The next is a mazulla person with close-cropped red hair and eyes as pale as the morning sky. Third is a short, wiry man with brown hair and spectacles. Last is a hulking figure as big as Thoa and Argus, whose cutoff shirt and pants reveal thick black banded tattoos wherever skin is shown.

The new man walks to the mazulla person and says, "I killed Abi."

The redhead's face pinches and they close their eyes, but give a nod. The man turns and leaves to sit on the other side of the room, these three words the only thing that passes between them.

As I watched each of them come in, I wondered which had killed Hiro. At least it wasn't this brute with fists the size of boulders.

Hiro is in no shape to fight any of them; he could barely stand as I helped him to the circle. Any of these fighters would have seen him as an easy target and taken him out. Georgia Keeney would still be alive if she had chosen him instead of me.

Even as I think it, I pray to the gods I don't believe in that I'm wrong.

When Alik stumbles up from level two, my eyes meet hers and I beg her in the silence between us to give me the news, one way or another. She takes a deep breath and tips her head toward me. At first I don't know exactly what it means, but then I see her lips tilted in the faintest of smiles and I know he is still alive. No matter what has happened between them, what they've done to one another over the years, Alik doesn't want him to die. I don't know if she loves him, but she doesn't hate him, try as she might.

When the next person comes up and it still isn't Hiro, I feel a pang of anxiety build up in the center of me. I look at the new person—bronze skin, wild black hair, soft cheeks—and though I see them, I don't *see* them. I take in all they are and dismiss it in a second. They are not Hiro, and until I see him and hug him and know my best friend is safe, I am not okay.

The final fight takes longer than all the others put together. Or that is how it feels. I no longer know the difference between what *is* and what *feels*. Maybe there is no difference.

I wait for either, for both; in Thoa's arms, surrounded by past friends and future enemies, I watch the door and live in this moment where hope has not yet died.

CHAPTER
TWENTY-SEVEN

HIRO

I have no idea how I made it to this point. It defies all reason. I came in already broken, already dead. Since they dropped me weaponless into a fight that had already started, I wouldn't have made it past the first level if not for the protection of others. Every fighter here can see it. Yet they leave me swaying on my circle, barely hanging on.

When there is only one left and I know I am at the end of my life, the old man steps out into the middle of the circle to face me. He is thin and haggard, his threadbare shirt hanging loose on his shoulders. The man's hair has long since vanished, and his white beard is sparse and unkempt.

"Will you fight me, young man?" he asks, his voice a hoarse whisper.

I swallow and force out the words through dry lips. "I don't think I can."

"But you must. Those are the rules. And we, too hurt and too old to fight the rest of them, have been left to decide who makes it through this challenge."

"Why did they leave us? We are too weak to pose a serious threat, and could have let two of the stronger ones win easily."

"That is why we remain. No one wants to win without giving their all."

Fools, I think. I would have taken the easy win. Probably. Maybe. Hiro from a year ago definitely would have, I have no doubt. Being with the

Raiders has changed me, but I don't know if it has fully stopped my propensity for taking the easy way out every chance I get.

I stumble towards where he waits in the middle of the room. It is so quiet now that the others are gone; the sound of existing is often deafening.

"I need you to tell Nova something," I say, my gaze meeting his.

"Who is Nova?"

"The first woman who fought, who was forced to kill the child."

"But who is she *to you*?" he asks.

I take a deep breath as if I'm inhaling his words. Finally, I say, "My best friend. The love of my life. The person who makes me both weak and strong."

"You love her."

"I do."

"Does she love you?"

I nod, swallow, unable to answer for a moment. When the moment for tears has passed, I say, "And I need you to tell her all that for me."

"Why can't you tell her?" the old man asks.

I shake my head. "I am too hurt to go on."

"And I am too old to go on."

"What a pair we make," I say with a chuckle.

"You have someone to live for, at least. There is nothing left for me inside this tower or out. That's why I'm here; I came to die."

I stare into his unblinking eyes for a long moment trying to gauge what his plan is, but I see no deceit, no hidden agenda.

"So, what? You're just going to let me kill you?"

He nods, a small smile curling the edges of his mouth and growing larger with each passing second. It is then that I see he has a brilliant, megawatt smile rivaling my own.

"I have spent my life sweet-talking and charming and being a delight to every person I passed. In all those years, I never found a person to love, and certainly didn't allow anyone to love me. If you have that already—so young! so much time left!—you need to live. And for you to live, you must kill me."

"I don't particularly want to kill you. You seem like a nice fellow."

"As do you," he says, flashing me another grin. "But we do what we must."

He bends his knees slightly as if he is preparing to get into a fighting position, but it never happens. I mimic his position, unable to do much more myself. I might have youth on my side but I can barely move.

The old man holds out a hand toward me and motions me forward with his fingers.

"Wait," I say, my brows furrowing. "At least tell me your name."

The man straightens up his old bones and asks, "What good will that do either of us? It's easier to kill a man without a name."

I shake my head. "I need to know. I'll never be able to let you go if I don't."

"You were willing to let go of the woman you love, but you can't say goodbye to a nameless stranger?"

I laugh at his words, at the absurdity and the truth of what he's saying. "I can't explain it. This feels important."

"Sid Hartman."

I nod my thanks for this courtesy, lower myself the tiniest bit into the fighting position that isn't quite right thanks to how beat up I am, and he returns to his.

"I'll probably fight back when instincts kick in," he says with a shrug.

Another nod to him. There is nothing left to say.

We circle one another slowly; it is not because we are strategizing or preparing for some great battle, but because we are tired and this is the only way we stay on our feet.

He lunges at me but there's no force behind it. Every move comes with a smile. When I return the action, it feels foolish; there's no weight to it.

"You've got to do more than that," he says.

I shrug one shoulder. "What happens if we just keep doing this until the audience ends up bored and we both end up moving on?"

"*Attention players,*" the voice says above us. "*We have come to the end of this level and the audience is indeed growing bored. We've cut away from your fight for commercials, and when we return in thirty seconds, you'll need to put in some real effort or we'll kill the both of you.*"

Sid and I stare at each other for a few seconds, then he drops to the ground and starts smashing his head against the floor.

"What are you doing?" I scream.

He looks up at me, blood spurting from his now broken nose. He smiles up with the wide smile of a man with nothing left to lose.

CHAPTER
TWENTY-EIGHT
NOVA

Hiro steps through the door to level three and all is right in my world. I feel lighter than I have in ages. With Thoa's finger tracing a slow comforting circle on my back and my best friend living through what certainly should have killed him, I can feel nothing but joy.

I don't have much time to revel in it before the announcer's voice cuts through the room.

"Welcome to level three, contestants. That was mostly entertaining. I hope you're prepared to step it up for our viewers in the next portion of the game. And if you're not, well, let me just emphasize that we have no issue eliminating players who are less than impressive. Does everyone understand?"

Around the room twelve heads nod their understanding. *Twelve.* Out of thirty-nine. Five of those twelve are my group, meaning they managed to murder twenty-seven on-worlders in two levels. And they have us nodding to agree to be more entertaining to the viewers while we kill ourselves. This world is messed up.

"Right then, let's begin level three!"

In the middle of the room, a panel in the floor opens and a narrow silver pedestal rises into the room. There is something in the middle of the small platform but it is too small to make out from where I am.

"Go forth, choose your color, and consume. Each will have a different effect,

but all will last approximately fifteen minutes. Long enough for us to have a grand ole time."

Seconds tick by and no one moves. Finally, Argus takes a slow, casual stroll toward the pedestal with all eyes tracking his languid movements. He stares down at the pedestal for the briefest second, then plucks something up and pops it into his mouth. He moves back to his former position in the same unhurried way, but now everyone else is abuzz with anticipation and race toward the pedestal.

The red-haired mazulla person arrives at the same time as Leah, and with the glares and growls shared between them I wonder if there will be a fight. Instead, they both pull something from the platform at random and move away to opposite sides of the room. Bets is there next, alongside the short man and the giant with the banded tattoos. The dark-skinned man, Alik, and the mazulla person with bronze skin come one after the other, leaving only me, Thoa, and Hiro to retrieve our items.

As the three of us approach, I notice Argus in the corner waving his fingers in front of his face. He stares at them as if they hold the secret to the universe. Maybe they do. Who can know what the star-people have given us.

There are three pills on the pedestal when we get to it: one striped yellow and black, one a violent shade of orange, and a third that is blue with a thin white triangle on it.

"Which do you want, Little Star?" Thoa asks.

With a sigh, I say, "The blue looks the most peaceful. I would like Hiro to take that one and hopefully get a few minutes of rest."

"Looks can be deceiving," Hiro says. "Besides, we don't know exactly what these things do."

I wave a hand in Argus' direction and say, "It's already kicked in for a few of them. The others might have a different reaction, but it appears to be mental rather than physical."

"But since the viewers want a show, I doubt any of these will be very calm and relaxing."

"Tick tock, children."

Hiro takes the blue pill, dips his head toward me, and puts it in his mouth. He stumbles away from the pedestal and finds a seat on one of the flat rocks scattered around the room.

"Just us, then," Thoa says.

"I don't know what to think of either of them. Neither looks safer than the other.

"Nothing is safe here. You know this."

I nod. "I do. But we made it out before, and we can do it again."

Thoa forces a smile. "I'm not so sure."

I reach for his hand and squeeze it. "Don't give up on me just yet."

"Never," he whispers.

Thoa takes the orange pill and swallows it, leaving the striped yellow one for me. I take it and move to a spot in the grass near Hiro. Whatever happens next, I want to at least be near the people I love.

I AM FLYING. SOARING. BUZZING. *BUZZING*? YES, THAT'S RIGHT. FOR THAT IS what I do. I am a bee. Bees buzz. I buzz. Buzz.

Flyyyying!

I don't remember this feeling before but I know it is what I've always done. How long have I been a bee? My whole life of course, but how long has that been? What is time when you are a bee? When you are flying? When you are buzzing? There is no time, only this. Only the beat of my tiny wings carrying my tiny body through this vast place, searching for that which gives me life.

I search for my queen. I work for her. All I am and all I do is for her. I can't remember having a queen, or not having a queen, or anything but the work. To live, to survive, to sustain the queen.

Oh, whoa. Maybe *I* am the queen.

It doesn't matter. I fly and soar and buzz and search.

Searching is familiar, even if flying isn't. I have always been searching.

Flying around, minding my own buzziness, and out of nowhere a massive shape swings toward me. Terror passes through me as I narrowly avoid whatever is swatting at me a second time. When the gargantuan thing comes at me a third time, I get pissed. I'm just over here looking for some honey, not trying to fight. But screw that. I'll show it what I'm made of.

I dodge back and forth, circling around and around as it aims for me.

I'm too fast. I land on it, feel the warmth of the slightly squishy surface under my legs, and shove my stinger into the bastard. Before it has time to react, I'm in the air again, soaring away.

I fly a moment longer, but stinging my attacker has tired me out. My wings are starting to droop, and there's a heaviness in my body as I sink closer to the ground. I tumble into the soft green land below me, my body weak and immovable. I close my eyes one last time…

When I sit up in the grass, my arms feel heavy, like they want to fall right off my body. Like they have moved without ceasing for hours, for days, for a lifetime. I lived a lifetime. And when my buzzing body was over, I died. And when I died I was at peace. And when I was at peace I was cast away from my perfect buzzing body and thrown back into this one. And when I was thrown back into this one I accepted pain and heartache and suffering again, because that is what this body knows. That is what my humanity costs. That is what I will pay, even if I'd rather be buried in the flowers, at peace, after a long, free life.

I look around and see some of the others returning to themselves as well. Leah is awake, shaking her head back and forth as if she's trying to deny whatever she's seen, and the short man with spectacles is rocking back and forth with his head tucked between his knees.

Thoa is sprawled on the ground beside me; I touch his wrist and feel his pulse thrumming under my fingers. It is good and strong, the pulse of a warrior, a Raider, my love. Hiro's fingers twitch where he lays, but otherwise he seems wholly relaxed. Maybe this level wasn't as bad as the others, as bad as it could've been.

Then I hear the wail.

On the other side of the room, the red-haired mazulla person is holding the man with the thick tattoos against their chest. Tears stream down their face as they run their hand along the face of the man who will not wake. A stake protrudes from the man, and without knowing how, I'm certain I killed him.

Bets is awake now. She approaches them before I get a chance to move. Bets puts a hand on their shoulder, making the person jolt in surprise and nearly drop the head of the man they're holding.

"I'm sorry," Bets says, and there is kindness in her tone.

I truly believe she *is* sorry, even if she is also guilty for having allowed such things to happen under her watch. It was easier for her to pretend these games don't hurt anyone and are only good fun for the viewership until now when she is face to face with those who are being hurt. There is a part of Bets that is kind—I have seen it, I have known it —and that part of her hates what is happening.

"Sorry?" the redhead asks. "You're *sorry*? Is that supposed to matter? Your *sorry* doesn't change anything. Quill was good, and now he is dead."

I understand how they feel, but part of me reels at their words. Yes, Quill is dead, but he knew that was a possibility when he came into the trials. His hunger drove him to this place anyway because that is what hunger does. These games are disgusting and I hate every part of them, but the people entering the doors weigh the risk versus the reward. Bets is definitely the enemy here, but she didn't make Quill sign up for the tower battle. Whether it was for glory or out of desperation, I will never know. So many come here because there is nowhere else to go, no other way to survive. Whatever reasons he had were his own, and they are as much the reason he is dead as the vicious off-worlders and their hunger for entertainment.

As much as I might want to say these things, I don't. I will not defend Bets or the star-people in even the slightest way.

Bets has moved to Alik's side and helped her sit up. The Captain's chest heaves violently and she clings to the Règle like a drowning person grasping for anything that will keep them afloat.

The dark-skinned man carries the smaller mazulla person in his arms. They are breathing and awake, but their dark eyes have a far off look, like their eyes can't reconcile the things they see. The man walks around another body still on the ground and nudges it with his foot. They do not move. He says, "I think this one is gone too."

I stand and peer over, strangely sad when I realize it is Argus. I have known him over the course of one level, but he would have made a good Raider, a good friend. A rush of panic courses through me all at once; whatever happened to him could easily happen to Thoa or Hiro, and there is nothing I can do.

Before these dark thoughts take me too far, Hiro sits bolt upright and stretches his arms above his head. He yawns, opens his eyes, and flashes me a megawatt grin.

"Hey, Squirrel," he says.

He looks like hell, but he's upright and talking and breathing and I'm just so thankful to see that he's made it through another level that a laugh bubbles up from my throat and I can't contain it. I know it isn't fair that he should live while Argus and Quill die, and it isn't fair that I should laugh while the red-haired girl cries, but it happens all the same.

Thoa coughs. My head jerks toward him. He is blinking away whatever insanity has clogged his mind, but he is okay. He is okay. He is okay.

There is nothing fair or right or good about this place. It just is. And we must do the best we can to survive.

CHAPTER
TWENTY-NINE
NOVA

The pedestal lowers back into the panel on the floor. When the panel closes below, a new one opens above. A cylindrical beam of pale blue light shines down from the ceiling, casting a shimmering glow through the room.

Thoa and Hiro stand on either side of me. I take their hands and pull them forward toward the light. Wordlessly, they follow.

As we step into the light stream, a feeling of weightlessness overcomes all other senses. Our bodies lift through the light, rising toward the ceiling. It carries us up through the panel and into the next level. We swim through the air, carried forward by a current that deposits us back on solid ground.

There is a wall of mirrors in front of us; each mirror looks to be a three foot square fit tightly against those around it. Were it not for the soft red light cast from behind the mirrors so that they give the faintest outline of each square, I probably wouldn't have noticed that it wasn't one piece.

I hear footsteps behind us and turn to see Bets and Alik stepping out of the blue air. Alik still looks unsettled, but she's moving on her own. I wonder what she saw that has her so distraught, and how it was entertaining for the star-people to see our unconscious forms. Aside from watching our numbers dwindle, what could they have possibly gained?

Before the thought is fully formed, the mirrors in front of us light up with images. Each square displays a different picture from a different point of view. Mine is easy to pick out, for it is the only one buzzing.

"That's me," Hiro says, pointing at one on the bottom corner.

From his viewpoint I see a blue sky with strange triangular clouds drifting above. It is a beautiful, clear day, and Hiro seems to be floating in water, bobbing up and down.

"Is that it?" Alik asks, eyes wide and wild. "That's all they did to you?"

Hiro puts his hand on my shoulder and says, "Nova chose well for me."

The Captain looks like she would murder me right where I stand if she thought she could.

I turn back to the mirrors and watch the other images. There is one where someone is running through a forest, their eyes darting behind them for whatever gives chase just out of sight. Another is nearly solid black, and at first I think there is nothing there, until I hear the shallow breathing and see their hands searching all around them only to discover they are trapped in a confined space and unable to use any sense but touch. The next one is the worst of all, for me at least, as it reminds me of a recurring dream I've had for years; I watch as someone's hands— Thoa's hands, I'm certain of it—hold back a vicious maw full of snapping teeth that bite and bite and bite without ceasing.

I feel the press of bodies as the rest of the group arrives. We have been funneled into a smaller area that I realized, and there is little room to move without touching someone. The closeness makes me uncomfortable, and I know I'm not the only one; it is impossible to feel safe while you're surrounded by those you don't trust.

We stand there silently, watching the screens display our torments. Some are small, like Hiro's and mine, while others are dark and violent and too intense for words. I see my screen in the moment I stung my attacker; on another screen I see a stake going into someone's body. I thought it was me, I *knew* it was me, and now I see for certain. This is the moment his screen goes dark. A moment later, the torture stops on another screen and it goes black as we witness the last moment of our competitors. We watch them die, like we have watched so many die, but this feels so empty and distant that I can almost understand how the star-people watch it without the remorse and heartsickness that death should bring. Almost.

Someone is puking behind me. I hear them gag, the splatter of it hitting the floor and the feet of those too close to them, and then the smell permeates the small space. In a strange way I find it grounding. Even after everything we've seen, it is still enough to affect some of us. We are the ones who need to make it through for this world to have any chance.

"Welcome one and all to the fourth trial. You're halfway there! First, I'd like to thank you for the exhilarating show you gave us on the last level. It was unlike anything we've tried before, and I dare say we'll be bringing it back in the future. Take a few minutes to watch the replays that were recorded with special neurotransmitters invented just for this event." When no one says anything, the voice continues, *"Only ten contestants remain, and we'll say goodbye to at least one of them on this level. Isn't this exciting?"*

We share looks between us, but still no one says anything.

I can almost hear the announcer rolling their eyes as they say, *"Well then, I guess we'll move on to the next portion of the show. If the first five contestants to enter the level could please move to the left of the room, and the remaining five could move to the right, we can get started."*

I move to the left with Thoa and Hiro. Bets and Alik fall in line behind us, while the other five move to the other side of the room. Any animosity that had been undone by our shared experience in level three is wiped away immediately as we stare at each other across the narrow aisle we've created.

"Now we're ready to begin," the announcer says. A panel on each side of the room lifts and they continue, saying, *"Choose the order your group will enter the funhouse and line up."*

"What are we supposed to do in there?" Leah asks.

"If I tell you it will ruin the surprise."

Leah sighs and says, "I'll go first."

"Me, too," Bets says.

Thoa says, "Then me, Nova, and Hiro."

"I guess I'll be in the back," Alik mumbles.

The other team looks at us as we line up and they put themselves in order accordingly. It isn't a bad plan; we don't know what will happen once we enter, so matching up based on who they think they would beat in a fight makes as much sense as anything else.

"*Bets, Thoa, Nova, Hiro, and Alik: you were the first five into this level, and the first team ready for the next challenge. You have therefore earned yourself an advantage. One time during your challenge, call out the name of the competitor you wish to use it against and it shall be done. Leah, Dante, Sam, Jai, and Romelia: your reaction determines how well their advantage truly works. Keep your wits about you and it will be nil. Good luck to you all.*"

The announcer's words had barely settled into the room but Bets and Leah were already walking through the open panels.

"Wait," I say. "Shouldn't we figure out a plan?"

In response, Thoa grabs my hand and pulls me through the door.

Inside the wall of mirrors is a corridor built the same way. There are reflective tiles everywhere I look, showing the faces of myself and my team.

"Well hello, handsome," Hiro says, smiling at himself in the mirror.

Even in his rough state, his smile is brilliant. I can't stop the grin that answers his, and as I catch sight of Alik standing behind him, I realize I am not the only one. She beams at his reflection, though he doesn't spare her a single glance. Some things never change.

The walls of the mirrored corridor lead us deeper into a room, I think, but I can't really tell. The reflections of us look back in confusion, changing with each step as if we're losing ourselves as we go. After only a few minutes in, I am well and truly lost.

Two or three minutes later, Bets turns around and puts her hands on her hips. "We are screwed."

"What are you talking about?" I ask.

"We're not just walking through hallways, progressing through another level. It's a maze. I didn't realize it soon enough."

Alik curses under her breath, then adds, "Of course it is. Level four. I'm sorry, Règle. I should have noticed."

"Enough with the apologies," Thoa says. "We know now. Let's figure out what to do about it."

"We? Since when is this group of assholes a team? You were going to kill me a few levels ago," Alik says.

"You were standing over Hiro with a laser gun!"

"I was *protecting* him."

"That's actually true," Hiro says.

All eyes swivel to him.

Hiro shrugs, eyes wide. "What?"

"What are you talking about? She was about to kill you," Thoa says.

Alik glares at Thoa. "If I wanted him dead, he would be dead."

"You don't know what you want," I say before I can stop the words from leaving my mouth. When her darkened gaze turns to me, I shrug and say, "I have no doubt you care about him. Maybe you even loved him at some point. But he's messed up so much and screwed you over more times than you can count, and somewhere along the way your love turned into something else. I don't blame you for being mad at the things he's done. I would be too."

"He's an asshole. That's been established repeatedly. But I've never wanted him dead."

"You sent him to the Règle," I say.

Alik's jaw clenches at my words and for a moment I'm certain she won't say anything. But then in a rush, she does.

"The only thing I have is my career. My entire life is built around it, because the other thing I thought I was building was all fake. It meant *nothing* to him. Less than nothing. Even now he can't admit what we had, what he turned his back on. So yeah, I've been pissed. And the thought of turning him over to face some sort of punishment for all the pain he has caused—and to further my position in the process—of course I wanted that. I wanted him to hurt the way I did. But after they took him and I saw what they did to him..." she trails off.

"You act like he was brutalized for no reason," Bets says, rolling her eyes. "Some of the guards roughed him up while they were trying to get information about his little girlfriend. And some of those guards were friends of yours and went a little wild on your behalf."

Alik shakes her head. "None of them are my friends. They tolerate me at best, and talk coups behind my back. I know who I am to them."

"She has no idea who she is to them," Hiro says, shaking his head. "If she would just let go of me, of who she wanted me to be, she'd see how she lights up the room for some of the other guys in her life."

"Instead, she pines for someone who can't love her the way she deserves to be loved," Bets says.

"Sounds like you," Alik says, meeting the Règle's gaze.

The ghost of a smile flickers across Bets' face but she doesn't reply. None of us do. We stand there for a moment in an awkward silence, eyes averted like we're afraid of what we'll see in each others' faces if we look too hard. Made all the more difficult by the fact that we're facing all these mirrors.

Finally, after far too long in this uncomfortable limbo, Thoa says, "So, we're in a maze. We didn't figure it out soon enough to do anything from the beginning, but we can work together going forward. If we're all willing, that is."

Murmurs rise from each of us and we come to the reluctant consensus that he's right. We can't start over, but we can go forward from here and figure it out as a team. Even if we don't feel like one.

"We need a way to keep track of our movements," Bets says.

My earpiece comes to life and Javian says, "*I can help with that. Just say the turns aloud and I'll track them.*"

"Holy shit," I mutter.

"What is it?" Bets asks.

I shake my head, not wanting to draw attention to the advantage sitting in my ear. I'll remind Hiro and Thoa when I get a chance, but it is not something for Bets and Alik to know, and I want the star-people to know about him even less.

"I can keep track of our movements."

"You couldn't even keep track of which corridor to take to get to the market," Bets says.

She's not wrong. Instead of giving her that small victory, I say, "I'm back at full capacity now that no one is messing with my head. I got this."

She clenches her jaw and nods at me. Without another word, Bets turns around and marches down one of the side hallways. Everyone falls into line behind her, and we begin our teamwork even more hostilely than we were a few minutes ago.

At first, Bets is slow to turn down each corridor. She pauses and considers, looking back and forth in the identical halls. It doesn't matter which way she looks; all we ever see is an unchanging block of mirrored walls. After a half hour or so, she stops looking. There's no rhyme or reason to the turns we make—or none that I can decipher, anyway.

"*Stop,*" Javian says, his voice jolting me in its suddenness.

"Stop," I say to the others.

"What is it?" Bets asks, her tone tinged with frustration.

"*Your turns, no matter how sporadic and random, are leading you to what I must assume is the center of the level. Even when you take a turn that should lead you away, you're still brought back toward the middle. They must have something planned for when you get there.*"

I repeat what Javian has just told me, but the eyes that meet mine silently question the information. They have every right to; there's no way I would know any of this on my own. I'm not sure how Javian has figured it out either, but Hiro trusts him, so I do too.

"How do you know?" Alik asks.

I try to give a disarming smile like Hiro would but I don't have the confidence so it looks more like a grimace. I see the expression reflecting back at me from the dozens of mirrors around us and know with certainty that this is not the way for me to win trust. Then again, maybe I don't need to win it. Maybe I already have it.

"I can't tell you."

Alik scoffs. "Then why should we listen to you?"

"Because you don't have a choice," I say. "You can trust me and we can figure out what comes next together, or you can keep heading toward whatever they have in store for us."

Seconds tick by while I wait for Thoa or Hiro to speak up and say they trust me, but to my surprise, it is Bets who responds first.

"Nova is a lot of things, but a liar isn't one of them. Let's use what she knows to figure this out."

"You don't find any of this suspicious?" Alik asks. "You said she couldn't even go to the market without trouble, so how has she worked this one out? There's literally nothing in this place to use as a marker."

Bets' lips quirk up in a half smile. "It's highly suspicious. Doesn't mean she's wrong."

"What do we have to lose if she is?" Hiro asks. "We're lost in this maze, and there's nothing else pointing us in the right direction."

Thoa nods as he meets my gaze. "If Nova is hearing voices whispering the way out, that's good enough for me."

I smile at him and give the tiniest nod of confirmation.

"So, what do we do? Knowing that we're being corralled doesn't do much good if we can't alter course," Alik says.

"*Use your advantage,*" Javian says. "*I might be able to track where the other team is if we hear something from their side. The statistical likelihood of both sides being mirrors of each other is—*" he pauses for a second, then says, "*ninety-seven percent.*"

"It's likely that both sides are built the same, so if we use our advantage maybe we can figure out where the other team is," I say.

"What good will that do?" Alik asks.

I shrug. "Whatever is waiting for us when we get to the center, wouldn't you rather have them face it first? Maybe they can take the brunt of it."

"And what if there are laser guns in the middle and they get to them first?" Alik says.

Hiro says, "They did give us the advantage for being first out of level three."

"Exactly," Bets says. "Nova is right."

We all turn to her and I ask, "I am?"

She nods. "They set the precedent that being first gets you a reward. By pushing that narrative, we've been rushing through this thing trying to find an end. But the game designers like to break whatever they've already established so it keeps everyone guessing. So, whoever gets there first will receive a punishment, not a reward."

"Right," I say, as if I had any idea what I was talking about.

"They said we can choose anyone," Alik says.

"Or we could choose no one," Thoa says. "Leave the blood on their hands, not ours."

Bets scoffs. "It would be foolish to waste the advantage. They would use it on us, if the situation was reversed. Who is the biggest threat?"

"The big brute," Hiro says.

I shake my head. "Muscle can be overcome. Leah, though, she's smart, and conniving. She's got her sight set on the end of this thing."

"Who is the one who lost their friend on the last level?" Bets asks. "They're the most dangerous."

"To you. They've got no love for off-worlders," Hiro says.

"And who do you think you are?" Alik says.

"Chief Hiro of the Old York Raiders."

She rolls her eyes. "You may have forgotten where you're from, but that doesn't mean everyone else can't see it."

"You showed up with the rest of us," Bets says with a shrug. "To them, we're all the same."

Hiro grits his teeth and growls, "We are not the same."

I place a hand over Hiro's heart in an attempt to calm him. He feels surprisingly solid under my touch, despite how fragile he looks. I whisper, "You are a Raider. It doesn't matter where you come from. Your heart belongs to your people."

He drops his gaze from them to me, but his rage still lingers on his furrowed brow and clenched jaw.

"You know who you are, Chief," I say.

Hiro takes a deep breath and lets his body relax, his brown eyes never leaving mine. "Yes, Chief."

Ignoring everything that just happened, Thoa says, "If we must go through with this, let's vote. It's the easiest way to decide."

"You know my vote," Bets says.

"I agree," Alik says.

"I still think Leah is the one to watch," I say.

Hiro nods and says, "I vote for Leah."

It takes everything in me not to smile at my victory. Any vote would always end up in our favor with three to two.

Thoa runs his hand through the dark curls falling over his face. When he looks up at me, confusion seems to mark his brows, but his eyes are hard. "I vote for Romelia."

My confusion matches his now. "Is that—"

"Yes. I side with the Règle."

CHAPTER
THIRTY

THOA

I don't know what she's doing. Every time I think we've settled what is between us, she does something else to make me question her. That kiss—gods!—I thought that was it for us. It felt so certain, so final, sealing everything into place. When our lips met, I knew we were going to work things out and be together, no matter what else lay ahead.

But then I see her with Hiro and I don't know what to think. I know what I feel though, and it's nothing good. I hurt when I see her hand placed upon his chest; I ache when I see her light up in his presence. They are friends—I know this—but I also know that he has waited for her return for the past year, taking no one else to his bed in that time. When they finally saw each other again, they kissed. She kissed him. She *wanted* to kiss him. But she did not kiss me.

Though I didn't witness it, the image is stuck in my mind. I can too easily imagine them locked in an embrace. The familiarity between them breeds contempt from me, and nothing I tell myself stops it. Jealousy rises, clenching my heart in its sharp talons and I am helpless against it.

I hold too much against her for what happened in the before time. *Before* there was a space station and off-worlders and violent games where we had to kill to stay alive. *Before* she fell in love with someone else, someone she didn't know; she had feelings for Krew, a complete stranger, though I stood before her bearing my entire soul to her in a choosing ceremony. *Before* we had brutalized one another's feelings because we didn't know how to love all of each other.

Maybe I still don't.

Maybe I hate her for what happened with Krew.

Maybe I love her because I have always loved her.

Whatever there was, and whatever there is, I can no longer say with any certainty that I have any control over who we are to each other. I thought I knew; I was wrong.

When she smiles in victory over who to use the advantage against, assuming I will take her side, I can't suppress the anger that pulses through me. Nova has no regard for what I want, only how she can use me. The messed up thing is that before now I might have taken her side without thought simply because I wanted to make her happy. I trust her, sure, but I have my own opinions on things. I have catered to her desires trying to win her heart, and the only time she's actually wanted me was when I followed a path that led me away from her.

I steel myself against her disapproval and say, "I vote for Romelia."

She can't fathom that I would choose anyone other than who she wanted. Part of me can't fathom it either. But it is done.

Her brows knit together and confusion is clear on her face. "Is that—"

"Yes," I say, my heart hammering in my chest. "I side with the Règle."

The look Nova gives me could level a building. There is so much anger there, so much certainty that she's right and no one else could possibly have any other point of view that's of value. There's also hurt, frustration, and a little bit of fear.

I hate seeing those things in her eyes, but I believe Bets is right about this. Maybe part of me also finds satisfaction in going against what Nova wants and acting out after she's hurt me. That isn't the whole reason for my defiance, though. I'm choosing based on what I think will most benefit the group. Eventually Nova will understand that. Probably. Then again, I spend a lot of time thinking and hoping for Nova to come around. I'm disappointed a lot.

"Right then," Bets says. "Announcer! We'd like to use our advantage."

I can hear a smile in their voice as they say, *"Wonderful. And who have you chosen to use it against?"*

"Romelia," Bets says.

"Ooooh excellent choice. They're a real firecracker. We'll set off your advantage momentarily. Enjoy the show!"

We look at one another expectantly, though none of us know what happens next. We wait for something to be different, to show us the way out, even if it means trouble from start to finish. We wait, hoping this will be our salvation.

CHAPTER
THIRTY-ONE
IVY

G amma is our salvation. Once Coco is coherent enough to state her own name, but medicated enough not to be in excruciating pain with every step, Gamma takes us back outside her apartment and into the corridor. It is no longer filled with excited people anticipating their independence day; instead, the place is eerily quiet and scattered with bodies in security uniforms.

The Raiders are nowhere to be found—neither marching through the station on the praises of the star-people nor lying on the floor underfoot. They vanished as if they had never been here.

Montana is visibly upset by this.

But his disappointment is short-lived; Gamma takes his tiny hand and says, "Not to worry, M. We'll still get to go with them. We just have to catch up."

Considering that Benjy and I had no real plans or options for what to do, following Gamma seems like the best choice to make. When she marches down the corridor like she owns the place, we follow in her wake, hauling Coco along with us.

She takes us into a service corridor that leads above the main halls. I've been through a handful of these places, and none are ever the same. Some run underneath, some alongside, some above. Many are unserviceable—full of miscellaneous junk from the past that few can identify. The corridors that are used regularly are well-lit and well-traveled, but mostly by people cutting through to try to bypass traffic rather than to actually service the station. Maintenance workers are more rare than one might think on a station of this size. Probably because the technology that put us here has survived longer than it was meant to, and the things that make it work are lost to the living.

Gamma knows this place. It is apparent with each step. She moves easily past every hurdle, directing us over, under, and through any barriers that block our path. Montana keeps up a running commentary of what is happening, but his tone is soft, almost reverent in this place. He seems to understand that this is not a normal place for a child to be, and he does not want to disrupt whatever has led him into this place.

A little more than half an hour after she led us into the service corridor we hear a loud commotion in the not-so-distance. Gamma motions for us to move quietly, and rather than speed up to see if we've caught up to the Raiders, we slow our pace. Gamma stations Montana in a corner with specific instructions not to move—a nearly impossible task for the child—while she tiptoes over the grates like she's done this a hundred times, light as a feather. She sidesteps a fallen conduit tube with ease as she stares down at the scene below. I can't read the expression on her face, but whatever she sees can't be good; the sounds we weren't sure about have resolved into screams.

Gamma holds up a hand to stop our progress but Benjy and I don't stop. We lean Coco against the wall near Montana and move toward where she is. There is nothing down there that we haven't seen before. When we are close enough to peer into the corridor as she has, we see the violent display she had tried to spare us. It isn't just that there are piles of bodies, it's the brutality of what is causing them. And the bodies aren't relegated to Raiders and the station's security; most of the people sprawled out below us are the star-people's children. The screams we've heard belong to the parents watching their babies being taken and murdered.

After years of hearing about the savages on-world, it is my people, the star-people, who are the worst of us. They are the ones prying children from their parents' arms. It is the security team who yells and threatens and kills. For what? To convince our own people *not* to go to the ground? To show them what happens to those who spread dissent? Do they not understand that all they're doing is creating more enemies in their own camp? No one will stand on the side of those who can perpetrate such atrocities with such little concern.

There are some security personnel on the floor, laser blasts through their brains. They must be the ones who would not obey their commands. We are not all bad, but enough of us are that wiping us out completely seems the only just way to root out the cruelty that lives in the star-people. If the Raiders kill every last one of us, I would not shed a tear.

"We must go," Gamma says, tugging at my elbow.

I hear the words but can't make myself turn away from the carnage.

"No," Benjy says, his voice a low rasp.

"There's nothing we can do," she says.

He growls, "We can try. There has to be something to distract them or delay them. Even if we only save one of them, it's better than doing nothing."

Gamma scans the area below us. "There are eight of them and only three of us. Not great odds, even if we had weapons."

"Like these?" Benjy asks. He pulls a laser gun from his waistband, bends down and pulls another from the leg of his pants, and retrieves a third from—well, I honestly don't know where he had it stashed, but it's in his hands now and that's what matters.

Gamma purses her lips like she disapproves, but she takes the weapon he proffers all the same. Wordlessly, she lowers herself on the grates and gets herself into position like any good soldier my father has trained.

He holds out a weapon to me, too, and I shake my head. "I'm not great with them."

Benjy shoves one of the weapons into his pocket and picks up my hand with his now free one. He puts the weapon firmly in my palm and curls my fingers around the trigger. "Do you know how it works?"

"Yes," I breathe.

"Can you point it at the bad guys and push the button?"

I nod, swallowing hard.

His gaze finds mine in the dim corridor, and there is pain and empathy and anger all wrapped up in this one look. "You've seen what they've done to those children. Can you walk away?"

"No." The word comes out before I have the chance to think about what I'm saying, to measure the weight of what this means.

Benjy simply nods and finds a position near Gamma.

I glance over my shoulder at Coco and Montana, still holding position against the wall. The little boy's face lodges in my mind; he is so small, so frail, so helpless in the world. Just like all the other children piling up below us. He tries to smile at me, falters. Tears creep down his cheeks instead. It is this that finally forces me onto my belly, pointing a laser gun at the people below.

When it was over, I couldn't say whether or not I'd hit any of them. My thoughts warred over whether I wanted to have killed some of them, or whether I didn't. For good or ill, there was no way to distinguish the shots in the middle of everything. They were all dead, and we weren't, and that was the only thing my shaking body and addled brain could comprehend.

They were no longer screaming in the corridor below us, but there were wails and cries and the sounds of pain beyond measure. Some of the children lived. Some of them will go on to have a future. We have done all we can do for the people below. We march on. Our business is with the Raiders.

CHAPTER
THIRTY-TWO
NOVA

R omelia's scream echoes closer than I would have imagined, the sound practically shaking the walls to my right.

"What are they doing to them?" Hiro whispers.

None of us want to know. Not really. If we knew, we would have to face that we had done that to them. We didn't *have* to use the advantage, but we did. We did. And Romelia is paying for it.

When their screams cease, the announcer's voice comes to life around us: *"Turns out Romelia just couldn't keep a cool head—or any head!"*

Their laugh is cruel, grating against my nerves. I would give anything to never hear it again. I'm certain I will.

"We killed them," Thoa says. His tone is matter-of-fact.

"Not us," Bets whispers.

"We are as much at fault as those running the trials. We had a choice." He turns to me and asks, "Was it worth it?"

"No. Of course not. There's nothing that could make it worth the cost."

"*I agree,*" Javian says in my ear, "*though it did provide us with some much needed information.*"

"Go on," I breathe, not wanting the others to hear.

"*The other team is moving at the same pace as you, but not together. Instead of working together, they split up and took different paths.*"

I want to ask how he knows but there's no easy way to do so without everyone else picking up on it. I make a humming sound to indicate I'm listening, but that's the most I can give.

"*I could try to explain this to you,*" Javian says as if reading my mind, "*but knowing won't help you, and Chief Hiro prefers briefer explanations. Suffice it to say, I scienced the shit out of where you are and what's around you.*"

"I think the other group split up," I say aloud.

Bets looks up at me. "There weren't any other screams."

"So, we know at least one member of their group was moving at around the same pace as us, but that doesn't help with the other four," Alik says.

Hiro says, "But it does tell us they don't trust each other."

"Neither do we," Alik says.

"Maybe not," I say, my gaze moving inexplicably to Thoa. "We can still work together, though. They can't. They're down a player, *and* their team is fractured. We have the advantage."

"That's what they called it when we killed Romelia, too," Thoa says.

I don't know what he wants me to say. We all made the decision, we're all guilty. I didn't want them to die, but if I'm being honest with myself, I knew that's what would happen if the advantage worked. The star-people aren't subtle with their torture. They might have *said* there was a way to overcome what they had planned, but the chances of actually doing so were slim to none. The viewers want blood.

"*There's a chance that someone could be ahead of Romelia and waiting for you at the end of the maze. Where were they in the initial lineup?*"

"Romelia was the last to enter the maze," I say. "We don't know how or when they split up, so every other player could be past them, or behind them. The other four could already be at the end waiting for us."

"We didn't keep to the line even though we stayed together," Alik says.

"*There's no way to confirm their positions at this—*"

Javian's words were cut off with a violent scream.

"Someone found Romelia," Bets says.

Hiro swallows, eyes wide, and says, "Or what's left of them."

"Who was it?" Alik says.

"Could've been any of them," I say. "I haven't heard any of them talk enough to distinguish one from the other."

"Are there any who might stick together?"

I think back to the level below and how Dante carried Jai until they were able to walk on their own. "Dante and Jai might have stayed together. He seemed protective of them on the last level."

Alik says, "Assuming you're right, since there was only one scream it probably wasn't them. That means Leah or…"

"Sam," Thoa supplies.

We sit in silence for a moment, trying to work out what, if anything, this means for us. I believe Leah to be the most dangerous person on the other team while Sam hasn't done anything to make a mark on my memory. I remember seeing him, but there's nothing remarkable to distinguish him from any of the other previous competitors. Except for the fact that he's made it this far. With Romelia dead, he's one of nine remaining. No one makes it this far without skill.

"Clearly what we're doing is working," Bets says. "We're navigating through, with no issues and no deaths so far. We all agree that trusting each other is out of the question but that doesn't mean we can't keep going the way we are and make it out as a whole. Can we agree to do that?"

"I thought that's what we were already doing," Alik grumbles.

"Sure, except now we have a better idea of what's happening. Slightly, at least, thanks to the voices in Nova's head."

My eyes dart to hers and Bets' lip curls up at the edge, the only confirmation I need that she knows about Javian. She might not know the details, but she's smart enough to know I'm getting information from somewhere.

"Let's do this," Hiro says, holding his hand out in the center of the group. "A real team."

Bets and Thoa put their hands on top of Hiro's. I hesitate for only a second before adding mine to the rest. We all look at Alik as we wait; her hesitation makes sense, as she is the one with the least connection to this group and the most to lose.

"I got you," I say. "As much as the rest of them. I know that might not mean much to you—"

"The only person I trust less than you is Hiro," she says.

"What about me?" Thoa asks. "Will you trust that I'll protect you?"

She nods. "You may have tried to kill me once today already, but I've seen you stick to your values even when you had to go against your friends. If you promise to look after me as much as you will Nova, I'll believe you."

"I promise to do my best," he says.

Alik puts her hand on the pile.

"*Excellent,*" the announcer's voice says, a smile in their tone. "*Though it took you far longer than the other team, who immediately agreed to help each other no matter what.*"

"Wait, what?" Hiro asks.

"But they split up," Alik says.

The wall in front of us shifts to create five doorways.

"*They did! And now, so will you.*"

CHAPTER
THIRTY-THREE

HIRO

Left, right, left, right—it doesn't matter. Every step takes me closer to the center and whatever waits there for us. I've tried walking in what should have been a circle, but no idea if it's actually done what I wanted it to. Sometimes there's an incline, sometimes I descend. It feels like I've been walking for hours but I'm sure it has only been a few minutes.

All at once the corridor opens into a small room. I immediately assume it is the center of the maze. After a moment with no one else entering and no apparent danger, I start to wander around. I can't see a way out at first, or even second glance.

Everywhere I look, I see my bruised and battered face reflected back to me. The mirrors show the horror of what the Règle's people did to me, and why everyone's eyes are filled with pity when they look at me. Even when they don't want to show it I can see it. They're not great at hiding how bad they want to wrap me up in a warm blanket and feed me soup. But I'm not sick, and their hands won't make me recover any faster. I got hurt doing something I'm proud of because it was good and right and completely un-Hiro-like.

I follow my reflection from mirror to mirror for several minutes before I finally see a small panel that doesn't line up with the others. I step toward it, outstretching a hand into the gap. The panel slides away and there's a door leading down into darkness; there are no mirrors.

This must be the way to the actual middle of the maze. There is relief in not seeing myself staring back as I walk down the hall. I pause and listen for anything ahead but there is only silence. My eyes are still adjusting to the change in light but I don't think there's anyone else there. Even after all the changes and upheaval, I still may be the first one here.

I step out of the darkened hall and into an octagonal room. The light isn't necessarily brighter here, just different. There's a soft blue hue to everything, casting the room in an eeriness that the mirrors didn't convey. They offered their own issues, like showing the group the reality of their situation and exactly who they are, even when they want to hide from themselves.

There's a quiet sound behind me, an exhalation of breath, and I turn to see Alik coming down the hall. I step towards her, a smile coming to my face. As much as she hates me and doesn't trust me, I still want her to live through this; I want her to find a life where she can be safe and happy.

We're only a few feet from each other when I see a flicker of panic cross her face. She jumps into action, sprinting the rest of the way toward me before I have a chance to react. I turn toward whatever Alik is watching just in time for the Captain to throw herself against me. I tumble to the side as a figure emerges from the hazy blue. How Alik saw them, I'll never know; she always was the best of us, even those who trained at her side under the same leadership.

Alik stumbles back from the figure who has resolved themselves into Leah. I expect a fight, relish the thought, even. Nova thinks Leah is dangerous, but I'm pretty sure Alik can kick her ass. She's certainly full of enough piss and vinegar to give it a go.

But there is no fight. Instead, Alik doubles over, her hand clutching at her gut. I look from her pained expression to Leah, who wears satisfaction like a crown. Her hands rest triumphantly on her hips, and I notice blood at her sleeve cuff.

"No." The word shudders through me as I move to Alik's side.

She has gone to one knee now, barely holding herself up. Her gaze lifts to mine and she mutters something from too-pale lips.

"What's that babe?" I ask, helping her lie down. I try to smile at her, to give her the only bit of comfort I can, but I feel it falter before it can take root.

Alik clutches at my collar and pulls my ear to her lips. "Knife."

I jerk my head up toward Leah. She has lowered herself in a position to pounce, the blade in her hand flashing when it catches the dim light.

"Run," Alik mumbles.

But I can't. I won't. I've left Alik over and over, every chance she gave me. I will not leave her now.

I stand to face Leah, assuming a defensive position Rego taught me. She doesn't wait for me to find my balance like he always did, but rushes to attack. I deflect her first charge, barely. Leah pivots far faster than I do; she continues her onslaught in the span of a breath. I scramble back from her, trying to find a position of defense while knowing there is none.

Rushing footsteps echo from the darkened hall and I catch sight of short red hair running toward me. Leah doesn't bother turning away from me, her eyes fixed on her prey. Better for her, really; the sight of a Raider, a *real* Raider, running toward you is terrifying. If I saw Nova charging at me like she is Leah right now, I'd probably shit my pants.

Nova slams into Leah and tackles her to the ground. They roll around, fighting for dominance. Leah's knife clatters across the floor and I dive for it. I tuck it into my boot for safekeeping and return to Alik's side. She needs me far more than Nova does.

Alik's skin is so pale she's practically glowing. Except her hands. They are stained with her blood. Gods, there's so much of it. It has soaked through her clothes, coated her skin, slicked the space around her with life, with death.

I kneel beside her and feel the warm stickiness seep into the knees of my pants. Up close, it is clear that she is not long for this world. If we were on the station, she could be saved. She probably would already be finished with her recovery and only a little sore. The medics could do wondrous things up there. Not so much on-world. Of course, they won't even try. That's the point of this place. Life is to be drained, not preserved.

Cradling the back of Alik's head in my hand, I lean close to her and say, "Hey, babe. Looks like you went and got yourself stabbed."

"Dead," she mutters, her lips barely moving.

"I don't know if it's that bad."

A faint smile lifts the corners of her lips. "Liar."

"I would never."

Her brows crease as if she's trying to work out an unsolvable problem. "Did you ever—" she coughs, red spittle gathering at the corner of her mouth, "—love..."

"Always," I say, the word falling out with ferocity. I am surprised to discover that I am not lying when I add, "I loved you from the first moment I saw you. I could have spent my whole life loving you, if I was a better man."

Her faint smile grows fuller. Between pained breaths, she says, "You were awful."

"You deserved so much more than who I could be. That was the only reason, Alik. I couldn't let you settle for me. I loved you too much for that."

Her creased brow eases and a peaceful expression replaces what was there. She is no longer questioning what was; she knows now how right she was. It might not ease the hurt I caused her, but it has surely given her some comfort.

Alik's head lolls to the side as the last of her gives up. I pull her against my chest as tears well up and flow down my cheeks. She didn't deserve this fate; in fact, the only reason she was here was because of me.

And the Règle. She's the real reason all of us are here. She threw me into this place, and Alik came after to try to save me. What a heroic dumbass. She would still be alive if...

Gently, so gently, I lean Alik's head back to the ground and I force myself to my feet. I did love her, even if I didn't realize what it was at the time. The things I told her were true, the way I felt about her was real, I just didn't know how to process those things while I had the chance. It was my new life that taught me that. If only she'd had the chance to know the man I became.

My eyes turn to the sound of running feet. Thoa and Bets are coming into the maze center. Anger rises in me at the sight of them. Bets is the cause of this, but Thoa promised he would keep her safe. I know he couldn't have—in my brain, I know this—but I still blame him for not being here to try.

I turn my back to them to see if Nova has killed Leah yet. I want her dead for what she did to Captain Alik. I want Bets dead, too, but I want it to be at my hand; I can wait for that particular treat.

There's a strange shaking at my feet and I realize the center of the maze is separating from everything else and lifting to the next level. At the edge of the room, a small figure crouches. They were out of sight until now, staying away from the fighting and the death. They stand now, and as the level above opens a beam of light shines down. It's the man with glasses—Sam, I think—and he wears an expression of self-satisfaction.

More running footsteps, but we're too far off the ground for me to see them. The small mazulla person with the lovely bronze skin comes into sight seconds later as she's catapulted onto the platform. I'm too numb to realize what has happened until Thoa squeezes my elbow and says, "Hurry."

I follow him to the place where they just came up. Thoa is lying on his stomach, hand extended to try to reach the large man below. The guy jumps up, trying to clasp Thoa's hand but missing. I join Thoa on the ground and reach down for the man. He jumps a second time, a third. Now we are too high. I'm certain he will never reach us.

The man has backed up and is running down the darkened corridor for one last attempt. He jumps, arms extended and misses Thoa again.

But not me.

His hand grabs hold of mine, hanging on for his life. His skin is sweaty and my grip is giving way already. I cannot hold him.

Then Thoa has his other hand and the weight of him lessens. His hand in mine adjusts itself and clings more firmly. Between the two of us, Thoa and I are able to lift him onto the platform beside us. The man pants, clearly exhausted, and all I want is for all of us to have a moment of rest before the next torture we must face.

Before the platform settles into place, a huge shadow passes overhead. I look up into a massive room that almost looks like it is outside except for the walls within view. Another shadow passes by, blocking the light that only just found us again.

"Holy shi—"

I turn in time to see a pale blue bird the size of a horse swoop down and grab the man with glasses. It carries him away in talons as long as my forearm. The man's screams carry down to us, pleading for help.

"We can still save him," the man we rescued says.

Thoa nods. "Let's go, before we lose him altogether."

"He's already dead," I say.

Thoa puts a hand on my shoulder and says, "I'm sorry about Alik. Truly. I wanted to save her."

"But you didn't. You couldn't. And we can't save that guy either."

"Who are we, if we don't try?"

"We are the star-people, they are us. There is no difference. We're all cruel killers, trying to save our own skin."

The other man says, "I don't want to be like them. There has to be more to us than that."

A thin scream sounds, and I see how small the bird has gotten in the distance. But that is not all I see. Above us, circling and diving lower and lower, are a dozen or more other birds. They are not as large as the one who stole Sam from us, but their talons can cut and their beaks can peck and our bodies can bleed.

"Fine," I say. "Get Nova and let's go."

I turn to see a small brown bird sitting on Alik's chest, pecking at her bloody gut. I chase after it, kicking and screaming. It flies up to join the others, but when I turn back to her two more have taken its place.

"She deserved more than this."

We all do. But all we receive are the deaths dealt to us from above, an entertainment for the masses. We are nothing more than the old movies I used to watch, showing a world I would never experience from the comfort of my bed on the temperature-regulated station. We die so the star-people can know the horrors of death while feeling relief at their own miserable lives.

CHAPTER
THIRTY-FOUR

NOVA

My nose is bloody and my lip is cut. Blood coats the inside of my mouth, a metallic tang that flavors the smile I give Leah. She got a few good hits in, but is in far worse shape than I. Leah is a thinker, cunning and quick, but not trained to fight. After this bout, I can see she *could* be trained—she'd make a fine Raider—but her survival in life and in the trials has been about outsmarting her competition and using every advantage she can. I respect that, even as I connect my fist with her jaw again.

Leah stumbles back blinking hard against the blow. When she gains her balance a few seconds later, she smacks her lips together and spits out a tooth. "That was a good hit."

"Thanks," I say, giving her a nod.

"Why are we doing this again?"

"You killed Alik."

"And?" she asks. "She wasn't really part of your team."

She's got me there. But I had promised to protect her, even if she wasn't one of my people, and now the best I can give her is revenge.

I dodge one of Leah's punches and ask, "Why did you do it? Isn't what they're doing to us enough?"

"I could ask the same thing of you. Why did you use that advantage on Romelia? Why did you laugh while we mourned Argus and Quill? Why did you murder Georgia?"

I don't answer; I can't. I know that none of those things were done with malice but does the intent really matter when the result is the same?

"It's not a trick question," she says. "The answer is as easy as it gets: you didn't have a choice. Whether it was them forcing your hand or a reaction to the situation you're in, there wasn't another option. You might spend years thinking about the decisions you made and how you could have done things differently, but in the end you did what you had to do."

"And you had to kill Alik?" I ask, throwing my fist at her half-heartedly.

"Not Alik, just someone. That was my task, and the only way I would live through that level. The gamemasters gave us a challenge to earn an advantage in this level. I took it. I figured my best bet was to attack whoever came down the hall first. I got lucky in that it was your busted up fella. I was confident I could take him."

"Hiro? But then Alik—?"

"She made a choice," Leah said. "One she can't regret. She dove in front of my blade."

The words slip from my lips before I can think about them: "She loved him."

Leah shrugs. "And I loved my little sister. I would've killed you on her behalf if I could have. But that's not how this place works."

"Your sister?" I look past the bruises and the blood, past the hungry eyes, and there I see the similarities. Angular, bird-like features look back at me with a coldness I hadn't noticed until now. "Georgia."

She nods and swallows the lump in her throat. "I know you didn't have a choice but I still hope you die. Violently."

"That's fair. But I don't think it's going to be at your hands."

"You might be surprised," she says.

A bird swoops down nearby, the wind from its wings blowing my short hair. I take my eyes from Leah for the first time in too long. Looking around I realize we've lifted up into the next level while she and I were fighting. This room must be the biggest portion of the tower; the ceilings are so high we might as well be outside. Swirling above us are dozens of birds in colors and patterns I've never seen before. They are a variety of sizes, too; some are large enough to cause a problem, others are smaller than my finger but swooping low and dangerously close to my eyes.

"Little Star," Thoa calls. "We need to go."

"Go where?"

"Away from here." He points into the distance where a bird flies away from us, something nearly as big as it is dangling below it.

I scan the space around us, half expecting Jai to be missing. No, they are there, tucked away at Dante's side. But the small man with the spectacles is missing.

"You want to do this together?" I ask, turning back to Leah.

She's gone. I spin around, looking for where she's run off to, but I don't see her. I don't have time to search if we're going to help the other guy.

Bets has moved to stand beside Dante and Jai, and Thoa is standing between me and them, waiting. Hiro hovers over Alik's body, trying to chase away the scavengers who seem to appear out of nowhere. I look between Hiro and Thoa, noticing the look that passes over Thoa's face when my gaze meets his. I want to go to him and run away from this place, escape out into the desert where we can finally find peace. Then I see Hiro and the brokenness that has taken over and I know I have to go to him. Thoa is strong and will understand why I make this choice; Hiro is a shell of the man he was only hours ago.

I walk over and put a hand on Hiro's shoulder. "We have to go."

"I know."

"We can't take her with us."

He sighs. "I know." A moment of silence passes between us as we look down at what is left of Captain Alik. Finally, he says, "It isn't fair."

"It's not," I say.

We move toward the rest of the group as a swarm of birds comes down at our heads. Though we swat at the air above us, though we should be able to fight off a handful of these small creatures, they continue to dive relentlessly without regard for themselves. Each time they dive, they get closer and closer to making contact.

The others are running now, and we fall in with them. If there is safety in our numbers, I can't imagine how secure the birds are. They've gone from a couple dozen to well over fifty in such a short time that I'm terrified to imagine how many will be here when I next look up. Each glance at the space above offers a fleeting impression of being outside. This level is taller than any of the others I've seen, possibly the size of two of them combined heightwise. It is immense and full and terrifying.

Everywhere my eyes turn is lush and green and full of trees and vegetation I've never seen. We barrel through the underbrush, thorns and briars tugging at our clothes with each step. The forest around us is thick and wild, a beautiful imitation of those I've seen in the real world. I long to return to them. I will.

A scream punctuates the air above us. Ahead, Dante comes to a stop. He scans the sky, his head swiveling back and forth. For the first time, I notice Jai clinging to his shoulders, their legs wrapped around his waist. I don't know what their connection is, but it is stronger than I realized. He isn't just protecting them, he is ensuring their survival. If they knew each other before this place, their alliance could be an issue as we progress. If not, when Dante picked Jai up on level three, it was the best thing that could have happened to them.

Bets and Thoa stumble to a stop behind him and turn their gazes up as well. Hiro and I catch up to them thanks to this stop, and nearly run into their backs. Thoa turns to us, his eyes narrowing. Hiro doesn't seem to notice. His eyes still hold a far away look, and I'm certain he's still seeing Alik's body on the ground, no matter what he's actually looking at.

"He's up there," Dante says, pointing.

High above the canopy that obscures most of what we can see, there are a handful of trees clumped together that have grown—or have been manufactured, at least—to stand three or four times the size of those that surround us. In the tallest of these, barely visible from my position, is a nest. A pale blue bird with yellow plumage on its head rests there. Its sharp beak and vicious talons tear at something.

No, I think. *Some*one.

"We'll never reach him," Bets says.

Everyone looks at her. It's an obvious truth. We all know she's right. Bets is just the one realistic enough to say it aloud.

She rolls her eyes. "We don't have time to sugarcoat this if the rest of us are going to make it out of here."

Sam screams again, a spine-chilling sound that feels like it should only be heard in a nightmare.

"We can't let him die like that," Dante says, a crease forming between his brows.

"He's already dead," Bets says.

The words seem cruel—especially since we are still listening to his screams—but they aren't. Not really. They are just another thing we all know to be true.

"Someone could climb—"

"Who? How? And what would they do once they got up there, other than be tomorrow's meal for that thing?" Bets says, cutting Dante off.

"I don't know!" he yells.

A flock of birds takes flight nearby. There's a silence that descends on us, smothering every emotion trying to take root. Dante is what we're all feeling, but Bets is what we all know to be true. We *want* to save the guy stuck up there being eaten alive, but we all know it isn't going to happen. If Sam is thinking about anything beyond his insides being pulled outside, he also knows it isn't going to happen. If he was down here instead, he would do and feel the same as we are now.

"We need to go," I say. The words leave my throat feeling raw, like they scraped their way out without permission.

Thoa's lip curls in disgust. I can see his frustration as clearly as I can see his bright blue eyes. He does not like what we must do, even if he knows it is the right decision. Thoa would save him if he could. And he's mad at me for agreeing with Bets that we can't.

He says, "I can make it up that tree."

Hiro steps toward him and puts a hand on his shoulder. "And then what, Bonecutter? By the time you get to him, the guy will be dead."

"He's not dead yet."

"Better if he was," Jai says.

It is the first and only thing I have heard them say and the sound surprises me.

Dante says, "You don't mean that."

"I do," they say. "It would be easier for him and us."

"We vote," Bets says.

"This is not a team decision," Thoa says.

Before he can say more, a shadow passes overhead and we all look up. Bigger than the bird that took Sam, the massive brown predator that circles overhead could pick up any of us. The bird seems to realize the same thing at the same time I do; its talons curl down in preparation to attack, and its eyes zero in on me.

CHAPTER
THIRTY-FIVE
NOVA

The bird is faster than I imagined. I want to run. I *need* to run. But my feet are rooted to the ground. My scream that will match Sam's is already lodged in my throat, ready to burst from me as soon as the beast grabs me.

My eyes are fixed on the sharpened talons, easily as long as the blades I have always loved. They grow ever-larger in my vision as they reach for me.

A sudden burning agony in my shoulder jolts through me as the bird's talons scrape against my shoulder bone. I scrunch my eyes closed against the pain and wait for the rest of this nightmare to end me. I should feel the rush of wind by now, I should hear the flap of the bird's wings as we rise higher and higher. But I don't.

Slowly—oh so slowly—I open my eyes. I look down to see a strong, tan arm wrapped around my waist. I feel the firm ridges and plains of Thoa's body beneath me. There is blood soaking through the clothes of my right shoulder where the bird's talons pierced the skin, but otherwise I am unharmed.

"It's coming back!" Hiro yells.

Thoa gives me a push up from his body. I turn to offer him a hand up, but he's already found his feet. I grab his hand, entangle it in mine, and we run.

"Deeper into the trees," Thoa calls to those ahead of us.

They turn and move farther into the forest, weaving through and around the bushes and brush that block the path. The bird circles above the canopy as if looking for the right place to drop on us again. It moves with us; even when we can't see it, the bird seems to know where we are.

Another scream fills the level. It is behind us now. Fading. As we run for our own lives, it is easier to forget the man who owns that voice. It shouldn't be easier, but it is.

From Dante's back, Jai points off to the side of the level. I can't see what they do, but Dante turns toward where they pointed and leads us away. We follow, none of us willing to split away from the group. Except Leah. She could be dead by now for all we know.

As soon as the thought enters my mind, I see her; she's a beacon on this stormy night. She's also what Jai was pointing at. Straight ahead, pressed against the wall a hundred feet in the air, Leah is climbing a rope ladder.

"What the..."

I hear the rush of wings only a second before the creature is upon us. I tug Thoa against a tree trunk and the bird's talons gouge the ground. It returns to the air empty handed yet again.

We stand there pressed together, panting. A sheen of sweat makes his tanned skin glow in the false sunlight of this terrifying paradise. Thoa looks down at me, his eyes questioning. I don't know what to read in his expression, what he wants to know, but I wish I could ease all of his troubles in one instant.

"Little Star," he breathes.

A squawk as loud as a siren on the space station echoes above us and we look up to see the blue bird who stole Sam and the brown bird who attacked me fighting mid-air. Each bird has their talons dug into something as they pull it back and forth, trying to best the other. It finally breaks, blood and viscera exploding between them. They separate, each taking a part of Sam, the brown bird winning the biggest piece with the spine dangling low as it flies away.

"To the ladder," Dante yells.

We're running again. Leah is nowhere to be seen, so she must have made it wherever the rope leads.

Bets gets there first. She starts up without question, moving with a speed I've never seen from her. Bets likes to move with languid precision. She wants to look casual but confident. Neither of those things are happening now. She climbs as if her life depends on it, because it does.

Dante and Jai are behind her, but not by much. Jai hangs onto Dante's back for dear life, and he climbs for both of them. That bastard is strong.

Hiro reaches the ladder ahead of us and turns back to see where we are. I wave my uninjured arm to usher him on. I see the pain on his brow before he turns back to the ladder; Hiro is no fool. He knows I'm asking him to leave me, because there is no way I can climb that ladder with my shoulder as hurt as it is. I am asking him to save himself, and it hurts him, but Hiro is good at saving his own skin.

When Thoa and I reach the ladder, I give him my best smile. "You go first."

"No," he says.

"Thoa," I say, "you have to."

"The hell I do."

"I'm right behind you. Just gonna catch my breath."

"I can carry you."

"No you can't."

He waves a hand above us and says, "He's carrying Jai. You think Dante is stronger than me?"

I nearly laugh at the words. "It's not about that."

"Then you want to die?"

"Of course not."

"Then get on my back and hold on."

"Jai is so small. They aren't as heavy—"

"Get. On. My. Back."

I do as he says and try not to worry when he grunts under my weight. Thoa is strong; he is Thoa-gra the Bonecutter. He has carried beasts for miles to feed his Raider brethren. If he says he can carry me, he can.

We ascend. Slowly. Though he won't say so, I know my weight is a burden for him. We are still so close to the bottom that a fall likely wouldn't kill me. Bets is near the top now. Hiro is closing in on Dante who seems to have slowed, likely due to the weight of carrying another person, even one as small as Jai. They seem to be readjusting, with Jai moving around to take the ladder for themself. They climb a few rungs above Dante on their own, then look down and smile at him.

"You got this," he says to Jai.

Jai gives him a nod, and I think we are going to keep going until I notice Jai reaching into their pocket. Silver flashes in their hand and I call out Dante's name in warning, but it is too late. Jai's hand drops to Dante's neck and crimson spurts from the wound they made. His hand leaves the rope to cover the wound; blood gushes through the fingers pressed against his carotid artery. While he hangs there one-handed, Jai climbs a few more rings and steps down hard on the hand on the rope.

Dante falls.

He is going to hit me.

Thoa throws himself to the side, the whole ladder moving with the motion. I lose my grip with the sudden movement. My left hand scrabbles for a hold, and barely finds purchase on the leather strap that crisscrosses Thoa's body. My right shoulder is trashed, so the only way I stayed aloft was by having my legs wrapped around Thoa's waist.

The ladder swings back in the seconds it takes for Dante's body to fall past us. I feel Thoa's muscles tense under me as he wills himself not to try to save the other man. He wants to reach out a hand and pull him to safety, but he can't. For himself, for me, he holds back. Not that there would be anything to save anyway. Jai's knife removed any hope of him surviving.

I look up at Jai and realize they're making great time. They've spent the last few levels conserving their strength, so now that they need it they are fully rested. It's genius, honestly, but also one of the most brutal things I've seen. They reach the top and turn back toward the ladder. Their knife glints as they saw back and forth on the rope.

"Damn it," I say.

"What's wrong?" Thoa asks.

"Jai is cutting the rope."

Thoa pauses and looks up. "Hiro will stop them."

"Why hasn't Bets done anything?" I ask.

The question is like sawdust on my tongue before the words are fully formed. Why would Bets save us? We're not really part of a team; if anything, we are Bets' biggest rivals in this place. There is a past hatred between us that eliminates any goodwill that could have been found by working together. She's letting Jai do her dirty work—a proud tradition amongst the Règles. Never get blood on your hands when someone else is willing to do it for you.

Thoa continues to climb but he will never make it in time. Not with both of us. I look down at the ground below us where Dante's body is sprawled, parts of him rising and falling at weird angles. Small birds are already pecking at him.

I release my legs from Thoa's waist and he immediately tenses. "What are you doing?"

"Trust me."

"Don't do this, Nova."

"You have to keep going. Move fast and you can still make it."

"I won't leave you."

"Take care of Hiro. When you get out of here, find Ivy and make sure she's safe."

"Nova, please," he says, his voice breaking.

"I love you, Thoa. I always have. Take care of my people."

I fall.

CHAPTER
THIRTY-SIX
THOA

I watch in horror as Nova's body falls. She tumbles through the air, and though I see her tuck into herself to protect her head, I can't imagine she will survive this. *What is wrong with her?*

I could go back down for her but what good would that do? We'd both die. As much as I want to, I can't carry her up the ladder if there's no ladder to climb. I'm not strong enough to save her. But I can protect Hiro through this, I can find Ivy, I can go back to the Raiders and take care of them. I can do the things she asked of me, even if I will be an empty shell of a man without her.

So, I climb. I'm much faster now that it is just me, without the extra weight on my back. By the time the first side of the ladder collapses, I'm more than halfway to the top. I don't bother looking up. If Jai cuts the other side of the ladder, it won't matter if I saw it coming or not.

It is hard going with only half the rope but not impossible. Easier than watching the love of your life sacrifice themselves for you.

I spare a quick glance above, and though Jai is nowhere to be seen, I see Hiro's head sticking out of the opening only a few feet above me. The bastard has that huge grin on his face and I have to clench my fingernails into the rope to stop myself from climbing up and punching him. There's no reason to smile, no reason to breathe anymore.

Taking a deep breath, I force myself the rest of the way up. Hiro reaches down a hand when I'm in range and I let him help me the rest of the way up. Without a word, he hands me the small pocket knife that must have belonged to Jai. It is still sticky with blood. I flip it end over end in my hand as I lean against the wall and close my eyes as my left-over adrenaline courses through me, threatening to make me puke. Everything is *wrong*.

"Where's Jai?" I ask, looking for the threat.

"Gone," Hiro says, his voice sounding so small and so far away. "But she made it. She actually did it."

My eyes shoot open at his words. "What did you say?"

"She fell—"

"She *jumped*," I interject.

He smiles. "Of course she did. She'd do anything to keep you safe. Even if it's as foolish as risking her own life."

"Why though? We could have made it."

The expression on his face tells me he is unconvinced, but he doesn't say so. "She landed on Dante. I'm sure it hurt like hell, but after a few minutes of lying still, she sat up, stretched her arms and legs, and stumbled off into the forest."

"Stumbled?"

"She'd just fallen thirty feet," he says. "Be glad it was only stumbling."

"Then what?"

Hiro shrugs. "I couldn't see where she went once she got under the canopy."

"So, one of those birds could have her already."

"You've gotta have more faith in her than that."

A growl comes out unbidden. "What did you say to me?"

"Whoa," Hiro says, holding up his hands. "Calm down. I know you love her, and she loves you. I thought *maybe* you dumdums had figured that out already and could start putting a little faith back into your relationship."

"I've never lost faith in her."

"Does she know that?"

I open my mouth to say yes, but the word gets stuck in my throat. I honestly don't know if she knows that. I haven't exactly had the chance to tell her, and she's been too busy to listen. We move around each other in circles; we protect, defend, and rescue each other, but it's been a while since we've *talked* about what we mean to one another.

"I don't know," I finally say.

"Well, keep believing in her, trust that if anyone can figure this out that it's her, and when she returns to us by some weird miracle, *tell* her."

"She doesn't listen."

"Make her."

I nod. When Hiro gives me his giant smile, I no longer want to punch his face. I do, however, need to clarify something with him before I can move on. "I thought there might be something between you two."

"Friendship," Hiro says. "That's all."

"Bets said you kissed."

Hiro winces. "Temporary insanity. We were just happy to see each other and it happened. But we knew right away it was a mistake. We love each other, but not like that."

"She didn't kiss me. In fact, I'm pretty sure I pissed her off within seconds of finding her."

Hiro sighs. "Can you blame her for being upset? Think about the last memory she had of you before seeing you on the station."

I have relived that memory often. The way our skin burned at each other's touch, the way our bodies melted into one another like they were one flesh, one end. I thought I was over her and trying to put her in my past, but she had already scarred her name upon my heart and never left. That moment at the Hole in the World where we were finally together reopened that old wound and made it clear I would never be able to be without her. She was—she *is*—part of me.

"There are a lot of things I wish I could go back and change, but not that. It's where I realized I was always going to be hers."

"It's also where she thought she'd lost you forever."

The words hit me in the chest and settle in. She didn't lose me, couldn't lose me even if she tried. She could tell me to leave, that she would never love me, and I would do as she asked; even then I would be hers.

I give Hiro a half smile and say, "I understand. Thank you. When I see her again, I'll make sure she knows all the things I've never said."

"Until then, let's try not to die."

"Any idea what comes next?"

"I looked through the opening but couldn't make anything out. After I took Jai's knife from them, they scurried in and I lost sight pretty fast."

"Is it dark?"

Hiro shakes his head. "It's… squishy."

"Squishy?"

"Yes? I don't know how else to explain it. Jai crawled into something that suctioned to their body. Then they were gone."

"That doesn't sound great."

"Yeah. I'm not looking forward to it. I'm not crazy about tight spaces. At least not in these circumstances," he says wagging a brow.

I close my eyes and sigh, but inwardly I'm thankful to have a little bit of old Hiro back. The swelling in his face has gone down a bit and he's starting to look more like himself, though I'm not sure he'll ever fully recover from what he's been through today. Some scars don't heal.

"I've got your back," I say.

"And I've got yours. Let's get through this thing and show them who the Raiders are."

Hiro climbs through the circular hole in front of us and disappears. I turn back to the trees and give one last look for Nova. I palm Jai's blade as I scan the area. There is little I can do for her at this point, especially without knowing what her plan is; the only thing I can be certain of is that she won't be climbing this rope. I saw through the other side of it and drop the ladder and the knife to the ground.

"Nova," I yell, my voice echoing through the level and sending birds scattering through the air. There is so much I want to tell her, so many things I need her to know, but I push all that away and call out the only thing she needs to hear. "Blade."

She is down there somewhere all alone, fending for herself, with no easy path to safety. The odds are completely stacked against Nova, and I have no idea how she's going to get herself out of this one. The star-people running this place should be terrified because I have no doubt that she's coming for them.

CHAPTER
THIRTY-SEVEN
NOVA

The sound of Thoa's voice calling my name is a comfort I didn't expect. A sob bubbles up and releases from my throat. He made it. Hiro made it. My boys are okay.

I'm okay, too. Mostly. I feel awful; my shoulder is throbbing and bleeding, the rest of my body is bruised from the fall, and two of my ribs are in bad shape but I don't think they're cracked. The drop wasn't easy but it wasn't high enough to kill me, and that's what I was counting on. Now I just need to figure out the rest.

"Blade!" Thoa yells.

I look out from my hiding place to see the rope ladder hit the ground. Good idea, considering there's no way I could climb it. Maybe I'll find something else to do with it. I scan the ground nearby the rope looking for the blade he dropped. That is a boon I was not expecting. Thoa could have—probably *should* have—kept it for himself for the next level. Instead, he sent it down with me, along with his hope. That is enough for me.

The knife is hidden from where I am. It could have landed anywhere, honestly. With Dante's body and the birds feeding on it lying near that same spot, I will need to get close to figure out where it landed.

I crouch low and move through the underbrush, ignoring the sharp pain in my side that hits me with each breath. As I draw near Dante, some of the birds turn toward me. There's a riot of color pecking into his dark skin—coral, cyan, sunflower yellow, sage, copper—their beaks stained with Dante's blood. These birds are smaller than the ones who fought over Sam but large enough to pose a problem if they all attacked at once. I stand to my full height and try to make myself big to scare them off. That works, or they decide I'm not worth the trouble when there's already a fresh meal in front of them.

Before I can stop myself, I glance at Dante's face. What is left of it. If Jai's knife hadn't already severed his carotid, the drop would have killed him instantly. His skull is cracked open, his face split in half with bones jutting out, and covered in so much blood it is unrecognizable. Bile rises in my throat; I turn my head to the side and heave up the contents of my stomach.

When all that is left is empty heaving, I spit away the taste of nutrition bricks and try to pull myself together. I'm too exposed like this. I need to get my stuff and get going while I still can.

Giving Dante a wide berth, I move to the wall where the rope once hung. I scan the area for the knife that should be waiting. I don't see it anywhere, but I know it is here. Thoa said so. A glance around tells me the birds haven't left Dante but that doesn't ease my mind. There are so many others who could swoop in at any time. The two big ones are probably still snacking on Sam. I'm not sure how long it takes to digest a man, or how much a bird can eat. He may not keep them busy for long, or he might fill them up for days.

I turn my eyes back to the ground again but I don't see the blade. I don't know why I need it, but in my gut I know I do. It's like a tiny voice whispering in the back of my head, telling me if I don't get the knife I'm as good as dead. I don't know if the voice is right, but it sounds confident enough to convince me to listen. Also I'm pretty sure that it is Cam's voice giving me steady wisdom, being the reasonable one of us who actually thinks things through rather than throwing herself off ropes in the middle of a level.

Kneeling down, I run my fingers through the grass in the hopes of feeling the metal I can't see. It's probably not the greatest idea; I don't know what kind of blade Jai had, and could cut myself if I'm not careful. I dart another look at the birds, wondering if they can smell blood. Or fear. With the gash in my shoulder and the unraveling ball of nerves in my stomach, I have plenty of both.

I crawl around for another few minutes without any luck. If it hit the wall it could have landed anywhere. I push myself to my feet, put my hands on my hips, and mutter a slew of creative curses under my breath. There's another option but I really didn't want to go this route.

Stepping toward Dante's body, I swallow hard at what I'm about to do and try not to let myself puke again.

"It's just his pockets," I say. "You don't need to look at any other part of him."

But I know I will. I can't stop my gaze from traveling to his ruined face, to the bones jutting from his broken body. The birds have eaten so much more of him than I thought they could in such a short period, and his ribcage is nearly picked clean.

"Damn," I say, scrubbing my hand down my face.

If it comes down to it, I could probably pull one of those bones free to use as a weapon. The thought wouldn't have phased the old Nova, but this version has a little more trouble reconciling what I can do with what I should do.

Some of the birds scatter when I get closer to Dante, but most stay right where they are. That's not exactly great news for me. If they aren't scared of me even a little, there's nothing stopping them from attacking the moment one of them gets a wild hair to do so. I can't think about it; this is the moment to live or die, and despite everything jumping from the rope says to the contrary, I want to live.

I plunge my hand into Dante's pocket. Empty. I can't force myself to reach over his body, so I walk around instead. A shiny-feathered emerald thing pecks at my hand as I reach into his other pocket and I haul back my fist and punch it square in the face. The birds around it flap their wings and chatter at me, but they pull back from where the other bird fell over. I didn't kill the thing, just stunned it. Hopefully it will deter the others for now.

Dante's other pocket is just as empty as the first. I move down to his boots and start unlacing them. They haven't been touched by the birds— too hard to get into, I guess. His left boot has nothing but bloody ankles and broken toes. Any hope I felt has gone, and I start to get my mind ready for the inevitable. I'm going to have to wield part of my fallen competitor.

Then my hand slides against cold metal in his right boot. My heart sings! I withdraw the rusty, battered blade as if it is a sacred artifact that must be preserved for future generations. I pop open a small, insignificant knife; in this moment, that sliver of knife feels like the most precious thing I've ever held.

I pull out Dante's boot laces and slip them into my pocket alongside the blade. As I turn from Dante's body to move back into the trees, a glint catches the corner of my eye. Of course I find it *after* searching the dead body. A dozen feet away I see the blade sent from the heavens with Thoa's blessing. I run toward it and am nearly there when a shadow passes overhead.

"Any suggestions?" I ask, hoping to hear the earpiece crackle to life. It doesn't. I touch my fingers to my ear and my heart plummets when I realize the tiny voice from the outside has been lost. It must've come loose when I fell.

I don't have time to look for it. I'm too busy trying to figure out how to not die.

I throw myself to the side, my body hitting the ground hard on my bruised ribs. The impact knocks the wind out of me. A massive mottled gray bird streaks past, claws outstretched. It's bigger than the other two giants I've seen so far.

Great, I think. *Just what I need.*

I push myself up and dive for Thoa's knife. I grab it and dive again, barely missing the talons that strike the ground where I was half a second ago. I roll toward the wall and push myself into a crouch. The bird is circling again, and I decide to let the wall do some of the work. Standing to my full height, I stretch out my arms and draw its attention. Its beady eyes seem to narrow as it careens toward me.

Steady, I think.

The seconds tick by as I stand there open-armed, waiting for the attack. My knees *want* to buckle but I manage to keep myself standing with sheer willpower. I have faced a variety of things that wanted to kill me through the years; so many creatures who became food for the Raiders, dozens of people who nearly ended me, and an entire space station full of pricks who wanted me dead. One bird isn't going to be the end of me.

The gray monster fills my entire vision. Every speck of green from the forest behind it is gone, every blade of grass has disappeared; even Dante's body has cleared away from my sight and all I can see is the shape looming ever closer. Staring so focused at it, I'm struck by how strangely beautiful the animal is. It has a long, slender neck that coils up from its body like a snake preparing to strike. The eyes are large and so glossy I feel like I could fall into them, like twin ponds. The thick black beak curves down and inward, a hook to dig into its prey.

I'm cutting it close. I know the timing has to be perfect.

"Three," I breathe.

The bird lets out a terrible squawk and the air around me shudders with the sound.

"Two."

Its talons rise up to grab me and I strain against the aching need in my belly to run.

I take a breath and say, "One."

I push off from the wall with as much strength as my legs can offer. The bird misses me by an inch, if that, as it crashes directly into the wall. The clang of its body hitting the metal echoes through the room and I smile at my victory. At least I won't have to deal with this thing again.

As I turn back to look at its crumpled form, I am sorely disappointed. And shocked, honestly. The bird must've swerved at the last second. It definitely hit the wall, and it definitely hurt itself, but not to the extent I expected.

What am I supposed to do now?

I reach for the daggers in my pocket as if those will help. Maybe if I get in close, but not close enough for its beak to reach me, I can stab it? There's already blood on one of the knives. The only thing left of Dante's life is crusted in the design set into the handle of the pocket knife.

It won't work, Cam says in the back of my head.

"Shut up," I mutter. "It's our only chance."

No it's not, you dolt. Stop thinking about killing it and look around you.

"You stop being so afraid of death that you can't do what needs done."

The rope, Nova. If you can't kill it, ride the thing.

My lips part to respond, but then I realize I probably look like a fool over here talking to herself. I have no doubt the star-people are watching. I wouldn't be surprised if the whole station had their eyes on me right now, glued to their screens as they root for my death. Besides, Cam is right. There are other options besides letting it recover and stab me with its many Nova-killing body parts.

I rush to the rope and start sawing through a section. I don't need a massive piece. If I can get it around the bird's neck, I can use one of the ladder rungs as a makeshift bridle and the rest of it as reins. Gods help me, I highly doubt I can get the rope in the thing's mouth for a bit, and even if I could, would it be able to snap through it?

I spare a glance at the bird and feel my chance slipping through my fingers. In the seconds I argued with myself, I lost the advantage of having it stunned. It isn't fully recovered though, so there's still a chance.

The rope separates and I lift the length I've cut, testing it in my hands. It's hard to guess what exactly I need for this—it's not like there's a lot of knowledge passed down in Raider camps about how to ride giant birds. I tiptoe toward the gray mass as it stretches each wing in preparation for flight.

I don't need to be close enough to touch it, I think. *Just close enough to throw my rope.*

And then what? The question gives me pause just as I'm about to toss the rope. I mount it? Can I do that? I've ridden a horse before but this thing has a completely different anatomy.

It stretches again and I know it's now or never. The bastard is about to take flight. Without so much as an internal countdown, I throw the ladder and hope with all my might that this works.

One of the rungs catches under the bird's beak and it swivels its head my way, one soulless black eye trained on me. I take two quick steps closer to it and shake the rope. It falls the rest of the way over the bird's head just as it turns and runs at me.

"No, no, no," I say, trying to dodge as it pecks at my midsection.

The beak catches my shirt and rips it, but misses my body. That was absolute luck and zero skill, and thank the gods for it. I don't think my ribs could have handled another blow.

The bird gives chase and I'm somehow able to hang onto the rope as it runs. With my bad shoulder, it feels like a miracle. It seems to realize that it will have the advantage if it takes to the air. With a sudden shift in direction the bird turns away from me and flaps its wings.

I run full force and throw myself at its back. My jump falls short—the thing is huge!—but I'm able to grab hold of some of the feathers on its back and pull myself up. My shredded shoulder burns with an intense pain that forces me to grit my teeth against it and pray I don't pass out.

The bird lurched forward from my impact but didn't stop its plan. We're airborne a few seconds after I crawl onto its back. I cling one-handed to the rope haphazardly around its neck as the bird banks to the side to try to throw me off. My thigh muscles clench tightly against the bird as I do my best to stay upright. It maneuvers again and again but can't shake me. I'm hurt and exhausted and I've almost been bird food more than once today, but I'm alive.

It rises higher, ignoring every pull of the rope. I can't direct the thing; the best I can do is hold on. Once the bird gives up on throwing me off and levels out, I adjust my position so I'm more comfortable. I can't move too much, despite the ache in my legs and the tension in my shoulders. It could shift at any moment and send me to the ground.

After a few minutes in this new position, I feel secure enough to look around and get my bearings. The room isn't nearly as big from up here as it appeared from the ground. It's huge in comparison to other levels, but having an overview like this lets me know it isn't unmanageable. If I end up on the ground again I'll have a much better idea of where to go. Not that I want to end up down there again if I can help it. Even knowing the lay of the land doesn't offer me a chance out of here unless I can spot an exit.

My eyes instinctively turn to the hole in the wall where the others crawled through to the next level. If the bird flies close enough, maybe I can make a jump for it.

It's like you want to die, the reasonable side of me thinks.

She has certainly made herself known during this level. I thought maybe I left that part of me on the station, returning to a simpler, brutal version of myself. Instead, it seems Cam has become part of me. She's the whispering part of my brain reminding me that I don't have to do dangerous, foolish things all the time. Sometimes I need to take a minute and think about things instead of acting on impulse, and sometimes my gut reaction is the only one that matters. There's room for both of us here if I am willing to listen.

"I don't want to die," I say. "I just don't see any other way out."

You haven't looked.

Fair point. As the bird soars around the perimeter of the room, I scan the walls for any sign of a door. They had to get this stuff in here somehow, and there's no way it all came in through that one little circle everyone crawled through. So, if there aren't any doors on the bottom…

My eyes turn upward. From the ground, it looked like a lovely blue sky on a clear summer day. But the star-people never expected someone to be this high. Those who *did* fly here would be too broken to notice what I see now.

The ceiling is painted blue for a background, but everything we saw from the ground was just a projection from the walkways above. I can see the devices clearly now that we're this close. The light pours from them and shows the poor suckers stuck below exactly what they want them to see.

The bird dips a bit and panic fills me immediately. I need to go higher, another fifteen feet or so, before I can get to the rafters. I pull hard on the rope around the bird's beautifully curved neck. Its head jerks back, and to my surprise, it flies upward toward the walkways that crisscross above.

When we're only six feet or so away, the bird lets out another violent squawk and pulls against the rope. Head down, it dives.

I dig my knees and boots into the body of the creature as I yank back with all my might on the rope. The bird fights me for a moment and there's a brief second when I think the ladder is going to come off its neck. As suddenly as it dives, it levels off and begins to rise again.

"What is wrong with this thing?"

I shouldn't have asked. As soon as I do, I see the dark outline in the corner of the room. As big as this thing is, there's something else here that scares it. I try to steer the bird to the other side of the room. Maybe there will be a better chance for both of us away from that corner.

We're only about three feet from the closest walkway when I feel the bird start to change course again. This might be my only chance. When Cam doesn't protest in the back of my head, I force myself to stand on the back of the creature. My legs are shaking for multiple reasons—the muscles burn from holding onto the bird, the wind buffets me and threatens to knock me over, the adrenaline from what I'm about to do is coursing through me, and the fear would put me on my ass if I let it. But I can't give my attention to any of those things. This is my only chance to get out of here, to return to Thoa and Hiro and the Raiders.

With them in mind and nothing else, I extend my arms above my head and jump.

CHAPTER
THIRTY-EIGHT
NOVA

My left hand scrapes against the bars above me but can't find purchase. I'm going to fall. I'm going to... No. My right hand catches the bar on the bottom of the catwalk. My body drops under the momentum of falling, putting all my weight on my right shoulder. I scream out in pain and throw my left arm back toward the walkway to relieve some of the pressure. The metal is so cold it stings my palm, but there is immense relief when my left hand takes most of the weight from my right.

I shimmy across the bar until I get close to where two of the walkways intersect. With every inch I move, I grow more certain that my right arm is going to fall off. Despite trying to use my left arm to hold most of my weight, the little bit I'm using my shredded shoulder is excruciating. The pain radiating through my body with each movement is unbearable; since the other option is death, I bear it. I kick my legs back and forth to get some momentum, swinging higher and higher until I'm able to pitch them onto the walk. My lower body safely in place, I release my handhold on the bar and pull myself the rest of the way onto the metal grates.

Panting and feeling like my arm is about to fall off, I lie there and rest. I can't believe I actually made it this far. When I said goodbye to Thoa on that rope, I thought it would be the last time I saw him. I hoped it wouldn't, I wanted to find a way out, but there was no way to know what would actually happen between dropping to the ground and now. *Now*. I'm far from safe, but I'm not on the ground beside Dante, and that's good enough.

After several minutes, I finally feel whole enough to sit up and look around. From here, the land below is quite beautiful. The viridescent vegetation blends emerald, olive, sage, grass, and sea green flawlessly into a landscape reminiscent of the real world. The gamemakers must study what it really looks like out there; there's no other way they could come up with something so close without ever having been there themselves.

Then again, who says they haven't been there? My dad was on the ground for years before the Chasseur came for him. Before they blew up my family. I shake away the wolves in my head, the snapping teeth that are always too close. If my dad was here for eight years illegally, and Krew managed to find his way to me by hacking his bracelet, surely some of the others visit here for various reasons. It's the only way a star-person would know how to create something so breathtaking after spending their lives surrounded by muted shades of gray.

But what about the birds? I've never seen anything quite like them. It's as if someone looked at a picture of a bird once, and created these creatures from the memory of that. I can't begin to think about *how* they created them, but here they are. Their wings catch the light as they soar below me, dotting the land with their vibrant colors. They are majestic and terrifying and absolutely not real birds. Yet here they are, existing right in front of me.

The dark shape is still looming in the corner across the room from where I rest. It doesn't look like it has moved an inch. The area is consumed by shadows, making it impossible to see what terror lurks there.

I tear my eyes away from the darkness, instead surveying the room for an exit. I'm certain there will be one, maybe more, reachable by the catwalk. I just have to find one that leads toward the next level. Getting to my feet, I spin in place until my eyes find the outline of a door. It isn't too far from me and I take a couple steps toward it before I look down to check the location of the level six entrance.

Of course it isn't on the same side. That would be too easy.

Based on where that door is, maybe there's one in the opposite position behind me. I turn, already knowing what I'll find there. Sure enough, there is a door on the side of the room where the other competitors entered the next level. And the walkway leads directly past the shadow in the corner.

I have to find out what the thing is. There's nothing else for it. There's a quiver in my gut at the thought. After seeing the way the other birds tore Sam in half, and staring at the bloodied beaks of those feasting on Dante, the possibility of facing down an even larger one is absolutely terrifying.

What else can I do? If I go backwards, the star-people will use it as a way to disqualify me. That may very well mean my death. Sure, I'm a citizen of the station, but that didn't save Alik on the last level. They could've gotten to her in time; instead, they watched her die. There's no reason to think they wouldn't want to watch me die, too, especially considering the trouble I've caused them over the last couple years. Gods, has it really been that long? How much time have they stolen from me?

My hands wrap around the bar in front of me, knuckles whitening at the thought of all that's happened since I found Krew in the desert. Before that, if I let myself truly think about what has been stolen from me and the rest of the on-worlders. They stole my father, killed my mother, and have watched us for entertainment so that we never truly have a moment to ourselves. It's impossible to know how long they've been doing that, how long they've monitored and chronicled our lives as if we were nothing more than fiction. I don't want to know.

And if I think further back, there are so many stories that I thought were fables and myths, like the tale of Zappho Curiosity and his plight when he fell from the stars. It wasn't a bedtime story, it was *real*. Somehow that story made it through generation after generation, and though it lost parts of it and others were made fantastical, I have no doubt that Zappho truly lived and tried to make things right for the people left on-world.

Maybe someday I'll be a story like Zappho. Today, though, *I'm* real, and I'm going to overcome whatever the star-people have in store so that I can make things better for the on-worlders.

I take a deep breath and release the bars in front of me. My hands sting from gripping them so hard, but that's the least of my trouble. I look around for anything that could be used as a weapon. If I have to fight that beast, the two knives in my pocket aren't going to do much damage. There's nothing useful or accessible nearby to help, so I resign myself to the inevitable—I'll have to outrun it.

I'm fast; well, I *was* fast. I've spent so much time on the station letting my body wither that I don't know my own stamina any longer. I was more out of breath than I should've been in the last few levels, and when I dodged the other bird it was closer than I liked. My instincts are taking too long to kick in. The longer I'm here, the better they get, but that doesn't mean my luck will continue to hold out.

I shake my head against the thoughts. It is just fear trying to talk me out of it, it's self-preservation rearing its inevitable head, its—

What if the door is locked?

It's Cam. She is the part of me that holds back, that thinks through her plans and works out possibilities and doesn't take chances. Cam sits in the back of my head and tries to keep me alive and safe. She was there long before I had a name for her; Cam was the one who made us sit a few more seconds in our hiding spot instead of chasing down a rabid wild cat in the forests, she learned the art of dodging when Rego taught us to fight, she turned us away from Thoa at the choosing ceremony. She saved us, she protected us, and she doomed us—over, and over, and over again. Now she tries to do it again. I don't know which of those things she is doing this time, and in the end it doesn't matter. Cam can't stop us from going forward. No one can.

I trace the pathways with my eyes while keeping the shadow in my periphery. Cam doesn't have time to object before I'm on the move toward the door. The metal clangs underfoot; I could slow my steps and try to slip past the lurking beast, but speed and surprise is the only thing on my side. If I run directly toward it, that could be enough to give me an edge.

The path turns left just ahead, putting me on an intercept course with the darkened corner. I don't stop to think about it. I cut left and keep running at full speed. My gaze is trained entirely on the shadows now but there still hasn't been the faintest movement from the space. I'm ten paces from the door and closing fast when a screeching caw reverberates from in front of me. The sound stops me short; I slide to a halt mere inches from the door, completely caught off guard by what *isn't* happening.

Despite the vicious sound and the giant shape that should certainly be rising to take flight and attack, nothing is happening. Nothing. Not if you're watching. If I saw this thing from below and heard the sound it makes, I would be shaking with terror. But I'm not down below, I'm staring directly at it. The fact that it hasn't moved an inch from its spot tells me way more about it than anything else could.

"It's a trick," I whisper.

Cam agrees.

The path I'm on takes us alongside the shape, but we're still several feet away from it and too far to make out more than just darkness. There is a different intersection back a few paces—one that I dismissed and ran right past—that would take me through the shadowed corner and into whatever the star-people are hiding back there. Because they're definitely hiding something.

I turn on my heels and head for the shadowed path. A speaker nearby crackles to life, and the announcer's voice comes out, muffled and unclear. I smile, knowing that whatever they're trying to say is likely meant to stop my progression. They don't want me to make this turn. I do it anyway.

After backtracking and turning on the new walkway, I pick up speed. No point slowing down now. I run past the shadow and around the side of it. Now that I'm here too, I can see that there is nothing there. Whether it is a trick of the light, or something set up that I can't see, I don't know. With the shadow gone from view I can see that it blocked another door. It's close enough to the level six door that I might go forward and join the others, but it was hidden for a reason, and could be so much more than what I expect.

What if—

"No," I say, shutting Cam down. "We're doing this."

"*Nova Kennedy,*" the voice crackles over the speaker. "*Turn around now and we will let you progress with the others.*"

"I don't think so," I call out.

My hand grasps the knob and I whip the door open. My eyes are met with a blinding white light and I throw my arm up to cover my face. I step inside the door and close it behind me. Spots blur my vision and try to blink them away. Before I can get a grasp on my surroundings, I hear a sharp intake of breath on my right and a soft voice says, "Hello, Nova. Welcome to the end of everything."

CHAPTER
THIRTY-NINE

NOVA

An elderly woman sits beside a flashing panel of lights and levers. She's petite, probably only coming up to my chest if she stood up, her bones prominent in her face and hands. Her gray hair is cut short and shaped to stand straight up in the middle of her head. Sharp green eyes watch every twitch of my hands, every turn of my head, forgetting everything else happening around us.

On the wall behind her are display screens showing the other competitors. In the center of the screens is one that has gone blank, the words *Please stand by* flashing across them.

"Is that one mine?" I ask, nodding toward the dark screen.

The woman smiles and says, "Viewers don't want to see how the sausage is made."

I have no idea what she's talking about but I say nothing. I give a quick glance around the rest of the room. There are three other stations set up like hers throughout the room, but she's the only person here.

"Everyone else left when they realized you were coming," she says, a crease forming between her brows. "They were scared."

"Not you?"

She slowly shakes her head. "You don't kill without a reason."

"You don't think I have a reason to kill you? I'm sure I could think of something."

"Not really. Not if you understand why I'm here."

I can't deny my curiosity. "And why is that?"

"Because I'm as much a prisoner here as you are. Most of us are. We aren't wielding weapons and fighting through mazes, but we live and die by the trials just like the competitors."

"Bullshit."

She smiles. "No shit. Most of the time we get signed on when we're too young to know better. They train us and give us a trade within their structure, they pay us well enough to have a life that isn't built around struggling for food, and in return we watch people murder each other over and over and over again."

"That last part is where things get bad."

"I know. Trust me, I do. I've worked in this room for forty-eight years. It gets moved to a different part of the tower each time, but it's always here. And so am I, watching dozens of lives snuffed out like they're nothing. It's awful."

"If you hate it so much, why are you still here? Find another job."

"Doing what?" she asks. "You've been out in this world. And up in theirs. Was any part of it easy for you? Could you just walk away and change everything because you felt like it?"

"So, you don't want to change because it's hard. When did that become a good enough reason?"

"It's not *hard*, Nova, it's impossible."

"I'm in the middle of changing my life right now. It's not impossible."

"And how is that going?" she asks.

I purse my lips together before conceding, "Not great. But at least I'm doing something."

"And I'm happy you get the chance to do that. I hope your story makes its way out and you become a legendary folk hero who shows the masses that change is possible. In the meantime, I have a family to feed. So tell me, are you prepared to stab me with the knives in your pocket because I want my granddaughter to eat?"

"Of course not."

She nods. "That's what I thought. You're not here to murder us all, no matter what lies make their way onto the feeds; you just want to survive."

"Wait," I say, my brows furrowing. "What do you mean by that?"

"Oh, are we finally done with the stabby part and we can move to the part where you get some answers? It took a lot longer than I expected."

I smile at the woman. Despite being on opposite sides of the battle lines, I respect the way she says what she's thinking and isn't afraid to risk pissing me off. Apparently she's the only one of them who isn't.

"What's your name?"

"You don't need it."

I shrug. "I guess not, but it puts me at a disadvantage since you know mine."

"I'd prefer for you to be at a disadvantage."

"Fair enough. Why did you call this place the end of everything?"

"It's where information goes to live or die. It's the end of truth or the end of lies—whatever we make of it. This is where we decide what people get to believe."

"What exactly do you do here?"

"It's the hub for all of the footage that gets shot for star-people consumption, including what they will see of the trials. Everything that gets recorded comes through here on a delay, so we can pause a feed before the viewers see something they shouldn't."

"The trials aren't live?"

"Hell no. There's too much that can go wrong on a live broadcast. I mean, there are people who see the whole thing live, but they're just grunts like me who are trained to flag and block content. The viewers see an edited program condensed to an hour or so. If it's a particularly spicy game they might split it into a two-night special. For the most part, the star-people have very little idea what actually happens in the trials. I thought you'd know that after being up there."

"My time there has been... fractured. And I didn't spend much time watching the screens. I tried to avoid them, honestly."

"I don't blame you. The stuff they watch for entertainment..." she trails off, shaking her head.

There's a few seconds of silence as we let those dark images fill our thoughts, then each shake our heads to dispel them. My mind goes back to something else she said, something that puts a spark of hope in my chest. "You see *everything* happening in the trials?"

"I do."

"Everyone?"

She gives me a sad smile but says, "They're all fine."

"All?"

"Thoa, and Hiro," she says, then adds, "and Bets."

"I don't give a—"

"Sure you don't," she interrupts. "None of it was real, it meant nothing, blah, blah, blah."

I press my lips into a thin line. Maybe I *should* kill her after all.

"Don't look at me like that," she says.

"Don't pretend to know me and what I've been through and I'll stop thinking about killing you."

She shakes her head. "I know more than you realize. I was the one editing the recordings of you two lovebirds. She might've deceived you, might've hurt you, but she *did* love you. And I think you loved her, even if you can't admit it anymore."

"It wasn't real."

"Except the parts that were," she says.

"There were too many lies to sort through. As far as I'm concerned, it was all just a means to an end for her."

"But that's also a lie."

"Then it will be in good company."

I am done talking to her about this, and she sees that by the expression on my face.

She gives a terse nod and asks, "What else do you want to know?"

"You record on- and off-worlders?" She nods, and I press on. "Who watches the star-people?"

"Other star-people. The ones who are higher up and think themselves important, mostly. They fill their feeds with things they shouldn't see, things that people should be able to keep private. Moments and memories that should belong to no one but those involved."

"Is anything off limits to them?"

"No," she says, clenching her jaw. "Their people don't know for sure that they're being recorded, but plenty of them suspect it."

"If they knew for sure, maybe they'd do something about it. An uprising."

"You think they don't watch for rebellion?" she asks.

"And they don't want to do anything? They don't want to fight?"

"Like this?" she asks.

She switches one of the screens from Leah's pinched, panicked face to a shot of the space station. There are bodies everywhere—dead and alive. So *alive*. The corridor is full of Raiders and star-people alike. I'd seen a little of what was happening when I was there, but this is next level. The star-people are *helping* the Raiders. They're escorting the Raiders through the halls, showing them the right paths and how to free prisoners on the station, and they're picking up weapons of fallen Raiders and standing shoulder-to-shoulder with them. It's beautiful.

"It's amazing," I whisper.

"A revolution. But we are two of only a handful who will ever see this. And then it will be forgotten."

"What?" I ask, jerking my gaze from the screen to her. "There's no way people will forget this."

The woman sighs, and I see the pain in her wrinkled face. "You'd be surprised how often people forget their hard-fought battles."

"Not this, though. Not with everything that has happened."

"Sweet child, this isn't the first time the star-people have stood up against the tyranny on the station. It's not the first time on-worlders have made it up there either, though they've never gone up in such force. It gets wiped away, the memories turn into myths."

"How can that be? People will be talking about this for generations. There's no way it can become just a story."

"Stories are what make us, Nova," she says. "And stories are easier to temper when you add something outrageous to them. The more unrealistic the tale becomes, the easier it will be to spread. The more the exaggerated version spreads, the fewer people will believe the truth of what happened."

"They can't do that!"

"They can, and they will. It's happened before and it will surely happen this time as well. I'm guessing you'll have magical powers in the version that makes its rounds, once this whole thing gets cleaned up. Or maybe you'll breathe fire and turn into one of the great lizards in the fairytales."

"A dragon?" I ask. "But those are just…"

The woman nods. "They are now, but some version of them made it into dozens of stories through the ages. How could that happen if they were never real?"

"And us, will we be like that? People will hear our stories and not believe all the things we've done?"

"You will become a dragon."

I let her words sit in the air between us while the revolution fills the screens around us. There are too many dead to let this become a myth. It is wasteful. Those people who sacrificed themselves for freedom, who gave their blood to rescue others from oppression, should have their stories told. They should be *more* than stories. If I let them fade away like those before then I'm no better than the star-people. I can't accept that fate for any of us.

"I will become a dragon," I say, meeting her gaze. "And I will show them my claws and teeth. I will show them my fire, and burn down everything their vile hands have built. If they wish for a myth, I will create for them a story that cannot be forgotten."

CHAPTER
FORTY
NOVA

Although the woman doesn't want to help me, she also doesn't try to stop me. She has me pull out my knife and hold it up to her neck while she raises her hands in defense, but that's about it. She says the cameras in the room still work, she thinks, but the sound has been on the fritz for a few months; anyone who watches the footage will know she and I talked but not about what, and it will look like I threatened her. I don't mind the deception. We're all doing what we must to survive.

I rip out the cords from the panel on the wall as she directs and cut through them with my knife. Bashing the panels is next. Once the room is thoroughly destroyed, I prepare to leave. There are two more hubs like this on the station, she tells me, but this will sever the main connection to the planet, disrupting recording, broadcasting, and communication. It won't stop them permanently, but it will be a helluva mess until I can come up with something more permanent. We'll have to address the others later; for now, I need to get back to my people.

My hand is on the knob to leave the room when I look back at her. The woman's hands are still raised, still holding up the falsehood. I nod at her and say, "Thank you for your wisdom."

"I gave you nothing but words."

"You didn't have to give me anything," I say. "You didn't have to help me at all."

She shrugs. "It was selfish, really. Figured it was time to give myself a way out of this mess. You're just a convenient excuse."

I give her one last smile, then turn the handle and leave. I hope she makes it out of this place before I burn the whole thing down.

Outside the door is another catwalk. This one isn't high above a level like the last one; instead, it sits a mere ten feet or so from the top of the other level. I can see my friends crawling around some strange sort of maze. From my vantage point their path is clear, but the intersections are frequent and have no discernable pattern from where they are. It looks as if they are surrounded on all sides by some sort of thick gooey material that clings to them as they crawl through.

Hiro is near the end but approaches an intersection that splits in six directions. Thoa is still lingering at the back of the maze as if he is waiting for me to follow behind him at any moment. The others move around the middle like bugs crawling in the earth.

The catwalk goes through another door. I could go to the next level and the one after, ending this whole thing as the winner. But what happens to the others if I do that? Instead, I climb over the railing and lower myself until I'm hanging by my fingers over the sixth level. I take a deep breath and release my grip, dropping the few feet to the clear surface of the maze.

Below me, Hiro jerks at the noise of my fall and looks around fruitlessly. They must have something preventing them from seeing me, despite me seeing them. That's okay though, because he can hear me. I move ahead of him and stand over the path he needs to take. I jump. He jolts again at the sound but seems to take the hint. Hiro crawls toward me, and I bounce a couple more times to encourage him to follow. When he reaches the end of the maze, a small door opens and light cascades into the sixth level. Hiro crawls through and enters level seven.

The light was bright enough to draw Bets and Leah's attention. They were close enough to see it, and possibly to hear me jumping. That's fine —they can figure the rest out for themselves. I walk back toward where Thoa is struggling to force his broad shoulders through. The tight space is probably hardest on him. Hiro is muscular, but Thoa is massive. He could pick Hiro up and toss him around if he wanted. Honestly, the thought is a pleasing distraction in the right context…

A few feet in front of him, I jump up and down a few times. He doesn't jerk like Hiro, but by the tilt of his head I'm certain he heard me. He moves slowly, forcing himself through whatever surrounds them. Though his progress is steady, I want him to move faster. I don't know what happens to whoever is last, but I think of Borah from the first time we came through the trials. I promised my allegiance to her, only to watch her get left behind on the level that was flooding, simply because she was last.

I tap the path ahead of him with more urgency, trying to prod him forward. He doesn't seem to take the hint. Or maybe he's moving as fast as he can. The space is clearly not meant for someone of his size.

From my periphery I see Jai crawling toward me. They're using my guidance too, and there's nothing I can do to stop it without compromising Thoa. We're about halfway across when I see a light cascade behind me. Someone else has crossed into the next level. My gut wrenches at the knowledge that he's one step closer to being last.

We keep going. I stomp, Thoa follows. There is no pause in his reaction, no hesitation when I lead him to the next tunnel. I wonder if he knows it's me.

The light comes up again after only a few minutes. There's only Thoa and Jai left. And me. I look around the room and wonder how I'm supposed to get out of here now. I can't get into the maze, so I can't go through the same door they do. And I jumped from the catwalk like a fool; it might be low enough for me to jump down, but there's no way I can jump ten feet up to get back on it.

Thoa is paused and I realize I haven't given him the next instruction. I back up a few feet and jump. He's nearly there now; so is Jai. One more intersection for Thoa and he's in the clear. Then I just have to figure out how to get out myself.

He's turned onto the last part of the maze now. Jai is close, but Thoa will make it out before them. Now that he's safe, I need to find my own way out. There's a door above, but no clear way to get there. I trace my fingers along the wall, searching for a handhold and finding nothing but smoothe, cold metal.

"There has to be a way," I mutter.

I rush around the edge of the room, my fingers tracing the wall for anything that might give me enough purchase to get back to the walk-way. When I'm almost back to where I started and every ounce of hope has been thoroughly dashed, I feel a tiny crevice in the wall that gives me pause. Normally I would have ignored it because it is so small, but at this point there is nothing else to check. That small crack might be my only chance.

Digging my fingertips into the space, I give my all to trying to pry it open. There isn't the slightest movement, the tiniest budge in the fissure. Despair wells up and sticks in my throat, a sob I won't release. This was the last possibility, and now it is nothing.

They made it out though, thanks to you, Cam says.

I hate her. I hate the logical, patient way she thinks about things and recognizes the good things coming out of the situation. I hate that she is right, and she is giving me one last thing to be happy about before I sit myself down to die. For that is what I will do now that all else has failed. Thoa and Hiro will go on, and that has to be enough. That has to be...

"Yooooooo, girl," Hiro's voice calls from above.

I look up and over to the open door in the wall that is halfway between me and the walkway. Hiro is hanging out, one leg inside wher-ever he is, and one hovering over me. Light cascades from behind him and a larger figure looms in the background.

"What are you doing?" I ask, a laugh bubbling up at the sight of him.

"Looking for you. I found a door."

"I see that."

"You wanna come with us or do you have some dangerous plans we don't know about?"

I laugh. "I want to come with you."

A hand grabs Hiro by the shoulder and pulls him back into the room. Thoa drops to the ground where Hiro had been and reaches down to pull me up. I grip his open palm and walk up the wall as Thoa hoists me through the door. We land in a heap, breathing heavily but giggling like children.

After a moment, Thoa stands and helps me to my feet. He pulls me tight against his chest and wraps his arms around me until I can barely breathe. Who needs breath when I have him? What is air in comparison with the feel of him pressed against me?

A moment later he pulls back, but only far enough that he can grasp my face in his hands and press his mouth to mine. It is ferocious, achingly so, forcing every ounce of relief we both feel into this too-brief embrace.

"Time to go," Hiro says, coming up beside us.

We break our kiss and I turn my face to my friend. He's beaming down at me with his megawatt grin and I feel my own smile curve up to mimic his. "Where to, Moose?"

Hiro shrugs. "Some ridiculous level to conquer before they'll let us leave, Squirrel. You know how it is."

"I do," I say, a heavy sigh falling from me.

"Let's go kick some ass then."

As we turn, my gaze lands on Bets. She's standing at the edge of the room, or whatever this area is, her arms folded across her ample chest. A dull throb aches in my gut at the sight of her. The old lady was right, even if I didn't want to admit it; I have a lot of anger toward Bets, a lot of rage for the things that happened, but that's not the only thing I feel for her. Even now, even after everything, I'm so, so glad she's still alive. I've absolutely thought about murdering her, but in truth I don't want to face what feelings might come if I lose her. I have no idea what will happen if we all make it through, either; that's a problem for future Nova.

She nods my way and says, "Told them you weren't dead."

"Yeah?"

"You're too stubborn to die when it's easy. When you go out it'll be the most complicated, unnecessary, violent act ever committed. And everyone will talk about what a hero you were." She rolls her eyes. "You're so predictable."

The corner of my lip lifts into a smile at her teasing, but I don't get a chance to respond before Thoa huffs and says, "You're wrong."

"She's just messing with me," I say, putting my hand on his forearm.

"I'm absolutely serious," she says, barely holding back her smile.

"When she dies many years from now, it will be as a gray-haired grandmother, surrounded by all who love her, in a house near a lake where fields are trampled by children running and goats grazing and lives well lived. She will not die until she has rested, until she has been rewarded for all she has done, until she decides there is nothing left to do but move on to the next adventure in the great beyond."

Bets brows raise at Thoa's words and she scoffs. "If that's how you think she wants to die—or live, for that matter—then we know two very different versions of Nova."

"You don't know her the way you think you do," he says.

She smirks. "Neither do you."

"Alright kids, that's enough," Hiro says. "We can talk about Nova dying after we get out of here. For now, let's figure out this level before the others finish the tower and we get stuck here."

Thoa's lips pucker and he gives a terse nod. Bets' smirk never fades, even as she turns to lead us back down a set of stairs and into the main portion of the seventh. The new area is below the last two. It appears that the bird level and tech hub were at the top of the tower, and now they've started leading us back down into the tower. The setup is strange, or at least different from the last time I was here. The previous levels were more narrow than I remember them being, so maybe they've aligned each new challenge side by side to offer more space to the bird level. When everything is recorded and cut to make it more entertaining, I guess it doesn't really matter how the tower is set up.

This new level is crossed through the middle with walkways, just like the top of the bird level. Everything is black or dark gray metal, and looks so similar it is hard to tell where the floor, walkways, and ceiling begin and end. I can't see anything below the walkways, but that doesn't mean there's nothing there. With all the colors bleeding together, it's impossible to decipher one thing from another.

The four of us stand in front of the walkways for a moment, silence surrounding us as we gather our thoughts. It takes longer than it should for me to look up and realize part of the group isn't with us.

"Where are Leah and Jai?" I ask.

The others look around at one another as if they hadn't realized the absence either.

"Leah definitely made it out of the sixth," Bets says.

"Jai was right behind me when we started looking for a way to get to Nova," Thoa says.

His words pique my interest and I ask, "How did you know it was me?"

"Who else would lead us out?" Thoa asks.

Bets says, "None of the gamemakers would interfere. My people are probably still trying to figure out where I am. And everyone else is dead."

"It could've been a trick," I say.

Hiro shrugs. "Didn't matter to me, as long as I got out of that goo."

Thoa nods. "It was hard to breathe in there."

"I couldn't tell what it was," I say.

"None of us could. It was pitch black, and there was something sticky along the walls. Every inch we crawled we were surrounded by the stuff, clinging to us." Bets shivers and adds, "It was disgusting to touch, but not being able to see made it so much worse."

"My size made it impossible to navigate. I didn't think I would find my way out," Thoa says, his face darkening.

"You were the farthest from the exit," I say.

"I tried to call for you," Hiro says. "A few times. You must've been too far back to hear me."

Bets says, "I think the goo dampened sound. I only barely heard Nova when she was guiding us out."

Heat burns in my cheeks at her words. I wasn't leading *her* out. I'm glad she made it through, but if Hiro hadn't been near her I'm not sure I would have gone out of my way to help her. I'm not going to take the time to dissect that particular scenario; I can't know for sure what I would've done, so there's no point giving it room to percolate in my mind.

"They both heard you though, and both made it out thanks to you. We all did," Hiro says.

A speaker in the corner crackles to life and my stomach clenches. I took out the control center for the footage, but the speakers transporting the host's voice into this place are still live. I wonder if the cameras are still transmitting anything to the station and if they can see where we are and what we're doing. Based on what the woman told me, I don't think they should be able to see what's happening unless they have a direct feed.

"*Back from the dead, our Raider in residence is still finding ways to cause trouble,*" the announcer says. "*She fell from the rope but managed to survive the bird level, and though we couldn't see her during that last level, we could see her handiwork as she led the others out of our sticky maze. Personally, I was hoping to see someone lose it in that last one, but Nova got in the way of that. Is she the hero or the villain? Only viewers can decide.*"

And it sounds like they *do* have a direct feed. But hopefully my damage is preventing this from being recorded or broadcast out beyond those working to transition this mess into entertainment.

"Oh gods," Bets says, rubbing a hand over her tired face. "Alistair, you left the tower channel open while you're filming an intro."

"What does that mean?" Thoa asks.

"They're setting up the tv show details," I say as the speaker crackles again. "Because our lives are nothing but entertainment for the star-people. Right, Bets? We're expendable once we're not amusing to them."

Bets presses her lips into a thin line and the glint in her eyes turn hard. "That's not fair."

"We don't do fair."

"I'm well aware. If we did, our lives would be a helluva lot different. But you and I both know you were never just an amusement for me. You were so much more. You *are* more."

The air between us is thick with all the things we've never said. Not as these people who aren't preoccupied with lies, at least. We owe each other so much more than what we can give here, now. We'll never give each other the things we should; we don't know how.

"I believe you," I say, my voice barely more than a whisper. My mind races with the things she did to me under the guise of love when I was in no position to consent. She still doesn't see anything wrong with what she did, but I don't think I can ever forget it. But this isn't the place for that talk. This is my chance to fix things for everyone else. "Your love for me means nothing when you treat my people the way you do."

"You act like this is my fault, but the tower was in place before my family had anything to do with it. Since I took over, I haven't done anything to your people."

"You haven't done anything *for* them, either."

"What am I supposed to do? They live down here, we live up there, and there's not much room for an in-between."

"Make room," I yell, my voice echoing through the level. "Leaving things the way they've been isn't good enough anymore. Not for us, not for you, not for anyone."

"I can't change hundreds of years of tradition overnight," she says.

"Maybe not, but you can do *something*. Start with small changes. For star's sake, just *start*."

She swallows hard, her wide eyes pleading with me as she works out what she wants to say. I give her the time to gather her thoughts as we listen to Alistair doing the next commercial. Yet again, they don't seem to realize we can hear them.

Finally, Bets says, "I don't know how to start. I'm barely hanging on as the Règle. There are so many people with pull, so many with power, and they all want something from me. More than one is actively plotting my death to try to take power for themselves. No matter what I do, I'm disappointing someone who can destroy me."

I take a step toward her and put my hand on her cheek. Her eyes flash up to mine and in her gaze I see the fear she's been living with despite doing her damnedest to hide it.

"What do *you* want?" I ask.

There is no hesitation as she says, "To help people."

I nod. "Who can do that better than the Règle?"

"Anyone would be better at it than me."

"You didn't ask for this. Remember? You were happy at the *Dirty Onion*, living a life out of the spotlight. But the moment you were thrown into this, it became your responsibility to stop living for yourself and start living for the people you can save. You have an opportunity to do something amazing. You just have to take a step; the people will follow."

She shakes her head. "They'll follow you."

"And I'll follow you," I say. "If you are good, if you deserve my trust, if you try to be more than what the Règleship has always been, I'll follow you."

Bets puts her hand over the one resting on her cheek and twines our fingers together. She closes her eyes briefly and takes a deep breath, then says, "I don't want you to follow me; I want you to be by my side.

Always. When I asked you to marry me, it was real. It's the truest desire of my heart."

Behind me I hear Thoa growl, but he makes no move to interfere. I can't imagine what he feels as he listens to this; I *won't* imagine it. I am sorry he has to hear these things, but this moment is for me and Bets.

"I will follow," I say, as gently as I can. "It is the most I can give you."

"You love me," she says, voice cracking.

I nod, not trying to deny it. "It isn't enough. Not when I've seen the darkness in you."

"Everyone has a dark side."

She's right. I know she's right. But what I've seen in her... I just don't think I can ever *unsee* it.

When I don't respond, she says, "There's light, too."

"Show me. Show my people."

"And then we can be together?" she asks.

I shake my head. "This isn't a recipe to win me back, it's a chance for you to redeem yourself and your office. Use this to prove to *you* that there is light, not me."

She glances behind me to Thoa and says, "You're really happy with him?"

"I'm standing right here," he says through gritted teeth.

"Yeah, you're kinda hard to miss, big guy. But I truthfully don't give a single shit where you are or what you're doing. I want to know if she's happy. I want to know if this is truly the life she sees for herself. Does she actually think she's going to end up at that little farm you talked about? Could she be happy with a life like that?"

"Of course she could," he says.

Bets crosses her arms and says, "Stop answering for her. She doesn't need you to do anything but stand there and look pretty. Nova is her own woman, and just because she's kissed you a few times doesn't mean you own part of her."

Hiro raises a finger in the air and says, "To be fair, we've all kissed her."

I roll my eyes and say, "Not the time."

"Not the time for any of this, probably," he says. "Leah and Jai are still missing, possibly already moved to the next level, and if we keep standing here debating your love life and potential future death, we may end up dying here while they move on."

"Good point," I say.

"Great point," he says, smiling. "Also, it's weird that everyone is in love with you instead of me and I can't listen to it anymore. I'm ready to get out of here so I can get back to having my own love life drama."

"That makes more sense," I say.

Whatever moment I was having with Bets is over now anyway. I hope she heard me. I hope it matters. The message she was trying to give me was heard too; when this is over and we are safe, I'll do my best to think through what she said and figure things out. I know I love Thoa, and I know I love Bets, but they represent two different parts of me and two futures where neither is completely right.

"We need to cross," Thoa says.

"Obviously," Bets mutters.

"I cannot handle listening to the two of you arguing for the rest of the time we're here. Let's split up and see if we can find a way out of here," Hiro chimes in, his voice too cheerful and bordering on frustrated. He puts a hand on Thoa's shoulder and guides him toward the walkway.

"I'm not leaving Nova with her."

"Nova can do whatever she wants, dude," Bets says.

Thoa takes a step toward us and I reach forward, placing both of my hands on his chest. "I'm fine. I'll *be* fine. Go with Hiro."

"You can't trust her."

I bite back the response I want to give him, reminding him of the time we were apart, the lies he told, the hurt he caused. There was a time not that long ago that I didn't trust him either. But I always loved him, and in letting that return from the depths where I'd buried it I found a way to trust him again.

"It has nothing to do with her," I say. "And everything to do with me. Trust *me*, believe in *me*. I'll see you on the other side."

He looks down on me, his azure gaze darkening a fraction before he nods and says, "As you wish, Little Star. Be careful." He pauses for a moment as if deciding whether or not to say whatever has crossed his mind, then he adds, "I love you."

Thoa turns to leave before I can say another word, and I watch his back as he and Hiro go to cross the walkway on the right.

"I love you, too," Bets says quietly from beside me. "In case you didn't know."

"I know," I say. It is my answer for both of them. It is not enough, but right now while my brain is reeling from all that was just said, it is all I have to give.

CHAPTER
FORTY-ONE
NOVA

Bets and I take the far left walkway. There's no strategy to it, no reason to choose it instead of following Thoa and Hiro, or to take it instead of the central path aside from wanting something solid and unchanging at my side. It is a meaningless decision, like so many others we have made, but in the end could determine life or death for us. What a metaphor for this place and the world at large.

"Do you want me to go first?" Bets asks.

My brows furrow. "You have far less fighting experience."

Her lips twitch into that familiar smirk again. "I can't stab you in the back if I'm in front of you."

"I hadn't even considered that," I say.

"Well that's progress, I think."

I shrug. "Or I'm more naive than either of us realized."

"No, honey, I know how naive you are."

I hear the teasing in her tone and smile in response. It has been far too long since there was a moment between us where we could joke with one another. Our relationship was full of playful banter in the beginning, when things were easier and there weren't so many lies and murders between us. It strikes me then how wild it is that casual murder between friends and lovers is a *thing*. How many people have died—good or bad, right or wrong—while we've been trying to figure this out?

"It's nice to see you smile," she says.

I look at her for what feels like an eternity before saying, "We really messed each other up."

"One hundred percent."

"We can't keep doing this to each other. No matter what happens after this place, we have to be better to each other."

"*For* each other, too," she says.

"Bets..." I say, trailing off. I could try telling her there is no "us" after this, but I don't feel like lying to either of us. I don't know what will happen. My mind tells me it would be foolish to return to her after all I've seen; hell, I've even said those words to her. But the truth is I don't know if my heart will let me walk away from her.

She says, "I want to be better, and as much as I'd like to lie and say I'm doing it for me and for those I can help, the truth is my heart is just screaming to be someone you could love again. Maybe eventually it will be more than that, but right now it's the best I can do. I will be better for you."

I think I want that too.

Still, there's so much more I want for her that is bigger than the both of us, but if this is what she can give right now, it has to be enough. I muster my best smile and say, "It's a start."

With a nod I turn away from her and start down the path. There's no way I can let her go first. I'm sure Thoa will give me a stern talking to when we get across and I'll listen to a full lecture about how I put myself at risk unnecessarily, but I just can't see this going any other way. If something comes at us, I need to be in the front to face it head on. If he doesn't understand that, he doesn't truly know me.

I take a few steps and within seconds the space looms up around me. It was impossible to see from the starting place, because everything here is the same dark color blending everything together, but this isn't just a path leading across the space. It is a maze, deceptively disguised and patterned in a way to make it look straightforward. After only a few paces, I can see that there will be nothing easy about this.

Glancing to the far side of the room, I look for Thoa and Hiro but they are hidden from view. There are hills and valleys of metal and plastic and whatever else this stuff is. Wherever they are, I hope they weren't as surprised as I am by this. I feel like a fool for thinking it would be anything other than a mess.

Bets hand presses against the small of my back and I jump, surprised by her touch.

"It's okay," she says. "Don't get overwhelmed. We can make it through this."

I swallow back the panic that had built in my throat. "I don't know what I thought this would be."

"There's nothing special about it. It's just one more level to get through."

"It's always just one more thing to get through. I'm ready to be through it. All of it."

"Then take another step," she says. "Every step gets you a little closer to being done with all of this. That was our agreement."

I bite my lip, thinking back to the words we shared before getting stuck in the trials again. She promised to let me and my people go. Bets said she would release anyone who wanted to go on-world. "No one else heard that agreement."

"Guess you'd better make sure I live through this then."

Her smile is thin but true. She will honor the agreement we made, but there is no agreement without her.

"You could tell the cameras now."

"It wouldn't matter. They'll just cut it out before it screens to the masses. No one would be the wiser."

It's true. After all I learned from the old woman in the hub, there is no doubt that what Bets says is true. I wish she was lying, or that I had the disillusionment that she was. After what I did in the equipment room, I don't know if anyone would see it anyway. Maybe those in the control room, the announcer, whoever is watching a direct feed. I don't know who that is or if hearing her words would matter to them. While she's here, she might as well be a worthless planet dweller like the rest of us.

"Let's get you out of here, Règle. I'd like my people freed by dinnertime."

We pick our way through the maze a few steps at a time. Occasionally we hear a sound like metal scraping metal; often, it is accompanied by a low growling sound, and a few times by a roaring. We know there is something prowling in the low spaces below us, but we haven't seen anything yet.

In the distance, I hear a scuffle. It is impossible to know whether it involves Thoa and Hiro or not. It could be the beasts below. There *are* beasts, I am certain. I wasn't sure at first, but now I have no doubt. I have glimpsed claw marks gouging the walls below us, mere feet from where we stand.

As we circle around a pillar of unknown material, I stop short. My stomach plummets at the same time bile surges into my throat. I turn back toward Bets and close my eyes but the horror of what I just saw still shines behind my eyelids.

Bets wraps her arms around me and I lean into her shoulder. I feel her tiptoeing to look over my shoulder; her body convulses against me at what she sees. We stand like this for a few minutes, neither finding words to comfort the other.

When she finally pulls back and our eyes meet, she says, "We need to go around them."

I nod. I don't know why the sight of Jai's body is so distressing. I have seen death before, I have killed. My body has been covered in blood from head to heel. But the sight of Jai slashed to ribbons, their entrails strewn across the path ahead of us, and bloody paw prints painting the ground around them... It is too much.

"Do you want me to take the lead?" she asks.

I do, I desperately do, but I shake my head. I am supposed to protect her. "I'm fine. Let's go."

I try to step into as little of their blood as possible, but the stickiness clinging to my boots as we move past Jai is unmistakable.

We go on for several minutes in silence. There is no scraping, there is no roaring; the only sound is the constant thrumming of my blood pounding in my ears. I need to calm down. In this condition, I am useless against whatever might come at us.

Breathe, I think. *Do your counts.*

I think of Rego and the way he taught me to center myself. Immediately I regret that I haven't asked anyone about him. I swallow back the emotion that rises, again, as I realize that I don't know if Rego is even alive at this point.

Out of nowhere, Bets slams into me and knocks me to the ground. We skid to a stop, my back scraping hard against something jagged. I reach back and feel the warm blood on my skin.

"What the hell?" I ask, shoving Bets off me.

She sits up, her face filling my entire field of vision as she says, "Run."

Before I can register what is happening, I watch a blade slide across Bets' throat. A river opens up and flows down the front of her as Bets' life fades away in an instant.

My eyes shift from her pale countenance to the woman standing behind her. Leah. She's standing above me, one hand holding Bets by the hair and one holding her bloody knife. She's breathing hard, her eyes wild with an animalistic panic, and I know there's no coming back from this for her. I've seen Raiders overcome with bloodlust, their souls marred by the lives they've taken, and madness filling their eyes. I see that on Leah now.

"I'll make it quick," she says.

I believe her. She killed Bets, and Alik before her, and possibly others that I didn't see. She was quick and efficient for both of them. Leah does not kill them because she enjoys it, and she does not allow them to suffer. She kills because it is the only way out for her, and she will do whatever she must to survive this place.

Leah takes a step toward me and I scoot away from her. My back presses against the pillar behind me and I can go no farther.

"I'm not ready to die." My voice comes out as a whimper.

"That's truly unfortunate," Leah says. "Because I am going to kill you."

She lunges for me, blade in hand. I roll to the side. Her arm jerks forward and hits the tower I was pressed against, and she lets out a groan.

"Hold still," she growls between clenched teeth.

"Screw you," I yell.

"You're making this harder than it has to be. Just let me kill you. You deserve this and you know it."

The words surprise me with how much they resonate. I *do* think I should die. I *do* think I deserve it. But that doesn't mean I'm going to roll over and let her kill me. If this is my time to die, she's going to have to give it her all. Because I have too much to do when I get out of here just to give up now.

Leah throws herself at me again. I jerk backwards away from her, throwing myself toward the edge of the platform. Fear squeezes my heart as I think about the condition in which I saw Jai's body. Whatever did *that* to them is down below. Going down there is not an option.

I scramble to pull myself away from Leah as she falls toward me. She has dropped her full weight into the fall and expected me to try to pull away. When her momentum pushes her forward, she does not miss.

Leah lands on top of me with a thud. Her arms and legs surge to find a way to hold me down, but I am throwing everything I have against her. We roll, body over body, too well-matched for either of us to win easily. I can beat her, I have no doubt, but I also admire her skill. She should have been a Raider.

She lands on top of me and straddles my hips. "Give up!"

I buck her off and tackle her back to the ground. I pin Leah's left arm down and bang her right arm over and over against the metal grates underneath her until she finally releases the knife. Once she is disarmed, I let out the breath I was holding and relax.

"We don't have to kill each other," I say.

"Of course we do," she spits. "There is no other way."

"I don't have a plan yet, but I'm sure we can figure it out. Work with us."

She laughs, the sound high and wild. "I would rather die."

I press my lips into a firm line. I don't want to kill her, but she's had so many chances to be free of this place and the constraints it puts on us. We don't have to live by the star-people's rules, but Leah is choosing to do so.

She doesn't know anything else, I think.

"I won't kill you," I say. She jerks against me and tries to throw me off, but I hold tight. Again I say, "I will not kill you."

Out of the darkness below, a huge shape bounds toward us. I see it jumping a mere second before it is on us, and I fall back from Leah to get away from it. The creature is massive, easily four-hundred pounds. The fur is golden and thick around its head, where three inch teeth protrude from its widening maw. The beast lets out a primal roar that sends my body quaking from the power it exudes. I have seen desert cats and large mountain prowlers, but nothing has prepared me for the sight of this magnificent animal.

Before I can say or do anything else, the brute pounces on Leah, clamping its mouth on her neck. Blood pours from the wound and bubbles out of her mouth. Her gaze searches for mine, and when we lock eyes, her lips twitch up in a smile.

I slowly step back from them, trying not to attract any attention. A low growl emanates from the creature, but it makes no move to attack as I slip away behind the tower I had been pressed against only minutes before. It has Leah's prone body, and Bets if it wants her too. It does not need me.

This is what I tell myself, at least, as I continue to back away. Even when I can't see it, I have trouble turning my eyes away from where it would come from. I know it is not the only one down there and another could come for me at any time. When I have moved far enough away that I can finally breathe, I turn toward where I think the exit is and run as fast as I can. There is no longer a need to be stealthy or worry about what lurks in the darkness; death is all around, and we are helpless to avoid it.

CHAPTER
FORTY-TWO
THOA

I hear her screams before I see her. I would go to her if I could. Surely she knows this. Nova knows that my heart is hers, that I would do anything to protect her, and that if I am not at her side it is because I can't be.

I hope she makes it to me before I die. I'd like for my eyes to look on her one last time.

CHAPTER
FORTY-THREE

NOVA

In the distance I hear Hiro yelling, "Hold on! Just hold on!" When I come around the next bend and the exit comes into view, I understand why. He's standing over Thoa, who is slumped against the wall, deep gashes cut down his abdomen.

I jump the gap between the path I'm on and the platform where they wait, skidding to my knees beside Thoa. His killing leathers are shredded. The same beast who killed Leah and Jai may have gotten Thoa as well, or it could have been something else. We heard many things below us, for they sent many things to kill us. The star-people would be happiest if none of us returned.

"Nova," Thoa says, his lips barely parting to form my name.

"Shhh, don't talk," I say. As if it matters. His silence will not stop the blood that flows from him.

"I love you," he mumbles. He tries to raise his hand to my face, but it barely lifts an inch from where it rests before it falls again.

Hiro puts his hand on my shoulder. I know what it means without him saying anything. He thinks Thoa is doomed, that he will die on this platform and there's nothing I can do about it. As I take in the sight of the strongest Raider I've ever known, bleeding, fading, I let out a stream of curses and prayers and pleas to any god who may be listening.

"Screw this," I say.

Hiro begins to say something, but his words do not filter down in a way that I understand. It is the faint smile on Thoa's face that has my whole attention.

"You're not dying today," I say.

He tries to say something, but coughs instead. Blood bubbles out of him with each convulsion.

I stand and step toward the door to the next level.

"Where are you going?" Hiro asks.

"Stay with him," I command.

I step through. There is fire and fury burning through my veins. My eyes take in the room and the random items scattered through it. There are pedestals lining the center of the level, each one seeming to have a different representation of the levels we've already passed. On the far side of the room is a plain wooden doorway just like the one that brought me here.

"Alright assholes," I yell, spinning in a circle. "I'm here again. I've made it to the last level. And yet again, you've destroyed me. You've broken everything; the only thing you haven't stolen is my life. What will it take to end it this time?"

The speaker above me crackles to life and I hear a woman's voice say, "Nova? Is that really you?"

Any pretense of courtesy is gone for whoever is controlling the games. "Yeah, it's me. Who are you?"

"It's Ivy."

"Ivy," I say, my eyes going wide. "Are you okay?"

"I'm okay. We're all okay, mostly. We've taken the station."

"You've… what?" I ask. There's no way I heard that right. There were so many of them, so much stacked against us.

Her laugh is sweet, though a little manic as she says, "Yeah, it's wild. But we're in charge, mostly. There's still some last holdouts but we're working on it. Someone the Raiders call Fatboy is negotiating for the release of the star-people who want to leave."

Okay, now I know I'm hallucinating. They must have pumped some psychedelics through the vents or something. There's no way Fatboy is in any way qualified to negotiate anything.

Ivy takes my pause as a reason to press on, saying, "Let's get you out of there. I can send someone to give you a bracelet and we can beam you up to help Fatboy. He's got the station leadership calling him Night Stalker now, and it's weird."

A laugh bubbles up for a moment, then the reality of what she said hits me and my breath seizes in my throat. "Thoa is dying. On the last level."

Ivy curses, then says, "He has to get through the door before we can do anything. I haven't been able to disable the settings yet. If anyone tries to reverse and go back to the previous level, the room will collapse, dumping everyone into a pit. I don't know what's in there, but it doesn't look good."

"I can open the door though, as long as I don't go through?"

She pauses, each second an eternity. After an eon of ten seconds, she says, "I don't know for sure. But if you get too close to the door, it'll open on its own."

"Send the bracelets," I say, making a decision. "Three of them. And if there are Raiders to spare, I could use a few. Just in case."

"On the way."

Seconds later, six figures appear before me: Zeb, who I rescued from prison, Drev and Karina, the former trial winners, Zulie, my counselor for the short time I was a Chief to the Raiders, the bad bitch from the Hole in the World with the blue-eyed attack cat—I can't believe I never learned her name—and Rego.

"We heard you need some help, Chief," Rego said, his eyes alight but his face serious.

I want to fall against him and let him comfort me like he has for so many years but I can't. There is no time for comfort.

"Through that door, Thoa is dying," I say, pointing. Zeb and Zulie take a step without another word until I call out, "Wait! We don't know how the mechanics are set up, and there's a high possibility that as soon as we try to go through it, we'll end up on the ground below where we'll have to face the beasts they put in to kill us."

"Can we save him?" Rego asks.

My eyes meet his and I swallow hard. "I don't know."

"But if we don't go, he dies for certain," Karina says.

With simple resignation and no regard for the danger to himself, Zeb says, "So, we go."

A weight lifts from my chest, letting me breathe. "We need to get a bracelet on him. Ivy can get him to medical once we do."

"And we can handle whatever comes while she makes sure he gets to safety. Easy," Zulie says. The tight press of her lips makes it clear she understands this may not be easy at all.

There's nothing else to say, and we can't waste any more time. "Alright then, let's go."

We move toward the door and it slides open once we are within a couple feet of it. I stand just outside, looking for a way to get the bracelets to Hiro. The Raiders close in behind me as they try to inspect the previous level for themselves. A roar echoes through the space, sending a chill up my spine.

"There," Drev says, pointing down the side of the room where we get a glimpse of something prowling toward us.

I unconsciously take a step forward at the sight, my need to protect Hiro and Thoa outweighing everything else. As soon as my foot crosses the threshold, the room begins to tip. The ground below us shifts and we cascade toward the middle. I catch Hiro's gaze as he realizes what is happening. He throws himself around Thoa's body as they slide down, shifting so that he can protect him from the fall. The sight sends a thrill through me; if Hiro is trying to protect him, Thoa is still alive.

I tuck my legs tight to my body as I slide, the floor collapsing back against the wall with a metal thud. We land with a thump against a surface of loosely packed sand. As soon as my feet hit the ground, I bounce back up and run to Thoa. Poor Hiro took the drop with all of Thoa's mighty bulk on top of him. Hiro is a tall, muscular man, but even he has had the air knocked out of him from having Thoa's mass land on him. Though he will definitely be bruised, his quick thinking might have saved Thoa's life.

Karina's long, thin fingers are around Thoa's wrist, checking his pulse even as she puts the bracelet around it. She gives a nod to Drev who taps his ear and says, "It's a go."

Before his words have fully passed his lips, Thoa and Hiro are gone. I hadn't noticed them putting a bracelet on Hiro but I'm so glad they did. They are safe and secure in Ivy's care, and I don't have to worry—

A roar fills the space behind me. I turn to see what the room has become: a giant pit, fully empty of everything but sand and monsters.

"Damn it," Drev mutters. He taps his ear again and says, "We need extraction when you have a minute." A pause, then, "No, we can handle things here. Taking care of Thoa and Hiro is the priority. We'll let you know when we're done."

His eyes meet Karina's and a look passes between them. Whatever they share is gone as quickly as it came, and was clearly the sort of thing that happens when you've known someone for a very long time.

With a sigh, Karina says, "Until they get the guys stable, we're on our own for a bit."

"Not the first time, won't be the last." Zulie shrugs one shoulder.

"Alright then, let's do this," I say, trying to sound braver than I feel. After seeing what happened to Leah, the carnage these beasts have caused, I have no desire to face them. But face them I must.

Karina pulls a long dagger from her boot and nudges my hand with the hilt. Zulie hands me the sword from her hip and unstraps her staff to hold it with both of her hands as she turns to face the animals. A sword in one hand and a dagger in the other, my blood sings with a thirst I haven't felt since I roamed the land to hunt for the Raiders. It feels like home.

The creatures are spreading out around the room, putting distance between themselves as they approach us. They don't want to be here anymore than we do; the star-people have captured and contained these animals and trapped them here, like they've done to us, and they are only doing what it takes to be the last one standing. Just like us.

"Nadja," Zeb whispers.

The first animal to reach us has closed in on the badass cat-lady, apparently called Nadja. She twitches an acknowledgement but doesn't turn around. Two curved swords are held wide, her arms outstretched. She and her cat stare down a dog-like creature, raised hackles, fur the color of the Mountain of Ushmor and the gods who live there, fangs bared and dripping into the sand. Her cat lets out a low growl that comes from deep in its chest.

The sound sends goosebumps racing down my arms. Nadja has this creature at her side, and though it seems to obey and even serve her will, that guttural utterance reminds me that her companion is still a beast.

"Steady, Khali," Nadja whispers.

Another animal slithers into view from the left, pulling my attention from Nadja and Khali's face-off. This one is some sort of reptile, long and sleek, its eyes glinting with a cold, calculating intelligence as it surveys its surroundings. The creature's pointed snout takes in the scent of potential prey. Its muscles ripple beneath olive-green skin, hinting at the power coiled within its frame. A hiss pierces the air, and as I stare into its open mouth I see sharp, serrated teeth protruding from its elongated jaw, gleaming ivory against the darkness of its maw.

"Hot damn," Karina says. "I'll take that one."

"That's a lot of teeth," Drev says, his lip hitching up at the corner.

"I'm going to make him smile," she says.

The screech of metal sliding against metal echoes above Drev, and all eyes turn toward the sound. Dozens of snakes slither from the opening above him; some stretch across the metal bars still extended across the top of the room, but many more fall from the opening into the pit around them.

"Guess I'll work on making those danger noodles grin," Drev says. He pulls the long sword from the scabbard across his back and runs off toward a clump of writhing serpents.

Zulie huffs and says, "They're not leaving much for the rest of us."

As if on cue, a scuttling sound finds my ears. A swarm of small, brown insects scurry across the ground toward us. Each has a multitude of legs carrying it forward, but it is their front claws and their curved, stingered tail that makes me gulp. Facing one of the larger beasts was one thing—I've trained for it, done it before, and come out victorious—but facing something so small and still dangerous is something else entirely. It certainly isn't something I've trained for.

"Oh, fun," Zulie says. She bounces on her tiptoes, her thick-soled boots thumping against the sand.

"I guess she's claiming those," Zeb says with a shrug.

"We've got our own trouble," I say.

Ahead of us, as if waiting for the lesser creatures to find their challengers before revealing himself, the king of beasts lets out a ferocious roar. The tawny cat I'd seen earlier, the one who had ripped Leah's throat from her body, stands with an unparalleled majesty. Its golden mane is crusted with blood under its chin. With eyes gleaming in primal instinct, it gazes intently at us, its muscles coiled like springs, ready to pounce at a moment's notice.

"Lion," Rego says, his tone full of awe.

My mouth turns up in a small smile at his use of the name in the old tongue. We spent so many days side by side whispering in that language as we guarded the camp while the others slept. He taught me so much about the Raiders, about taking care of myself, about fighting and family and love, and the only thing I had to give him were a few secret words and the devotion of a little girl who had lost everything.

I swallow back the fear rising within me as I watch Rego square his stance and prepare himself for a fight. He has spent years fighting, taught so many Raiders to do so, and now he is facing down another challenge like he would any other. I should not worry about the fierce warrior at my side; he can handle anything.

I turn back to the lion. Its stance exudes confidence and dominance, its massive frame imposing and formidable. Every movement is deliberate, calculated, as it assesses us with a mixture of curiosity and caution. There's a palpable tension hanging between us as we are locked in a silent standoff, a primal dance between predator and prey. I've never felt so weak and small in my life.

Zeb stands to my left, Rego to my right, and I can see the grim determination in both of their faces. They are ready for whatever comes, but I'm not sure that I am.

Without warning, the beast lunges forward. Rego reacts first, jumping between me and the cat. He has a shortsword in his left hand, and his trusty spear in his right, and he swings both at the animal in quick succession. Claws slash down but Rego falls back, deftly avoiding them.

While Rego has it distracted, Zeb comes up alongside it and swings his blade at the massive cat, narrowly missing as the beast leaps aside, its claws raking across his arm. With a scream of agony as blood gushes from his arm, he stumbles backward into Rego, who steadies him for only a second before lunging forward and thrusting his spear into the beast's side with a primal yell. As the creature roars in pain, I come up on the other side and drive my knife deep into the cat's flank. We might have a chance if we can disable those massive claws.

The lion, enraged by the combined assault, whirls around, its eyes burning with fury. With a fierce growl, it charges at Rego, who barely has time to brace himself. His spear shatters under the force of the lion's charge, leaving him momentarily defenseless. Reacting on impulse, I throw myself at the lion's side, aiming to distract it from Rego. My blades dig into the lion's side, but it barely seems to notice as it continues to press against Rego.

Seizing the opportunity, Zeb regains his footing and charges forward, his determination shining through the pain. With a primal roar of his own, he launches himself at the lion, driving his blade deep into its shoulder. The lion's head jerks back and it roars in agony. It swipes a powerful leg toward its attacker and knocks Zeb aside, sending him crashing to the ground once more.

Rego, undeterred by the loss of his weapon, stabs forward with his shortsword in an attempt to draw the cat's attention from Zeb. Before the beast can choose which target to attack, I rush forward, my heart pounding with adrenaline. With a final burst of energy, I leap onto its back, driving my sword into its neck with all my might. With a thunderous roar, the lion collapses to the ground, defeated but still dangerous as it thrashes about.

We watch in silence for a moment as we wait for the beast's life to pass. In the quiet, I hear a low chuckle bubbling up from Rego. I glance to him only to see him staring at me, a smile on his lips.

"We did it, Little Star."

I return his smile, letting myself relax into the idea that we are done. We have won. Drev is speaking into his earpiece now, and as I survey the area I see we were all victorious. Pride and relief swells within me, and I am so, so grateful for these brave people who came to the rescue.

A violent sound erupts behind us, one final roar as the lion's primal instincts take over, and in a desperate act, it lashes out with a swift and deadly swipe of its paw. I can't move away in time, and as I watch the cat's claws strike toward me in a moment that feels stretched and distorted, Rego throws his body in front of me and takes the blow. With a sickening crunch, the lion's razor-sharp claws tear through his chest, leaving a gaping wound that seeps crimson. Rego staggers backward, a look of disbelief crossing his face as he clutches his mortal wound.

"No," someone yells behind us.

A swarm of weapons erupt around us as those who have finished their battles come to our aid. They finish off the big cat, but it is too late. My gaze locks with Rego's as he falls to his knees. Screams pierce the air, fill my ears, and after a moment I realize it is me calling Rego's name. I drop in front of him, my hands covering his as they rest over the opening in his chest. Blood pours out between his fingers, coating mine in sticky red warmth.

"No, no, no," I mutter, my voice coming out in a broken whine. I glance over my shoulder to Karina, the only one with even a little medical training, and I croak, "Do something!"

She presses her lips into a thin line and shakes her head, her brows knit together.

Rego's voice slips through the raging helplessness, through the convulsing sobs shaking my body, through the wrenching of my heart.

"It's okay," he whispers.

I shake my head as I mutter his name. "It is not okay."

"You're okay," he says, his lips turning up ever so slightly. "My girl."

Nothing is okay. But here he is, trying to comfort me, giving me what he thinks I need. Rego, my protector, my friend, my father for so many years. "I can't lose you," I whisper.

"I'm with you," he says, "always."

As I sit there helpless, I watch Rego's life slip away.

CHAPTER
FORTY-FOUR
IVY

Thoa is hooked up to a dozen machines keeping him alive. Hiro is a little better, though not much. He's breathing on his own at least. They're in a small room next to a sleeping Coco, who has been receiving fluids for the last couple hours. Her skin is already regaining some of its glow, and I have hope that she'll be fine with time.

I leave them in the care of the station doctors with Benjy keeping guard. We aren't sure who we can trust but I need to get back to command. We've taken over the station, and reports are coming in constantly about the state of affairs. Plus, I have no idea what fate I've left for Nova. She insisted I take care of her guys; now that they're stabilized I need to see what I can do for her.

I walk through blue-fourteen-square. Pœwani market is full of people, like usual, but these aren't shoppers out for an evening stroll to evaluate the goods. There are celebrations throughout the place, but there are tears and wailing in others. Pockets of sound rise up and die within a breath, and I wonder what the impact will be when everything is totaled.

The market sounds fade as I move into the next set of corridors, but it is much the same everywhere I go, though perhaps on a smaller scale. Bodies, bodies everywhere and not a one that breathes. So much destruction. I can see the horror in the faces I pass as they hover over those they've lost, and the elation in others who feel the freedom that comes with the Raiders. Though I see and recognize these things, the only thing that continues to cross my mind is wondering who will clean up this mess and take care of the leftovers. Surely there will be people who want to stay. Not because of a love for the leadership or the way things have been run in the past, but simply because this station is home to so many and change is terrifying.

"You!"

I hear the shout and spin around. His white coat is covered in gore, and the bandage around his head is absolutely disgusting, centered on his eye. I can't help the smile that comes to my lips at the sight of Doctor Shaw looking absolutely destroyed.

"Well hello there, Doc," I say.

"Where is she?"

"Who would that be?"

"Your bitch of a sister. I'm going to wring her neck with my own two hands."

I laugh at the thought. Shaw has caused plenty of harm to both of us, and with the right amount of power he could cause plenty more. But he doesn't have that power anymore. The idea that he would even try to fight Nova on his own is laughable. His only hope against her was sedation; at full strength, she would destroy him.

"I would honestly love to see you try," I say.

He lifts his hand and trains a laser gun on me. "Unfortunately for you, that won't happen. I've had enough of both of you. This ends right now."

A force blasts into my side and I know I'm dead. I always thought it would be because of faulty wiring. Not a sexy way to die, but true to me. Dying in service to the station, in setting people free, in saving my sister and her found family—

"Are you okay?"

I stare into dark eyes, a creased brow full of concern. I've seen him a few times on the screens as he worked with the station leadership, but this is the first time I've been this close to him. "Night Stalker?"

The smile that blooms across his face sets him alight. "I knew it would catch on."

I can't help but smile at that. "Fatboy—"

"You don't have to call me Night Stalker," he interrupts, "but please, not Fatboy either. I don't like the sound of it on your lips."

I'm not sure what to say to that. That he is considering my lips at all seems strange. "What should I call you?"

"Maybe you can use my real name."

"I'd like that," I whisper.

His smile seems to grow shy, and he says, "My name is Rufus."

"I'm Ivy."

We stare at each other for a soft, silent moment, where everything around us seems to disappear. With a jolt I realize he is still on top of me after saving my life, his body covering mine in its entirety. My heart hammers wildly in my chest, though I can't place the reason for it. Heat fills my belly and a blush creeps up my body until I feel the color in my cheeks.

Rufus seems to realize it at the same moment and push himself off me. He stands and reaches a hand down to me. "Can you walk?"

I reach for his hand and allow him to pull me up. "Yeah, I'm good. But Shaw…"

The doctor's brain is splattered across the side of the station, his body slumped on the grates. A red-haired woman stands beside him, her eyes flickering back and forth in the corridor.

"No longer a problem, lass."

"You killed him." I say it as plainly as possible, though even I can hear the accusation in my tone. I add, "Don't get me wrong, I'm glad he's dead."

"He was a prick, aye."

I laugh, unable to hold it back. A second passes and I say, "Thank you. I'm Ivy, by the way."

She nods. "I know. We were sent to find ya. Wynda MacNally's my name, but my friends call me Red."

"Are we friends, then?"

"By proxy. Your sister freed me, gave me a fine goal of sowing chaos and making a mess. I think I'm serving our friendship well."

"Agreed."

"Right then," Red says. "Let's get you where you're going."

"And where is that?"

"To the voting room," Rufus says. "They're calling representatives in for each group to make some decisions."

My brow furrows at his words. "Voting for what? I thought the station was free now."

Rufus' lips are a flat line, and I can see he is not happy with what is happening. "We control parts. But there's still enough opposition to keep us struggling for a while. If we can stop the killing, we have to try. The station's leadership is willing to talk, but they're not eager to do much else. They've had success with how things have been, and they don't want it to change."

"That's bullshit," I say, anger coursing through me.

"Aye," Red says. "But that's politics."

As we continue down the corridor, Rufus says, "Ultimately they want to take things back to normal. They're even planning to nominate a new Règle."

"Nothing will change. We'll have done all this, and they'll erase it."

"They want us to bring people in to make the decisions for each group, but even in that they're being strategic to try to sway the votes. You were named as a rep, because they think they can control your vote."

I laugh. "There's nothing they can do to influence how I vote."

Rufus and Red share an unreadable look between them as Red says, "I hope that's true."

Before I can ask what she means, we're walking past two guards and through a door that leads to an elaborately decorated room. There are beautifully crafted panels along the walls, a mix of actual wood and metal with a lovely patina. It's so different from the stark, plain metal throughout the ship that the coloring surprises me. There are paintings hanging around the room. They look older than anything I've ever seen. In the center of the room is a long table with a dozen cushy chairs surrounding it. Almost half of the chairs are filled with old white men, and there's a squirming within me at the sight. They truly do want everything to be as it has always been.

Rufus guides me to an empty chair on the far side of the table and he sits beside me. I can feel Red hovering behind for a moment, but then she seems to fade into the wall for later use. To my absolute horror and also shocking relief, Yosh Okada is to my right.

"Good to see you, Ivy," he says, though he doesn't look my way.

"You too," I whisper. "I thought they might have killed you for your part—"

"I don't know what you mean," he interrupts, eyes darting around to see if anyone else is listening to us.

"Of course," I say, taking the hint. "I just mean that as Nova's doctor, the previous Règle had certain expectations of you that weren't fully realized."

He gives a terse nod. "It seems that all of the doctors failed in one way or another. For that, I am terribly sorry."

It is my turn to nod. I know Yosh didn't want to see me hurt, he didn't want to be part of the things Shaw did to Nova—stars, that's why he saved her in the first place—but there was only so much he could do. When everyone else was in prison or in the padded rooms, Yosh was free and walking about. I don't know how he managed it, what parts of him he had to sacrifice to make that happen, but I do know he's as much the reason we've had a revolution as Nova is, and no one knows it. It was his shot that stabilized her memories and let her return to herself, and he did that with a huge risk to himself. But he did it. That's what matters. And if I tell myself that enough, I can forgive the rest.

I study the rest of the room as they whisper amongst themselves as we wait for the final chairs to fill. Next to Rufus is a tall black man with thick braids pulled into a high ponytail. He is not dressed like the other Raiders with their leathers and coverings; instead, he embodies a posh, eccentric gentlefellow in a rich, green tux that is splattered with blood. I can't make out much about the person to his left, other than that they are significantly slighter than the hulking rich boy, and their face is far more open and kind.

Across the table are four white men in a row who are vaguely different from one another while remaining completely indiscernible. Even their clothes are shockingly similar—fine-cut suits in dark colors— with their only real variation being the color of their pocket squares.

When my eyes land on the woman to Yosh's right, I nearly squeak in surprise. I whisper, "Gamma?"

Her eyes meet mine and a faint smile tips the edges of her mouth. "The name is Blaire," she says. "Asher Blaire."

The name tumbles around in my head for a moment until it crashes against understanding. "Oh," I say, eyes going wide. It's the most I can offer her, but it seems to be enough.

Yes, I know *exactly* who Asher Blaire is. I've heard the name in hushed conversations between my parents for years. This sweet grandma who took us in earlier and helped us get through the corridors with Coco also happens to be the biggest name in reformation politics for the last forty years. She worked with my father long ago, and when she left the Chasseur, she immediately went rogue against the station's leadership and tried to organize underground movements to challenge the Règle's authority. She was imprisoned for a while for starting a riot that covered four residential blocks and one of the larger markets. After release, she stayed dedicated to the cause, though mostly through speaking engagements rather than provocation.

I honestly wasn't aware she was still alive. Her name hasn't made it into the feeds for several years. *Montana,* I think. She's his primary caregiver now. She can't risk getting herself in trouble and having him taken away. And then I dragged her into trouble.

The door opens again and another old white man enters. Thin. White-blonde hair parted to the side. Cornflower blue eyes boring into mine.

"Looks like we're all here," Ledwin Kennedy says.

Rufus motions to the empty seat on the Raiders side. "We're missing one."

"Don't worry," my father says. "Nova is on her way. We can get the preliminaries out of the way before she arrives, I think."

"She's safe?" I ask, clutching at Rufus' hand to ground me.

Ledwin nods. "We pulled her out of the pit a few minutes ago."

"And the others?" I ask.

A crease forms between his brows in a look I am quite familiar with. My questions have annoyed him enough through the years that I know when he wants me to be quiet. A couple years ago that look would have silenced me. Unfortunately for him, I've grown more like my half-sister every day since we met on that ship, each recognizing something in one another that we didn't have with our father: family.

"They were all pulled out," he says. Turning to the rest of the group, he says, "Now gentlemen—"

"'Esteemed guests' works much better when addressing an assembly, Ledwin," Asher Blaire says. "Especially if you're willing to pretend to respect people's pronouns."

I fight to hide my smile at the twitch in his jaw. A few seconds pass and he says, "You're right, of course. My apologies to all of my *esteemed guests*."

Asher waves a dismissive hand at him and says, "Think nothing of it."

My father presses on, saying, "We are here today to sort through all that has happened on the station."

"And on the ground," Rufus says.

At his words, I realize my hand is still intertwined with his. I move to pull away, but he squeezes ever so slightly. Maybe he needs me to ground him now as much as I needed him a moment ago.

"We have a lot to figure out. Let's start with the most pressing for the station, because that is where we are," Ledwin says, directing a gaze to Rufus that drops to our hands a second later. "We need a new Règle."

"We don't," Asher says, while I say, "No!" Meanwhile, the white male quadruplets all speak words of agreement with his pronunciation.

"Sounds as if we have the numbers to proceed," Ledwin says.

Rufus looks to those at his left, then says, "We are with your daughter."

"Which one?" Ledwin asks.

"Both," Rufus says. His hand is warm in mine, and I feel comfort and strength pouring into me through that connection. "Currently, the one who is here. The one who is right."

"The numbers favor us," I say.

And then Yosh clears his throat.

I want to strangle him. I know before he speaks what he is going to do, and I would do anything to stop him. I can't understand why he would sabotage his own interests.

"I'm with Mister Kennedy," he says.

My father eyes him with a mix of suspicion and gratitude. "Thank you, Mister..."

"Doctor Okada Yoshinori," he replies.

Ledwin smiles. "Thank you, Doctor, for recognizing the needs of the station above your own desires. Let's begin the nominations."

"An easy task," Yosh says, nodding at my father. "The obvious choice, sir, is you."

"Are you kidding me?" I whisper. "What are you doing?"

Without even a glance my way, Yosh whispers, "Better the devil you know."

"You do understand that he is *actually* the devil?"

The corner of Yosh's mouth tips up ever so slightly. "There's always more than meets the eye when it comes to your family."

"Nova," I murmur. I never understood exactly what his feelings for her were, but I knew it was more than he was willing to admit. Maybe more than any of us guessed.

He nods. "Never bet against a Kennedy when death is on the line."

"There's a lot more on the line here than just our deaths," I say.

"I know," he says. "That's why I sided with your father. We need him to keep us moving until Nova gets here."

"You really think she's coming?"

"I'm counting on it. Without her, we're screwed."

CHAPTER
FORTY-FIVE
NOVA

The sounds of the station blend into a steady hum of nothingness as I sit on a metal slab in this makeshift hospital. A woman in a blood spattered medical coat looks me over, prodding at my wounds. Her touch is clinical, but surprisingly tender. It's clear she has been doing this work for a long time.

"You're fine," she says with a sigh. "We stitched up your shoulder, but you'll want to avoid using it for a few weeks. You've got some bruised ribs and a nasty cut on your thigh, but you'll heal."

I open my mouth to speak, but no words come. Something awful rises in me, an emotion, I guess, and I can't stamp it down quick enough. It feels like there's something stuck in my throat, rough and coppery and hard as a rock. It tastes like grief.

The woman puts her finger under my chin and tilts my head until our gazes meet. "What you've seen, felt, and experienced... those things will heal too."

Her dark eyes are kind, honest. I believe her words as much as I can; the numbness I feel prevents me from accepting what she says as the full truth. It would be nice if I could, but then my mind flashes with Rego's face and I know I will not heal, no matter what she says. The trials stole something precious from me, again, and they served no purpose. We were thrown in as entertainment, we were cut down as an amusement.

Rego sacrificed himself for my life; I lost him for something that wasn't worthy of his offering.

I pull away from her touch. Her mouth is downturned in resignation. She moves away from me to put her things away. Outside the room I can hear raised voices, though I can't make out what they're saying. It's as if they're filtering down from some faraway place.

There's a knock on the door. The doctor opens it and a thin man with silvery-purple hair pokes his head in. When his green eyes meet mine, half his mouth turns up in a smile.

"Benjy," I say with a nod.

His brow creases, his smile dying as the scar on his face pulls his lips back down. "You okay?"

I shake my head once but say, "Yes."

"She will be," the doctor says. She gives me one last look and leaves the room.

"Well, the bad news is that you're back on the station," he says. "The good news is that you're basically in charge of it now."

His words pierce my heartache and remind me there is still much to do, and no one else to do it. I want to sit and hurt and feel this emptiness deep in my bones; I want to rest. Rego would shame me for wanting to give up, so I can't. I have to live for him. I have to sacrifice myself in service, as he would have. As he did. If I can't, how could I possibly live with myself after seeing what he did for me?

I don't know how long I sit here drowning in sorrow but enough time passes for Benjy to say, "I don't know what happened, or what will help you, but we really do need to get going."

"Nothing will help," I mutter, but I get on my feet anyway.

He leads me out of the small evaluation room, and into a larger adjoining area. There are a handful of makeshift beds and seats in this space, as well as doors leading to other rooms like the one I was in. Nadja and her cat rest on one of the beds. Khali is curled up at Nadja's side, and though there's blood matted in her fur, Khali's breathing seems steady as she licks her paws and occasionally nuzzles Nadja's hand for pets.

Another door opens nearby and Drev steps out, his arm slung over Karina's shoulders for support. They both seem to register Benjy at the same time. Despite Drev's injury, he dives for him first. Karina is right on his heels, her weapon already drawn.

"Stop!" I yell, stepping between them.

They do, reluctantly. Karina's rage is palpable as she meets my gaze. Her words sound like they're being dragged across broken glass. "He is the reason the Huntress is dead."

"He got them all killed," Drev says.

"His sins are not forgotten," I say. I feel him tense beside me and I know he hears the truth in my voice. "But he has done good here too. Without him, I would be dead. My sister, too. And others, I'm sure. It doesn't wash away what he did, but it does stay his execution in this moment."

Drev shakes his head. "I can't let him walk out of this room."

I sigh, so overcome with weariness that the thought of this conversation drains me of any tact I might have otherwise. "You are in no condition to fight."

"I could take him," Drev says.

"Only if he can get to him before me," Karina adds, her voice low.

I say, "And I would be forced to intervene. It's not a road we need to take. You might be able to take down one of us, but not both, and not without cost. And I have other stuff to do that doesn't involve fighting two people I respect."

Benjy's throat bobs as he says, "You deserve justice for what I've done to you and your families. I don't expect to go free, but I'd like to do some good before I die. I know it isn't enough to make up for what I did—"

"Nothing will ever be enough," Karina says, cutting him off.

Benjy nods. "I know."

There's nothing more from him, nothing to try to redeem himself or explain his actions. I appreciate that he doesn't make the attempt. It means I don't have to let myself forgive him out of obligation. I could forgive him, I think, if enough time passed. Perhaps we will never know, because time is not on my side. I plan to finish this while I can, and then succumb to death long before my heart has time to rationalize the reasons we've all committed the atrocities we have.

"We're going now," I say.

Their eyes follow us as we cross the room to the exit but neither of them move. In the corridor, Benjy lets out a relieved breath.

"I thought they were going to kill me."

"If they didn't understand the importance of what we do next, they would have."

He shakes his head. "They respect you."

"Not enough to still their blades."

His lips tug up in a half smile. "You really have no idea the effect you have on people."

"I get people killed."

"You give them hope."

"A curse," I say. "Hope is the worst thing they could have."

"You don't really believe that."

I shrug. "I didn't always. Now, I'm not sure. It hasn't served me well these last few years."

"If you didn't have hope, you wouldn't be walking with me to this meeting. You wouldn't be planning ways to fix things."

"I don't even know where we're going," I say. "Or why you need me."

"Oh, right," Benjy says. "I guess I should give you the quick version: the fighting has stopped, the Raiders and station leaders are in a closed door meeting to figure things out, and your dad is doing his damnedest to usurp as much authority as he can. So, you know, an average day."

I pause for a beat, swallow. "I didn't know he was alive."

"Of course he is. The station could drop from the sky and that man would still walk out unscathed. Nothing seems to touch him."

Not nothing, I think, remembering the last few times I saw him. He was fighting against the Règle and the ways of the station. He was siding with his daughters, raising an army, trying to change things. Is that still who he is, or has the last year changed him? Could they have altered him the same way they did me?

"I don't know what his endgame is but I'm ready to find out. Let's get there before something else blows up."

"Or we could *help* something blow up," he says, smiling again. "I sure love it when things go boom."

CHAPTER
FORTY-SIX

NOVA

W e arrive at the conference room without anything going boom. Benjy tells me it's a travesty, and part of me agrees, but I'm just so tired. I don't want to think about the chaos around me, and I certainly don't want to cause any right now. I want to sit down in a quiet room away from everything and everyone and rest for at least a week straight. I can't, but the idea is still nice.

There are guards stationed outside the room. I recognize both of them. With a nod, I say, "Hicks, Jackson."

"Cam," Hicks says, nodding in return. "Good to see you."

I tilt my head, letting my confusion at his words show on my face. The last time I saw him, he was my commanding officer and regularly tried to befriend me so that he could gain favor with Bets. But she's dead now, and there's no one here to help his career. Unless my presence is a shift in the tides for him, I can't imagine him actually meaning what he said. "Is it?"

His brows furrow as if he's surprised at my question. He probably is. Cam was always respectful—Nova, not so much.

"Yeah, it is. With everything going on..." he trails off, waving a hand at the hallways still bathed in blood. "Being alive feels like an accomplishment at this point."

"Or a curse."

Hicks presses his lips together in a tight line, clearly done with me. I turn to the other guard and say, "Long time no see, Jackson."

He nods, his lips frowning at the edges. "Well, I was in prison for a while. Put a damper on my social calendar. Guess that's what happens when you side with a bunch of rebels."

"I don't know that I'd call us that," I say, my gaze finding his. "We are just a group of like-minded individuals who would prefer it if we could live without being watched, without being controlled, without the hand of the Règle on everything we do. That should be a right, not a crime."

"Can't say I disagree," he says.

"Yet you're here, guarding the very ones who held our people captive."

"Nah, that's him," Jackson says, pointing at Hicks. "I'm here for everyone else."

Everyone else? I think. *Who else would be in this meeting?*

They usher us through the door and into a fancy room full of wood and metal and paintings and decorations that do nothing but put wealth on display. My brain only has a second to recognize all this, and then I shove it to the background as I take in the people assembled. My gaze flits from person to person, recognizing some and promising myself to return to their faces in celebration that they are alive, but I keep searching until my green eyes meet hers. It is only then that I let go of the breath I'm holding and give myself permission to relax.

Ivy is alive, and I am looking at her with my own eyes, seeing her dare to exist despite everything that has happened.

She stands, her face beaming back at me. She pulls her hand out of Fatboy's and moves away from the table. We close the gap in an instant, my arms wrapping around my little sister's shoulders.

"You're here," she whispers against my shoulder. "You're okay."

"Of course I am," I say, trying to reassure her. "I will always come back for you."

"Thoa is alive," she says. The words rush out of her like they couldn't be held back a second longer.

"Thank you," I say, breathing a sigh of relief. We stand locked together for a moment, relishing the comfort of knowing the other is safe. Finally, I break the spell and ask, "So, you and Fatboy?"

A laugh bubbles out of her. "Shush," she says. "He's nice."

"No judgment," I say, pulling back to study her face. "I'm for it as long as he treats you well."

"And if he doesn't?" she asks, raising a brow.

"I'll kill him." When she laughs, I purse my lips and say, "I'm not joking. Make sure you tell him I said that."

"You get us out of this mess and I'll make sure to deliver the warning."

I peek past her at the rest of the room. They're all staring at us with various expressions ranging from joyous to annoyed, with one or two that are downright angry. I pull from Ivy's arms and say, "Let's get to it, then."

"I trust you," she murmurs, giving me a little nod. "Whatever you want to do, I'm with you."

Ivy moves back to her seat, her hand sliding into Fatboy's as soon as she sits. The sight fills me with warmth; something about them makes me *certain* there is a future after this for those who seek it. No matter what happens here today, people will still thrive. Hopefully this conversation we're about to have will make it easier.

I take the empty seat next to Leer. Though it has been a long time since we spoke, and even that last encounter was brief as I convinced him and his neighbors to fight on my side, the space between us remains comfortable. It has always been so with Leer, and I expect it will remain so until we both pass from this life.

"Hello, friend," he says, his soft voice exactly as kind as I remember it.

I put a hand on his forearm and say, "I am truly happy to see you."

"Same. You've been away too long."

I smile at Leer's words. He speaks as if I've been away on a hunt and have finally returned bearing fruits and gifts for my people. I say, "I will try to do better next time."

"See that you do. Your god-daughter shouldn't have had to wait so long to meet you."

"God-daughter?" I ask, my brows going high.

Leer's face lights up. "She is the most perfect thing this world has ever seen. Her name is Star. If I do nothing else with my life, I will have done enough."

"Congratulations," I say. "I'm happy for you."

"That's enough joy for now," Herol Hamrick says from between Leer and Fatboy.

I smile at his growled words. "I missed you too, Herol."

"Been a while, kid."

"Still running that floating city into the ground?"

"Aeroport is flourishing at my hands, thank you very much."

The corner of his lips twitch ever-so-slightly but he doesn't give up his normal smile. He's all business in his green suit, even with the red splatters covering him. I look past Herol to Fatboy, whose gaze is focused on Ivy. The rest of the room holds nothing for him.

My eyes slide past them and it is only now that I realize Doctor Okada is sitting on Ivy's right. I stare at his profile, warring with myself about how to feel toward him. He wasn't a prisoner with the rest of them, and suspicion colors my impression of him because of it. But I also know he had a hand in helping me escape the mental prison that Bets had built for me, and he rescued me from the hospital the first time I was trapped there. When I was lost as Cam, he tried to reach out to me, even if just in a small way so I didn't feel so alone. Somehow Okada has been both friend and foe, the lines blurring between the two.

"Can we please get back on track?"

I slowly turn to face the speaker. His voice seems to echo in my head long after his words have ceased. The last time I heard him speak, he was winning people to our side at Coco's family farm. He had his wife and daughters by his side, and he seemed more whole than any man had any right to be. What has happened since then to have him back here seeking power from the star-people?

"Apologies, father," I say, my tone cold. "I've only just escaped death, and am learning that some people I love are still alive as well. I doubt you can imagine how that could make someone feel."

His cornflower eyes meet mine, and for a moment I think he's going to break down and show some real emotion. Then his eyes narrow into a squint, as if he can't quite stand the sight of me.

"As happy as you are, perhaps you can tame those feelings in light of the devastation wrought on the station today. While your loved ones are fine, there are hundreds dead and thousands grieving."

Whether he means his words or they're only for show, his chastisement hits me hard and leaves an ache in my chest. I hate to admit it but he's right. There are so many dead, so many wounded, so much loss. I'm certain many of them are my own people, and the pain of it will haunt me as long as I live.

"She can feel both," a woman by Okada says. "The duality of the heart: it can ache for others and feel relief for itself. That's a perfectly rational reaction."

She turns her gaze to me and gives me a small nod. I don't know who she is, but I'm thankful for her words.

"Our *feelings* mean little in the grand scheme of things, Asher. Not when there's still so much at stake."

"Feelings are what your whole world is built on," Asher says with a laugh. "Pride, arrogance, resentment, jealousy, fear—I could go on and on."

Ledwin's jaw clenches. "I am here to serve the station and the people who call it home. Any other claim proves you know nothing about me."

"You know nothing about yourself. If you think you're trying to become the new Règle out of some selfless, altruistic act, you've deceived even yourself."

The whole room watches them banter back and forth, holding its collective breath to avoid disrupting whatever is happening. I've never heard anyone speak to my father in this way. Even when I told him to go screw himself, there wasn't the same level of intimacy shared between us. Listening to him and Asher, it's clear there is a history there that can't be unraveled in the amount of time we have.

"What terms are we discussing today?" I ask. Maybe if I put it out on the table in such a way, I can lead them to a more productive conversation.

"We voted on the new Règle," Fatboy says. "Without you."

"Intentionally," Asher says in a mutter that doesn't attempt to be quiet.

"And you won?" I ask my father, no hint of surprise in my tone.

He nods. "I have been granted stewardship for now."

"For now," I repeat. "The last few Règles haven't had much success."

"It seems someone was murdering them," he says, eyes giving me a pointed look.

"Maybe it's an indication the station doesn't need a Règleship."

"Or that the station needs better criminal reform."

We stare at each other for a long moment before Fatboy speaks up and says, "I don't care what the station needs. I want to know what we're going to do to make things right with the Raiders and the people on-world."

"Wait a second," Ivy says, pulling her hand from Fatboy's. "The station has people who are innocent of all the damage done by the higher-ups. They need resolution as much as your people."

The room explodes into chaos. There are arguments between friends and allies, between enemies, between everyone with breath in their body. My eyes dart to my father amidst the tumult. He sits in his chair, quiet and still, a smile lighting his face as he surveys his work. It is then I know that another Règle will die today.

CHAPTER
FORTY-SEVEN
NOVA

A surprising amount of things happen in the meeting room despite the disagreements. Though my father attempts to use his influence to control the proceedings, it is clear he does not have the power he wants. Sewing discord has not been to his advantage.

Of all the people in the room, it is actually Fatboy who seems to broker the most attention. Once he takes control of the conversation we quickly come to an agreement on several things, including letting the Raiders return to the planet. The eagerness of the star-people to remove them would be comical if not for the things that happened to get to this point. They are also urgent to remove any technology that would let us return. I insist on tabling that portion of the discussion in case we need to use it later to our advantage.

When it comes to releasing the star-people who do not want to stay on the station any longer, they are more resistant. I do not understand their reasoning, no matter the arguments they give. In the end they agree to give the people the option to leave because there is nothing else they can do. Many people have already made their decisions about leaving, and nothing this committee says will change that. It will take time to get them to the ground, a concern brought up by Ivy, but she seems fairly confident we can sort it out if we can get some other techies on board. I have no doubt she would start solving this problem right now if we would let her leave the meeting.

Things are moving along well now, and Ledwin's face grows more sour with each victory between the groups. He does not want us to agree, does not want success without his hand in it, knowing that each step forward takes a little more of his power away.

"The trials," Hosh says, drawing my attention. "It's time to do away with them."

I nod in agreement, as well as the others near me, at the same time the other part of the table begins shaking their heads. I'm certain my eyes are deceiving me. What possible reason could these men have for not wanting to end such a barbaric custom?

"Too many have died already," Herol says.

"For nothing," Asher adds.

"I disagree. The trials are an important part of our culture," one of the men at the end of the table says. His face is scrunched up as if this is something he has given a great deal of thought, as if it impacts him in the same way it does the rest of us.

My hands sitting on top of the table clench at his words, and I find myself staring daggers at him. The dumbass is lucky I'm not *throwing* daggers his way.

"Forgive me for saying so," I say, forcing the words out through clenched teeth. "But what do you know?"

"Excuse me?" he asks, his pale eyes going wide.

I grit out, "You heard me."

"I think I know what my people want," he scoffs. "The trials stay."

"The trials stay if you are the ones going in them," I say.

Dumbass looks to the others next to him for support. They all look uneasy and won't meet his gaze.

"I don't think you understand," he begins.

"You sure as hell don't," Yosh says. He waves a hand in my direction and says, "Nova is the only person here who has actually been in the trials. She is the only one qualified to make this decision. So, no matter what any of the rest of us say, even those of us who agree with her, it's just empty words. Nova lived it."

"Twice," I say.

His head whips toward me. "Twice?"

"That's where I was," I say, my voice cracking. "Watching more on-worlders die. Losing people I love."

"Why? How?" he asks.

"The previous Règle wanted a show. It was supposed to be one last hurrah before she shut down the trials for good."

The man next to my father asks, "Where is she? Why isn't she here to tell us this herself?"

"She's dead. Bets fell through the portal when she forced us through, and ended up in the trials herself."

"And she…" one of them starts.

"We can watch the screens. I'm sure I can bribe someone for the footage before they process it for the masses," Dumbass says. "Then we'll see what happened for ourselves. The ratings when we show that—"

"I tore apart the recording room in the tower," I say. "There may be some footage from before that, but you won't capitalize on her death. And once we're done here, I'm going to rip out whatever you have left so you can never do this to my people again."

"You think that's enough to end the games?" Dumbass asks, a smile coloring his voice. "We can rebuild those in a matter of days."

He must read the horror registering on my face because he laughs, letting me know how impotent my rage truly is.

"All that room is good for is storing the data until it gets processed into something palpable. You might've ruined your own show, but it won't stop the next trial, or the one after that."

Either the woman lied to me so I wouldn't kill her, or this old bastard is downplaying what I did. I don't know which it is, but my blood is boiling either way.

I look up at him, hatred seething from me when I do. "I will burn this place to the ground with you in it. I will destroy everything that has ever pertained to the trials, and I will kill every last one of you who wants it to continue."

He blinks at me, mouth ajar, but says nothing. There is nothing he can say. The tower will never again see the bloodbath it did today.

"Let's vote," Ledwin says.

It's the first thing he's said during this conversation, and I hate him for it.

"Those in favor of keeping the games?" Ledwin asks.

The Dumbass raises his hand. A growl rumbles in my throat and it takes everything in me not to catapult myself across the table. But then I realize his is the only hand raised. The man next to him looks like he's wrestling with what to do, but ultimately decides not to vote with his neighbor.

Dumbass looks to the man beside him and asks, "Preston, are you really changing your stance because of these people?"

The man mumbles something the rest of us can't hear, and the white Dumbass face goes red.

"Things change," the man at the corner of the table says. He has been quiet so far. Though he sits with the station's community reps, he has mostly voted with the Règle and the former leadership. "Sometimes when new information comes to light—"

"Shut up, Royce. You're only here because you vote how we want you to," Dumbass says.

Royce does shut up, but the surprise he wears is jarring. I feel a twinge of pity for him; the poor guy clearly thought his opinion was valued, not that he was just another puppet in a long line of controlled votes.

"This is bullshit," Dumbass says, slamming his hand down on the table.

I open my mouth to speak, but my father's words are reverberating through the room before I have a chance. There is no mistaking his stance when he says, "If you think we're going to continue with the same strategy used by the last regime, you're out of your mind. I had to sit back and watch my daughter nearly die when she went through the trials, and I will not put some other family through that."

"But the viewers—"

"They can find something else to entertain them, Warren," Ledwin says. "There's plenty of mindlessness on the screens; they don't need brutality to let them *feel* something."

I say, "My father and I don't agree on a lot of things but we do on this. You might think you're being brave to stand against one Kennedy, but believe me when I say you don't want to stand against us both."

Ledwin smiles and adds, "We handle things in different ways but the result will be the same."

Dumbass looks back and forth between us before seeming to decide that we are, in fact, not someone he wants to mess with. With a sigh, he drops his gaze and stares at his hands like they are the most interesting things he has ever seen.

"Anything further on the agenda?" Ledwin asks.

Eyes dart around the room, but everything of consequence has already been settled. Ledwin opens his mouth as if to adjourn the meeting, but then we hear the soft sound of Ivy clearing her throat, and everything pauses.

She stands, meets my eyes for a second as if pulling at some strength that lives between us, then turns to our father. "There is one more thing."

He smiles at her in a way he has never smiled at me, and says, "What's that, dear?"

In a voice as sweet as sap, she says, "The space station. We need to blow it up."

CHAPTER
FORTY-EIGHT
IVY

The looks they give me range from shocked to furious, with a little bit of laughter coming from Asher a couple seats away. I try to take all of it in while keeping my focus on my father. His opinion is what matters right now, because it can sway everyone else. He might be an arrogant bastard obsessed with power just like Asher said, but right now it's the support of the Règle that I need, not the love of my father. The latter is welcome though, despite all he has done.

I don't know how Nova feels about our father. Not truly. She's had such a strange history with him. Knowing and loving him for the first few years of her life, only to be ripped away from that life and raised by her aunt, then to lose that connection as well and end up with Raiders. Her life has known so much heartache, so much hunger for family and belonging. Then one day we show up again, and suddenly she has her dead father back, and a sister nearly grown. It couldn't have been easy to know what to do or how to feel about any of that, but she's done her best. She loves me, despite the little time we've had together, and I have no doubt she would spend her life getting to know me if we had the chance.

But we don't. Not if the Règle listens to what I'm about to propose.

My father's expression hasn't changed. There is no surprise in his pale eyes, no confusion written on his face. I doubt he expected me to suggest blowing up the station, but he also doesn't seem nonplussed that I did. He knows me. We don't always agree, but he knows whatever I'm planning is purposeful and has been reasoned out. Nova's feelings for him might not be clear, but my love for him is absolute. There are things about him that I don't like, things I rebel against and wish could be changed, but in the end we know the other is trying to do what is best. Sometimes we end up on opposite sides of what that means and find ourselves as situational enemies, but in the end we always come back together as family.

"Explain," he says.

I swallow back my nervousness. I don't have the confidence that he and Nova always display. But I know I'm right about this. I *know* it.

Starting with the most basic information, I say, "The station was never meant to last this long in one place."

One of the old white men rolls his eyes and says, "You're talking nonsense."

"Quiet, Bernard," my father says. "Ivy is young, but she's got more brains in the tip of her nose than you have in your whole head."

Bernard makes a strange noise, like a scoff and a shriek had a baby. I dismiss him and continue: "When the founders made this place, it was meant to be a starting point for the future. Instead, we settled in, got comfortable, and stopped pursuing who we once dreamed of being."

"And who is that?" Asher asks.

"Adventurers. Pioneers. Trailblazers at the forefront of discovery. We went from being free-thinking creatures with chaotic minds that led to exploration to being small-minded and docile, so content with what we had that we stopped wondering what could be. As years passed, our souls began to rebel against the lives we made. We created tame things that long to be wild."

"Blowing up the station will fix that?" Warren asks, raising one brow.

I don't bother glancing his way. My eyes trained on my father, I say, "Yes, it will."

"How?" Yosh asks from beside me.

"The station was built to keep humanity from dying out after the cataclysm. It was created so we would have a home to rebuild and get our lives together. But it wasn't supposed to *stay* together. The original engineers built it in segments, knowing that someday we would lose the parts that didn't serve us and take off into the stars in search of the next great human adventure."

"This is preposterous," Preston says. "You expect us to give up our lives and go off through space because you *think* that's what people from hundreds of years ago wanted?"

I shake my head. "I don't expect everyone to want to go. Those who don't are welcome to go on-world and figure out how to make the planet a home again. But there are people on the station and on the world who will want to do this. There are people like me who know that there's more to this life than what we've been handed. We deserve the chance to seek it out."

"Wait," Nova says. I turn my eyes to her, watching as my words sink in. There is hurt on her face when she swallows and asks, "You plan to go, to leave the world behind? You're not going to stay and help me sort things out?"

I try to put as much of my sorrow into my expression as I can. I want her to know that this isn't a decision that I've come to easily. She has been abandoned by so many through the years, and even though they didn't mean to leave her, she's been cast off like a broken thing. Now I'm doing the same thing. I'm not leaving her because I want to, but because I must. I want her to know it isn't her fault.

"Someone has to," I say, my voice cracking.

"You speak as if it's already decided," Bernard says.

"It is," Ledwin says. His tone sounds breathless, as if speaking the words stole the last bit of air from his lungs.

"This is too far. I can't accept this. I won't," Warren says.

"Gun!" someone yells, while another voice calls, "Get down!"

Rufus throws his body over mine and pulls me to the ground just as an explosion of sound fills the room. Someone screams, and my world goes dark.

CHAPTER
FORTY-NINE
NOVA

S everal things happen at once: Ivy rips out my heart, Dumbass jumps up and pulls a gun, and people around the room are throwing themselves in various directions. In the chaos, while everyone is jumping into action or catapulting themselves out of danger, I just stand there motionless wondering why Hicks and Jackson didn't check us for weapons. The thought is so strong, my brain narrows to that one thing and I can't take anything else in.

A body rams against me and I fall to the ground. I look up into the pale blue eyes that used to rock me to sleep, that told me adventure stories, that made me feel brave when I faced a bug without flinching. I look up into eyes that seem to be losing their light and the same rate that blood trickles out of the hole in his side.

Time catches up with me, and whatever shock I'm in disappears long enough for me to realize my father is dying.

"No," I whisper. "No, we can save you."

He shakes his head. "It was never about me, Nova. It was always meant to be you and your sister."

"What are you saying?" I ask.

"You never understood..." he trails off, a cough racking his body. "Everything I did was to get *you* here. Not me. *You* are the future."

I open my mouth to speak but a sob takes the place of my words. Finally, I'm able to call out, "We need a medic!"

Asher is beside me a moment later. She rolls my father off me and applies pressure to his wound. There's so much blood. Her hands are coated in it. Her eyes meet mine and she gives her head a slight shake. He's not going to make it.

I swallow back the lump in my throat, plaster a smile on my face, and lean over my father. Though I want to lie to him and pretend he's going to be fine, I can see the resolve on his face. He doesn't need me to lie to him, he needs me to love him one last time.

"I know you did everything you could for us," I say, surprising myself with how true the words feel as I say them. "It couldn't have been easy for you, but you did your best. And I know you love us."

His lips turn up at the edges ever so slightly. "I do. You're the best thing I've ever done."

"Dad?" Ivy says, falling to his side.

"Hey, baby girl," he says.

She clutches his hand and holds it to her mouth, whispering against it as she says, "I love you so much. You need to stay with me. I can't do this without you."

"You'll be fine." Another cough rattles through him. "You and your sister will both be okay. Be bold as you go into your destiny." Tears pour down Ivy's face as we sit beside him for what feels like hours but in truth is only a few minutes. In one final breath, he mutters, "I love you," and falls silent for the last time.

Minutes pass as we sit by him in silence. Fatboy comes to Ivy's side and wraps his arms around her. She falls against him and he picks her up, carrying her away to find refuge, I hope. No one comes for me—I'm not sure if that's a blessing or a curse.

At some later time I force myself to stand and leave my father's side. I walk to the other side of the table where Dumbass sat. His body is on the floor, a long knife protruding from his neck. One of the other old men is dead on the floor beside him—Preston? Bernard? They all look alike. The one who lived through it is pressed against the wall with the quiet one, both looking shellshocked.

Doctor Okada and Asher are leaning over a third body, and I move

THE RAIDER WITHIN 277

around them until I can see Benjy's face. I'd forgotten he was even in the room. Once he escorted me in, he vanished into the background. Now, as I replay the events in my mind, it was his voice calling out the warning about the gun. He must've charged Dumbass when he started shooting, but not soon enough to keep my father from getting shot. Benjy stabbed him, but got shot in return.

Okada looks up at me, and whatever he reads on my face changes everything about him. The crease of his furrowed brow smoothes, his frowning mouth turns up, and though he's not smiling exactly, he no longer wears anger or fear as he did a moment ago. He stands in front of me, putting his warm hands on my shoulders and forcing me to narrow my view to him. He says, "Your friend will be okay. He's hurt, but he's stable."

"My father..." the words tail off in a sob.

"I know," he says, pulling me against his chest. Okada wraps his arms around me and holds me tight, his body encompassing me while the rest of the room fades away. After a long moment, he whispers against my head, "I'm sorry I couldn't save them both."

I let the words sink in. He knew he could save one of them, and he chose Benjy. I don't know what made the choice for him, or if it was just a matter of who he could get to first. I'm not sure I want to know. For now, standing in his arms is the only thing I want, and I'm unwilling to complicate that.

The door opens and someone comes in. I hear their voices but I don't look to see who it is. I don't care. Even when I see them carting Benjy away, I don't bother looking to see who has him. Maybe this makes me a bad person, if I wasn't already one, but I can't find it in me to move away from the safety of Okada's arms.

He holds me until I can breathe again. The front of his pale blue shirt is wet from my tears. I pull my face back from his chest and look up at him. His dark eyes meet mine, and there's a question there that I can't parse. Okada is looking at me like I could answer the question to his universe if I would just open my mouth to speak. I look back with questions of my own.

Whatever answer he's looking for, he finds it. His hand slides up my back, and though I miss the warmth from him holding me, there's a new sensation when his palm fits against the back of my neck and tips my face toward his. His lips claim mine, and though his kiss is gentle, there is also a firmness here that speaks of finality. It's as if this is the first and last kiss I will ever receive, and I am okay with that. I kiss him back, abandoning myself to this moment where grief and heartache and loneliness and self-hatred and fear can simply have a break from existing in me, and I can feel nothing but the way Okada fits against me like he was always meant to be there.

He pulls away after too short a time, pressing his forehead to mine as we catch our breath. I stare at his lips, plump and red from having my teeth graze across them, and turning up at the corners like he can't believe what just happened.

The doors open again, and again I don't spare a glance that way. But then I hear a voice I recognize piercing through whatever moment we're having. "What the actual hell, Squirrel? Keep it in your pants."

CHAPTER
FIFTY
NOVA

I stand with my sister at the Mountain of Ushmor. A funeral pyre dances with firelight ahead of us, and we watch the smoke carry the souls of our loved ones to the great beyond. I have never believed in such a place, but Rego did, and as I watch the pyre where he and my father lay side by side, I hope he is right.

There are many others on pyres nearby. The bodies of the dead have burned for days, and will burn for several more; the mourning will continue for long after that, and then the real work can begin.

When the fires die, Ivy takes my hand and we walk silently toward home. Over a small hill, tucked within a copse of trees, there is a house with fingers of smoke curling from its thatched roof. We go inside where my family waits.

The homesteader sits in a chair by the fire, speaking quickly in her native tongue as Krew smiles back at her over the skein of yarn in his hands. He answers her in the same tongue as he gestures at the poor attempt to make a scarf. Her attempts to teach him to knit are not going well, but it's clear she enjoys having someone to talk to.

Thoa and Fatboy—*Rufus*, I correct myself, though it doesn't come easily—enter the small cottage with a brace of conies and a basket full of fish. Rufus drops the basket as soon as he sees Ivy, picking her up and spinning her around. It is lovely and silly and perfect. I may never have thought of pairing the two, but their affection for one another is undeniable. He's going to the stars with her when she leaves, and it eases my fear a little. When I see the way he looks at my sister, I know that she will be loved and protected as long as she wishes for Rufus to be at her side.

I glimpse Thoa's smile as he watches them, and I do not miss it when he casts a look my way. He has not spoken to me of our arrangement, nor of his plans for the next stage of what is to happen. He is waiting for me to bring it up, I think, but I haven't yet had the courage to examine my feelings. *Tomorrow*, I promise myself, secretly hoping that time will stop moving before it comes.

When Hiro comes in looking for me, I decide there are far too many people in the homesteader's cottage and invite him to go for a walk. He follows me out and we stroll in companionable silence for several minutes. There are houses being erected in a nearby clearing. One of them belongs to me. When all was said and done on the station, when the blood stopped flowing and we saw who still remained, returning here was suddenly the easiest decision I've ever had to make.

When I appeared in Kavis' front yard with a group of Raiders and star-people at my back, she took it all in stride. It did not matter to her where we'd come from, what we'd seen; she offered us a warm place to sleep, a comforting hand on our shoulders, and a belly full of vegetable stew. She and I sat in her garden the following morning. I told her I wasn't sure where I'd go next, and she placed her wrinkled hands on my face and said, "Stay." I could not say no.

Others felt the same. This place is one of refuge, and under her care we are able to replenish what has been lost. Hiro has been leading some of our people to build houses here for those who wish to stay, dotting the hills around us in clusters of four or five.

Not everyone wants to stay. Many of the Raiders are breaking off into groups and beginning to roam. Zulie and Leer left this morning, taking two dozen Raiders with them, and Zeb's group is planning to leave tomorrow. He'll take little Sarah with him—though they are no longer little and no longer Sarah, as they go by Kif now.

"The three houses near Kavis will be finished tomorrow," Hiro says.

"That's good news," I say.

"Tired of sleeping on the ground?" he asks. "You're awfully spoiled for a Raider."

I smile at him, but he's not wrong. I've been living on the station for long enough to have gotten used to the comforts of a real bed. I definitely miss it. It's the only thing I miss about that place.

"What about you? Looking forward to having a place of your own?"

He winces at my words and says, "Yeah, that's something I wanted to talk to you about."

I furrow my brows at this, fearful of what may come next. "Are you thinking of moving to the next hill over? I honestly wouldn't mind having a little room between our houses so I don't have to listen to all the moaning coming from your place."

He smiles, but it doesn't reach his eyes. "You know I love you—" he begins.

"Just say it," I cut him off, the words strangled as they fight their way out of my throat.

"Javian is going with Ivy."

"I'm sorry," I say. "I know you care about him."

"I love him," Hiro says.

I stop walking and look up at him. He is as handsome as ever, his skin darkened by his time in the sun, his dark hair and beard grown out in the fashion of the Raiders. Tattoos scroll up his arms, cut off by his leathers. I stare at him, memorizing every aspect of this man who has become my dearest friend. Though our time together has been short, my life will forever be altered by knowing him.

"The guard I met in that prison would have never said those words."

"He was a fool."

"And you're not?" I tease.

He smiles. "Oh, I definitely still am. Maybe a little less so, because I'm not going to let this one get away. He's too good to say goodbye to him."

"I understand."

Hiro takes my hands and stares down at me, his eyes pleading. "I need to know that you really do understand. It's not that I want to leave you—"

"We promised," I croak. "Never again."

"We did," he says, voice cracking.

"I get it," I say, a little too fast. And I do. He has to go, just like I have to stay. It doesn't diminish our love for one another or the bond between us, but it does mean we have to say goodbye. "There's still some time before you go. Let's not waste it on thinking about missing each other."

"I will miss you Squirrel, so damn much."

"I'll miss you too, Moose."

Hiro pulls me against his chest and we both fall apart. When the tears finally stop, we walk hand in hand through the village that's coming together, admiring a future that we won't share.

———

I MOVE INTO MY HOUSE FOUR DAYS LATER. YOSH FOUND SOME PAINT ON THE station and now our front room and kitchen is yellow. When we stand there together, his hands tangled in my hair as he presses kisses down my neck, it truly feels like home.

I can't explain the sudden affection that has bloomed between us. Perhaps it is that we are both broken people who have done things that no one else fully understands, and in each other we are not looking for perfection. Yosh doesn't try to fix me or hide my flaws away; instead, he embraces them. And though I never saw him as a possibility before, I can't unsee it now. He doesn't complete me—he sees me as complete, even in my brokenness, and complements me in ways I never would have thought possible.

Krew moves into the house next door. We've had a walkway built between our dwellings so that Yosh can go where he pleases. When we realized the connection between us and what it truly meant, we had a long, awkward talk about what would happen next. It was clear immediately that Krew needed to be part of the conversation. Yosh and Krew were in a strange place, and there were explanations that needed to be made. Krew hadn't known how and why Yosh had remained free when the others were imprisoned, and Yosh still has a lot that needs accounted for. He did things he isn't proud of, compromised parts of himself, because he knew he needed to be useful to the Règle in the hopes of helping me and Ivy. It paid off in the end, but he still wakes up shaking, thinking about the things he had to do.

Yosh and Krew are not engaged as they once were, but there is still love there. The feelings between them never died, though perhaps they have changed into something else. Either way, I want them to have room to explore what remains and build upon that foundation if they can, hence the walkway. I worried I would feel jealous, or that Krew would, but so far there are only brief flickers of it. Yosh says it is a natural emotion and we must talk through those feelings. Talking is not my favorite thing to do, but somehow when he proposes it I know it is right.

Krew and I still need to talk about what happened between us, and what that could mean in the future, if anything. But that day in the forest when our bodies joined feels like a lifetime ago, and we are in no rush to figure things out. For the first time since we met, we have time.

HEROL HAMRICK CALLED AEROPORT TO PICK HIM UP AS SOON AS HE WAS able, and after several days, his floating city shone like a jewel on the horizon. It leads the way to the Mountain of Ushmor, followed by half a dozen others that will be ready to set down in the next few hours. Gearhaven is among them, and I wonder if Nigel Weatherfield will be with them. His presence seems to complicate things with Thoa, and things are muddled enough as is.

Copperhill is also among the floaters. Coco will go with them when they depart. I have only seen her twice since we returned; once when she was too deep in her mind to know me, and another time when the sight of my face caused her to burst into tears. She is broken, and though every part of my heart longs to help her, I am the cause of her pain. Though it wasn't my hands that hurt her, she was tortured because of the possibility that I could have loved her in another life.

Doctor Davie will help her. The love at Copperhill will heal her. Maybe I will see her again someday, in another life.

When they arrive, I will finally have the chance to thank them for saving Rego. There is so much more they did for me without ever knowing it. Watching their family and how it connected, how they were free to love each other without restrictions, made me realize that I could have more and be more and love more.

More Raiders will be with them. Some may want to stay, some will want to go. Wherever they end up, all want to see the Chief from the stars. I've heard a few of the stories that were told while I was gone and it sounds as if Hiro's skill as a wordsmith served him well. They regard me as highly as if I am Zappho Curiosity. Maybe to them I am. I hope to dispel those myths soon, so that I can slip into a real life, one built around what I need and what I want, one without duty impacting every decision I make.

I stand in the space behind my house where a garden will be one day, and I watch people disembark the floating cities. There are more of them than I expected. My initial reaction is to worry where they will shelter but then I remember that they are Raiders.

A warmth at my side lets me know I am not alone. I turn, expecting Yosh's lithe body, but instead I find Thoa at my side in all his bulky glory. He has traded in his killing leathers for canvas pants that Kavis made for him and a tight, thin shirt. I am certain she enjoyed every second of taking his measurements.

"We'll need to feed them," Thoa says.

"They're Raiders," I reply.

There's a low rumble in his chest and it takes me a moment to realize he's laughing. "We were too, once upon a time."

"No longer?"

He shakes his head. His azure eyes are distant, but I'm not sure if he's still watching the people from the ships or if he's lost in a memory.

"Not me. Not since the trials—the first time. I lost all of me in there."

I swallow back the lump in my throat. I know what he means. "They took that from us but it doesn't mean you can't get it back. You can have everything back if you're willing to work for it."

He turns to face me, his gaze locking on mine. Sadness is etched on his face when he says, "Not everything."

Thoa's mouth moves in a mockery of a smile, then he turns and walks away. I watch him traipse toward the copse of trees by Kavis' house, the tall grasses parting with each step. He doesn't look back.

"TONIGHT, WE HONOR THE SUN WHO GIVES US THE DAY, WHO WITHDRAWS SO we may have night. Like the sun, we give ourselves to whom we choose as we share the right to wed. Like the sun, we turn away as we desire, offering instead a period of rest."

Hiro's voice echoes across the land, and others take up his words throughout the assembly, repeating them in languages I've never heard. He shakes his walking stick in the air. Beads and teeth scrape together, creating a melody that carries on the wind.

Before Hiro can continue the ceremony, one of his advisors steps up beside him. She is a Raider I do not know, but she exudes power. Though Hiro is her chief, she will lead her own band of Raiders soon. I know this with one glance.

"Chief Hiro," she says, her voice carrying more confidence than anyone I've ever heard. "It is your right to choose first. Who will you have as your mate?"

His face breaks out in his megawatt grin. "Raiders, friends, family: I have been Chief while my mate, Nova-du, has been among the stars. But now she has returned, and I will remove myself from being your chief." Murmurs echo through the valley, but he simply smiles and motions for them to quiet. They still instantly, and he says, "You have taught me much, and I will forever treasure my days with you, but my time has passed. Tonight, in my final act as a Raider, I wish to honor the Raiders' way of love."

He steps down from the makeshift stage and wanders through the crowd. Women and men watch him as he passes, and I have no doubt that many are quietly begging any god that will listen that Hiro will stop in front of them. But he doesn't. He walks toward me, his steps sure and true. Well, not me exactly, for I am standing beside Javian Balunovic.

When Hiro reaches us, he takes my hand in his and says, "My mate, my best friend, my Chief. I promised my loyalty and devotion to you, and I have not wavered. My love for you continues now and will always persist, but my heart belongs to another. Will you set me free of my oath?"

I smile at him, despite the tears that trail down my cheeks. "Chief Hiro, you have honored me with your promise, with your love. And though I release you from your oath and bid you to follow your heart, always know that you carry part of my heart with you, wherever your path may lead."

I glimpse tears on his face too, just before I release his hand and turn my back to him. The words he speaks when he leans close to Javian are quiet, just for them. I hear Javian laugh, a full sound that fills me with delight. He will love Hiro, he will take care of him, and they will be happy. They will fly off into a new life, and they will be happy.

As Hiro and Javian walk arm in arm toward one of the mated tents, the confident Raider woman calls out, "Chief Nova-du, it is your right to choose your mate."

My heart beats wildly in my chest. I wasn't sure they would call me, wasn't sure I'd need to make this public declaration, but here I am walking toward the front of the assembled Raiders, my palms sweaty and dry at the same time. When I reach the platform and look out at the faces staring up at me, my heart fills with pride and wonder.

"Many of you know me," I say as cheers rise around me, "and many of you do not. You have known my friends, my advisors, my mate. You have known the people I love. Through them, and because of them, you have known and loved me. You saved me and so many others from the star-people. You gave me hope, and a reason to fight. But now, tonight, my fight is over. Those of you who wish to continue as Raiders may do so, with new chiefs leading you into the future. Those who wish to stay and build permanent homes, or return to the floating cities to make lives there, or whatever else you may want to do—you are free to go and live and do as you wish. You are free. Raiders will always be free."

I step down from the stage and walk toward my home. Yosh and Krew are there waiting for me. They are not Raiders, they do not love like Raiders, but their love is the balm my heart requires.

As I pass the last of the crowd before I reach the trees that surround our small community, I find azure eyes on me. Thoa stands on my path, blocking the way. I cannot hide from this any longer.

I step in front of him and he says, "I know this is goodbye. I know you will never choose me, no matter how much I wish for it."

"Why do you wish it?"

"I love you."

"And I love you."

"But it's not enough. No matter how much I want it to be. And that's okay."

I look up into his eyes. There is no hurt, no judgment. For the first time in a long time, he doesn't look haunted or broken.

"I have found peace with Doctor Okada."

"And it doesn't bother you that he also belongs to Krew?"

The question makes me smile. "No, not at all. He gives me what he can, what I need, and finds his needs with me. Though he assures me I am enough, there are times I cannot give him all of me, cannot navigate who I am versus who I am trying to be. There are times he finds things with Krew that I cannot offer. But my love is bigger than possessing him simply to call him mine."

After a moment, he says, "Then I am happy you have found him."

"What about you?" I ask. "What have you found?"

His lips tip up in a crooked smile. "Myself, I think. Took me a while."

"Is that enough?"

"It has to be. I tried everything else. And I'm done with that."

"Will you ever try again?"

He shakes his head. "There's nothing else for me, Little Star. Not another thing, not another person, not another cause. I filled my life with so many things that didn't fit, and only one thing that ever did. But you were too big to press into the little space my heart can provide. So even though I need you, even though I don't know what I'll do without you, I know I'll still be okay in the end. That's the first time I've been able to say that and mean it."

"I need you, too," I say, swallowing my pride and my fear and admitting what I want, like Yosh has taught me. "Even though I don't know how it will work, and we'll have to sort it all out to give this a real chance, I don't want to go another day without you in my life. Wherever that end is where you're okay, I want to be there with you. Can you accept me as I am, and understand that my heart will never belong only to you?"

"Yes," he whispers.

"Will you walk with me through sunlight until the solstice marks the end of our path?"

Thoa smiles down at me, putting every one of Hiro's megawatt grins to shame.

It takes four months for Ivy's plans and preparations to go into effect. The space station is broken into two dozen usable sections, with each piece preparing to go in a different direction while the rest of the station is used as scrap. There are around twenty thousand people on each ship, sending humanity out into the stars. Ivy and Rufus are the youngest of the starship captains, but if I were a betting woman, I'd put it all on them. Hiro and Javian will be with them too. My heart is heavy with their upcoming departure, but I know it is something they must do.

There are star-people, on-worlders, and plenty of Raiders piling on the ships. Ivy was right when she said we needed to let people be pioneers again. The hunger for adventure is palpable all around us.

The remaining Raiders—and some of the star-people who have joined them—have begun their travels. Our village is now a regular stop for them as they make their way through the land. We share and trade, and even the floating cities have started flying near to trade with the Raiders. There have been struggles, for nothing will ever be perfect, but it certainly feels closer to *whole* than it ever has.

"Nova!"

I turn to see my sweet sister walking up the hill toward me. Her blonde hair trails behind her, the wind blowing it back from her flushed face.

"Hi sis," I say.

She steps up beside me and smiles. We face the Mountain of Ushmoor in the distance, staring at the smoothed stone faces of the gods. For a long moment neither of us say anything, and not for the first time I wish I could freeze time and hold this moment forever.

"The ship is readying for takeoff," she whispers.

"I know."

"I wanted to say…" she trails off.

I force a smile as I turn my gaze to her. I reach forward and take her hands. "I am so proud of you."

"Me?" she asks. "You're the hero."

"I wouldn't have made it without you."

"Yes you would have. There were so many people—"

"No," I say, cutting her off. "You were the reason I came back to myself. You kept bringing me back, and I will always come back to you. Even if you are a million miles away living amongst the stars and the mystery of everything you've ever wanted. My heart will be right there with you. It will always come back to you. And someday, when we're old and gray and life is done, I hope to see you again."

"In the great beyond," she says. "I'll look for you there."

Ivy pulls me to her and we hold onto each other for a long, long time.

Rufus comes for her when they can wait no longer. I hug him too, my mind flashing to all the times I kicked the snoring kid in the unmated tent beside me. I walk with them to the spot where Hiro and Javian are saying their goodbyes to the rest of the village. Hiro and I have said goodbye a dozen times already, but he pulls me to his chest one last time and whispers, "I love you, Squirrel." He ruffles my hair and pushes me away, giving me one last grin.

Then they are gone.

My heart aches already, knowing it will never be whole again.

Then Yosh's arm wraps around my waist, his hand resting on my hip, and Thoa's hand takes mine. They ground me, reminding me that there is still love here.

There is love, and I am home.

ALSO BY SHELLY JARVIS

The Dreamwalker

"Space Harry Potter"

Or get the Boxed set: Duology Boxed Set

This World and the Next

"A short story collection with gems such as *Hillbilly Necromancer: a Love story"*
and *"Grandma Assassins in Outer Space"*

Black Sea Bright Song

"The Little Mermaid **if it was told from Ursula's point of view"**

The Fall of Water House

"The Last Airbender meets the Bachelorette"

ABOUT THE AUTHOR

Shelly Jarvis began working on speculative fictions thanks to a writing assignment in Mrs. Bettijane Burger's eleventh grade English class, but her passion for writing developed at seven when she wrote a Halloween tale about a witch and a ghost who became best friends.

An avid science fiction and fantasy reader, Shelly spends a large portion of each new day dwelling in other worlds.

Shelly enjoys spending time with her wacky spouse, her wonderful nephews, and her rescue pups, Gimli, Fergus, and Goose. She currently resides near Charleston, West Virginia, in the wild and wonderful mountains that have her heart.

Learn more about Shelly, including other books and how to contact her, at ShellyJarvis.com.